RED TIDE

MARK JAMES MILLER

BLACK ROSE writing™

ISBN: 978-1-61296-582-6

PUBLISHED BY BLACK ROSE WRITING

www.blackrosewriting.com

Printed in the United States of America

Suggested retail price $20.95

Red Tide is printed in Adobe Garamond Pro

Dedicated to Corey Miller, 1976—2009

RED TIDE

"This way to join the lost people." –Dante's Inferno

Chapter 1

Tom's Big Idea

Looking back after so many years, I'm surprised it didn't happen sooner than it did. Tom always was a guy full of big ideas.

He'd had big ideas before, but never one that would cause so much trouble.

It came upon him out of nowhere, striking suddenly, the way a *chubasco* strikes in the Sea of Cortez: He stopped, clapped his hands together, and turned so he stood facing me.

"You know what I'm going to do?" he cried. "I'm going to climb to the top of that smokestack!"

"You don't mean the smokestack on top of the old power plant, do you?" I asked.

"That's the one," he affirmed, grinning excitedly and wagging his big head back and forth. "I'm going to climb all the way to the top and shout so loud they'll be able to hear me over in Hawaii!"

"You're crazy," I said, giving him my-you-can't-really-mean-that-look, the one I reserved for moments when he came up with his most outlandish ideas. "I always knew it. Now I've got proof."

"And you're coming with me," he declared, grabbing me by the shoulder and shaking me, something he did when he had one of his ideas for adventure. "It won't be any good to do it alone."

"Dream on," I said, disengaging myself from his grip. "There's no way."

We were walking down Main Street, as we did nearly every day after school, and he had been singing his favorite song, *Sloop John B*, in that off-key way of his, for while Tom was someone who can do just about anything they set their mind to, you could fit his musical talents into a thimble and have plenty of room left over. His singing grated on your ears like someone scratching their fingernails across a blackboard. I had just been about to ask him to give my ears a break when he started on this business of going into the old power plant and climbing to the top of the smokestack.

Tom's plans for adventure usually involved ditching school and driving up the coast to Redondo Beach or Malibu to spend the day surfing, or else he would want to take a whole weekend and go as far north as Santa Barbara so we could go surfing there, sleeping on the beach or in the back of my van if it got cold. His more outlandish ideas—he often suggested we run away and go to Hawaii—he often forgot about, but I could see that he had this one fixed firmly in his mind.

"Let's go tonight," he said, still filled with enthusiasm and the wild, manic sort of energy that he had when one of these ideas possessed him. "We can go after it gets dark. More fun that way."

"More fun," I said caustically. "If you want to have that kind of fun, why don't you swim to Catalina?"

"That's been done already," he said impatiently. "I want to be the first to do something, like the first guy to climb Mount Everest, or the first guy to reach the North Pole."

"Oh, so it's that way," I said, still trying to be ironic. "You want to be remembered, you want people to think about you."

"Of course," he admitted. "I want to be immortal. Don't you?"

We had passed Harbor Surfboards and were in front of Clancy's Bar by now. Across the street was the old Bay Theatre. Above the marquee were those ornate windows that look down on the street like big oval eyes, never missing anything that goes on. The sun was setting, for it was late afternoon, and it glinted off the glass, reflecting brightly as a searchlight. The door of the bar opened and an ugly, wizened little man in a baggy rumpled suit came out and stood blinking in the light. With a small gnarled hand he pointed first at me, then at Tom.

"It's the end of the world!" he proclaimed. "Are you ready? Are you prepared for Judgment Day?"

"Get lost, you drunken bastard," Tom said good-naturedly.

The little man swallowed hard and backed away, then turned and went down the narrow walkway that leads into the alley behind Main Street. A gust of wind blew some newspapers around in front of him. He passed a big battered metal trash can that overflowed with garbage, and a large gray rat scurried from behind it before dashing out of sight again. I scooped up a rock from the gutter and threw it overhand like a baseball so that it hit the trash can, making a loud banging sound, and the little man jumped in surprise before disappearing around the corner.

"What good did that do you?" Tom asked.

"I hate drunks. They remind me of my father."

"Want to go tonight?" Tom asked eagerly.

"Go? Where?"

"Oh, come on!"

"I have homework to do tonight. Just because you never crack a book. I don't have to flunk out too."

"Oh yes, I forgot," Tom said. "You're the guy who gets such good grades. You're the guy who doesn't even have to study most of the time like the rest of us poor dummies. But listen Pete," he went on plaintively, "you've got to go with me. I don't want to do it by myself, and besides, you know how to get in there. I can't do it without you."

"I am not going into that place again, ever, long as I live," I declared. "And if you have any sense at all, you'll stay away from it too. Something bad always happens to people who go screwing around in there."

"You mean you think it has a curse on it?"

"Worse than that. It might even be haunted."

"Haunted? You mean by that kid that got killed? You don't really believe in anything like that."

"When it comes to that place I do."

"Why? Just because that guy died in there?" He stopped, and looked at me keenly. "I'm sorry," he continued. "He was a good friend of yours, wasn't he? But that's no reason not to go back."

"I can't think of too many better ones."

"Tell me again what happened."

"I told you about it once already."

"I know, but it was a long time ago and I've forgotten some of the details. So come on, tell me again."

"I don't want to talk about it," I said, waving my hand in the air as if could wave away his request, consign it to the same place I wanted to consign his idea of going into the old power plant.

"But look Pete," he said earnestly, "you'll never get shut of it if you don't talk about it. It's going to haunt you for the rest of your life if you don't get it out of your system."

"Drop it," I said sharply. "Just let it go. End of story."

Tom turned to look toward the ocean, where the sun was getting lower in the sky. His St. Christopher medal, which he wore around his neck, flashed slightly when the sun hit it. *"We come on the Sloop John B,"* he warbled, off-key as always, *"My grandfather and me/Around Nassau town we do roam…"*

• • •

I don't know where Tom's family came from originally, although I suspect his roots ran deeper in California than mine did. When he and I met he had just come to Angels Beach from San Diego to live with his "Uncle" Neal and "Aunt" Marianne, although they weren't really his aunt and uncle. I know he was related to them in some way, either by marriage or by blood, and he had been sent to live with them when his real mother and father, who still lived in San Diego near Mission Bay, decided they were unable to deal with him any longer.

He had run away to go to San Francisco in the summer of 1967, the Summer of Love. He wanted to be part of that migration of kids that were going to the Haight-Ashbury district of the City by the Bay that summer, to just be there when it happened. There had been a feeling in the air that Spring, a murmuring that you heard, that something big was going to happen in San Francisco in the summer, and he wanted to see it, in spite of his parents' warning that if he did, it would be the last straw.

He did it anyway, knowing what the consequences would be, knowing that it was only one of a long line of sins he had committed that had brought him to this point. He preferred surfing to school, girls to reading books, and sports over any kind of study, and while he was a born athlete, and starred on both the swimming and water polo teams, his grades were such that he was perennially in danger of not being allowed to play due to his almost failing every class he was enrolled in. So the coaches were always just as exasperated with him as everyone else was, although they wanted him on their teams so badly they were willing to overlook his mischiefs and his aversion to class even if his parents and his counselors weren't.

I wouldn't say he delighted in getting in trouble, it more just part of his nature. Like the time he was caught *in flagrante delicto* with the Vice-Principal's daughter, in the Vice-Principal's house and in the girl's bedroom. The look, he said, on that Important Person's face was worth all the trouble that resulted from it. (Tom had an aversion to people who took themselves too seriously, referring to them as Important People, and the vice-principal of his high school in San Diego was one such person. He had the same feeling about his Uncle Neal. When he encountered someone like that he had an overwhelming desire to take them down a peg if he could, to puncture their air of self-importance and remind them they were as human as everyone else.) The girl, whose name he didn't even remember, was sent away to live with relatives in Phoenix, and Tom was warned—again—that a similar fate would befall him if he didn't stop all his nonsense. So when he came back from San Francisco at the end of that summer his mother and father had packed him off to Angels Beach and Neal and Marianne without, he said, much fanfare.

The truth is, he didn't like talking about his past—the future was what concerned him, he preferred to look ahead rather than backwards. I was more introspective than he was, and so I was more inclined to wonder about where my family came from and how I happened to be in Angels Beach rather than New York City or Chicago or Buenos Aires or Sydney or any other place on earth.

I was a first-generation Californian. My father, George, came to the Golden State when he was nine years old, brought here by my grandparents from Kentucky during the Depression. My mother, Laurie Anne, came from Illinois at about the same time, and in the same circumstances. Both families settled in Los Angeles, within a few miles of one another. When World War II broke out George, who was 19 then, joined the army and spent the war years in the Pacific. He came back when the war was over, met Laurie Anne, and after they got married they bought a house in Angels Beach. Houses were cheap at the beach then, and a lot of young veterans were using their GI benefits and moving to the coast to raise their families. You saw it and felt it everywhere—new housing tracts being built, new office buildings, new shopping centers and malls, new schools, new roads, new highways, and new people, coming, as I said, from all over. The past was being pushed aside to make way for the present and the future.

There were still some remnants of the past to be seen in Angels Beach: The Bay Theatre, built in the 1920s, the old City Hall building, the old airport on the northern outskirts of town, no longer in use, with patches of weeds and other debris growing over what had once been a landing strip, and the old power plant, the one Tom wanted so badly to explore, which sat on alongside the San Gabriel River, its smokestack jutting into the sky, built of brick like an old factory that now sat abandoned and alone, a relic of the past, forsaken but not entirely forgotten, a place I had vowed I would never go back to.

Chapter 2

Brian

I wouldn't go back there because of Brian.

Brian was my best friend, back in that summer of 1966, more than two years before Tom had his Big Idea, and one Saturday afternoon he and I had gone into the old power plant that sat on the northern edge of town.

Brian was like Tom—always looking for adventure, always wanting to do something no one had ever done before. "It's too bad I was born in this time," he used to say, "instead of 50 or 100 years ago. There were still unexplored places in the world then, mountains that had never been climbed, places that nobody had ever been to, things nobody had ever seen before. Here I am, stuck in this time when there's no adventure left."

But there was the old power plant, sitting just outside of town like an old medieval castle, looking broodingly down on the bay where the San Gabriel River empties into the Pacific Ocean, and on top of it was a smokestack that jutted two hundred feet into the sky. If you stood on the end of the pier when dawn broke you could see its silhouette outlined against the sun, and if you were on the beach near the 1st street jetty you could look up and there it was, massive and made of red brick, with that smokestack looking like a beacon, calling you. The plant didn't operate any more. It blew its last whistle in 1959 and since then it had sat there, silently, surrounded by a ten foot high chain-length fence with barbed wire on top and big "Danger—Do Not Enter" signs every twenty feet or so. Each year the weeds that grew around it got taller and more of the big levered windows were broken so the glass lay on the ground with the weeds, and some of the boys who lived in town had gotten inside and seen what was there and a few had tried to climb all the way to the top of the smokestack but each one had gotten part way up and then gotten scared and come back down. Brian was determined to be the first one to climb up all the way.

Just getting inside was hard enough. There didn't seem to be any way in unless you had a key to the padlock on the gate. But there was another way, and Brian and I had discovered it one day while we were hanging out around the 1st Street jetty, watching as the Long Beach Marina and Yacht Club was being built on the other side of the San Gabriel River. Ever since then Brian had been able to think of nothing else but getting inside there and getting up on the roof and then climbing to the top of that smokestack. He talked about it night and day, and so finally one Saturday afternoon we decided to go for it.

We had made our way inside, going under a fence by the jetty and then coming into the plant by going into a tunnel that must have been used for drainage once, and we went inside the plant and up one flight of stairs after another until we were on the roof and stood looking up at that smokestack and wondering if this was really a smart thing to do. You didn't realize how tall it was until you stood there looking at it like that. We started climbing, Brian going first, me behind. And with each rung of the ladder I held on tighter, and I looked and saw the rusty bolts that held that ladder to the smokestack and saw the way they were popping loose and pulling away from the stack, and when I tugged on the rung it wiggled back and forth. It seemed like the stack went straight up forever, like the Tower of Babel, there was no end, and there was nothing to hold on to except the ladder that seemed in danger of coming apart the further up we went. I looked down, a bad mistake, and felt myself getting dizzy.

"Brian, wait," I called up to him. "I'm going back down."

"What are you, chicken?" he called from above me.

"No, I'm not chicken," I yelled back. "I'm just not going any farther."

"Chicken!" he taunted. He was like that, taunting you if you hesitated about something.

"Go to hell!" I yelled back, and then I climbed down.

By the time I got back down to the roof and looked up I saw that Brian was nearly to the top. That he had kept going, and that I hadn't been able to, made me angry and ashamed all at once. So without saying anything, or waiting to see if he made it all the way or not, I turned and left, going back down the stairs and through the plant and the tunnel and then home.

I didn't hear from him the next day, or the day after that. He must be as mad at me as I was at him, I thought, but when I didn't hear from him the following day either I began to fear something was wrong. That was when his father called, because Brian hadn't been home since Saturday.

I told everyone what we had done. Brian's father called the police, and I went with them over to the power plant. The policeman unlocked the gate and we went in and up the stairs to the roof and there he was, lying at the foot of the smokestack.

I still saw him in my dreams. There was a pool of dried blood around him. Then there was his face. It wasn't a face anymore, because of the way the birds had been at him. And I had seen it, and was sure by now that I would keep on seeing it for the rest of my life.

The police investigated, and figured out that he had made it to within one rung of the very top. But what must have happened was that the rung he put his foot on gave way at the same time as the one he was grabbing with his hand, so he had nothing to hold on to and fell, backwards, away from the stack and two hundred feet to the roof.

I didn't like thinking about any of it: The way his mother screamed when she saw him, and the way his father gasped as if his life was being torn out of his body. Brian had been their only child. They were old when he was born, and he was all they lived for, all their hopes and dreams and plans were focused on him. Then his father cried out "You!" and went for me, and before I knew it he had me down and was choking me, and it took two policemen to get him off.

Brian's mother and father demanded the police arrest me for murder. But the police and coroner said the fall had killed him and even if I had been there nothing could have been done for him. They didn't believe it, and kept saying I was a murderer, and said it must have been my idea to go in there at all, and they kept on saying it until they moved out of town and were never heard from again.

I thought it was my fault too. I kept saying to myself that if I had stayed there I could have talked him out of it. In my dreams he would fall past me, and I was helpless to do anything about it, and sometimes I woke up screaming and covered in sweat, grateful that my bedroom was on the other side of the house away from everyone else so they couldn't hear me.

I had other dreams as well, and in them Brian spoke to me: "Pete," he would say, "it's OK, I made it, it's all right." He forgave me in those dreams, which I often wished were real, and there were times when I told myself they *were* real. They made me feel better

Chapter 3

Deacon

Pete is what everyone called me then, but that isn't really my name. My father took to calling me that when I was very young—as far back as I could remember, that was what he called me. I never knew why. For many years I thought perhaps he didn't like the name my mother gave me when I was born, for he wasn't there when that event took place but was somewhere in Korea and so she had to think of a name for me all by herself. When he came home he started to refer to me as Pete and the nickname stuck. People were often surprised to find out it wasn't my real name.

The only clue I ever had as to why my father insisted on calling me Pete instead of my real name came from some old pictures I saw once. I was in the garage, searching for something, and I came across a trunk full of junkie old things that had been left there years ago and forgotten. Among them were a lot of pictures of my father in Korea (he had been called back in the summer of 1950 after the North Koreans came screaming across the 38th Parallel). Several of these pictures were of him and a young fellow, arm in arm, smiling with some mountains in the background and looking as if they must have been the best of friends. "Pete and me, August '50," was written on one, and another said, "Pete, September '50, near Pusan." Then I came on another one that read, "Pete—killed—January '51—may he live on." The month and year were clearly written, but I couldn't see the day, for the ink was smeared. This hit me with a real wallop, since I was born in January 1951 and I wondered, and later became convinced, that this guy Pete was killed on the same day I was born and my father must have started calling me that to remind him of his dead pal.

I also wondered if there could be even more to it than that. Not only was I born on the same day he was killed, what if I was born at the same *time* he was killed? Perhaps I was him, in some strange way, or he was me, maybe his soul had been looking for a place to go and had found me, freshly minted, so to speak, and had come to rest there. Maybe he was part of me. Could that happen? As the years went by I became sure of it. He was there all right, and he was trying to tell me something. But what was Pete trying to tell me? I tried and tried but I couldn't make it out. I used to ask Casey Jones about it, since he knew about things like that, but he could never give me any real insight on it either.

I wanted to ask my father about it too, but by the time I discovered those pictures he hardly spoke to me, so asking him about that wasn't an option. When I was small he and I were close—he took me fishing with him and coached my Little League teams—but when I reached my teens his attitude toward me changed. He began to dislike me, and with each passing day this dislike festered and grew to the point that when he saw me he scowled and his face took on a look of revulsion. He hardly spoke to me, and when he did it was to say how he couldn't stand the sight of me and that he should beat the tar out of me just to teach me a lesson. So I didn't get an opportunity to ask him about Pete until much later, and under less-than-ideal circumstances.

• • •

It was September 1968 when Tom had his Big Idea. Our senior year of high school had just started. We were supposed to graduate next June. I was planning on going to UCLA. Tom had other ideas.

Tom was a surfer. He often said surfing was all he lived for. This was an exaggeration, for he did have *some* other interests, and he had learned a long time back that one-half of the human race is made up of a sex tantalizingly different from his and there were a number of things you could learn from the female of the species if you were willing to take the trouble, and he wanted to find out all there was to know. So it wouldn't be accurate to say he lived *only* for that next ride on his Yater longboard. But while other people our age were making plans for college and careers, his goal was to get on the first boat or plane bound for Hawaii after we walked across the stage in our caps and gowns, find a grass shack on Oahu's North Shore and spend his days surfing. If there is such a place as Paradise, he would say, that would be it. For him, anyway.

He had won contests in Huntington Beach, and Newport, and Malibu, and he had the trophies in his room to prove it. At the hotspots from San Diego all the way north to Steamer Lane in Santa Cruz people knew who he was, and said that if he kept at it he might rank with Mickey Dora or Butch Van Arksdale as one of the best surfers ever. We went surfing just about every morning, getting up before school started and loading our boards into the back of my 1965 VW van and going down to the beach by the pier in our wetsuits to catch some waves in the cold water. If the waves weren't so good in Angels Beach we would drive down the coast to Sunset or Surfside or even to Huntington, catch a few waves and then drive back in time for our first classes.

When I saw Tom on his surfboard I could see this was something he had been born to do. There was magic taking place when he rode the waves. He was made for it. Casey Jones, who said our lives were written in the stars long before we were born, said surfing was Tom's destiny. (He said seeking the truth was my destiny, which did not seem nearly as glamorous, and he had given me a necklace with the Rune of truth and the sun's energy, Sowelu, on it, and later a set of Runestones, and began teaching me to read them. This, he said, would help me find my true path in life.

Tom looked like a surfer: Tall and blond, he would shake that big head of his all around when he got especially excited or happy about something. "Some of the best waves in the world are over there in the Islands," he would say when he got to talking about Hawaii, and that big head would wag back and forth. "Just think of it, Pete. The North Shore. The Pipeline. Waimea Bay. The Big Island. Imagine us there, going surfing every day. Wouldn't that be the life?" On the walls of his room he had posters of the Hawaiian Beaches, complete with dark-skinned native girls dancing in grass skirts, another reason he was itching to go there. Once he even got a record of Hawaiian music and tried to learn to do the hula. He moved about awkwardly, his motions fractured, unlike his usual graceful manner, with his arms flailing about while his head moved in another way altogether. It looked so ridiculous I couldn't help laughing out loud.

"Go ahead, laugh all you want," he said. "When I get to the Islands I want to know how the natives live. I'm going to surf Waimea Bay, and the Pipeline, on the north shore of Oahu. Those are the greatest waves in the world. And I'm going to enter the Duke K. classic, too, just to say I did it."

He lived in a big house in the best and most expensive part of town, called East Park Estates, with his guardians, Neal and Marianne. He had a large room on the second floor, and often we would be up there, doing our homework, or more precisely me doing my homework while he lay on his back, staring at these posters and visualizing himself riding the waves and frolicking with the native girls. Surf music would be coming from his stereo, for he loved Duane Eddy, Dick Dale and the Del Tones, the Surfaris and The Beach Boys and had collected almost all their albums. "Sure you don't want to go with me?" he would say. "Think of the adventures we could have!"

"I can't. I'm going to college."

"That's right. You're going to UCLA. You've been accepted there. You're just so damn smart. Being smart isn't all about books, you know. It's also about how you live your life. Well, when I get over there I'll think of you."

He could swim like a torpedo. His hands and feet were both one size bigger than they needed to be, and they propelled him along the lanes of the pool in a swim meet or a water polo game with such sureness of purpose that he had acquired the nickname "The Barracuda." He had been on the water polo and swimming teams at his old school in San Diego, and he had been the most valuable player on Angels Beach High's water polo team last year. He had been on the swimming team too, setting records in the freestyle and the backstroke. Great things were expected of him this year in both sports, and he had even been slated to be captain of the water polo team. Several colleges had tried to recruit him. But he wouldn't play. The coaches phoned his house night and day and told him how he was letting the school down and the team down, but nothing swayed him. He had no more interest in sports, and wouldn't change his mind no matter what anyone said. "I'm done with all that," he said.

His other passion was karate, and he had trained at one of Ed Parker's studios in San Diego. He had been teaching some of it to me, showing me how to do basic blocks, kicks and punches. We practiced together in his garage, and I got to where I could do an upward block, followed by a reverse punch, with some authority, as well as a front snap kick and an X-block. I practiced at home, too, in my room, whenever I had time, doing the techniques over and over.

Tom got picture books of Hawaii and other islands and places he hoped to see someday, and sat turning the pages and looking at them raptly, seeing himself there. He even learned some words of the Hawaiian language, like "Aloha" and "Mahalo," and bought a ukulele which he tried to learn how to play. But Tom couldn't even play Chopsticks on a piano, and his efforts with the ukulele didn't sound much better than someone twanging on a rubber band.

He had a deep reverence for the beach and the ocean. They were holy places for him, the places where he had his deepest and most meaningful experiences in life. So when we walked down the ramp beside the pier and out onto the sand and saw that Waldo Erickson and Stan Karlovitch were there, Tom's face took on a look that was partly disgust and partly amusement, as if he were seeing something profane going on that he couldn't do anything about.

He nudged me with his elbow. "Hey Pete, there's your buddy. Young Waldo. What's he doing here?" Usually Waldo and Karlovitch hung out in Ocean Avenue Park with the rest of the town drunks, druggies, prostitutes like Sleazy Mary and Horrible Helen, and other assorted derelicts that made the place their second home. Or else they cruised around town in Waldo's 1956 Buick convertible, which had bald tires and sounded like a washing machine with a motor about to give out, yelling foul names at people they didn't like and asking every girl they encountered if she wanted a ride.

"Do you think," I asked, "he'll ever grow up and become *Old* Waldo?"

"He'll never live that long," Tom predicted. "Neither him nor his pal, Dog-Face Karlovitch."

"We can always hope," I said.

"That Waldo really hates your guts," Tom declared.

"How long since you caught on to that?"

"It's not normal. That guy just *burns* with hate for you. But I can't figure it out."

"The feeling's mutual," I said.

"Yeah, I noticed that too, and I can't figure that one out either, because that isn't like you to hate anybody, not that way."

"It goes way back," I said.

They were cavorting about aggressively on the sand under the pier and we walked closer so we could see what they were doing.

They had cornered a cat, a small, starved-looking black-and-white cat. They chased it one way, hitting at it with sticks, and when it hissed at them and tried to get away they would laugh cruelly and hit at it some more.

"Grab him!" Karlovitch yelled.

"I can't!" Waldo yelled back. "He'll claw me."

"So? You some kind of a pussy or something, afraid of a little fucking cat scratch? Come on, get him, then we'll kill him!"

"Yeah!" Waldo said gleefully. "We'll catch it, then we'll kill it, we'll make a sacrifice out of it, we'll put him on the altar!"

Waldo dove headlong for the cat and managed to catch it by the tail. He scrambled ungracefully to his feet, holding the cat triumphantly out in front of him. The cat howled in terror, fighting desperately to get free, and at last it was able to dig its claws into Waldo's arm.

"Ouch!" Waldo cried, furiously, shaking the cat up and down. "Stop it! Stupid fuckin' cat! I only wanted to play with you. Here, cat, let's see how you like to play in the water!"

Waldo flung the cat toward an onrushing wave. The cat turned in the air so that it landed feet first, but just as it landed the wave rolled in and washed over it, and the cat let out a fearful yowl and fled crazily, its fur matted and stuck to its body. Waldo and Karlovitch laughed.

"What a man," Tom said. "What do you think they'll do next, Pete? Pull the wings off some flies?"

Waldo began doing a dance in the sand and singing a perverted version of a child's nursery rhyme. He did that when he was feeling especially good, like when he had wrecked a little kid's bicycle or gotten somebody down and punched their head until the blood flowed and they screamed they'd had enough. Waldo could do that. He didn't come into this world blessed with too many talents, nor did he begin life with an overabundance of advantages. He grew up in the ramshackle trailer park near the old lumberyard on the north end of town, out where the airport used to be, and on his best day he couldn't read any better than a second grader or get past six times five on the multiplication tables. When he was called upon to read out loud in school he struggled to pronounce the simplest words while the rest of the children laughed and imitated his pitiful efforts and his face grew redder and redder until the teacher had mercy on him and told him to sit down, which he did, burying his face in his hands. But put him in a dark alley with someone and he would be the one I would bet on to come out first. When he fought there wasn't going to be any gentlemanly shaking-hands-and-no-hard-feelings-afterwards. He fought for all the marbles, winner-take-all and no holds barred.

"*There was meat goin' in,*" he chanted, "*an' juice comin' out. If that ain't fuckin' you can count me out!*"

Karlovitch joined in. "*Meat goin' in,*" he echoed, "*juice comin' out—*"

"*If that ain't fuckin' you can—*" Then Waldo noticed us. He scowled, and pushed his black bowler hat decorated with a peace sign further back on his head.

"Well Cowabunga!" he shouted. "Just lookit what we got here. If it ain't Surfer Joe and his buddy, little Petey-boy. You two are in the wrong place. This ain't Surf City. Hey Stan. Lookit here. Two little surfer boys who lost their way."

Karlovitch, as tall as Tom but heavier and darker, came lumbering over and stood beside Waldo, leaning his elbow on his friend's shoulder and sneering.

"They hain't got their boards with 'em," he observed. "You know somethin', you two just don't look right, 'thout your boards. You guys look kind of—half gone, man, I mean, just not all *there*, without your *SURF* boards. If you know what I mean."

This sent the two of them into wild spasms of laughter, as if this was more hilarious than anything they had ever heard in their lives. They leaned on each other and pointed at us, saying, "They ain't got their surfboards," and "Two little surfer boys—they look half gone," thumping each other on the back and laughing until the tears ran down their faces.

Then Waldo stopped laughing long enough to say, "Hey Stan, know what I heard?"

"What'd you hear, Waldo?"

"Surf City burned down!"

Now they started laughing again, even harder this time, cackling and doubling over. I could feel my face turning red. But Tom was never at a loss in a situation like this. With the most marvelous *sangfroid* he said:

"Hey Waldo. I see you brought your *dog* to the beach with you today."

This stopped the laughter, just like pulling the plug on a radio. "Now you did it," I said, *sotto voce.* "We are both going to die."

"What did you think? That you were going to live forever? We all gotta go sometime."

"It doesn't have to be today, does it?"

Karlovitch, like Waldo, wasn't a great talker even when he was calm, and the number of memorable things he said in his life could be fitted onto the head of a pin. But now he seemed to have lost the power of speech altogether. His uncanny resemblance to a dog was the subject of many jokes, but Tom was the only person who would dare say anything about it when Karlovitch was close by. His face contorted and turned dark red, and the lips worked furiously as he tried to think of something to say. "One of these days, Surfer Boy," he managed, "one of these days I'm gonna…"

"Down boy," Tom said. "Speak! Roll over! Good dog."

"Will you stop it?" I said.

"But I'm having so much fun!"

There's no telling where this might have gone if Dave Myers, who had been lounging against one of the pilings along with his brother Larry, boredly smoking a long black cigarette that smelled of jasmine and watching this with an amused expression, hadn't tossed his cigarette aside and stepped between us. He moved with the lithe delicacy of a prowling panther, looking down on us with a disdainful expression, his big white teeth bared like fangs and then retracting when his mocking smile faded. Waldo and Karlovitch froze. I felt an intense desire to get away from there. Even Tom stiffened.

"Hi Dave. What's happening?" Waldo said weakly.

"Do you know where you are, Waldo?" Dave asked. "You're on my beach. This is my beach," he declared. "This is my town. I won't have any fights on my beach."

Waldo and Karlovitch simply listened, the way true believers listen to the word from on high.

"Sure, Dave," Waldo said. "We didn't mean nothin'."

Dave turned to us, friendly now, smiling. "You see what I have to put up with?" he asked. "What can I do with guys like this? '*They didn't mean nothin','*" he mocked. "I've tried to improve your mind, Waldo, and yours, Karlovitch, but you can't improve something that doesn't exist."

"But Dave," Karlovitch started to protest, but Dave cut him off.

"Quiet, you two Neanderthals. I want to talk to your two acquaintances here," Dave said. His voice always surprised me, for it was two tones too high, it just didn't fit a man his size.

"Let's get out of here, Pete," Tom said, touching me on the arm.

"Stay a little while," said Dave. He looked me mesmerically in the eye, and said, "What if you could have anything in the world that you wanted, what would it be?"

"Don't listen to him, Pete, he's evil," Tom said.

But I couldn't take my eyes away from him. His eyes were black, black like deadly nightshade, deep and bottomless as a portal leading into infinity, looking at you from behind a pair of clear pilot's glasses, and when he fixed them on you they were like a promise of great things to come but that could only be fulfilled if you were willing to pay the price. I wanted to see what was in there, what that promise was, but I had always been afraid to look too deeply, fearing that once drawn in I would never be able to get out.

Tom said Dave was evil, and always told me never to talk to him. Whenever Dave came around Tom couldn't get away from him fast enough. It wasn't fear; Tom wasn't afraid of too many things, and he wasn't afraid of Dave. It was more of an instinctive repulsion, like trying to push the same two poles of a magnet together. But they were curiously alike, strange reflections of one another, both possessing a radiance that drew people to them just as surely as iron filings are drawn to a magnet. But where Tom was light and fair, Dave was dark and forbidding, like a mountain peak with clouds all around it. Tom was open-faced and square-jawed, with light blue eyes that flashed merrily when he laughed. Dave's face was closed, and although he smiled a lot he almost never laughed and the smile did not extend to his eyes. Tom was like the morning of a sunny day, fresh and clean and full of promises of good things to come. Dave was like the twilight as darkness begins to fall and long shadows are cast over everything and you don't know if what's lurking in the shadows is good or bad, but you are curious to find out what is there and a little bit afraid of it too. So if people were drawn to

Tom for the Light, they were drawn to Dave for the Dark, and if Tom was like the Sun, Dave was like the Moon.

They were both good-looking, born lady-killers, but in different ways. Tom might have been a poster-boy for what masculine good-looks are supposed to be. Dave was so handsome he was almost pretty, and he was also a little effeminate, something you could never say about Tom. If he was especially impressed by something he would throw his arm out in a limp-wristed fashion and exclaim, "Oh, you don't say," in a rather feminine manner that wasn't an act but seemed, as far as I could tell, genuine. This made him all the more sinister, and yet fascinating to me at the same time. And Dave knew how good-looking he was. He was as vain as the proverbial peacock, and something of a dandy too. He wore black leather boots that came up to his knees, lavender shirts with long billowing sleeves, and silk scarves tied around his neck or his head, and many times I saw him looking at his reflection in a mirror or window, or noticing the way the eyes of women followed him when he strode down the street, leaving a blazing trail of blue or lavender behind. Sometimes he wore clear rimless pilot's glasses that allowed you to see into his eyes and other times he wore mirrored sunglasses that reflected your image back at you and made it impossible to see what was behind them. He appeared to have no difficulty seeing whether he had glasses on or not and I wondered if his wearing or not wearing them were meant to manifest difficult facets of his personality.

Waldo and Karlovitch had become his disciples soon after he came to town. They did anything he said and took all the abuse he gave them— and he abused them frightfully, calling them Neanderthals and Cro-Magnons, cretins and morons—without ever talking back and always returning for more. He ripped around town driving a bright red Porsche, tearing down the streets like a magenta bullet and then coming screeching to a halt when he got to where he wanted to go. When I looked at him I had the strangest feeling that what I saw was not the real thing but an illusion, that hidden beneath the fancy clothes and the pretty face was something else, his real self, and that if I ever saw it I would be frightened to death. He was always friendly to me, engaging me in conversation whenever I happened upon him on Main Street or on the beach or near Strawberry Fields, the headshop where the hippies hung out. But he always made me uneasy.

And sometimes on the beach at night, near the jetty at the far end of town, I had seen a bonfire burning. If my father beat on me when he was drunk or my mother came into my room late at night and sat on my bed in her sexy nightgowns and I had to ask her to leave, knowing she would come back again if I didn't keep my door locked, I would sneak out through the window and I would walk down there close to the jetty and I had seen that fire burning. I got close enough to it to smell marijuana being smoked, and I had seen, by the glow of the fire, Dave in the center of a circle. Waldo and Karlovitch were there, and so was Larry, Dave's brother, and other people I didn't know, for by now Dave had assembled a regular coterie of acolytes around him, lost souls who believed he had some wisdom to impart to them that would make their lives better. I heard them chanting in a language I didn't understand, and a day or two later, when I went there in daylight, I had found strange markings on the rocks and the remains of an animal that had been cut to pieces.

"I'm not evil," Dave said to Tom. "All I do is give people what they want. I know what you want," he went on.

"No you don't."

"You want to be the best surfer in the world, you want to be known in all the hot spots, everybody will know your name. And you want to go to Hawaii, too, and surf the big waves there."

The expression on Tom's face told Dave he was right. "Don't be surprised," he said. "I know everything."

"You can't know everything," Tom declared.

"Oh yes I do."

"He knows, Surfer Boy," Karlovitch called from over where he was. "He knows everything."

"He can read minds," Waldo put in.

"I read what passes for a mind when it comes to you, Waldo," Dave said. "I can read minds and I can tell the future."

"I don't believe it," said Tom.

"So you want proof. How about this: Want me to tell you what's about to appear? A smelly, stinky old ragbag of a man is coming. He slept in the gutter last night and he got drunk on cheap wine that he bought from panhandling money on Main Street. Here he is now," and Dave turned and spread his arms like an announcer introducing a juggling act, and right then Deacon Christopher came staggering out from beneath the pier, like Lazarus rising from the dead, and stood blinking in the sunlight. "What did I tell you?" said Dave.

"How the hell did he know that?" Tom whispered.

How could Dave have known? His back was to the pier and Deacon hadn't been there when he was leaning against the piling. Months afterwards Tom and I talked about it. "Say," Tom said one day (we were living in the commune in Laguna Beach by then, sitting upstairs in our room) "you remember that day we were on the beach and Dave knew Deacon was coming without even looking?"

"Sure, I remember."

"How did he know that?"

I just shook my head. "I don't know. I saw it, though, same as you did."

"But how did he know?" Tom persisted. "He doesn't have eyes in the back of his head. Do you believe those stories people tell about him, that he can read minds and all that?"

"I never did believe it. But I've seen that guy do some funny things."

"There must be some explanation," said Tom.

"Such as?"

"I don't know, but there must be one. Still," he said, shaking his head, "there is something real spooky about that guy."

Deacon was a familiar figure in town, an embarrassment to the store owners and city fathers who wanted to clean the town up and make it respectable so they could bring in business and tourist dollars. When he stood on Main Street near Clancy's Bar or by Strawberry Fields on Ocean Avenue, his filthy hand stuck out, badgering passers-by, saying "Some spare change? Some spare change?" the people who ran Angels Beach, like Tom's Uncle Neal, cringed and turned red and vowed to do something about it. When someone gave him a dime or a quarter, placing it in his skeleton-like hand with its long ragged nails with the crescents of dirt beneath them, the dirt spreading from the end of his fingers onto the nail like a spot of ink, he would say, "God bless you, God will reward you," speaking out of a tangled greasy black beard, his head bobbing up and down on his chicken neck.

He stank horribly and wore ragged clothes that hadn't been washed since Eisenhower was president: Torn jeans and old motorcycle boots, a ragged shirt and a sleeveless denim jacket with a skull and crossbones on the back. His hair was as black and greasy as his beard, although there was more and more gray mixed in with it nowadays, and hung wildly from his head in long waves.

When he had begged enough money he would get a bottle of the cheapest wine or whiskey he could find and get drunk. Sometimes when he got drunk he would go up and down Main Street yelling and beating on a trash can lid with a stick, shouting that the end of the world was near and it was time for everybody to do their penance. Eventually someone would call the police, and they would throw him in the drunk tank until he slept it off. When they turned him loose he would go right back at it, begging and drinking and carrying on until he got locked up again.

That was the way he lived. Sometimes he tried to change: He would go to the New Faith Chapel on Main Street and get food there, and he would attend the Reverend Jim Feather's sermons and sing "Hallelujah!" with all the rest of them, and he would say he was swearing off booze and would turn over a new leaf. But that never lasted long. In a few days or at most a week he would be back to begging and carrying on again.

He hadn't always lived like this, this pathetic scarecrow of a man who staggered all over town begging and sleeping with the alley cats. I was one of the few people who could remember that he was the remains of a once proud man, although it seemed like an awfully long time ago, almost in another lifetime. But when I was a little kid Deacon had lived on 14th Street, two blocks over from me, and he would fix my bicycle when I had a flat tire or the chain was broken. His garage was made into a workshop, and he was always out there, fixing cars, fixing motorcyles and drinking beer. There was a smell of solvent in the air, and music playing from a radio, for Deacon liked listening to American Bandstand. He would be out there in his undershirt, his long arms with their elongated corded muscles bare, a pack of cigarettes rolled into the sleeve. Sometimes he wore a Harley-Davidson hat on his head a la Marlon Brando in *The Wild One*, and he had a beard and kept pictures of naked women on the walls of his garage. There was a swastika flag hanging from the rafters, which he had brought back from the war. "I had to kill a goddamn Nazi to get that flag," he used to say.

A lot of people in town said Deacon had a fortune put away somewhere, that when he had gone crazy he had forgotten where it was. Everyone had heard the story and so it probably wasn't true. But it was the kind of story that wouldn't go away, like the Lost Dutchman Mine or the city of El Dorado. People believed it, and that made it true in a way, gave it a life of its own. But it wasn't the same now, things had changed. I wasn't that little kid anymore and Deacon wasn't like he used to be. Now he was an emaciated skeleton, afraid of his own shadow.

Deacon didn't remember me anymore, but once in a while I thought I saw a trace of recognition in his eyes, as if he almost remembered. He would look down at me and smile, the way he had back in the old days when we were friends. A few times he had even gone over to his old house on 14th Street, and had stood in the street in front of the house, looking in vacantly, and stay there until somebody ran him off.

But all that was long ago, another time, it seemed.

I watched, with a rising sick feeling rising inside, as Dave, Waldo and Karlovitch began to look closely at Deacon, as if they were inspecting him for something. Waldo and Karlovitch forgot about Tom and me and began to grin. They were anticipating some good clean fun here, why, this might even beat hitting dogs with their car.

"What are you doing here, Deacon baby?" Dave asked.

"Oh, I walk here sometimes."

"Oh you do, do you?"

"Yeah, it's somethin' I like to do. I been walkin' here for years, when

I'm here."

"When you're here? Is there someplace else you go?"

"Yeah. I go over by the jetty sometimes, and I talk to seagulls an' sit on the rocks."

"Some of them seagulls are his friends, aren't they, Deacon?" asked Waldo.

"Sure, some of 'em are."

"An' they talk back to you, don't they?"

"Oh no. They never gimme no sass. They're real mindful of what I say."

This made Waldo and Karlovitch laugh. "He goes other places too, don't you Deacon?" asked Waldo. "He even goes to other planets. Ain't that right, Deacon?"

"Is that right, Deacon?" asked Dave. "You go to other planets?"

"You think this is the only world?" Deacon said indignantly. "There's others too! I know, 'cause I been to 'em."

"He's been to 'em," said Karlovitch. "What do you do when you go there, Deacon?"

"I'm so far out of this material world it's like I never been here at all," said Deacon, his voice rising even as the laughter from his tormentors grew. "I talk to rocks and trees—"

"And they talk to you, too, don't they?" asked Waldo.

"You goddamn right they do!"

"He's been to Tibet," said Waldo.

"Tibet?" said Dave. "What does he do in Tibet?"

"What do you do in Tibet, Deacon?"

"I been to Tibet an' got buried alive, an' I left my body and floated way up there" he pointed, "in amongst the stars—"

The three of them were stooped over with laughter by now. Dave took off his aviator glasses and wiped his eyes. "Oh Deacon," he said with a wrist-flipping motion of his arm, "You just slay me. Hey Larry," he called to his brother, who was lounging on the sand nearby, sitting there vacantly with his back against a piling, "come on over and get hip to this."

Larry, the knuckle dragger, short and built low to the ground, as broad in the shoulders as two ordinary men and twice as strong, came stalking over. He could bend nails with his bare hands and tear telephone books in half. He had a wide, brutal face with a broken nose—the reminder of a brawl with some Hessians in a Long Beach bar—and small pig's eyes that glared sullenly out at the world like two dead lamps. He stayed in the background, rarely speaking, only coming forward when his brother called him to frighten somebody. When Larry passed by, people froze and held their breath and didn't breathe again until he had gone.

He came over and stood next to Dave now, arms folded thickly across his chest, silent, deadly.

"You think I'm nuts, don'tcha?" Deacon demanded. "You think I ain't never been to where I say I been. Well, lemme tell you. You don't need nothin' but your spirit to go. Your body can stay here."

"Does your body stay here, Deacon?"

"I ain't in this world!"

"No?"

"Oh, hell no! My body is stuck here, but the real me can go anywhere in the whole universe."

"Do you go by taxi or flying saucer?"

"You think it's funny but it ain't!"

"Deacon, you been on one too many acid trips," said Karlovitch.

"I was somebody 'round here once," Deacon yelled back.

"Deacon, baby," said Dave. "My ears. You're hurting them."

Deacon stopped yelling, and stood mumbling to himself. "I ain't in this world. I ain't, I ain't."

"Hey Dave," said Waldo. "Let's throw him in the water."

"Why, whatever for?"

"Just so we can see what happens."

"Waldo, I keep waiting for you to have an intelligent thought. Think that ever will happen?"

"But Dave, listen. Wait'll you see what he does!"

"What'll he do?"

"You gotta see it! It's too much! Please, Dave!"

"Get Larry to help you," Dave agreed.

Deacon had begun to wander off, but they weren't long in catching him. Larry went over and caught him from behind, clamping on like a machine, and Waldo took hold of one leg and Karlovitch caught hold of the other. In an instant Deacon was lifted off the ground, it all taking place so quickly he didn't know what to make of it.

"Hey, what're you guys doin'?"

"Oh, shut up," said Waldo. "Just get ready to feel real good."

"We're just gonna take you for a ride, Deacon, just a little ride, that's all," said Karlovitch.

"But what for?"

"Quit squirmin'!"

"Lemme go! Lemme go!" he cried. "What did old Deacon ever do to you guys? Lemme 'lone, why don'tcha? Please lemme go, I ain't in this world no more, oh let a poor old devil alone!"

But the more he begged the more Waldo and Karlovitch laughed. Even Larry chuckled a couple of times. Tom and I stood watching, following as they got closer and closer to the water. The whole thing was making me sick and I didn't want to watch anymore. I didn't know who I was more disgusted with, Waldo and Karlovitch for tormenting a poor old fool like Deacon, or Deacon for letting them do this to him. He looked like some sort of human sacrifice being taken to a pyre.

It bothered Tom, too. "You guys having fun?" he shouted.

"It's just some harmless recreation," Dave said. "Why don't you join us?"

"What are you going to do next?" Tom asked. "Take fish out of water and watch them die?"

But Dave wasn't paying any more attention. He followed the others closer down near the water, where the real fun was about to take place.

The closer they got to the water the more Deacon began to understand what they had planned for him. "No, no, please!" he cried, and he began to thrash all around, trying to get free. But they had too tight a hold on him, and he had no strength anyway. He begged something pitiful, but this just made them laugh all the more.

When they got to the edge of the water they began swinging Deacon back and forth, chanting "One-Two-Three!" and then they let him go like a sack of dirt. Deacon sailed through the air, flapping his arms like wings as he desperately tried to avoid the water. But he landed right in it, and he screamed as if the water was liquid fire on his skin. Standing there on shore, Dave, Waldo, Larry and Karlovitch roared with laughter at the sight.

Deacon flailed about frantically, screeching, trying to get on his feet and get out of the water. A wave came in and washed over him. "Not yet, not yet," said Waldo, and as Deacon came out of the water he and Karlovitch grabbed him and threw him back in, like a fish they didn't want, getting wet up to their waists. "Let's drown him," said Karlovitch. So they went further into the water, caught him, and held his head under.

When they let Deacon up his hair was all matted and wet, his beard stuck to his face. He was puffing and blowing and howling with terror. Water came out of his nostrils and mouth. Then Karlovitch hit him in the stomach so that he doubled over, and they grabbed him again and ducked his head back under the water and this time they kept it there and didn't let him up.

"They're gonna kill him," I said helplessly.

When they finally did let him up he was limp and heaving, and they let him go and didn't hinder him this time when he came out of the water and fell like a rag onto the sand, retching out salt water in big gasps. The four of them stood around him and laughed.

"Let's get out of here," I said disgustedly.

"Don't go away mad, surfer boys," Waldo taunted. "Just go away."

There followed more mocking laughter. "That fucking Waldo," I said.

We went back the way we had come. I felt as if I might throw up.

When we got to Pacific Coast Highway Tom said, "I feel kind of sick."

"Join the club," I said.

"Forget about it," said Tom. "Sure you won't go with me tonight?"

He pointed to the north, where the old power plant sat.

"I told you."

"If you change your mind, call me or come over."

"I won't change my mind."

"All right," he said wistfully. "But it would have been so much fun."

Chapter 4

The Baby Bird

Angels Beach was founded by the Reverend John James Jones, who claimed he had a vision of angels dancing on the beach near Alamitos Bay. He was one of the town's earliest residents, and established its first church as well as its first business. The story of the reverend's vision spread, and by the time the city incorporated in 1910 it was so well known as Angels Beach that there was no point in naming it anything else.

The Reverend Jones was having more than just visions of angels. He also said he saw burning bushes and heard voices. Perhaps these were the result of his domestic problems, because one day not long after the city incorporated he went to a hotel in Long Beach near the Auditorium and killed his wife and her lover. He then went to his house on Studebaker Road and shot himself.

So Angels Beach was born, and in its early years it was known as a little fishing village with about a thousand permanent residents. They lived on small streets in little houses with vacant lots between them. The streets were rough and narrow, and each had an alley separating it from the next one. It was as if they had been built with the idea that only small cars would traverse them, and not very often at that. On the northern end, toward Long Beach, there was a lumberyard and later, a trailer park, and on the other side of Pacific Coast Highway a small airport from which biplanes and crop dusters took off and landed. It closed in 1950, but the hangers and other buildings were left behind and when I was a boy I used to play there, and you could see the remnants of the runways that now had weeds growing over them.

The streets began at Pacific Coast Highway and ran in a straight line to the beach, intersected by Electric Avenue (which went, along with the railroad tracks, to the old power plant that Tom wanted so badly to explore). There were seventeen streets, each, as I said, with an alley in between it, starting at 1st Street and going all the way to 17th Street at the southern end. 1st Street ran parallel to the San Gabriel River, which emptied into Alamitos Bay. Big rocks lined both sides of the river, and a bridge ran across it, over to Studebaker Road, where the Long Beach Marina would eventually be built.

On the other side of the river were more fields, empty and barren, no different from the fields on the far side of the highway near the old airport, mile after mile of tumbleweeds and tall waving grass. There was a rise, known as The Hill, on the far side of the highway, that rose gently and then sloped into a big, dense grove of eucalyptus trees that was once a sacred spot to the Indians that inhabited the area before the Europeans came.

In the late 1950s the area began to grow. People came from everywhere to live at the beach. The vacant lots I had played in had new houses and apartments built on them. The city of Long Beach built a marina right alongside Alamitos Bay, where boating enthusiasts moored their yachts and schooners and cabin cruisers. On The Hill and beyond new housing tracts were built, three, four, and five bedroom ranch-style homes with connecting garages and no alleys in between them. Everyone drove new cars, everyone lived in a nice house. So why were they all so unhappy?

I lived in Old Town, on 16th Street, near the southern end and a few blocks from the ocean. The houses were small, built in the 1930s and 1940s. On quiet nights when I couldn't sleep I could hear the waves crashing on the beach, a few blocks away.

Many times I had heard Laurie Anne nag George about selling this house and moving into one of the new developments. A lot of the old-time residents were doing that. But he wouldn't budge from where we were, and so we stayed there.

When I got home that day it was getting close to dinner time, and I found Laurie Anne holding my brother Darren on her lap and playing with him as if he were a baby. His arms were around her neck and she was petting him and cooing over him, saying he was her baby, and her love, and her bitsy-poo, and then she would kiss him and coddle him like was a big, brand-new doll she had brought home to play with. She had kept his hair long and curled all the way up until he had started kindergarten, saying she had always wanted a little long-haired boy, and she dressed him in sailor suits and bunny suits for years after that, and said he was *so* cuddly in his bunny clothes she just wanted to hold him close to her and kiss him again and again. She had a lot of make-up on and her long red nails glinted in the light.

"You like to sit on Mama's lap, don't you, Funny-Bunny?" she said, valiantly trying to bounce him up and down, although this wasn't easy, for he was eleven, almost twelve, now. "You're Mama's bunny. Won't you always be Mama's funny little bunny?"

"Yes Mama," he said. Then he saw me, and when he did he put out his tongue and sneered, his beetling-black eyebrows coming together as he did so. Our mother saw none of this, and she kissed him on the mouth, then pressed him to her chest the way she would a newborn.

"Pete home, Mama," Darren said. "Pete home now."

"Oh," she said, turning, and seeing me standing there. "Oh, Pete, there's something in the backyard I want to show you." To Darren she said, "You get down from Mama's lap now, Funny-Bunny. She has to tell big brother something."

She got Darren off her lap, and stood up. "We're playing our baby game," she explained, and when I didn't say anything, but just looked disgusted, she became defensive. "But he's my baby," she said. "Isn't he just a cute baby? Did you ever see such a cute baby in all your life? Hmm? Did you? So cuddly, so soft and precious." She tousled his hair. "Come on, big boy," she said to me, "let's dance, dance with me, come on," and then she tried to dance me around the living room, going "La-da-da-dee-dah," to the tune of *The Blue Danube* and pressing herself against me. I pushed her away.

"Why don't you want to dance with your mother?" she said poutishly. "Your poor mother, you don't care about her at all, do you? You're a mean kid."

"What was it you wanted to show me?"

I followed her hip-shaking march into the backyard and stopped beneath one of the elm trees. There was something on the ground and she pointed at it. "There it is," she said.

A baby bird had fallen out of its nest. It lay on the ground, unable to move, chirping pitifully and fluttering wings that were too small to carry it into the air. At the sight of it Darren let out a squeal of cruel joy and charged, his fingers outstretched like claws.

"Don't touch it!" I said sharply. "Its mother won't take it back in the nest if you touch it."

Darren stopped short, glaring at me resentfully.

"There's no need for you to talk to your brother that way," my mother reproved. "He wasn't going to hurt it. Why can't you ever just be nice to him?"

I didn't answer that but knelt down beside the baby bird, looking in wonder and curiosity at its tiny wings and beak. I could feel the terror it felt at being away from the only home it had ever known. I was touched by it, for it was so small and helpless, and I decided the only thing to do was get it back into its nest someway.

"I thought you might want to help it," she said. "You are always wanting to help strays. Sometimes I think you like strays better than you like your own mother."

I looked up into the elm tree, which swayed slightly in the late afternoon breeze, looking for the nest, which I saw at last, high above.

"I'll get something to put it in," I said, "and then carry it up there and try to get it back into its nest someway."

"Just don't try to bring it in the house. I'm going in to fix dinner."

She left, and I went into the garage and found a woven basket my father and mother had brought back from Tijuana years ago. I can climb the tree, I thought, with the basket in one hand, and with any luck I can roll the bird into the nest without touching it. If a stray dog came around I wanted to feed it, I left milk for the neighborhood cats. I wasn't like Tom, who preferred to collect bugs—I liked small animals, and always had. I went out of the garage and back into the yard.

Darren stood a few feet away from me, staring, intense, not speaking, waiting with his mouth open.

I knelt down expectantly, the basket in one hand. Blood oozed from the beak of the baby bird. It kicked and twisted, the little wings flapping weakly, like the last flutterings of the wings of a dying angel.

I turned on my brother, who stood like a runner at the starting blocks.

"Is it dead yet?" he asked, breathlessly. "I only stepped on it hard enough to break it. I wanted it to still be alive when you came back. I wanted it to suffer, and I wanted you to see it die." He smiled at me with a cruel, mocking triumph in his face, his black eyebrows arching.

"Why?" I said, not getting it yet, not wanting to believe that anyone, even Darren, who liked to tease tied up dogs until they were foaming with rage and who smashed other children's toys just so he could watch them cry, could be *this* cruel. "Why did you do that?"

"I felt like it," he declared, smiling still. "I didn't want you to have it. So I killed it and now you'll *never* have it."

I flung the basket aside and charged for him. He turned and ran for the house, screaming, "Mama! Help! Mama!" But I ran hard, and just outside the back door I grabbed him by the shirt and flung him face down onto the grass. He kept screaming, "Mama! Mama!" over and over, kicking and howling wildly in his terror, and I hadn't even begun to start giving him the pounding I so badly wanted to give him before our mother was there between us, rising, it seemed, from the ground like a maternal savior, determined to protect her baby.

"What are you doing to him?" she cried, throwing her arms out and back so he could hide behind her.

"He killed the baby bird!" I yelled.

"I did not! It was a accident, Mama!" Darren bleated, scrambling to his feet and getting behind her. "I dint mean to, Mama," he said. "Mama, I dint. I dint mean to hurt that birdie, Mama. Why, I would *never* hurt no baby bird, Mama. I would never." And finishing this, he sneered at me again, and stuck out his tongue.

"Liar!" I yelled, reaching past my mother, making a fist and extending the knuckle of my middle finger and thumping Darren on the breastbone. Tom had shown me how to hit that way. Darren howled obligingly, throwing his hands up over his chest, tears streaking down his face. "Mama! Mama, my heart! He hit me right in the heart!"

I got slapped ringingly across the face. "Why are you always so mean to your brother?" my mother cried. "Why do you always humiliate him and bring him down? Why can't anyone ever just be nice to him?"

"He killed the little bird," I repeated. "He killed it, he did." I held my hand up to my face. But my mother wasn't listening to me anymore. She had turned away, she was gone, back into the house. Darren, still crying and holding his hands to his chest, went with her. But at the door he paused, and turning so our mother couldn't see, he sneered at me one last time.

• • •

I decided to bury the baby bird. It seemed important, to me, that this tiny bird, so cruelly killed, be placed in the ground. So, I got a small shovel from amongst my father's tools and took the dead bird out near the far back fence, right next to the alley and the eucalyptus tree, and dug a hole perhaps two feet deep, and laid the little bird inside.

I wondered if I should pray. I would have, perhaps, except I didn't know how, for I had never done much praying or gone to church.

I had lived in this house all my life and while I dug the hole I remembered that this eucalyptus tree, whose smell always made me think helplessly of cough syrup and being home in bed with the flu, had been there for much longer than I had been on this earth. When I was small I had built a tree house out here, and looking up into the green leaves and sun-spotted shadows I could still, amazingly, see remnants of it—a piece of a plank here, a rusty nail there--proclaiming mutely that I had been there too, I had left my mark, however small, behind me.

I remembered that my father had sawed the wood for the tree house for me. He had used his table saw that was in the garage and he cut the planks to length, saying that this wood was pine and pine wouldn't last as long as oak would last, but it was good wood all the same. Now that's funny, I thought. He liked me, back then. He hates me now but he liked me then. I wondered why he hated me now just as I'd wondered that at least a million times over the past couple of years, and I wondered if I was different, in some way, compared to how I'd been then, when he liked me and took me fishing with him and helped me build a tree house.

I buried the baby bird my brother had killed and when I finished I put a little marker over the spot, just a few twigs, nothing more. If you didn't know they were there for a reason you wouldn't give them a second glance. If Darren knew why I'd put them there he for sure would kick them over.

In the corner of the yard, right next to the fence by the alley, off a ways from the eucalyptus tree, was an oak tree, no more than a sapling still, with a small round fence made of chicken wire surrounding it. I had planted it there years ago, and I watered it faithfully, wanting it to grow. Now I went and got the watering can from beside the garage, filled it, and watered the oak.

One day when I was in the fourth grade the teacher had taken our class out of our room and over to the auditorium, where classes from different grades had gathered. One of the teachers set up a television in the front of the room. They told us they had brought us here so we could watch the new president of the United States, John F. Kennedy, being inaugurated. That was in January, 1961. I had just turned ten.

I had watched. I wasn't all that interested, but I had watched. I saw the old, outgoing president, Eisenhower, standing tiredly on the platform, and then there was the new man, Kennedy, bareheaded and much younger, taking the oath of office. People made speeches and bands played. I couldn't figure out what the big deal was.

After the inauguration we went back to class and the teacher had passed out some little packets of acorns. On the back of these packets it said, "Hello. I am an acorn. Plant me in the ground and water me regularly, and in about 100 years I will grow into a full-sized oak tree for everyone to love and enjoy." So I had taken the package home. I was probably the only kid in school who did, because the ground around the bicycle racks was littered with them, but I took mine home and did as the instructions said. I watered the acorn week after week and one day, to my great delight, it sprouted confidently out of the ground and began to grow. But it was a slow process. It had been nearly eight years now, and it looked pretty puny to me. If you're going to grow, I said to it silently, you better get going, you only have ninety-two years left. But what would be here in 100 years? What was here 100 years ago? Where was I? Was I anywhere? Where would I be in 100 years? What happened to life, where did it go when it was over? In the corner of the yard, a few steps past the back gate, stood the remains of the incinerator. It was crumbling and falling apart now. We used to burn our trash in there when it was still legal to burn your trash outside. George kept saying he was going to tear it down but he never got around to it, so it just sat there, year after year, crumbling away a little more. Did life get burned up like the trash that we used to burn in there?

"Hey, Ugly, Mom wants to know are you going to eat dinner here tonight?"

Darren stood a safe distance away this time, just in case I decided to come after him again.

"What are you doing, Ugly?" he sneered, his black eyebrows coming together again. "Tending to your stupid tree? That tree is stupid and ugly like you are."

Darren had black hair like our mother, and he also had her small, oval-shaped eyes. We were a real contrast, Darren with his dark hair and prominent black eyebrows and me with my blond hair and light complexion—people had a hard time believing we were really brothers.

"You know what I'm gonna do sometime? Sometime when you're not here? I'm gonna get the ax and then I'm gonna chop that stupid tree of yours down so it dies and you'll never get to see it grow like you want. What would you do if I did that, huh? How would you like that, if I chop down your stupid tree?" He took a couple of steps closer, tense, in case he had to run. "What would you do about it, huh?"

"You touch this tree, ever," I said, "and I will kill you."

"I'm gonna tell Mom you said that!" Darren cried joyously. "You just wait! You're really gonna get it for saying that to me, you big ugly stupid moron!"

I still had the aluminum watering can in my hand and I flung it sidearm by the handle. About two inches of water remained in the bottom, just enough to give it some velocity so that it flew straight as an arrow. Darren stood frozen as the missile shot his way, and then at the last second he tried to leap aside. But it was too late, for the can hit him at the knee and he responded with the most satisfying jump and scream. "Mama!" he cried, running for the house, holding his hurt leg and limping. "Mama! Pete hit me! He hit me with a water can! Mama, my leg! My leg hurts, Mama!"

I retrieved the watering can and put it back in its place next to the garage. I heard Darren in the house, yelling and crying, and I didn't have to be psychic to know what was going to happen if I hung around: In a moment my mother would be back out here, yelling at me and maybe even slapping me again. So I went toward the back gate, past the remains of the old incinerator and into the narrow alley, got into my 1965 VW bus and drove over to Tom's house.

Chapter 5

The Old Power Plant

"You want a job?" asked Tom.

"I always avoid work whenever I can," I said. "You know about one?"

"Where I work. Over at the Marina, at the gas dock Denny Lockhart's old man owns. He wants to hire another guy and I told him you might be up for it."

"I'll think about it," I said. "Maybe if I got a job my Dad would get off my back. He's always saying what a lazy good for nothing I am. Does it pay anything?"

"'Bout a buck-seventy an hour."

Night had fallen by now and we were walking along Ocean Avenue toward the far end of town. We could hear the surf rolling in and out on the beach, a dull, constant roar that after a while you really didn't hear at all, it was just there in the background.

When we came to the First Street entrance to the beach we turned and went across the sand where there weren't any people now, the waves breaking on the silent deserted beach and the moonlight playing on the water. A small bay formed where the San Gabriel River empties into the ocean and it looked very quiet and peaceful, as if you could walk or ice skate on it. The coastline swung outward in a broad arc, past the lights of the Marina, and we could see the lights of Long Beach Harbor and then beyond, to the Palos Verdes Peninsula.

"Why are you so set on doing this?" I asked Tom.

"It's like this," he said happily, "I want to be the first guy to do something, like the first to climb Mount Everest, or the first man to walk on the moon."

"Did you bring a flashlight?" I asked.

"I brought two," he grinned.

We stopped, for we had come to the jetty. "Which way from here?' he asked.

"Over the rocks," I said. "But be careful. There's a place where we can get in under the wire."

We jumped up onto the huge granite boulder that had been laid here years ago to form this jetty. I led Tom to the spot where the chain-length fence curled up at the bottom like the yellowing pages of an old book, lifted so he could crawl under, then scooted through after him. Above our heads hung a sign with a skull and crossbones on it that proclaimed, "Danger!" along with some other words of warning that had faded out over the years. We scrambled down off the rocks and were standing on a dirt service road, with the plant looming high above.

"Man," Tom whistled, "you don't see how big it is until you get close to it, do you? How long's it been here?"

"I remember somebody telling me it was built in 1910."

Tom whistled again.

"They shut it down back in '59," I said. "I can remember when it was running. You could hear all this grinding going on inside, whistles blowing, smoke and steam coming out the stack."

The plant was made of red brick, and high overhead were some old-fashioned levered windows, broken out long ago by kids throwing rocks. The size of the place, and the heavy red bricks it was made of, gave it a look of permanence, as if it had always been here and would always remain, like a medieval castle or one of the pyramids of Egypt.

"This was the easy part," I said. "Everybody knows how you get this far. Getting inside is a lot harder."

"It's like with women," Tom agreed. "Getting started with them is easy, but getting in all the way is tough."

"Except for you," I said. There were times when I was envious of the way the girls flocked to him like repentant sinners seeking absolution. He didn't even have to try.

"Hey, isn't there a watchman here or anything?"

"Oh, hell no," I said. "If there was, half the kids in this town would have been busted by now."

"Which way from here?"

"Follow me."

We walked through the moonlight, dogtrotting softly on the dirt road that ran alongside the building. It was an unusually clear night and more and more stars appeared in the sky until it seemed every star in the universe was out, twinkling and sending down its light. There was a gentle stillness in the air. I looked at the sharp weeds that grew up next to the building, yellow and green weeds that made me think of the vacant lots I used to play in when I was small.

"Wait till you see the inside," I said.

"I can't wait. Hey, that kid who got killed here, do you think he wanted to die?"

"'Course not. Nobody wants to die, Tom, why do you say that?"

"I don't know, only that I think sometimes people can't stand to live anymore. Or maybe they lived as long as they're supposed to."

"Now that's a crazy idea," I said.

"You think so? Maybe it is, at that. But I'll tell you this. You know how I ran away summer before last and went to San Francisco, to the Haight-Ashbury. That was what finally convinced my mother and father they couldn't deal with me anymore, so they shipped me off here, so I could live with dear old Uncle Neal and Aunt Marianne, whom we all know and love."

"That was nice of them."

"Yeah, wasn't it? They're all heart, the whole bunch of them. But anyway, while I was in San Francisco I met this woman named Monica. She was into all this strange Oriental philosophy. She used to try and tell me about it but it didn't mean much to me, it all seemed sort of weird to me. But I do remember her saying that you know what your entire life is going to be before you're even born."

"Now that is far out," I said. "Crazy too. I don't believe it."

"Me either. But I've thought about it sometimes. What if it was true?"

The road led down an embankment, where we stopped and I pointed. "Okay. We go down to the end of this path, see? Down to the water's edge. There's a seawall there. We walk on top and then we come to some stairs that look like they lead right into the ocean. But there's a tunnel there. We're gonna go inside, where it's so black you can't see anything, and I do mean nothing at all."

"Okay," Tom agreed. "What comes after?"

"More stairs, and if I remember right, some long passageways. We're going in through the bottom of the place, you dig?"

I pointed at the plant and then at the place where we were going in the darkness. Tom nodded.

"You slip," I went on, "and you go right in the bay. There's sting rays in there, and they've been known to bite little boys like you on the ass. You still want to go?"

"You think sting rays scare me?" he asked indignantly.

"I just wanted to give you one last chance to change your mind."

We made our way down the steep path toward the water. Then we mounted the seawall that was beside the bay. It was narrow and slippery and we walked with short, careful steps. Occasionally there would be a slapping sound coming from over the still water. On the other side of the bay were the lights of the Marina.

Tom, walking along behind me and balancing himself easily, noticed all the stars too. "Look at them all," he said. "So many stars. And I hear we don't see but a fraction of them.

"Remember that woman Monica I was just talking about? Seeing all these stars made me think of her again. She was one of those people who want to be hip but don't really know how. You ever meet anybody like that? They want to be with it but they aren't, they can't let go and loosen up enough. That's how she was. Miss Uptight, 1967, but trying not to be. She had this big house in the hills up around Berkeley, and she would come to the Haight sometimes all dressed in black and hang out.

"I think she was really just lonesome, because she was divorced and had gotten a lot of money from her old man, but still she didn't have anybody to talk to. She lived all alone in that big house, and sometimes she would start crying for no reason I could see.

"One time she took me up there and we got high. I sat on the couch looking out at the hills and the view from up there. That was something to see, too! But then I started to look at this clock she had. It was a real expensive clock, have you ever seen them, they're like in a bell jar and you can see all the mechanisms working inside? Well, I was zonked like I said, and I just sat there staring at this clock, and I was thinking of how perfect every piece was, each one designed to do just what it was supposed to do, nothing wasted, everything just balanced the right way. Man, I really tripped out on that clock for I don't know how long.

"Monica came around, and asked me what was I doing. I told her I was contemplating this clock of hers. She laughed, in this sad way she had, for she was sort of sad all the time even when she was happy, and then she wanted me to make love to her."

"And did you?" I asked, still walking ahead of him in the moonlight.

"Not right then. Later on I did. But even while I was making love to her I couldn't stop thinking about that clock, and what I'd seen inside it. I started thinking that so many things are like that, balanced, you know, just the way they are supposed to be. And looking at those stars, I'm thinking the same thing, each one has a job to do, each one is helping the rest of the universe stay in balance. Does that make sense?"

"You're in danger of becoming a real deep thinker," I said, "just like me. Here we are. Watch your step now. This is where we need your flashlights."

I went—very cautiously—down some narrow concrete steps that were even more slippery and covered with moss and slime than the seawall, Tom following behind me, and we stood in the entrance to the tunnel.

"This must have been used for waste," I declared. "See how it still stinks?"

"Maybe it's getting to be red tide," said Tom, wrinkling his nose.

We went a few feet into the tunnel, and then, as the darkness enveloped us, I said, "Okay, Tom, put on the light now." The darkness was getting thicker with each step we took. I heard a click as Tom worked the button on the flashlight, but no light came. He cursed and tried again, with the same result.

"Batteries must be dead," he said.

"Try the other one."

He did, but with no better luck than before. "Shit," he said. "This one doesn't even have a damn bulb in it."

"For God's sake, Tom," I said, exasperated, "you mean you brought two flashlights and neither of them work?" He was silent and we stood in the near-total darkness of the tunnel for a moment while he cursed and kept monkeying with the flashlights in a vain effort to get one of them to function. "Listen Tom," I said. "We gotta go back. We can't go in there without flashlights."

"Can't use the batteries in this one," he muttered, still examining the two flashlights. "Wouldn't you know, a bigshot lawyer like Neal doesn't even have a damn flashlight that works. But hell, Pete, let's go anyway."

"In the pitchdark? Not me, buddy. You can have it. Take a look in there," I said, gesturing with a wide sweeping motion at the uninviting total blackness of the tunnel. It looked as if we would be walking into ink.

"What are you afraid of?" Tom demanded. "The boogeyman?"

"Yes," I admitted. "I've always been afraid of the boogeyman, if you want to know the truth, and if there really is such a thing then this is exactly the kind of place where he's likely to hang out. Besides, this place has always given me the creeps."

"Oh, come on, Pete," Tom begged. "Don't go off and leave me here now. We've come all this way, we can't go back. Come on, please, let's keep on."

"No," I repeated.

"All right," said Tom. "Fuck it. I'll go on by myself."

I was frozen now, remembering how Brian had yelled down at me from that stack. No, I couldn't do it again, I couldn't go off and leave Tom here. I couldn't do it two times, not in the same lifetime.

"Well," I said, relenting, "I do have a book of matches in my pocket."

"You would," said Tom, "for smoking your damn cigarettes."

"If you're sure you still want to do this," I concluded.

"Hey, that's it! I knew you wouldn't let me down, Pete old buddy," Tom said happily. "Are you ready? Then let's do it!"

With every step the light behind us got dimmer and the darkness all around us got thicker until we were immersed in it. Beside me I heard Tom's breathing and his footsteps, but I could barely see him, he was just a movement in the dark.

"Hey Pete," Tom said in the darkness, "there's something I've been meaning to tell you."

"What is it?"

"I lost the good luck charm Casey gave us."

"You mean the magic circle?"

"That's the one," he affirmed.

"*You lost the magic circle?*"

"It isn't really lost," he said. "I just can't find it. I think it's in my room somewhere."

"That can't be good," I declared.

The magic circle was a disc about the size of a silver dollar that Casey had given to us last summer. He claimed it dated back to the Middle Ages, but there was no way to be sure of that. It had a magic circle engraved on one side and some astrological signs engraved on the other. Casey had said it would guide us on our journey through life and help us find our destinies. It would also protect us, he said, and bring us good luck.

After what seemed like hours my foot collided with something and I fell forward, skinning my knees and my elbows. I yelled loudly, and cursed, and said I wished I'd stayed home tonight. The sounds echoed off the walls eerily in the heavy darkness, frightening us both.

"Hey Pete, where are you?" Tom called in a loud whisper. "You all right? What happened?"

"I don't know. Wait a second." I lit a match, and the sudden brightness revealed that we had come to another concrete stairway. At the top was a large double door. We went up these stairs slowly, opened the door, and stepped into a long narrow hallway that was even darker than the tunnel, if such a thing is possible. I lit another match and we found our way to a set of doors, several of which were locked, and then we managed to get one to squeak open. It did, reluctantly, as if the hinges and mechanisms had so rusted over the years that they preferred to be left alone and unused, sitting peacefully in this darkness that was as unending and eternal as the dark inside one of the pyramids of Egypt. Those pyramids are thousands of years old, I thought, and I wondered if this plant would last that long. What would be here in a thousand years, I wondered. Where would I be? We pushed the door open and stood on the plant's main floor.

Moonlight filtered in through the windows high above, illuminating the huge oblong room so it sat in a kind of half-darkness, a deep twilight that clearly revealed everything from the floor to the ceiling. There were huge machines lining both sides of the walls, silent giants, sitting there like statues erected to some unknown electric gods, each one complete in itself and separate from the others, but identical also, long rows of inert mute Titans that had served their purpose and now sat, silently waiting for the end of time. Tom and I stood close to the wall, awestruck, as if we had entered the lost tomb in the Valley of the Kings.

"Wow," Tom said in a whisper, "what a place. Kind of gives you the shivers, doesn't it? I keep expecting those things to turn on, you know, to start up and make noise. Let's walk around some, come on. Why do you think they left them here?"

"Maybe they're no good any more."

We walked around toward the far end, looking up at the huge machines that towered over us and listening to our footfalls on the dust-covered floor.

"What did you say the name of that kid was?" Tom asked, still whispering.

"What kid?"

"The one who got killed in here, your friend, what was his name?"

"Oh," I said, softly. "Brian. Brian was his name."

"Do you suppose," asked Tom, "that he's still here, someplace?"

"What do you mean, still here?"

"I mean his spirit."

"I thought you didn't believe in ghosts, Tom."

"I don't," said Tom. "But they still scare me. Looks like we've come to the main entrance."

We stood in front of some big, factory-type double doors, but they were locked up tight and there wasn't anything we could do to get them open. Then Tom noticed a doorway off to the left, and we went through there into a black, maze-like collection of corridors and cubicles where the offices had been when the plant was in operation. We discovered old wooden desks left behind, long since rifled through, their contents dumped rudely onto the floor. "Toni and Frank, '60," was written on the wall with spray paint, "Jesus Saves," on another.

We found more stairs, and went down them, back into the inky darkness, walking slowly so as not to fall. When we got to the bottom there was another long corridor. This led toward a doorway, silhouetted by light from the windows. On the floor, near the end in the corner, we saw, as best we could see in the faint light, what looked like a shamble of objects strewn about. They looked out of place here, they didn't belong, like coal on a landscape of purely white snow.

"What is this?" Tom whispered, looking around. We saw a tangle of blankets laid out beside a wall, and a ragged pack that served as a pillow. There were some clothes--really just rags--piled up. There was garbage, too, old empty Hostess cupcake wrappers and boxes of Ritz crackers.

"Somebody lives here," I declared. "A bum, a tramp."

"I know who, too," Tom rejoined. Bending over, he picked up a tattered blue denim jacket, and showed me the skull and bones on the back. "Good old Deacon," he said. "So this is his hangout. I might have guessed. He must know some other way in here, he couldn't go through all those tunnels and everything like we just did every time he comes home."

"I wonder where he is now?"

"Who knows? Probably out panhandling on Main Street like always. Look." He gestured toward a jungle of cast-off wine bottles in the corner, and shook his head, thinking, as I was, of the human wreck that went by the name of Deacon. Suddenly he stiffened.

"You hear that?"

"Cut it out," I said.

"No, I mean it!"

"Get lost!"

"Listen!"

Now I heard it--the click of a lighter. I listened, and now I heard footsteps. They were heavy slab footed steps, crunching their way across the gravel and the weeds outside. They were accompanied by the sound of a person singing mindlessly, like a happy imbecile singing to himself inside a padded cell.

We barely had time to retreat down the corridor, down to the far end where the light didn't penetrate, and leaned against the wall, covered by the dark, before the door squeaked open and the footsteps rang dully to us. There was a flare of light, and then Deacon stood in the doorway, smoking and singing to himself.

I was struck, once more as I looked at him, with a feeling of revulsion, of shame, at this repulsive creature who was, like me, a member of the human race. He lived, and liked to live, in this squalor, a denizen of the darkness, a troglodyte who was happy amidst the dirt and the garbage. For a moment I hated him, hated him for allowing those guys to torment him the way they had on the beach today, hated him because of the way he stunk and the way he let people whack him around like somebody's dog, and then came back for more, begging, hands outstretched, wanting it.

In the dim light we could see Deacon's long emaciated frame moving about, accompanied by the glow of his cigarette. I recalled the stories people told of him having a treasure buried somewhere, and I wondered, wildly, if that could be true and if this could be the place where it was stashed. But I didn't believe those stories, they were just tall tales told so many times they had taken on a life of their own. I looked over at Tom, who grinned back at me.

"Let's jump out and startle him," he whispered mischievously. "Think of how far he'd jump!"

"He'd die," I whispered back.

"I know," Tom agreed. "But think of how funny it would be."

Now, like a sun exploding on the very first day of creation, the door squeaked open and the corridor was flooded with light. Tom and I instinctively jerked back and around the corner, then poked our heads out, me laying low, Tom above me. The light did not come down to where we were but filled up the other end, so we could see and hear what was going on.

Deacon gave a shrill cry of surprise. The cigarette tumbled from his lips and he flung himself against the wall, hands upraised. Cops, I thought, they've come to evict him from his dusty, dirty home. I expected to see flashlights and uniforms come through the door, carrying with them all the weight and heaviness of the Law.

But there weren't any uniforms, nor any flashlights. A tall figure in a brown leather jacket stepped in first, moving with the lithe delicacy of a prowling panther, sniffing the foul air and looking about disdainfully, shaking his long leonine head. He was followed by another figure, short and squat, with shoulders so wide and arms so long the knuckles almost dragged the ground.

Deacon stood against the wall as if pinned there, not speaking. The tall lithe figure, arms akimbo, said, in that strangely high voice of his, "What absolutely exquisite taste you have, Deacon baby. It leaves me-- speechless." He held up his hands searchingly, as if the unanswerable had been stated out loud.

There was snickering outside the door. Waldo and Karlovitch, I thought, even though I couldn't see them I knew they were there.

"You guys," Deacon said in a quavering voice. "What do you want?"

"Deacon, my smelly friend, we've come to pay you a social call," Dave said mockingly. "You've never invited us to your pad before. That's a shame. Friends should treat each other better than this. You should have had us over for tea long ago, but that's as may be.

"I keep hearing a rumor about you, Deacon," Dave went on. "I've heard it often enough and in enough places that I think it bears looking into. People say you have a fortune put away somewhere. I want to know where it is. Money," he lectured, like a professor speaking to a class of economic majors, "is of no use lying about. It has to be put into circulation, where it can generate more money. Haven't you ever read John Maynard Keynes?"

Deacon made no answer to this but remained where he was, attached to the wall, taller, even, than Dave, dirty and frightened. Dave kept waiting for him to reply. When he didn't Dave gave a loud sigh, hands still on his hips.

"So tell me, Deacon baby," Dave said. "Where is this money?"

"I got no money," Deacon replied in a shaky voice.

Dave sighed again, and this time there was a note of impatience in his voice. He gave a signal with his hands and his two disciples came inside. The four of them surrounded Deacon in a semi-circle.

"You lie, Deacon," Karlovitch said. "Everybody knows you got money stashed."

"No I don't!" Deacon pleaded.

"You lie!" Waldo roared.

"Think hard, Deacon," said Dave. "For your own sake I want you to think very hard."

Deacon didn't reply but just shook his hairy head back and forth.

"He's a fuckin' liar," Waldo said. "I say we make the bastard talk."

"This is your last chance, Deacon old boy," said Dave, and when there still wasn't any answer, just more babbling that there was no money, Dave sighed again. "You know what I think, Deacon? I think you just can't remember where the money is. That's all. That's the whole problem right there, men, he can't remember. He needs something to help him remember. Close the door," he ordered.

Waldo closed the door and we couldn't see what happened next, but we heard it all. The darkness enveloped the corridor again and there were sounds of scuffling. I sensed they were taking hold of Deacon, just like they had on the beach this afternoon. He cried out, like an animal, and there were sounds of blows.

"All right, Larry," said Dave. "Make him remember."

There followed after that an awful sound, long and drawn out, like an animal crying. Up above me Tom was tensed, just like I was tensed, and we listened and wondered what was should do.

"Want to charge in?" I said halfheartedly.

"You want to die?" Tom rejoined. "There's four of them. And Larry's got a gun, I've seen it!"

"We can't just sit here and listen to it!"

"Come on, Deacon," Dave was urging. "Just tell us where the money is and it'll stop. I'll get you a nice bottle of wine. No? You still don't remember? Okay, Larry, do it again, see if he remembers this time," and there was more of that terrible screaming. Then it stopped, and Dave spoke once more.

"Deacon, you're forcing me to do this. I don't want to, but you just won't be reasonable. So it's your own fault. All right, Larry, *cut him*, maybe then he'll see the light."

Tom's hand was on my shoulder and it squeezed painfully, harder and harder, as the screaming began again and kept on. There was no end to it this time, it kept going and going, and just when I thought I was going to go mad if it didn't stop there was a cry of "Oh shit!" from Karlovitch and something fell heavy and solid to the floor.

Then there was absolute silence for a moment.

A lighter clicked on, and the four of them surveyed their work. There was the sound of a slap, and Dave's angry voice.

"*Cretin*! I didn't mean for you to do that. I wanted him to talk, damn you!"

"He didn't know a goddamn thing anyway," came a new voice, Larry's, which I almost didn't recognize because he spoke so seldom. "Don't hit me again, David. I'm warning you."

"Why'd you do that, Larry?" Waldo said in a terrified tone. "You wasn't gonna do nothing like that, you only said—"

"Shut up, you imbecile," said Dave. "I've never understood how a person as stupid as you are ever learned to talk at all."

"But Dave—"

"I said shut up!"

"You was just gonna make him tell about the money!"

"What's the matter, Waldo, you scared?" Larry taunted.

"I never figured on nothin' like this!"

"Well, you better get used to it, because you two morons are in, you are in this all the way up to the cracks of your lily white asses. You got that? Both of you got that?" Dave asked.

"Dave, you shouldn't of let him do it," Waldo protested.

In the dark I could barely make it out when Dave, fast and lithe as a cougar, took Waldo by the collar and slammed him against the wall.

He didn't say anything but just held him there, and when he was satisfied Waldo had gotten the message he let him go.

"Too late for regrets," he said philosophically. "I don't believe there was any money at all, just the result of some greedy fool's imagination and tale-telling. Now let's get the hell out of here. But you two," he said warningly, "you don't forget what I said."

There was a terrible deadliness in the way Dave spoke and from where I was, hiding in the dark only a few feet away, I didn't envy either Waldo or Karlovitch. Nothing in the world could have made me trade places with them.

The door opened brightly into the moonlight and they trooped out, one by one, and then the door was shut and all was darkness again. Dave was the last one to go and before he did he paused, looking right down the corridor toward where Tom and I were hidden. He stood, outlined against the light from the doorway, looking toward us, and my breath stopped in my chest and my heart pounded like it never pounded before. Then he turned and went out.

Now we heard nothing, nothing save the sound of our own breathing.

We didn't move, but waited for what seemed the length of time it takes Pluto to revolve around the sun. Finally Tom touched my arm and we went, cautiously, into the darkness, walking slowly and carefully, until we were near the door.

"Light a match," Tom whispered, for we couldn't see anything.

Deacon lay on his back amidst the garbage and the debris of what he in his madness and his misery had called his home, his throat slit from ear to ear. The razor that had been used to do this nasty work--it was an old fashioned straight razor like I had seen in my grandfather's bathroom, alongside a shaving brush and mug and a thick long razor strap--lay nearby, covered with blood but still able to gleam evilly in the dim light. We saw, too, where his shirt had been ripped open and his chest slashed. His arms were out to either side sprawlingly, and blood had soaked the front of his shirt and dripped down onto the dusty concrete floor to form a pool beside him.

The life that was in Deacon had fled, gone, I thought, as the match burned down and went out. Just a few moments ago it was there, encased in that emaciated body, but now it was gone. Where did it go, what happened to it? Those eyes, still open, no longer saw, the nose no longer breathed, the heart didn't beat anymore. He didn't crave cigarettes and booze, he didn't have to be afraid of water now. Was life a spark that went out the way a light was turned off, or was there something more, was there a part of Deacon still lingering in this foul-smelling lair?

Tom seized my arm and jerked at me violently. "Run for your life, they're back!"

I ran. I ran back down the corridor and into the darkness, seeing, in a scissor-flash instant, Larry's thick form coming through the door. Then behind us there were shouts of rage and surprise.

Now, in this time-stopping instant, frozen there for all eternity, there were two bright and distinct flashes of yellow and orange light, each one as bright and deadly as that first flash of atomic fire at Alamogordo in July 1945. They were followed by an obscenely loud "Blam!" and in that micro-second I felt something shoot past me and hit the brick wall, splattering red dust and chunks of brick in the air.

Tom and I ran back up the stairs, through the maze of offices and back onto the main floor of the plant. Then we went down the stairs and into the tunnel that led outside. We ran faster and longer than either of us had ever run before, or thought we could run. We came out the tunnel into the light, neither of us speaking, then made our way along the seawall, then back to the jetty and under the fence. We were onto the sand now and still running, both of us panting and gasping for air, sprinting across the deserted beach toward the clump of palm trees that rose like an oasis about a quarter-mile from the pier, and when we got there we both collapsed, neither of us able to move another inch.

Chapter 6

The Promise

We lay there like that for I don't know how long, wheezing and gulping air. After a time we sat up, leaning our backs against a palm tree, both of us utterly spent, still gasping.

Even when we were at last able to speak neither of us did for a long time. We sat looking at each other, seeking reassurance that what we'd just seen was real and not a nightmare we were somehow in together. Tom's face was filled with fear, his crystal eyes wide and alarmed. The moon had come out and was bathing us in a long white blanket of light. This light was somehow comforting but I thought, It's such a beautiful night, how could something like this happen on such a beautiful night? Tom's blond hair and fair skin shone in the moonlight.

"Do you think they saw us?" he asked at last. "No," he answered himself, "it was too dark. They couldn't have."

I didn't say anything, but kept looking up at the moon. Once I had seen the moon through a powerful telescope and had seen the craters and valleys that mark its surface. It had brought me so close I felt I was actually there. Could someone on the moon, looking down here at the earth, see what was going on? There was a pulsating red light in the sky which I took to be Mars. I remembered what Tom had said about the universe being in balance. Did Deacon's death balance anything, or did it put things out of balance, so that they would have to be put right again? I had just seen a person killed, I had been shot at, but the planets just kept right on in their orbits around the sun, the universe continued to expand and grow without noticing. Or did it? Was everything marked down in a book somewhere, a long accountant's ledger, with a credit column and a debit column, to be added up on some final day of reckoning? Was that what Pete was trying to tell me?

"It all happened so fast," I said. "We were going around the corner when Larry came through the door. Why do you think they came back?"

"Doesn't matter," said Tom, leaning his head back until it rested against the trunk of the tree. He closed his eyes meditatively, those big diamond-shaped eyes the girls found irresistible, some of them not even girls at all but real live grown up women, with husbands and children even. He sat there that way for a moment, as if in deep contemplation, before his eyes popped open again.

"If they did see us," he said, as if this was a thought he didn't want to give voice too, "our lives aren't worth jack shit anymore. You know that, don't you? If they know it was us we better get on the next plane to Alaska, and figure on hiding out there until we get old. We don't have to worry about your buddy, Dummy Waldo or Dog- Face Karlovitch, they're more scared than we are. But that Dave—he's the smart one. And he's got that gorilla brother of his to do the dirty work for him."

"But they will know," I said. The words just popped out. Tom's face lit up with alarm.

"What do you mean?" he demanded.

"Because we gotta go to the police station right now," I declared, "and tell what happened."

Tom made no reply to this, but simply sat staring at me, his mouth open.

"We gotta go to the cops right away," I repeated, and when he appeared to still not have gotten this I stood up, weary from the long run we'd just made, my legs quivering and my armpits wet. I took several steps away from the palm tree. He'll follow me, he'll be right along, I said to myself, he's in shock, I'm probably in shock too. But I knew what I had to do and that was propel myself along the sand over to the stairs beside the pier, climb them, and then go along Main Street to Electric Avenue and over to the police station that was next to the City Hall on 8th Street. There was a park across the street and next door was the City Recreation Center, and my mother went there for her Women's Club meetings. When I was small she used to leave me with these babysitters and I always feared she would never come back, I would be left with these strangers forever.

Then Tom yelled "No!" and rose all at once from his half-sprawled, half-seated place at the base of the towering palm tree, all in one motion, launching himself like a rocket, leaving the ground completely and becoming horizontal in the air. He tackled me around the legs and brought me down onto the sand. Then, being bigger and stronger than I was, he dragged me back over into the shadows of the trees and held me there until I quit struggling and he was satisfied I wouldn't go anyplace.

We sat, staring at each other in the moonlight. In my head I could hear the music of Beethoven's *Ode to Joy* echoing across the empty sand to the waves that pounded the shore. Carolyn, who had brought me to the knowledge of the Great Secret, had also taught me about classical music, and when I went to her townhouse she gave me vodka gimlets to drink and she would listen to Beethoven's *Pastoral* or Richard Strauss' *Also Sprach Zarathustra*. She turned it up later when we went into her bed, because that was how she liked to do it. She had told me about the Ninth Symphony, how it was an ode to brotherhood and peace, and about the German poet Schiller, from whom Beethoven had gotten the words. I could hear them now, coming to me like figures dancing on the sand:

"O Freunde, nicht diese tene..."

Tom sat staring at me, his eyes wide open, his head cocked to one side slightly as if he could hear the music too. The waves were hitting the shoreline and I thought, there's a man dead over there, right over there he's dead he's dead he's dead can't you hear me he's dead! But the waves just keep rolling in, they don't care they don't care they don't care...

"How old are you, Pete?" Tom asked at last.

"Why," I said, "you know damn well how old I am, Tom."

"You want to live to see your next birthday, don't you?" he asked seriously.

"I suppose I do," I replied. "Sometimes I'm not so sure."

"Don't you want to graduate next June?" he went on. "Go to college, get a job, get married, have a wife that gets fat and wants to put out less and less as the years go by? Pay taxes, have kids and a house that looks like everybody else's with a dog that shits in the backyard? You want to do all those other fun things they say we got to look forward to? You want to do all that, don't you? If you don't want to live that long, you just march right over to that police station and tell what you saw. By this time tomorrow you'll be where Deacon is, if you tell."

"Where do you think Deacon is now, Tom?" I asked.

"I don't know, and I'm not anxious to join him," Tom replied. "Are you?"

"But we gotta tell," I insisted. "Those guys are murderers."

"That's exactly why we can't tell," Tom said fiercely. "If we do they'll murder *us*. I know how the law is. I've watched Neal in court. We go and tell and those guys will be out of jail in a few days and then they'll come looking for us, man, don't think they won't. Where the hell are you gonna hide, Pete?"

"But we saw it..." I said, weakening even as I spoke the words, picturing Larry coming at me with a switchblade in his hand, the blade honed to where it could cut like a scalpel.

"What did we see?" Tom asked. "It was pitch dark in there. Can you say for sure what happened? That's what their lawyer will say. That Dave is no fool, I'm telling you, he knows all this. Hell, he can probably prove he was a hundred miles away when it happened. And then he gets loose, and so does Larry. And Larry will come and cut your motherfuckin' balls off some night. I'm telling you, Pete, you're killing yourself if you go and tell."

He saw now that I was giving way, and relaxed a bit. My shoulders sagged and I looked away from him and stared at the sand. My fists were clenched tight, the nails digging into the palms, and I realized the rest of my body was tensed up like a spring wound past the breaking point. I saw he was right.

And then something else came to me. What, when you really thought about it, did I care that Deacon was dead? He was just a smelly old bum, a ragbag who lay face down in the gutter dead drunk most of the time. He was of no use to anybody. To me he was nothing. What if he was my friend once? Maybe he was better off dead. Maybe the world was better off without him. Who was I to say?

Still feeling uneasy I said, "Okay," to Tom.

"All right," he said. "Let's shake on it. Let's swear right here and right now that neither of us will ever tell what we saw or heard at the old plant tonight.

"Do you swear?" he said. "Swear to God?"

"I swear," I said.

"Say it again."

"I swear it."

"I swear it too," he said.

We shook hands, and then stood up.

"What time you got?" Tom asked, since he never wore a watch.

"Ten," I replied. I was shocked. Ten o'clock! It was only ten o'clock. I had thought it must be three in the morning by now. Years, it seemed, had passed since we went into that plant, it was a whole lifetime ago. But it was only ten o'clock. I had to go home now, I had to get up and go to school in the morning. And I would know in my heart what had happened and I couldn't tell anybody. People would be walking down Main Street, my father would be asleep in front of the television if he hadn't already gone to bed drunk, and over there was a body lying in a pool of blood.

"Let's go home," Tom suggested, and we began trudging toward the pier. We went up the stairs and along Ocean Avenue.

"The best thing to do," Tom said, "is forget about it."

"Yeah," I agreed. At his house we shook hands again and I got into my van and drove home alone.

But how, I wondered, could you *ever* forget about something like that?

Chapter 7

The Lost People

I always thought of red when I thought of Carolyn Hoskins. The color automatically popped into my mind whenever I said her name to myself. She had red lights in her townhouse that made everything seem red inside and even the sheets of her bed were cherry-colored. All was red and we were like two black figures silhouetted against a brilliant red sky, red like a desert sun, blood red, with *The Beautiful Blue Danube* or Tchaikovsky's *"Russian Dance"* playing in the background.

"Do you know how to waltz?" she asked. She always asked me that.

"No. I've never waltzed before, will you show me?" That was how I always answered. It had become a ritual.

She was willing to show me, and while I didn't think I would like to waltz it turned out I liked it real well. We would waltz all over her living room and then up the stairs to her bedroom. That was where the best part of the dance happened. When she put her hands on my shoulders with the music going and looked into my eyes there was only one thing I could think of. And I knew she was thinking of it too, but she wanted to waltz first.

"Come on," Carolyn said, breathing hard as the music played downstairs. "Come on, now, inside of me. I want to feel it, right there, and I want to sin! I want to be in sin, and live in sin, and wallow in sin!"

She moaned and cried out as if she were dying, squeezing me so hard that I thought she would break my ribs. She's devouring me, I thought, she's swallowing me whole, she's taking something from me, something I'll never get back, something precious, and I don't want to give it to her, and yet I keep coming over, to give it again and again.

I had known, that morning, that I would come over to Carolyn's house tonight and get drunk and be with her. I had known it when my father, as we sat down to eat breakfast, had opened his newspaper and begun roaring. "A bum!" he bellowed, his face red. "A stinking goddamn bum! Living right there! Right there!"

Carolyn lived in a townhouse in one of the new housing developments near the Marina that were very trendy and expensive and smelled of fresh paint and new carpeting. There was a skylight directly over her bed and from there you could look straight up into the sky and see the stars and the moon on a clear night. But tonight it was overcast and you couldn't see anything. In the distance I heard a foghorn blow, long and mournful, from someplace on the ocean outside the Marina.

On the table beside the bed sat a picture of a square jawed, brown-headed man with chiseled rugged features who stared disapprovingly at me. What would he say if he knew about this? What would happen if he were to show up here all of a sudden? I didn't want him staring at me anymore so I turned his picture over.

"Don't do that," said Carolyn.

"He's staring at me."

"I don't care. I want him to see. I want him to see what we do in my bed."

"Why?"

"Because it's so wicked. Because I want him to know. Do you know what he'd do if he found out about us? He might kill both of us. He'd definitely kill you. He's crazy. He always says the idea of another man touching me makes him insane. That's what I like to do. I like to make him insane."

"Does he know about this?"

"He suspects I have someone else. He suspects because I drop him little hints, leave clues around, just to torment him. I like tormenting him."

"Why do you like tormenting him?"

"Because it's fun. It makes me feel good. I like how crazy it makes him."

"What does he do?"

"He's an artist. A visual artist. I told you. Why are you so interested in him now?"

She had told me. His name was Rudy and he was German--Swiss and he practically worshipped the ground she walked on. And she was a poet whose work was published in poetry journals and literary quarterlies and was talked about in coffee houses and on university campuses where people gathered to talk about such things, she was an up-and-coming New Poet who was going to shake up the poetry scene so that it would never be the same again.

Her red hair was spread out on the pillow like liquid fire. Carolyn Hoskins, I said to myself, Carolyn Hoskins carolynhoskins, making one word of it. Carolyn, I thought again, wishing I had more to drink. I loved her desperately once, maybe I still did but I wasn't sure of that or anything else anymore.

She was a poet. She was unconventional. People expected her to be different. She was very chic and stylish and hip, dressing in a manner other women wished they could, always with an extra dash of style and class thrown in: A bright sash tied around her waist, or a scarf fastened about her head, vividly colored but not too loud, not on her. I had seen her and fallen in love at once, there was no stopping me. And she led me, step by step, down a path that could only end in one place.

Not that I minded going. I had seen her at a poetry reading at Long Beach State this past summer and she had come up to me and laid her small cool hand on my arm and asked me how I liked it. That seemed an eternity ago now. "How old are you?" she asked. "Twenty? Twenty one?"

"No," I said, pleased that she was noticing me and flattered that she thought I was older than I was. "No," I said. "I'm seventeen."

"Oh no," she said. "You must be older than that. You seem so much older and mature." Her red hair hung down dangerously to her shoulders, and later she invited me over to her townhouse and gave me cognac to drink and asked me if I knew how to waltz. She had said I was such a handsome young man, so nice to look at, and she gave me books to read by Rainier Maria Rilke, e.e. cummings, and Allen Ginsberg. She opened up a new, exciting world for me, a world I was only on the fringe of but hoped, one day, to enter. She read my stories and poems and said they had potential, and asked me what I wanted from her.

I closed my eyes, and when I did Deacon's head, disembodied and bloody, grinning a horrible lifeless grin, came toward me, floating, hideous, propelled by some unholy force that I knew would never rest. A week had gone by since that night in the old power plant. I feared I was going mad, there were times when I was certain it had never happened at all but I had just dreamed it, imagined the whole thing, and that thought, that I was crazy, was strangely comforting to me.

The morning after the killing I was amazed to discover the world was still the same. I knew I had changed greatly, I would never be the same person I had been before Tom and I crawled beneath the wire on the jetty and gone into that black tunnel. I had seen a man killed, shots had been fired at me by someone who wanted to snuff out my life the same way he had snuffed out Deacon's. How could I not be altered in the most profound way after that? And yet the world just went on and on, the same as it always had. I knew I would never look at the world the same, after seeing what I had seen in there. I was different and I felt the world had to be different too, and yet the world stubbornly refused to acknowledge this.

I had emerged from the depths of the plant with a story to tell, and yet I couldn't tell it. But as day after day went by and nothing was said about it, no one knew, I wondered more and more if it really happened. I kept expecting the news to sweep over town, but not a word was said, the body just lay over there, rotting on the dusty concrete.

I didn't sleep much, but lay in my bed looking up at the big crack in the plaster ceiling of my room and listening to the wind gently rustle around outside. Sometimes when it was real late I could hear the waves crashing on the beach, for our house was less than a quarter-mile from the ocean and at night when it was quiet the sound of the waves breaking carried a long way. I stared at the surfing posters I had on the wall and at the horoscope Casey had done for me last summer. One night I remembered with sudden shock and horror how he had predicted that something profound was going to happen in my life in the fall, and I stared at the astrological signs and wondered what else they could tell me. As the long nights went on and the days passed I began to feel that the horoscope had a protective power, it was guarding me from all the fear and terror I felt, and when I woke up after one of my nightmares I would be grateful that it was there watching over me. The strange astrological signs of the zodiac danced and writhed about as if possessing a will of their own, each one infused with its own personality.

I was tormented by bad dreams, night after night: Dead people chased me, graves opened and the dead emerged, grinning heads with no bodies floated in the air like butterflies and followed me wherever I went. Sometimes I woke with a shout, covered in perspiration, and was glad my room was on the far side of the house, away from the rest of the family.

At school on the sixth day I ran into Tom.

"Are you sure we didn't hallucinate what happened that night?" I said to him. "Maybe it was a dream, it never happened at all. Can it be? Say it," I pleaded. "Say it was a dream we were in together."

But Tom wouldn't say it. His face was haggard, his big crystal eyes were red and puffy.

"You saw it just like I did," he said hoarsely.

"I'm not sure, now, what I saw."

"It was no dream," he maintained. "No dream. Unless it's all a dream, everything in life, I mean."

"I know," I agreed unhappily. "I just keep on wishing it was. But how come nobody knows about it, how come nobody's said anything? Maybe we should go back there, just to be sure."

"Like hell," Tom said. "Like hell I'll ever go back there, long as I live. I wish I'd never gone there at all."

"Well, it was your big idea, remember?"

"Don't remind me. You don't need to remind me. I remind myself of it every day. And I won't go back. And you," he said, putting his hand on my shoulder and squeezing until it hurt for emphasis, "don't you go back there either. You hear? Stay clear of that place. I think maybe you were right, it is cursed. First your buddy got killed in there, and now this. Stay away from there, don't you ever go back."

I had gone back, although he didn't know about it, nobody did. I had driven my van down Ocean Avenue to where it ended at Marina Drive, parked and then gone over to the chain-length fence and stared past the "Danger—Keep Out" signs to the old red bricks and broken windows. That was as close as I could get and I couldn't see anything out of the ordinary in there. The old plant looked peaceful enough, during the daylight hours, there were birds chirping and I saw they had built nests under the brick easements. They fluttered back and forth unconcernedly, circling in the air, and being born aloft by the updrafts. I got back into my van, still wondering what there was different about me now, for nothing on the outside had changed.

That morning my father came to the table for breakfast as he always did, precisely at 7:15 am, wearing a tie and smelling strongly of Old Spice after shave. No matter how drunk he'd been the night before, he always made it to the table at exactly the same time every day, although there were some mornings he looked like he wished he could stay in bed an extra couple of hours and stared at his food as if he had never seen anything quite so revolting in his life. He would hurriedly drink some black coffee, massage his temples with both hands, rub his hands together as if trying to wash them, then open the newspaper. That was when the roaring began, for he would go into a tirade, cursing and bad-mouthing everybody and everything he didn't like, and that took in just about the entire world. The country was going to hell, he said, and it was the fault of the people protesting the Vietnam War, the rioters in the black ghettos, the hippies and the students who were demonstrating on the college campuses. His face would turn red, then purple, as he shouted and cursed and beat his fist on the table in his indignation, and come close to hyperventilating with outrage at the state the world was in.

He often concluded his morning rant by taking after me with his fists, for he held me responsible for most of the world's ills and the sight of me alone was enough to send him into a towering rage. He treated me worse and worse over the past several years, and seemed to hate me more with each day that went by. Since my fifteenth birthday I had been taller than he was, a fact that did not make him proud but only fed his resentment of me. "Look," I said one day, "I'm taller than you are now." His only response was to glare at me, and say sullenly, "Don't ever think you're so big I can't whip you." In the morning I could see it coming: He would scowl at me belligerently, his face red, his chin thrust forward with his fists clenched, chest heaving as he sat regarding me as if I were an enemy that had to be fought.

"If I ever hear about you messing in any of this hippie-longhair stuff, I'll tear you apart," he would say. "I better not ever see you wearing love beads or a peace sign or a flower in your hair! I'll wear you out, so help me." If he came after me I would flee out the back door, leaving him far behind, but more often he cursed and yelled and threatened until I lost whatever appetite I'd had and left to go to school with a sick feeling in my stomach that didn't evaporate for several hours.

He had boxed during his Army days and even though he was by now fat and out of shape as he went into his late forties he could still hit somebody and make it hurt. Both Darren and I went around with bruises on our upper arms or shoulders where he had struck us during one of his drunken rages or just because he felt like it. He worked as a salesman for a construction company in Long Beach, and his work often involved taking clients to lunch or dinner where little food but much alcohol was consumed as contracts were negotiated, and he frequently came home from work so drunk he would pass out in his car and I would have to carry him into the house and put him to bed.

He spoke so often and so fondly of his time in "the service" that people wondered why he had ever left it. When asked about it he was vague and evasive, causing me to suspect there was something connected with it that he did not want to talk about.

He had won an award for bravery in Korea—the citation said he had saved some members of his squad that had been ambushed while on patrol. He was very proud of this, grandly displaying it whenever the opportunity presented itself, and often told me and then Darren how badly we would fare if we ever had to go (a not so far-fetched idea in those days when there was still a military draft). "You wouldn't last very long in the service," he would say disgustedly to one or the other of us, as if it were a dreadful failing. Darren was so frightened of him that he talked baby talk to him nearly all the time, and I simply avoided him whenever I could so I wouldn't get hit or yelled at. But if I wanted anything to eat in the morning I had to come to the table and be there with him, and endure his ranting and raving.

As he sat looking at a section headed "Local News" he suddenly started to roar. "A goddamn, stinking, lying, thieving stew-bum of a transient, living right there in that old power plant! Living right there!" He glared at me belligerently. "Did you hear me?"

"What?" I said dazedly.

"A transient!" he roared again. "Can't you understand English?" he demanded, his eyes bleary. He rubbed his hands together, glaring at me.

"What about this transient?" I asked, still not understanding.

"He's dead, goddammit to hell! Committed suicide!"

"Let me see that," I said impulsively, grabbing the paper away from him and looking at a small article, one that was certainly not the big story with the banner headlines I had envisioned. "LOCAL MAN FOUND DEAD." David "Deacon" Christopher had been found in the old P G & E plant outside town, where he had evidently been living illegally for some time. His body had been discovered by a company representative who had come to the property to take an inventory of the equipment remaining there since the facility's closure in 1959. An investigation would be made to determine the exact cause of death but the police were at present calling it a suicide, since there were no signs of foul play.

"Give me that back, damn it," George said. "Living right there all that time!" Evidently the knowledge that Deacon had lived inside the old plant was the most upsetting to him of all, for he kept on ranting about it between slurps of his coffee, going on about this stinking vagrant and bum and rubbing his temples. That Deacon had lived there, and not on the streets or in an alley, seemed to be of great importance, for he beat on the table with his fist and kept yelling about it.

I excused myself, saying I had to leave for school, and left without eating anything. I crept out of the house feeling sick. I went through the yard and past my oak tree, then into the alley where my van was parked. I started the engine, the sick feeling growing, along with the feeling of wanting to blot it all out with alcohol.

I had hoped, the way a person drowning will cling to anything he can grab for, that it would, still, turn out to be not true, unreal, but here it was. They'd found him, and I couldn't run away, anymore, even from myself.

Something was moving along the wall beside me. A spot, I thought, a spot that moves, how about that. A spot, he thought, see how I can rhyme things even when I'm drunk, and realizing in spite of my drunkenness that it was not that funny. I tilted my head slightly and saw it was a large brown house spider. It was moving along the wall right above an end table with a statuette of red and blue glass of a man and woman doing a tug-of-war.

The spider stopped, as if unsure of which way to go next. It worked its fangs open and shut several times. I sat up. Tom might like to collect spiders and bugs, but he could have them. I cast about for something to squash the spider with.

"What are you doing?" Carolyn murmured. She was far away, deep in the pillows and the half-light of the room.

"There's a spider on the wall."

"So?" she murmured sleepily.

"I'll kill it, that's what I'll do."

"No!" She sat up sharply, her red hair flowing. "No, don't kill it. Put it out the window."

"Why? It's only a spider."

She wouldn't let me kill the spider. Instead, she threw on a silk robe and getting out of bed, found a piece of paper, shooed the spider onto it, then put it out the window, into the night.

"What's that all about?" I asked.

"Never mind," she replied, rather sullenly, getting back into the bed and lighting a cigarette.

"Oh come on, tell me," I wheedled.

"Maybe I like spiders."

"Bullshit."

Carolyn seemed so strange to me that nothing she did surprised me too much anymore. I settled back into the pillows once again, prepared to forget about the spiders, when she began to talk.

"When I was small," she said tautly, with a hesitant air, "I lived in this little town in Massachusetts."

"I know, you told me that. Near Boston."

"Don't interrupt, let me tell this," she said. "One day, when I was out playing, I saw, beneath one of the eaves of our house, this big mass of spiders. It was a whole ball of them. It must have been the size of a baseball. There were thousands of them. And this ball of spiders was alive, it was pulsating.

"I looked at it, and I started screaming. I felt like those spiders were crawling all over me. Oh, it was horrible. I couldn't stand it.

"I yelled so much my father came outside. He was very sick and could barely walk, but he came out anyway to see what was the matter with me. I said, 'Daddy, look at all those spiders, kill them kill them!' But he wouldn't kill them. He looked at them and said he'd never seen anything like that before either, but that the spiders must be doing something important, maybe they were helping us somehow, and we should just leave them alone.

"But I couldn't stop thinking about all those spiders. I couldn't sleep that night because I kept thinking they were going to get in my bed. So the next day I got a broom and I went out there and I broke up that nest of spiders, I just broke it all up, and I killed as many as I could.

"I didn't tell my father what I had done. And later that day he got worse, and that night he was really bad, and the doctor came to our house, and the next morning my father was dead. And in my mind I have always associated his death with those spiders—maybe they were doing something important, just like he said, maybe they were taking on some of his illness, helping him to stay alive. But I made a vow never to kill another spider, or let anybody kill one. Now do you understand why I wouldn't let you kill that spider? Oh, what does a kid like you know anyway?"

"I think it's very noble," I said, "and moving, and I'm sure all the spider lovers of the world will always be grateful to you."

"Where are you going?"

"I want some more to drink," I said, fumbling about for my clothes.

"Don't you think you've had enough tonight?"

"No-I-do-not-think-I've-had-enough-tonight," I replied bitchily. "If-I-thought-I'd-enough-tonight-I-wouldn't-want-anymore."

"I only asked you," Carolyn said from the pillows, the smoke rising above her head. "You don't have to be rude. I don't care if you drink yourself to death. I just asked."

"Well," I replied, pulling on my shirt, "I only told you."

That Tom, I said to myself, he thinks he's the only one who has ever been with somebody older than him. I have definitely done him one better in that department. But he doesn't know about this, nobody does. I looked at Carolyn drunkenly. Her red hair was tousled from the pillows, and the robe she had put on was white silk with Chinese lettering on it. I thought she was very beautiful although there were times I hated her and didn't know why.

"Nobody knows I come over here," I said. "Nobody."

Carolyn didn't respond to that, only took another drag on her cigarette.

I turned and went down the stairs and poured myself some cognac. I drank it, then drank more, because I wanted to be drunk, to blot things out, to obliterate them, all of them, and not see and not feel anything anymore.

I sprawled heavily on the couch, drinking and smoking and looking around. There were lots of books in a wooden bookcase, some of which I'd read and others I wanted to read: *Madame Bovary, For Whom the Bell Tolls, Tess of the d'Ubervilles, The Catcher in the Rye, War and Peace, Anna Karenina, The Magic Mountain.*

One of Rudy's creations sat on a table nearby, he had given it to Carolyn as a gift, and was, she said, worth a lot of money. It was a maze of pipes and valves inside a glass aquarium, and the aquarium was filled with rocks of all different colors. There was a pilot light, and a length of flexible hose that tapped into the gas line from the kitchen, so when the main switch was thrown flames of different colors came shooting out, licking over the rocks and spreading out like napalm, rolling here, going there, the flames leaping and dancing about. It was called The Inferno, and there was an inscription on it that read, "This way to join the lost people...Abandon hope, all ye who enter here." It was supposed to represent hell, Carolyn said, and the words were from Dante. Many nights Carolyn and I had sat looking at it, after smoking some Panama Red I'd gotten from Tom, and I would wonder who the lost people were.

The thought had occurred to me many times that I was doing an awfully mean thing and I didn't like myself for it. But I kept coming over and experiencing the secret delights of Carolyn's bed, delights that were made all the more exciting by the idea that Rudy could show up anytime. Carolyn had told me a lot about him. He was rich and lived on a yacht that he moored in the Marina nearby. One day soon, when he had cleared up some business matters, he would take her on a cruise to the South Pacific and they would be gone for months. That would mean there was no place for me in her life anymore. "This is probably the last time I'll ever see you, because Rudy says we could be going any day now. And I don't know when I'll be back. Do you understand?" I would say I understood all right. And then she would put on the music and we would waltz and go upstairs to her bed and fall into it wildly. She would raise her voice up to the ceiling and beyond with her cries of pleasure that sounded sometimes like she was dying. And I didn't like myself for what I was doing, because it seemed low and underhanded, I remembered what Tom always said, that a stiff dick has no conscience.

I drank more and more cognac, realizing deep in the recesses of my mind that if I drank much more I was going to be sick, but I just couldn't seem to get to that place where nothing hurt anymore. If you smoked enough pot or drank enough booze there was a certain magical place you got to where all the hurts were gone, at least for a while. But I couldn't seem to get to that place. I drank more and was still drinking when Carolyn came downstairs, still clad in her robe.

"Why are you drinking so much tonight?" she asked. "It isn't like you."

"I don't know," I replied dully, not even looking at her. "Maybe I hate myself."

"Do you think drinking like this will change how you feel about yourself?"

"What are you trying to do? Be my mother?"

Carolyn slammed her glass down, nearly breaking it. Then she lit another cigarette with short, angry gestures.

"I think," I said, drinking the last of what was in my glass and knowing I had just said the wrong thing, "I'd better be going now."

"Yes," Carolyn said icily, "of course. You'd better be going. What else could it be? You're not leaving so soon, are you? You don't mean to tell me you're going already? Oh," she went on, "you're too much. You're not even grown yet, and you're like all the rest of them, typical man, you got what you want and then you're going. All you care about is someplace to stick that dick of yours, it doesn't matter where, any old place will do."

"Yeah," I agreed, "any old place will do. Even yours."

Carolyn's eyes blazed erubescently. "All right," she said furiously, "go on, get out. Go away and don't come back here, ever. And take your juvenile junk with you, your stupid adolescent attempts at putting words together on paper." She stormed over to a desk on the other side of the room and took out several folders, all stuff I had given her, filled with my poems and stories. "Take this crap," she said, flinging them at me. "Take it and get out."

Now I was devastated. "So this is crap. You said you liked them."

I bent over to pick them up, for they had scattered when she flung at me.

"I only said that," Carolyn stated coldly. "I didn't mean it. I only said it to be nice."

I picked up my poems and stories and slunk out. I couldn't think of anything else to say. She shut the door behind me with a certain decisiveness, a kind of finality, and I knew this, whatever it was, had come to an end, I wouldn't see her anymore.

I made my way down the stairs carefully and out to where my van was parked. I drove home slowly, then parked in the alley and went in through the back, my usual way, noting happily and with relief that my mother was not waiting up for me as she sometimes did. She would wait up for me and want to know all about where I'd been and what I'd been doing. When I had been going with Rena she had gotten extremely interested and wanted to know all about it, for Rena was the first serious girlfriend I'd had. My mother would be waiting for me, wearing one of her short nightgowns with the spaghetti straps, and would say, "Well, how did it go with Rena tonight? Did you make out very much with her? Have you gotten to first base with her yet? Did you feel her up?" If she was drunk she would giggle and say all this and keep on pestering me for details. I would never tell her, and she would get angry, and hurt, and say she just wanted to be friends with her son, and I was so mean not to tell her, why was I so mean to my mother?

But tonight she wasn't awake, and I made it to my room and shut the door and locked it so she couldn't come in. Sometimes she came in when I was in bed, clad in one of her nighties, and sit on my bed and want to play with me or tickle me, saying I was such a big boy now, she just couldn't believe how big her little boy was getting to be. I didn't like it when she did that, it made me feel funny inside, and I kept the light off and the door locked at night so she couldn't get in. Sometimes she would scratch and knock softly at the door but I would pretend to be asleep and not answer.

I hoped the cognac would put me to sleep and keep me from having the nightmares. But it didn't do me any good. I was restless all night long. Deacon kept coming to me in my sleep, his head a great mass of crawling spiders. He implored me to go and tell the truth. He couldn't ever rest until the truth of how he died came out, and people knew he hadn't taken his own life but had been murdered by those two maniacs, Dave and Larry, and assisted by their flunkies, Waldo and Karlovitch.

I got up in the morning feeling sick, my head throbbing. At breakfast George went into a tantrum right away. Students were demonstrating at Columbia University in New York, and his face didn't even get red this time but went purple immediately.

"Why don't they send all those goddamn people over to Russia?" he bellowed. "If they hate it here so much they can go live there!" He glared up from his newspaper, and when his bleary eyes settled on me I got that familiar sinking feeling in my stomach.

"What the hell are you looking at?" he roared. "You and your goddamn surfboard! I'll show you whose boss around here!"

He flung his newspaper aside, and getting up from his chair, he came toward me, his fists flailing. From where he sat Darren grinned in delight, glad it was me getting it and not him as I turned and fled through the kitchen, past my mother who was standing there in her robe and her hair in curlers fixing eggs and frying bacon, and out the back door, hearing my father shouting behind me, "You better run! You better run!" I went out the back gate and got into my van and drove down the alley.

Before I went to school I went by the old power plant. It, too, looked the same, but I knew it was changed on the inside, since Deacon wasn't in there anymore. I wondered if the dream I'd had could be real. Could Deacon's restless spirit be out there, somewhere, in a dreamy netherworld, with all those spiders on him, tormented like that until I told the truth? No, no, no, I said to myself, that can't be. It can't be because I can't bear the thought of it. It's all the booze. That's what it is.

It had to be that.

Who, I wondered again, are the lost people?

Chapter 8

Tom and Tiffany

Tom and I worked at the gas dock that Denny Lockhart's father owned at the Long Beach Marina. We still went surfing every morning before school started, and when the last bell rang at the end of the day we went over to the Marina and stayed until ten or eleven o'clock every night, working at the dock. While the weather stayed warm we sat in folding chairs outside the office and drank wine or smoked Panama Red, which Tom seemed always able to get, and looked into the sky when the night was clear and counted the stars. We watched the lights of the Marina and of Long Beach Harbor beyond, watched them flicker and dance and move about as if driven by some power and will of their own. We could also see the old power plant, standing there silhouetted against the skyline, but neither of us mentioned that anymore.

The dock was at the edge of the Marina. You crossed the bridge over the San Gabriel River off 1st Street and made a left turn into a parking lot, then went down some stairs toward the water. There was a gangplank and then the dock, made secure to some pilings so it wouldn't float away. There was an office, and three pumps outside on a wide wooden deck. At the end of the day when the channel gate got ready to close there was a regular parade of all the boats from the Marina, all shapes and sizes: sailboats, motorboats, yachts, houseboats, schooners, catamarans. Then the gate closed and night fell, and the lights of the Marina came on, lighting up everything with all the colors of the spectrum.

I saved all the money I made, for I had nothing to spend it on and I didn't care if I spent it or not. I did my homework there, and I helped Tom with his, just to keep him from flunking out. And when I was there alone I sat listening to the gentle slap of the water against the pilings, and felt the slight rocking of the dock on the sea, and stared at the old power plant until I couldn't stand to look at it any longer.

I marveled at Tom, at how he was able to go on without letting this bother him. He appeared to never think of it, while I couldn't think of anything else. I couldn't sleep, in fact I was afraid to sleep, for when I did the nightmares plagued me. I kept seeing Deacon with his throat cut, over and over, and his head covered with spiders, crawling in his eyes and nose, and he came to me again and again in my sleep, begging me to release him from this torment, to go and tell the truth. And I couldn't, I couldn't tell, I had sworn not to and besides, I was afraid.

Then I started to dream about Brian again. I saw him lying there on the roof of the power plant. And once he and Deacon were together, floating along side by side and coming after me. Go away, I would scream silently, go away and leave me alone!

He was a bum, I thought. He was no good to anybody. The town drunk. He stank to high heaven, people used to hold their noses and shrink away in horror when he came near. What did it matter to me what happened to him? And yet I could never get free of the feeling I'd done wrong by keeping quiet and swearing I'd never tell. I felt ashamed, because I wouldn't tell and because I'd been there and done nothing while those guys killed him.

It seemed to me it was all about lying. To not tell, when I knew the truth, was the same thing as lying, when you got right down to it. And lying was not a good thing to do even though I had done my share of it in my life. But I always told myself I only did it when I had to. Even when you had to do it, lying was a bad thing. I hoped I could get through my life without any more lies.

That probably wasn't realistic. Lies were everywhere, untruths all around. One day in October I arrived at Tom's house to pick him up on my way to the Marina. I saw the front door open and a tall blond girl wearing a black dress came out and walked through the archway. She walked past the white snakeroot and bitterweed plants in their big round pots and the small stone statues of angels that led toward the front garden, pulling at one of her sleeves and smoothing her dress with both hands, then feeling at one of the buttons in the back as if she wanted to make sure she had done it up right. She didn't notice me and she walked quickly down the driveway and across the lawn and got into a 1967 Pontiac Firebird. She had turned the corner and gone out of sight when I knocked on the door. "Hey there, old pal," Tom smiled. He was pulling on his shirt and his hair was disheveled. He smelled of Chanel Number 5 perfume. "You ready to go?" He hummed and sang a few lines from *Sloop John B.*, and we got into my van and drove to the Marina.

The next day I got there a few minutes early. I saw the same Pontiac Firebird parked a couple of doors down from Tom's house. Then the front door opened and the same girl came out, going hurriedly over to her car and driving off.

As soon as Tom opened the door I said, "I think I left my copy of *The Sun Also Rises* in your room the other day." I was in an honors English class and we were reading about Jake and Brett and learning about The Lost Generation. I brushed past Tom and hurried up the stairs to his room.

"Wait a minute," Tom said. "The Sun Does What? You didn't leave anything up there, park your board for a second Pete," but I went before he could stop me. The scent of the Chanel Number 5 got stronger as I went up those stairs, like a trail a bloodhound could follow. His bed lay in disarray, with pillows scattered and the blankets turned over. He bounded up the stairs behind me.

"There's no book of yours here," he said. He looked a little uncomfortable. His shirt was unbuttoned and his hair was tousled again. He fiddled with the St. Christopher medal around his neck.

"No, the book isn't here," I agreed. "We better get going."

As we were driving toward the Marina I asked, "Is Denny going to be there today?"

"I think he's coming by later."

"Is Tiffany going to be with him?"

"Tiffany? She usually is. He likes to take her everywhere he goes."

"He wants to marry her," I declared. "Can you imagine?"

"They've been going together a long time," said Tom.

"Think she wants to marry him?"

"How would I know? But I guess I wouldn't be surprised if she did. He's the kind of guy girls want to marry. Steady, dependable, the kind you can count on. Plus he'll be rich someday."

"He's crazy about her," I said.

"He must be, if he wants to marry her."

Tom didn't look at me while we were talking but kept his face averted and looked out the window. We were turning off Studebaker Road, the one that led to the Marina, and I drove into the parking lot.

"She looks good, Tiffany does," I said. "But she flaunts herself. And she's a flirt."

"She flirts with everybody," Tom agreed.

"But Denny doesn't seem to mind. Or else he doesn't notice."

"He doesn't notice," said Tom. "He doesn't notice a lot of things. That's the way he is."

"He doesn't notice a lot of things that go on right in front of him," I said. "He's a great guy, though."

"Sure, he's a great guy," Tom agreed.

That night about nine o'clock I heard footsteps on the gangplank. The door of the office opened and Denny came in. Tiffany followed him. She wore a black dress and the scent of the Chanel Number 5 came in with her.

"Check this out," said Denny, waving a piece of paper about like a flag. "It's my acceptance to Long Beach State. I made it! See? Look at it Pete."

"Terrific," I said.

"I know it probably doesn't seem like such a big deal to you," he said, "with you going to UCLA and all. But my grades haven't been that great and I didn't know if I would get in or not. Pete's the smart one of our group," he said to Tiffany.

"I'm not so smart," I said.

"Anybody who can get straight A's without even trying is smart," Denny insisted. "I wish I could be as smart as you are, Pete."

"Let's have a drink," Tiffany suggested. "Is there anything here to drink, Tom?"

"Yeah. We should have a drink," Tom agreed. He went to the refrigerator and got out a bottle of red wine. "This will do, won't it?" he said. He turned the radio on to one of those underground FM stations that were broadcasting out of Long Beach and Pasadena in those days. Jimi Hendrix came on, singing "Purple Haze." Tom poured four glasses of the red wine. "What'll we drink to?"

"Let's drink to Denny's going to Long Beach State," I said.

"It's a good school," said Denny. "Not as good as UCLA, or USC, or Stanford, but it is a good school. They have a great business program there."

"Business sounds so boring," said Tom. "Why are you majoring in business?"

"That's what I'm going to do," said Denny. "Business. I'm going to go to work for my Dad, marry this wonderful girl here," he took Tiffany by the hand, shook it back and forth, all the while smiling at her, "and make lots of money. That's how my life is going to be."

"That will be nice," said Tiffany. "Having a lot of money will be nice. I've always wanted to be rich." She looked at Tom all the while. "Isn't there anymore of this?"

Tom poured more wine for her. She drank part of it and smiled at him. He didn't smile back. We all went outside and sat in the folding chairs and looked at the lights of the Marina and the Palos Verdes Peninsula.

"Are you two engaged?" I asked.

"No," Tiffany said quickly.

"We're engaged to be engaged," Denny said, smiling at Tiffany, who smiled back at him weakly.

"We're all so blonde here," she observed. "Tom, Pete, me, we're all blondes. Except you, Sweetie," she said to Denny.

"I guess I'm the odd one," Denny said.

"I still like you, even if you are odd," said Tiffany. "You should wear these," she continued, picking up an old pair of sunglasses that had been lying around the office and gathering dust and putting them on Denny's face. "There. Now you really look odd."

"I can't see," said Denny. "I'm blind." He took the sunglasses off and blinked. "That's better."

"You two look so much alike," Tiffany said, meaning Tom and me. "You could almost be brothers."

"We're not so much alike," I said.

"Sure you are. You're both tall, you're both cute. You're like apples from the same tree. Don't you ever see Rena anymore, Pete?"

"Not for a while now," I said.

"Did you know she's been going to that church on Main Street?"

"What church?"

"Oh, you know, the one all the hippies and junkies go to, I think it's called the New Light or New Faith or New Something-or-Other. I think she goes there mainly to get away from that stepfather of hers."

"I know him," I said. "Spiro. When we were going together and I went over there I saw him breaking plates against the wall and throwing dishes at the back fence."

"What kind of a name is Spiro?" Denny wondered.

"He's Greek," I said. "Like in Homer."

"Homer who?" asked Tom.

"Oh yes, Homer," said Tiffany. "Didn't he write part of the Bible? Oh no, that was Virgil."

"I never could understand this religion stuff," Tom said. "Some people get so worked up about it. Does anyone go to church anymore?"

"I do," Tiffany said. "We go to church every Sunday." She had just about finished her glass of wine. She kept looking at Tom. She wore a little cross around her neck, made of pewter, and it glinted in the moonlight.

"If there is a God," said Denny, "then I should thank Him for all He's done for me. I've got this great girl," he put his arm around Tiffany's shoulders and pulled her over to him, "and I've got these great friends, Tom and Pete, why, we're like the Three Musketeers, aren't we? Let's drink to friends," he proposed, holding out his glass formally. "To good friends," he said.

"To good friends," I echoed, holding my glass out and looking at Tom.

So we drank to good friends, although Tom had some trouble keeping the smile on his face and Tiffany quickly drank the remainder of her glass and asked for more. Tom went inside and opened another bottle. He came back out and sloshed more wine into everyone's glasses.

"What about you, Tiffany?" I asked. "Where are you going next year?"

"I'm going to Long Beach State too," she said, "and I'm not sure what my major will be. I'm also trying to get into modeling school."

"That way we'll be together all the time," said Denny. "What's your major going to be, Pete?"

"Not sure yet," I said. "Maybe English."

"Talk about boring," said Tom.

"So speaks someone who isn't going to college at all," I said.

"English is still boring," Tom declared.

"I guess it would be, to someone who never reads a book."

"Aren't you worried about getting drafted, Tom?" Tiffany asked. She was still looking at Tom, and the more she drank the more she looked at him. It was becoming so obvious that it would soon be impossible to pretend it wasn't happening. But Denny, cherub-faced and round-eyed, didn't notice anything.

"Yeah Tom, what about that?" he said. "You'll be draft bait if you don't go to college."

"If they ever try to draft me I'll tell them I have homosexual tendencies," Tom stated. Everyone laughed. "That's all you have to do.

They don't take queers in the army."

"We should go," Denny said when he had finished his wine. "Come on, my love," he said, still holding Tiffany by the hand. "See you guys tomorrow," he said, waving to us and then heading up the gangplank, dragging Tiffany behind him. She followed, but turned and looked one last time at Tom as they left.

Tom fairly gulped down what was left in his glass, then poured more and drank that down too. The bottle was almost empty.

"What do you think you're doing?" I said.

"Nothing. Just finishing this bottle is all."

"Not that," I said. "I didn't mean that."

"No? Well, what do you mean?"

"Never mind," I said. "Forget it."

"You look like hell, Pete," Tom said.

"Do I?"

"Oh, yeah." He sat down beside me. "You got these bags and black circles under your eyes, your shoulders are all hunched up all the time. You're really a mess. What's the matter? Don't you ever sleep anymore?"

"Not for a long time now," I said. "Can you?"

"Sure."

"How?"

"It's easy. I just close my eyes."

"I can't close mine. Whenever I do, I see it all over again."

"You shouldn't think about it," said Tom.

"Don't you ever think about it?"

"No."

"Well, I can't stop thinking about it!"

"There wasn't anything we could do!" Tom nearly shouted.

"You're wrong, there was! We could have rushed in, yelled, thrown a rock, anything! We shoulda done something, I tell you. Instead, we just stood there like a couple of flakes, and we let those bastards do it."

"Yeah, and we'd be dead now, too," Tom reminded me grimly. "Have you forgotten how Larry shot at us? We'd be with Deacon now, wherever that is."

"Maybe I'd rather be with him, than here, and thinking about it all the time."

"Stop talking that way," said Tom. "You're gonna go crazy, you keep on talking that way. Here. Take another swig of this wine. It's good wine, Pete. I stole it from Neal's liquor cabinet. It cost a bundle. Have some more, it'll cheer you up."

"We can't just stay stoned and drunk all the time," I said.

"Sure we can," said Tom, taking another drink of the wine. "What else is there?"

I wondered if I might be wrong about him, maybe all this gaiety was just an act. I felt, as time went on, that I detected a sadness in his eyes that had never been there before. All the laughter and joking he did seemed forced, he was *too* happy, there was an almost manic wildness to him that didn't seem right, it was out of kilter. I wondered if he would do anything as low as what he was doing with Tiffany if we hadn't seen what we'd seen that night. Maybe it affected him too, more than he knows. What happened changed us both.

• • •

Not too long after his affair with Tiffany began Tom started suggesting we run away.

School began to be a real burden for him. He did less and less of his schoolwork, and even with me helping him his grades sank lower and lower until he was failing just about every class he was in. Tom had never been what anyone would call a scholar. He had trouble just sitting through a class and he couldn't concentrate on his studies for more than a few minutes at a time. But if it was something he found interesting the story was different.

Tom had an overriding interest in biology. He loved to collect insects and study marine life. Under his bed were jars and collecting boxes of wasps, bumblebees, garden spiders, and other bugs he found interesting. He could sit beside a tide pool and tell you the names of all the creatures that lived in it, and he could tell you where their cousins and distant relatives lived. He even knew the Latin names for some of them.

His favorite, though, was Hercules, his pet tarantula.

Hercules was fat, striped, multi-colored, and came, according to Tom, from someplace down in Mexico. Tom fed him crickets and small lizards, and claimed his bite wasn't poisonous, but I never wanted to put that to the test. Hercules would sit in his glass terrarium by the window for days without moving a single *trichobothria* hair, but when there was food nearby he managed to move just a shade under the speed of lightning. Once in a while he would slowly raise one of his forelegs, as if testing the air, and then lower it back down. Tom said he might live as long as twenty-five years.

"They don't see hardly a thing," Tom said, "and they don't hear, either. But put food nearby and they know what to do.

"Look at this," he went on. "Look at Hercules' worst enemy. You think you got problems? How would you like to have *this* coming after you?"

He reached under his bed and got a quart jar with air holes punched in the top. From inside came an angry, frightening buzz that made me shiver, involuntarily, all up and down my back, and when I saw what was in the jar and making that sound my shivers took a quantum leap.

"Look!" Tom said again, with a touch of awe in his voice.

Inside the jar was the biggest wasp I'd ever seen, shiny black with bright red wings, pounding furiously against the glass, trying to get free. "Check her out," Tom said reverentially.

"What do you call it?"

"She's the digger wasp *Pepsis*."

Pepsis red wings buzzed like an engine. "Never saw anything like her before, did you?" asked Tom. "Isn't she awesomely beautiful? Know what she'd like to do, better than anything else in the whole world? Sting poor old Hercules there, sting him and paralyze him, then lay her eggs on him. Then the wasp grub will eat him alive. *Alive.* How's that for creepy? But isn't she beautiful?"

"How do you know it's a she?"

"'Cause I just know. The female is always the deadly one."

"You oughta know."

I didn't share Tom's enthusiasm for bugs in general, and I loathed spiders, but when he began to unscrew the lid of *Pepsis'* glass prison I had an immediate desire to run for my life. "Hey!" I cried. "Don't let it out in here!"

"Oh, don't be such a sissy." Tom fearlessly undid the cap, like Pandora opening the box to release the demons. He stepped over to his open window and the wasp flew off into the air. I breathed a little easier.

Sometimes Tom carried Hercules around on his head. Once he greeted his Aunt Marianne that way, standing there with Hercules amidst his blond hair as she came in through the door after a long day's work. She saw the spider and let out the most awful scream, which wasn't like her, for she was a cool professional woman, usually very reserved and unemotional. But now she began to yell something terrible. Her briefcase, purse, and the papers that had been in her briefcase flew in all directions and she flung herself backward to ward off the monster. Tom, startled, tossed his head back and Hercules fell to the floor. This only increased Marianne's terror. Hercules, not knowing what to do, began to scuttle along the carpet in her direction, heading straight for her. It looked to Marianne as if he intended to crawl right up her legs and burrow in. She threw herself backwards and landed on a couch that was fortuitously behind her. She whooped and hollered for Tom to do something, which he did, scooping Hercules up and taking him back upstairs, laughing silently to himself.

That was the end of Hercules, for Neal made Tom get rid of the spider, but Tom was unfazed. He and I took a trip to the Mojave Desert not long after that and he caught a hideous green scorpion, which he put in Hercules' old terrarium. He would get a big magnifying glass and look at the scorpion with it. "Check it out," he said, "if you want to see something that is pure ugly." Neal made him get rid of the scorpion too, when he found out about it, and the black widow spider he'd caught to keep the scorpion company, that had to go also.

Sometimes he would astonish me by reading a book. I found him reading books about insects, marine life, even the stars and planets of the solar system. He read about dinosaurs and reptiles, along with the books about Hawaii and the other islands of the South Pacific he wanted to see. I told him he should read *A Tale of Two Cities*, which I had just read and liked, but he set it aside after getting about one-third of the way through. "Boring," he said.

There were times when I would find him in one of the gardens of Neal and Marianne's house, (the house had several beautiful gardens, for Marianne loved growing flowers) watching a spider spin its web, and once, a blue jay building its nest in a plum tree. He could sit and watch that for hours, going into a meditative kind of state. But afterwards he would be filled with a manic kind of energy, and would want to go surfing, or, if the waves weren't up, we'd go to the park and try to find a game of touch football.

Or else he would be in the garage, waxing or repairing one of his surfboards. He would set the board on sawhorses and work over the cracks and dings with liquid resin and fiberglass, his practiced eyes missing nothing. When he wanted to, he had great concentration. He seemed unaware of my presence, sometimes, as he stood contemplating the board, dressed in his usual fashion: Cut off jeans, colored t-shirts with no sleeves, sandals or tennis shoes with no socks, his St. Christopher medal around his neck. He had the tell-tale knots of a real surfer on his knees and ankles, knobs that come only come from hours of sitting on the board, waiting for the waves to come up. He would hum *Sloop John B.* to himself as he worked, although as I said he was always out of key.

He had surfed all the hotspots of the West Coast, from Ensenada down in Baja to Steamer Lane in Santa Cruz up north. Now he wanted to go to other places and surf, see new beaches and the world at the same time. Hawaii would be the first, and from there he would go to Fiji, Tahiti, Australia, New Zealand--there weren't any limits, as long as the weather was warm and there was a beach, he knew he'd be happy.

But school began to drag him down more and more, and his fling with Tiffany bothered him too, even though he didn't admit it. But the longer it went on the more obvious it became, and as the weeks passed they weren't even bothering to hide their affair anymore. Not from me, anyway. Denny still didn't have any idea. With his round face and innocent eyes he saw nothing but goodness all around him. He believed everyone's heart to be as pure as his own.

He had his life planned out. He would go to Long Beach State, get his degree, go to work for his father, and marry Tiffany, in that order. His father owned several businesses besides the gas dock and eventually he would take them over and maybe start some new ones of his own. He even knew how many children he wanted--four, he said, because that was a nice round number--and he planned on living right here in Angels Beach all the rest of his life. "There isn't any better place to live that I know about," he said. "Everything I want is right here."

"But you've never even been to any other places," I said. "How can you know?"

"I don't need to. You and Tom can go out and see the world, have all the adventure, it's okay with me. I'll be here when you come back. It's just how things are.

"But you gotta promise me one thing. You gotta keep in touch with me, no matter where you go. We have to stay friends, always, loyal and true, the way friends are supposed to be."

When he talked like that it was all I could do to keep from grabbing him by the collar and shaking him and yelling, "Open your eyes, you fool!" I couldn't understand how somebody could do that to someone he called a friend, and I couldn't understand how that friend could be so blind as to not see what was going on right under his nose practically, and then I couldn't understand how another friend could know about it and do nothing.

What is right, I wondered, what is wrong, and what do you owe to somebody else? What is the line between truth and lies, sanity and madness, life and death? Maybe life *is* death, and we don't know it. Maybe it is all just a dream. Was that what Pete was trying to tell me? That life is just a dream, as the song said? At night I would look up at the stars and ask them what they knew, wondering if they could hear me, if they would ever answer me.

And when the answer came I didn't like it, for it always came back to

Deacon, and those dreams I had: The spiders were on him, and he was begging me for help.

But I couldn't help him.

I was ashamed, because I hadn't helped him. I had just stood there while those four bullies roughed him up and threw him in the water that day, and I had stood by that night while they killed him. I hadn't helped, I reflected, because I was afraid. I was afraid of Dave and Larry, I was a little less afraid of Waldo and Karlovitch. I was afraid of what they might do to me if I butted in, they might have taken me into the water and ducked my head under until I almost drowned, they might have slit my throat the way they did Deacon's.

Why did they choose that night of all nights to go after Deacon's non-existent treasure? Why couldn't they have gone the night before, or the night after, or a month after? And why did Tom get his big idea to go that day, and not some other day? It didn't make any sense to me. Maybe it was all an accident, or maybe there was some design to it, some plan, but I couldn't see what it was. And now I was ashamed because I knew about Tom and Tiffany and I didn't tell Denny, and that made me part of the wrongness too.

One night in late October I was alone at the dock when the door of the office burst open and Tiffany came in. It had just started raining and her hair and face were wet.

"Is Tom here?" she asked breathlessly.

"Tom?" I replied.

"I mean Denny."

"Neither of them are here. I'm all by myself."

She paused a moment, as if thinking something over, then said, "I know about you and that woman."

"Who?"

"That Carolyn Hoskins. I saw you go to her house. I live on that same street. But don't worry. I won't tell anybody."

"It doesn't matter," I said. But I still didn't want anybody to know about it. "I appreciate you not telling," I said. "Thanks."

"I knew you'd understand," she said. "I gotta go find Tom."

"I thought you were looking for Denny."

"I'll find one of them," she said from the door.

So after that I had an understanding with Tiffany. I wouldn't say anything about her and Tom and she wouldn't say anything about me and Carolyn.

Right away it began to rain even harder. I stayed in the office and looked out the window at the drops hitting the water. They pitter-patted down at first and then got louder and stronger until the rain turned into a regular storm. I looked out the window at the ocean, which was all gray and cold-looking, and saw the waves tossing up and down, rolling back and forth angrily. There was a flash of lightning, but no thunder. Then I saw a tall blond form moving through the rain, walking along and shaking his head to keep the rain off, and I realized Tiffany hadn't found Tom when she went off to look for him.

"You just missed her," I said when he came into the office and closed the door behind him, the water dripping off him and landing on the floor.

"Who?" he asked, shaking his big head to get the water off.

"Your great love, Tiffany."

"Hah," he said derisively. He poured himself some coffee after setting his schoolbooks down. "Wanna help me write a report?"

"Not especially. Why can't you write your own report?"

"Because it's boring as hell and you're better at it than I'll ever be."

He drank the rest of his coffee and made a face, as if he hadn't enjoyed it at all. "God," he said, "this school stuff sucks. I've gotta write a report on *Macbeth*, which we are reading for this English class I'm in. How did I ever wind up in an English class where they read *Macbeth*, I'd like to know? What did I ever do to deserve that? *'Lay off, MacDorf, until Norwegian Wood comes to Dullinsane.'* See, I know my Shakespeare, you can't say I'm a brainless California surfer boy anymore. Pete, I don't think I can stand this until June. Let's run away."

"Where to?"

"I don't care, anyplace. Anyplace is gotta be better than here, I tell you. Let's do it, what do you say?"

"Later," I said.

"I want to live in a grass shack on an island someplace," Tom said. "All I want to do is surf every day, live off the land, fish in the ocean. Is that too much to ask from life? Doesn't sound like it to me. There's gotta be a place like that somewhere, what do you think?"

"How would I know?"

"Let's go find it."

"It's called Paradise. Shangri-La. The Garden of Eden. People have been searching for it since they crawled out of the caves. But it sounds too ground to be true."

"He wants to graduate," Tom said. "You and Denny, the college boys. Hell, if you won't go with me, I'll do it myself. Or else I'll join up. That's what I'll do. I'll join the Army, go to Vietnam."

"You're crazy," I said.

"Or," he went on, "I'll drop out. I'll go back to the Haight. I was happy there. I'll grow my hair long again, be a hippie. A flower child, that's what I'll be."

The rain stopped and night fell. We closed the dock, locked the pumps, counted the money and put it in the safe. Tom turned the radio to an underground FM station. "How about my report?" he asked. "It's due tomorrow."

"I've got one at home I did for the same class last year," I said. "You can copy it."

"Thanks, Pete." He got a bottle of wine from the refrigerator and drank some. "You say Tiffany was here?"

"Yeah, just before you came."

"Did she say she was looking for me?"

"Either you or Denny."

"What he doesn't know," said Tom. "I think they'll be very happy together, don't you?"

"I don't know. Maybe you and her will be happy together."

"Me and her?" Tom looked at me astonishedly. "Man, you got a screw loose, Pete old pal, if you even *dream* of a thing like that."

This apparently triggered something he was feeling, for now he began to tell me about what he and Tiffany did together, leaving nothing out. This wasn't like him and I didn't want to know this. The world was filled with things I didn't want to know, that was my discovery for the year. But the whole idea of what he was doing with Tiffany made me angry now.

"Well," I said testily, "Denny tells me he does the same things with her. The very same things, all the time. So it doesn't sound to me like you're getting anything special, Romeo."

"Hah," Tom snorted. "She only gives it to him when he's desperate, and even then she makes him beg for it."

"How do you know? Were you there watching?"

"I don't have to. She tells me. She tells me all of it. And she gives it to me anytime I want it, see?"

"Well, la-dee-dah," I said. "Don't you know he wants to marry her?"

"So?" said Tom. "Let him marry her, what do I care? I sure don't want to marry her."

"Does she know that?"

"'Course she does. She wants to marry him, too."

What a pair, I thought. Aloud, I said, "Don't you think it's wrong, what you're doing?"

"A stiff dick has no conscience," he replied flippantly. Then he added, "Maybe it's better that it's me who's doing it, because if it wasn't me, it would be somebody else, somebody who doesn't care about Denny at all. I do care about him, and so I won't let it get out of hand and nobody will get hurt."

"That sounds like an awful lot of bullshit to me," I declared.

"Since when did you get so fucking holy?" Tom said, becoming angry now. "Mind your own business from now on. Don't talk to me about this anymore." He had never spoken so fiercely to me before and I decided I had better drop it. What did I care, anyway, when you got right down to it. It was just more lies, that was all. But I was getting so sick of lies.

Tom turned away from me morosely now, and sat staring at a pile of newspapers that had gathered on the old wooden desk below the window. Some of them went back months, all the way to the start of summer: *LBJ Orders Bombing Halt, Proposes New Talks; Rocket Attacks Rip Saigon;*

Humphrey Gaining on Nixon in Latest Poll. "These papers oughta all be thrown away," he said, "before Denny's old man sees them and gets pissed." We heard footsteps on the dock outside and then the door opened and Denny bounced in.

"Hey, you guys," he said cherubically, his round features lit up with his usual good cheer and friendliness toward everybody. "You're still here, I was hoping you would be," he went on, clean of hands, pure of heart.

He shook hands with us both, happily, beaming. "I just saw Tiffany," he said. "I wish you two could have seen her face. She thanked me over and over for the necklace I got her. That's the best thing in the world, to give somebody a gift and make them happy, especially when it's someone you love."

I couldn't help but smirk ever so slightly and look at Tom when Denny said this. Tom wouldn't meet my eye but sat there looking uncomfortable.

Denny drank a mouthful of wine and then got out a joint of Panama Red. We sat smoking, Denny and I doing all the talking, Tom not saying much, but looking embarrassed and uncomfortable and trying hard not to show it.

"This is one of the best things in the world," Denny declared. "To be with your friends this way. What could be better? In about eight more months our high school days will be over and everybody we know will go their separate ways. We've been together all these years, some of us, since kindergarten even, and now we won't be here anymore. And some will go away from here and some will stay, and some will get married and some won't, but it won't be like it was, it won't be the same anymore. But we gotta remember things like this, and times like this, and not forget, because it'll never be like this again, never. Don't you think so, Tom?"

"I guess so, yeah," Tom said uncomfortably."

"I mean, think about how things change," Denny said. "Pete and I have lived in Angels Beach all our lives, and look at how the town has changed in that time. All sorts of new houses have been built, new people moving in. Pete, remember how there used to be bait-and-tackle stores along Pacific Coast Highway? Nearly all of them are gone now. And the old liquor stores where the bums used to hang out? They're almost all gone too."

On the ocean a foghorn sounded. Jim Morrison sang "*People are strange*" from the radio. "I get worried sometimes," Denny said, "that we won't see each other anymore after school is out. I'm staying here, but you two are gonna go out and see the world. But I got a feeling that sometime we'll all be back here again, together, that somehow you'll have to come back to the place you started from. And who knows what it'll be like here in ten or twenty years. It could all be different, things change so fast. Hell, ten years ago this Marina wasn't even here. You remember that, don't you Pete?"

"Sure," I said, "I remember. It was just fields here then."

"Where do you think we'll be, in ten, twenty years?" Denny asked dreamily. "It sure would be nice to know. What will we be like, what will we be doing? But if we knew that would take a lot of the fun out of it. But how many of the people we know will still be around? How will they turn out? I guess you can't ever tell. Hey! I just got a great idea."

Denny leaped out of his chair and got the wine bottle, then poured what was left into each of our glasses. "Let's drink a toast," he proposed, "and swear, right now, that in twenty years, no matter where we are of what we are doing, we'll come back here, to Angels Beach, and meet in the park by the pier. Twenty years from today, October 20, 1988. Okay?"

"Okay," I said, smiling and raising my glass.

"Okay," Tom said uncomfortably.

We all drank and swore, Tom doing his best to look enthusiastic and not guilty. Denny got a piece of paper, tore it into three equal parts, and wrote the date and time on each, then put down that the three of us promised that we'd meet again in the park in Angels Beach in twenty years. We all signed, and he gave each of us a copy.

"Anybody got a pocket knife?" Denny asked.

"What for?" Tom wanted to know.

"I was thinking we ought to make a mark in blood."

"No," said Tom. "I don't like blood."

"Because that would make it more lasting, more permanent," Denny said. "We'd be like blood brothers. But I suppose this is enough. We'll meet in 1988. Seems like so far away, doesn't it? We're really lucky, you know, to have a friendship like this. Not many people do, I mean have friends they can really count on, that will always be there, be their friend no matter what. I know we'll be friends always, just like I know we'll meet in twenty years." He raised his glass suddenly and threw it so that it hit the wooden wall of the office and smashed, the pieces going all over the floor. "That's to our friendship!" he cried. "So it lasts forever!"

I threw my glass too. It was just an ordinary water glass and it broke easily. Tom did the same thing, and we both said, "To our friendship!" the same way Denny had, although I thought I detected some hesitation in Tom's voice.

"I think," Denny said, "that I am one of the luckiest men in the world. I've got it made. To have friends like you guys, a nice girl like Tiffany who loves me--I'm so lucky I can hardly stand it."

Tom stood up. "I gotta go," he said abruptly.

"How come, Tom?" Denny protested. "It's early yet."

"I'll see you guys tomorrow." Tom went quickly out the door.

"Now what do you suppose is the matter with him?" Denny asked. "Do you know, Pete?"

"I don't have any idea," I said.

I supposed one more lie wouldn't matter.

Chapter 9

Casey

I went walking by myself. I walked by the San Gabriel River, alongside the rocks that lined both sides. The water looked choppy and gray, just like the water of the ocean did, and I looked at where the river runs under the bridge and then empties into the small bay next to the Long Beach Marina. I always ended up at the same place: Standing outside the chain-length fence, staring at the red bricks and broken windows of the old power plant. *It happened in there,* I would say to myself, and once again I feared I was going mad.

I didn't want to be at home because of the way things were there, and so when I wasn't working or at school I would walk, aimlessly, in places where there weren't any people and I could be alone. I walked along Pacific Coast Highway over to Dolphin Avenue, which is the last street before the town proper comes to an end, and then I would turn right and go along the fence beside the Naval Weapons Station. Once in a while a ship would put in, to load up with supplies for Vietnam, for the base had become more of a supply depot by then, but otherwise there wasn't much going on inside the base that you could see from out here.

In this old part of town the streets were narrow and crooked. Each street had an alley behind it (the streets in the newer parts of town, where Tom lived and where Carolyn lived, didn't have any alleys) and I'd played and roamed and ran in these alleys for as long as I could remember. The sidewalks were cracked and jutted upward in some places, as if the ground beneath was trying to split them in half, and I looked at the words "C. H. Ryder Construction 1938" engraved on the squares every thirty feet or so and wondered how new it must have seemed back then and thought of how old it seemed now. This had all seemed old when I was small but the world at least was new then, every day fresh and full of promise. Now it didn't seem that way anymore. It was dreary and worn out. Days which had once felt always sunny and bright were now overcast and full of clouds, I saw the sun less and less. It rained almost every day that fall and winter and there were mud puddles all around. The vacant lots were masses of mud and dying tumbleweeds. Black clouds loomed over the ocean, and the sea itself, which I would often stand and stare at, was gray and cold-looking, not blue and inviting like it used to be. Funny how I had never noticed that before, how the ocean changed colors so dramatically, and I'd been living here next to it all my life. But the world itself seemed gray, losing its light and its laughter.

If that baby bird had not fallen out of its nest, my mother would not have seen it and decided she wanted to show it to me. And if she hadn't done that, my brother wouldn't have killed it, I wouldn't have hit him, my mother wouldn't have slapped me, and I wouldn't have felt I had to get away from home and accompany Tom on his Vision Quest to climb to the top of the smokestack. Then none of this would be happening. I wouldn't be standing here, thinking I've gone crazy. Deacon would still be dead, but I wouldn't have anything to do with it, he could rest in peace and it wouldn't make any difference to me.

And it got worse, everyday it seemed to weigh more. It was with me when I went to sleep and it was there when I woke up each morning. Nothing I did could make me free of it.

I did not want to be around people unless I had to be, so I avoided Main Street and the more populated parts of town. Sometimes I did go past the old Bay Theatre and looked up at the two big windows that always made me think of two great big eyes watching me, but when I did go by there I scurried past as quickly as I could. I went on by Clancy's Bar, pushing my way through the drunks that were always congregating there, and then turned into the alley that ran parallel to it so I could get off the thoroughfare and be by myself again.

• • •

"Just what is so interesting about that old pile of bricks that you want to stand there contemplating it for so long?"

I turned around and saw a man standing a few feet away from me, leaning on a cane and smiling. He wore a leather jacket and his long white hair blew in the wind.

"Casey!" I shouted, and skipped over to shake hands.

"Where in hell you been?" he asked. "I can't remember the last time you came to see me."

"I've been busy…"

"You couldn't be that busy. Don't you know an old fellow like me gets lonesome for his friends? You used to come to my house all the time, you and Tom and that girlfriend of yours. I haven't seen any of you for ages."

I told him once again I *had* been that busy, and, afraid he would ask me why I was staring so intently at the old plant, began telling him about my job at the gas dock. He listened patiently and nodded, and then suggested we get out of the wind and go to his house, which wasn't far away.

"It's too cold to be standing out here gabbing," he said, and we began walking along 1st Street, Casey able to move fast for someone who had to use a cane to walk, as the wind blew in off the ocean and some seagulls flew overhead toward some forbidding-looking clouds.

"Jesus! Coming Soon!" read a sign in an upstairs window as we went down an alley toward Casey's house on 1st Street. We both saw it at the same time. Casey made a scornful face.

"Must be a follower of that new reverend that's come to town," Casey said. "That guy reminds me of a used car salesman. But people are flocking to him like kids to the Pied Piper. I'm not surprised. The stars predicted it. It's the time we live in. False messiahs will be coming. We're in a transition period, going from one age to another. It's a dark age now."

"I've heard about this guy," I said, "but I've never seen him."

"I've talked to him," said Casey. "He's got a slick delivery. He's selling his message, all right, and he's good at it. I went to a few of his sermons, just to hear what he has to say, and it only took me a little while to figure out this guy is a total fake. You know who I saw there?"

"Rena?"

"Oh, so you've heard."

"People keep telling me about it."

"She's a nice girl, how come you dropped her?" Casey asked seriously.

"I don't want to talk about it." That was my standard answer whenever anybody asked me about Rena. It always seemed to work and got me off the hook. I had never told anyone about Carolyn.

"Nice girls don't come along every day," Casey commented.

"I still don't want to talk about it," I said, smiling so he wouldn't think I was being sullen.

I had avoided Casey since that night in the old power plant. Once I went to his house almost every day. I would bring Rena over when I was still going with her, Denny would be there with Tiffany, Tom came around with whatever girl he had picked up, and we all sat on the big front porch at night and watched the sun drop down and turn into an orange disk over the ocean (Casey had a spectacular view of the ocean from his house) and then Casey would get his guitar out and we sang songs long into the night. We sang and clapped our hands to the music, and Rena and I had gone up the stairs to the balcony on the third floor and looked out at the stars and the lights playing on the ocean and kissed and pressed our bodies against each other until it was time for me to take her home and I was so worked up I thought I would explode.

As if he could read my mind, Casey said, "Sad about Deacon, isn't it?"

"Yeah," I said, quickly, "real sad."

"Poor bastard. I never thought he'd kill himself. I thought he might waste away to nothing, but I never thought he would take his own life. I guess you never can tell what people will do."

We crossed the bridge that spanned the San Gabriel River from 1st Street to Studebaker Road and then went on up the street toward Casey's house. Casey's white hair blew in the wind. He sported a goatee and moustache so that he looked a little like Wild Bill Hickock, and when the wind blew his hair back you could see the stump where his left ear had been, and the long, jagged scar that trailed down from his ear to his jaw line. A reminder, he always said, of his past, when his life had consisted of motorcycles and women and fights in bars on Saturday nights. Below me I could see the currents of the gray water, going this way and that, rippling back and forth as if they couldn't decide which way they wanted to go.

Casey lived in the house built by his grandfather, the Reverend John James Jones. The old reverend built it back in the 1890s, when he had helped found the town of Angels Beach. Once it had been the biggest and most expensive house in town, and the neighborhood the most exclusive. Now the paint was peeling, the houses were getting old and decrepit and some were being torn down to make way for condos and townhouses. It was on the 3rd floor of this house that the good reverend, after catching his wife in *flagrante delicto*, had blown out his own brains. That never bothered Casey. Let the dead bury the dead, he would say. But it used to bother me. I spent many a night there and more than once I woke up during the wee hours and listened with my heart pounding and was certain I heard the ghost of the reverend spooking around up in the attic or else right outside the door in the hallway. There would be creaking and bumping and knocking sounds and then I could see a light outside the door that was there and then gone and I knew damn well there had to be *something* out there. A couple of other times the flame on one of the candles Casey had burning would turn blue—a sure sign, Casey always said, that there was a ghost nearby. He just laughed it off. He said a ghost was only a restless spirit that, for one reason or another, hadn't made the transition all the way from this world into the next one, and was trying to find its way. Ghosts never hurt anyone, only scared them because people are always afraid of what they don't understand.

Well, he would know. Casey lived in a world of spirits, familiars, crystals, witches, spells and incantations. He knew about magic and the occult, about astrology and alchemy, sacred circles, mojo bags and juju. He kept large round candles, the kind you see in cathedrals, burning night and day in different parts of his house. He grew mandrake in his garden, kept rosemary in pots near his front door to keep witches away, and as we went up the wooden steps I saw the old familiar horseshoe nailed in the upright position above the door to bring good luck. Crystals hung from the ceiling, for he said they could keep a Black Magician from putting a spell on you and would also ward off the Evil Eye. He did white magic and juju magic, but never, he swore, black magic. He believed in past lives and reincarnation, and said he had once been a Druid priest, and also a Runemaster with one of the ancient Germanic tribes of Northern Europe.

Casey eased himself into his wooden rocking chair, the only place, he once told me, where he could be comfortable. As I sat myself down in a dusty old chair with a glass of Casey's wine in my hand it occurred to me that being constantly in pain must be a hard way to live. And Casey had never been free of pain since his accident fifteen years ago, in 1953. His body ached, especially his back, but so did his shoulders, where the surgeons had to dig deep to put him back together. He didn't complain about it, just endured it stoically, saying this was just the way it had to be and that, as Carl Jung said, there was no coming to consciousness without pain.

Behind him, on the wall, hung a photograph I tried my best not to look at. It was a black-and-white picture of Casey and Deacon, taken in 1952 at Big Sur. They stood beside their Harley-Davidsons, proud and young and in their prime, the pines and the cliffs and the flat sprawling ocean in the background. Whenever I saw that picture I had a hard time believing I saw the same man who went about town begging spare change. I turned away and sat so I wouldn't have to look at it.

"Want to listen to something?" Casey asked. "Put some music on."

I went over to his stereo cabinet, and from the myriad of albums by Pete Seeger, The Weavers, Peter, Paul and Mary, Phil Ochs, Bob Dylan, Woody Guthrie, The Brothers Four, Buffy St. Marie, The Chad Mitchell Trio, and Joan Baez, I selected The Kingston Trio. He also liked the blues, and he had old 78 rpm albums by Muddy Waters, Ma Rainey, the Memphis Jug Band, and Sonny Boy Williamson.

Casey's house had three stories and an attic, a big stand-up-and-move-around-in attic full of boxes and bed frames and old pictures, the kind of attic kids play in on a rainy day. You don't see attics like that in California too often, just like you don't see cellars or storm windows or doors with keyholes you can see through. Not that many of them were built and those that were have been torn down and something new built in their place. Casey lived a strange combination of New Age and Old Times: In spite of all the crystals, Runes, Tarot Cards and the hint in the background of spells and magic that were always a part of being in Casey's presence, I always had the sensation when I went into his house that I was stepping into a time portal and being transported back to another era. I looked around at the old furniture, at the sinks with their separate faucets for hot and cold water, at all the old books and magazines and newspapers, and at the creaking hardwood floors and the walls with the big cracks in them. Right outside the backdoor was a wash tub with a hand-operated wringer on it. There was a radio from the 1920s in a big wooden case with an enormous dial on the front and whenever I turned it on I expected it to start broadcasting news from the past: The Scopes Trial, Lindberg making his flight across the Atlantic, Babe Ruth hitting his 60th home run, the crash of the stock market, Roosevelt telling the country it had nothing to fear but fear itself. Then one day it occurred to me that Casey was one of those people who never gets rid of anything, and besides, it was hard for him to get around, he could barely keep the place clean, so it was easier for him to leave all that stuff where it was.

"So," I said to Casey, "what about this new reverend? What's his trip? Is Jesus really coming soon?"

"Any day now, according to this guy. He says he's got a special hook-up to God, and that God has told him the day and the hour when Jesus is returning to earth. Only trouble is the good Reverend doesn't want to share the precise day and hour this is going to happen. Says it was given to him in confidence, ho-ho, and he can't reveal what God said to him. Sort of like Moses on Mount Sinai. But people believe him, for better or for worse. We're at the end of an age, the Piscean Age, which began 2,000 years ago. We're entering a New Age, the Aquarian."

"When does it start? This year, '68?"

"Oh, hell no. We are just on the cusp of it now. Some astrologers say it begins in 2001. Others say it starts in 2012, or 2157, or even 2374."

"What do you think, Casey?"

"It can't start too soon," he said. "We're in a Dark Age now."

"Why do you say this is a Dark Age?"

"Anytime you are fighting a war is a Dark Time. Pluto is due to enter Scorpio in 1984, and that's a combination for profound change. And Saturn, Neptune, and Uranus will have a conjunction in Capricorn in 1988 and '89, and that will bring great changes in the world too. Nixon is going to be a very bad influence. People are going to be sorry they voted for that man. Be careful what you wish for, Pete. When you get it you might be sorry you did."

"Does it always happen that way?"

"Most of the time," he said.

He smiled in a world-weary way, the smile of a man who has seen a lot and learned from what he has seen. When he took that awful spill on his motorcycle in 1953 his wife, who had been riding on the back, died instantly and he came out of the tangled wreckage more dead than alive. After the doctors worked on him he lay in his hospital bed staring up at the ceiling for weeks, his body encased in a cast from his neck to his heels. One day he had a revelation. It may not have been as dramatic as the one Saul had on the road to Damascus, but for a man whose idea of a good time had been stomping somebody's face to a pulp on Saturday night, it came as a life-changing experience: He saw the universe as One. Everything connected, all worked in harmony, everyone is part of the same divine plan. Like a butterfly escaping from its cocoon, another self-emerged from the body cast when it finally came off. His biker days over (he could barely walk, let alone ride a chopper) his life took an entirely new direction. He moved to San Francisco, took up the guitar and began writing poetry. He became part of the folk music and Beat literature scene there, singing in coffee houses and reading his poems at small gatherings of fellow Bohemians (he had been at City Lights Bookstore in 1955 when Allen Ginsberg read "Howl" for the first time). He lived in a studio near Golden Gate Park, all the while contemplating the implications of his revelation. This led him to his study of the stars and astrology, magic and the occult. He came back to Angels Beach when he inherited the house, and took up magic and astrology as a full-time vocation. He lived there alone, except for Taurus, his big German Sheppard, and never remarried, for he confessed to me once (in a manner that indicated he didn't want this to get around) that his Big Fall had left him in such a state that he had difficulty consorting with the ladies. He didn't elaborate, only said that things didn't work the way they were supposed to, which explained why I had seen Sleazy Mary and Horrible Helen going toward his house every now and then.

The nickname Casey stemmed from his biker days, for his real name was Andrew, but he had taken Casey from the song "Casey Jones," when he had been a member of a motorcycle club of boisterous World War II veterans who called themselves "The Pissed Off Bastards," and later changed the name of their fun-loving group to the "Hell's Angels," going on into infamy after that. He had pictures to prove it: Photographs of himself with Ralph "Sonny" Barger, Terry the Tramp, and others who had made their way into fame and the pages of police blotters, and pictures from the runs to Hollister in 1947 and Porterville in 1951, and pictures of them all hanging out in Big Sur and Mammoth Mountain.

His bookcases were filled with volumes on magic, astrology, and the occult. He loved the existentialists: Sartre, Camus, Nietzsche, Kierkegaard, Spinoza, as well as Carl Jung. There were books by the Beat writers: Jack Kerouac's *On the Road* and *The Dharma Bums*, William Burroughs' *The Naked Lunch*, and poetry by Allen Ginsberg, Lawrence Ferlinghetti, and Gregory Corso. Casey didn't play his guitar professionally anymore but he enjoyed having people over and playing and singing the old songs he loved: *This Land Is Your Land, John Henry, The Wreck of the 97, They Call the Wind Maria, So Long, It's Been Good to Know You,* or *The Lemon Tree.* Even now I can never think of Casey without the words *"Lemon tree, very pretty/And the lemon flower is sweet/But the fruit of the poor lemon/Is impossible to eat,"* coming to my mind. One of his acoustic guitars sat in a nearby corner, and another hung on the wall.

"Is everything written in the stars?"

"You'd best believe it is."

"You mean, it's all predetermined, before you're born?"

"Sure. Like Deacon."

"Deacon?"

"Yes. If I were to go back, and find out just when and where he was born--and I could, if I wanted to, 'cause he gave me all his papers and everything before he totally lost his mind--I could find his death in his chart. In fact, maybe I'll do that, now that you mention it.

"You know," Casey said, from amidst a growing pile of books and papers, the smoke from one of his filterless Camel cigarettes rising above his head, "he knew what was happening to him."

"He did?"

"Yeah. He got worse and worse as time went on. But he still had some moments when he was together. One day he came over here. 'Case,' he says, 'I'm losing it, my mind just doesn't work like it should anymore.' 'You're gonna get better, Deak,' I'd say, trying to cheer him up, but he knew better and so did I. He says, "Case, here's all my papers, the deed to my house, my car registration, all that stuff. I don't want it all to get lost.' So he gave it all to me. But it was a sad thing to see."

"What caused it?" I asked, lighting a cigarette.

"Who knows? One day you got it all, house, money in the bank, a nice scooter to ride, women—and the next day you're in the street, all dressed in rags, no place to go. I used to give him money whenever I could, so he'd at least have something to eat. Mostly he spent it on booze. He'd come knock at my door. 'I got an awful headache, Case,' he'd say. I'd let him in. I let him sleep here sometimes. Not too much, though. I knew he'd never leave if I did that. Kind of like if you feed a stray cat. There's only so much you can do. Did make me feel bad."

"You ever hear that story everybody told about him?" I asked, thinking that if anyone would know about it, Casey would be the one.

"The one about him having all sorts of money, a treasure?"

"Think it was true?"

"Who knows? He had a decent amount of money once. He just might have buried some someplace."

"How would he get a lot of money?"

"He was a fence. A risky business, but he had a natural talent for it. Our biker friends would rip off bikes, part them out, and sell to him. He would turn around and sell this stuff to chop shops, or even legitimate places. He made a lot of money which he never put in the bank. He didn't trust banks. So he just might have buried it like some pirate's treasure."

"Where would he keep it?"

"Who knows?"

I drank the wine Casey had given me and wondered if I should have any more. Probably I shouldn't. I'd been drinking an awful lot lately. I got drunk just about every day. And if I wasn't drunk I was smoking Tom's Panama Red. And often I did both together, which blotted everything out nicely. But I had some wicked hangovers when I got up in the morning. My head would be pounding and my stomach doing somersaults. The only thing to do was drink some more wine and smoke some more Panama Red as soon as I left the house and got into my van and headed off to pick Tom up for school. Once I was so sick I threw up in the alley. My mother and father never noticed, and for that I was grateful.

But should I have any more? I guessed one more wouldn't hurt. Just a little bit. I poured it carefully into the glass, only filling it up part-way. I looked at the bottle. The wine was a vin rose, blush colored. Being drunk is a good thing, when you're drunk you don't have to think about anything. Yes, to be drunk is a fine thing. There isn't anything better, except to be drunk and stoned at the same time. Even thinking of Carolyn didn't bother me. Or did it? When I thought of her I felt a pang in my chest, a kind of empty aching feeling that I had trouble getting rid of. What's the matter with you, why don't you take an interest in girls your own age? What about Rena? You ditched her. You hurt her when you did that.

Thinking of Carolyn gave me an abandoned feeling, like I was lost. It wasn't the first time I had ever felt that way. Most of the time I didn't know what was going on inside of me. I did my best not to feel anything, but you can't keep feelings away forever, sooner or later they surface, and I had to admit Carolyn still had a hold on me.

I felt terribly alone now. What kind of life was this, that all these things could happen? People went crazy and had their throats cut by maniacs. And if everything was written in the stars like Casey said, why wasn't it written better than this? Was there a meaning to it all, was there something in charge, or did it just happen, randomly, like water drops bouncing around on a hot griddle?

When I looked up into the sky I thought about that idea of the universe going on into infinity. Once, when I was small, I'd asked my mother about that. She said the universe went on forever, with no end. That was the craziest idea. I had thought about it over and over. How could anything go on forever? She had said heaven was up there, and that was where you went when you died. But how could that be, if there was no end to the universe? I never did get it figured out even though I spent a lot of time worrying about it. I didn't sleep for weeks, for fear that when I slept my soul would leave my body and fly upward into that infinite darkness above.

"So, has anything strange, out of the ordinary happened to you recently?" Casey asked.

"What do you mean?"

"Remember when I did your horoscope last summer?"

"Sure. I put it right up over my bed, just like you said."

"The position of the Outer Planets when you were born contained an opposition that points to a massive life-change right about now. They indicate something traumatic, either this year or next year. Has anything like that happened to you, Pete?"

"You must be kidding," I said. "Nothing ever happens to me. I just go along the same old way, every day, without anything exciting going on."

He looked at me skeptically. "Remember, you can always come and talk to me," he said. "You know that, don't you?"

"Sure," I said. I had some more wine. "Say," I continued, to change the subject, "you told me that I'm a Capricorn, since my birthday's in January, with Virgo rising. What is Tom?"

"Tom's a Leo, the sign of the Lion. His birthday's on August first. Leo is ruled by the sun. It's the sign of the King, too. Leo's are usually proud, fiery, energetic, leader types."

"That sounds like Tom." I finished the wine I had and got up. "I gotta go, Case."

Casey moved painfully out of his rocking chair and went over to a cluttered old desk, opened a drawer and searched inside. "Here," he said. "Take this," and he handed me a crystal attached to a short chain. "It'll protect you."

"From what?"

"From whatever it is that's going to happen."

I stepped out onto the front porch, lurching just a little, as Taurus came up and stuck his big head at me as if he wanted to be petted. "You should always tell the truth, shouldn't you?" I said. "Shouldn't a person always tell the truth, no matter what?"

"I'm in favor of telling the truth," he agreed.

"Even if you promised," I said, faltering now, realizing I had said what I didn't mean to say, "promised not to? You gotta tell anyway, don't you?"

"Are you all right?" he asked.

"Never been better."

"Is there something you want to tell me?" he asked. When I just shook my head, he said, "All right, well just be careful, OK?"

I went out the gate and started walking, the crystal in my pocket. But my step was heavy, and I felt there was a big load on my back. When I looked up at the sky I saw nothing but dark clouds overhead, and the water in the river looked cold and uninviting

Chapter 10

Rena

After I left Casey's house I decided to go to the Indian Camp. To get there you had to walk past Pacific Coast Highway and up by the part of town called The Hill, past the new housing tracts and roads that were being built until you stood at the crest of a long sloping street and then you could see an enormous grove of trees, a mile long and more than a mile wide. In the clearing were the remains of some old farm houses that had been there when all this had consisted of nothing but farmland. Beyond you could see Signal Hill, some oil wells, and the back end of Long Beach State College. The trees aren't there any more, all torn down to make way for more houses, but they were there then and had been standing there for hundreds of years.

The Indian Camp was actually a clearing deep in the trees that you couldn't find unless you knew where to look for it. I remember hearing how the Indians used to migrate up and down the coast and the archaeologists found relics in various places around The Hill. I always thought this clearing must have been a sacred place for the Indians, for there was a flat rock that was ringed by other, smaller rocks laid out around it, and Indian markings on the sides. Then there was the peaceful feeling the place had, as if this was somewhere to leave all your troubles behind and just feel good. The sunlight filtered down through the trees and cast long shadows on the ground.

Deacon, of all people, also knew about the Indian Camp. He had told Brian and I where it was, and when we were still into playing cowboys and Indians we had gone looking for it. Deacon had said it was a holy place. But Brian was the only other person who knew about it for a long time. And after he got killed I would come there sometimes and sit, and look at the trees and listen to the wind. Brian had scratched his initials onto one of the rocks, and I would sit and look at that: "Brian the Great, 1964," he'd written, and said that in a thousand years somebody might come in here and see that, and they would know he had been here. And by that time we'd outgrown playing cowboys and Indians and were starting to notice that girls had shapes that were round in some interesting places and moved in some interesting ways, facts that become our number one topic of conversation. Brian wanted so much for people to know he was alive, I thought, and now hardly anybody does. That seemed a kind of raw deal to me. Take Deacon. Nobody remembered him either. But he was best forgotten.

Then Rena came along, and I used to bring her here too. But that came later, after Brian was dead.

I stood there holding the crystal Casey had given me in my hand. It sparkled in the dim light and the more I looked at it the more it seemed to be giving off a light of its own. I kept gazing inside the crystal and it was like infinite space was contained in there. I could see planets and moons and stars, all drifting off into infinity. If everything was written in the stars then there wasn't any sense in struggling over it, all was going to happen just as it was meant to happen. I felt better, looking at the crystal. Maybe it would bring me luck.

I felt a little more peaceful now and sat down to smoke a cigarette, the crystal still in my hand. On the rock opposite from the place Brian had scratched his initials I saw where I'd scratched "Pete and Rena '68." Rena and I had stood here and kissed after I scratched that in there. I had brought Rena here after we had been going together for a while, telling her she was the second person to know about my secret place.

"And who was the first?" she wanted to know.

"Brian," I said, and she looked at me somberly, for she had known Brian too. We had all grown up together, Rena, Brian, Denny Lockhart, Waldo, and me. We had known each other from first grade onward.

So it became our special place. After we had been at Casey's singing and carrying on we would come here, walking across the open field in the moonlight, holding hands, going carefully onto the paths and between the trees.

"This is our place," Rena would say, and she would brush back her long hair. "It's our secret place and nobody else knows about it. And we won't tell them, will we?"

"No, we won't tell," I agreed.

"Do you feel that?" Rena would ask, while we were holding each other tightly. "Do you feel my heart pounding?"

I could feel it, all right. I could feel her heart pounding the same way my own heart was thumping away. Rena's hair was long and light brown and cascaded gently to her shoulders with a slight curl to it, and it bounced rhythmatically up and down as she walked. She wore makeup sometimes but mostly she didn't need it, she was very fresh to look at, blooming into her womanhood like a flower opening up for the first time in all its majesty and glory.

One day I had told her I wasn't going to see her any more, and she began to cry. "Promise me one thing," she said through her tears. "Promise me you won't take any other girls to our secret place. You won't, will you?"

"No," I had promised. "I won't."

I had kept that promise and it was an easy enough promise to keep. I hadn't dated any other girls, for I was seeing Carolyn by then, and she certainly would have never wanted to come to a place like the Indian Camp.

"Just tell me this," Rena asked, still crying. "Is it someone else?"

"Yes," I said, and I would say no more, and Rena didn't go on with it but dropped it then. For I was trying, in my own way, to be honest. It didn't seem right to keep on seeing Rena and continue doing what I was doing with Carolyn. That didn't seem right at all and so I decided I wouldn't do it anymore.

I had cried some too when Rena and I broke up but I was too macho to do it in front of her. And I missed her as well. I missed Carolyn now, but in a different way—I missed the thrill, the excitement, of it all, the never knowing what she would do, or when her mad boyfriend, Rudy, might show up, I missed the utter wickedness of it all. That had been what drew me in, until Carolyn was done with me I was her slave, I couldn't help myself, it was an addiction I couldn't break free of. When I was with her and we were panting and moaning together it was like trying to hold back the ocean.

Nowadays I missed Rena more and more, and as I sat there smoking I wished she was there with me now. I saw, through the trees, that the sun was down and it was dark out. I did not want to go home because I didn't like the way things were at home but I supposed I'd have to go pretty soon.

Now I heard a noise and saw something rustling in the trees. I looked up, startled, and Rena came out into the clearing. I stood up, staring, open-mouthed.

She stared back at me, equally surprised, wearing jeans and a sweater. Her hair was tied back, showing her face and high cheekbones, red now from the wind. Her eyes were wide, partly from surprise and partly because they were large brown eyes and tended to have a wide look to them. They stared, drilling into me in wonderment.

"Am I seeing things?" I asked.

"I could say the same thing," Rena said. "I've dreamed about this."

We stood staring for a few more seconds and then we were into each other's arms, holding on as tight as we could. She always smelled of rose petals and violet, and as I held her I realized that I had missed that smell, for it always seemed so fresh, like when you've just stepped out of a lake of clear water high in the mountains.

"I've dreamed of my coming here and finding you and then it would be like it used to be," Rena whispered. "But I never thought it would really happen. It feels so good to have your arms around me again."

"I've dreamed of it too."

"I come here a lot," she said, still whispering.

"Yes?"

"Almost everyday, sometimes. I used to come in here and say to myself that you would come too. And then when that didn't happen I would sit on the rocks and watch the trees. Then I didn't come back for a long time. But then I started coming again. I don't know why, but I just couldn't stay away."

"I've come here a lot too," I said, caressing her hair. "Oh, Rena, I'm so glad to see you."

"Are you really?"

"I couldn't be any gladder, I don't think."

She broke away from me now, smiling in her sun-bright, sun-sweet way. Rena really did have a wonderful smile. Her face was very tan, for she was one of those people like Tom who tan easily and well, it looks good and natural on them, not artificial like Tiffany, who always looked as if she had been under a sun lamp so she could enter a who-has-the-darkest-tan contest. Rena's smile lit everything up, like the sun appearing on a gloomy day.

She took my hand in both of hers, then reached into my pocket playfully, something she always used to do when we were going together, and took out my crystal.

"What's this?"

"Casey gave it to me. He said it would bring me luck."

"Do you believe him?"

"It's worked already."

Suddenly my feelings for her were overpowering, and I moved to gather her in my arms again, but she stepped aside playfully.

"It's getting dark out," she said. "I have to go soon."

"Want me to walk you home?"

"Not yet...Why don't you kiss me?"

I kissed her, and her mouth was like melting honey against mine.

"I've missed you kissing me," she said softly. "It takes my breath away, sometimes I feel like I might faint."

I felt her breasts rising and falling against me as I held her.

"Kiss me again," she said.

"Sometimes," she said, "sometimes when you kissed me I would feel things I never felt before, stirring deep inside of me. They weren't like any feelings I ever had before. I wanted to know if I would feel them again."

"Do you?"

"Yes," she said, still speaking softly. "What do you feel?"

For an answer I kissed her again, then moved my hands around the front to touch her breasts, but she pulled away now.

"No," she said, "no, not now. Walk me home now."

I climbed up on the rock above and then turned to help her. A snake slithered across the top of the flat rock ahead of me. Rena saw it, at the same time I did, and let out a shriek. The snake disappeared into the tall grass.

"I didn't know there were any snakes around here," Rena said.

"They're here," I told her. "We just don't always see them."

"I never saw one before."

We walked along the path and out of the trees and then alongside Bay Boulevard toward Pacific Coast Highway. Rena lived on 13th Street. Her house was shabby, the paint peeling and the yard full of dead grass and weeds. Her father had taken off with a Chinese woman who had run a mah-jongg game at the Pike and never came back, leaving Rena and her mother to fend for themselves. Her mother had been struggling ever since, working two waitress jobs in second-rate restaurants in Long Beach so they could keep the house. Then she got a new husband, an overweight, unpleasant man from New York named Spiro. Spiro sometimes worked as a welder at the Long Beach Naval Shipyard but he always managed to find a way to get laid off after a few months and spent the rest of the year drawing an unemployment check. He would lay around the house all day in his shorts or bathrobe, unkempt and unshaven, and whenever I came over to get Rena he would rouse himself long enough to give me a long interrogation, coming at me fat and greasy-looking, his chin thrust forward. Tossing aside the newspaper, he wanted to know what kind of a young man I was. Did I know how to behave properly around a young lady? This child meant everything in the world to him, just as if she was his very own, and he put his arm around Rena's shoulders and squeezed protectively in a way I didn't like and which made Rena shudder. Spiro looked me challengingly in the eye. Rena stood looking mortified. He reeked of beer and body odor, and everyone stood in silence until he finally nodded and said, "All right then. Just so we all know where we stand," and at last Rena and I could leave. It got so bad I wouldn't come to her house anymore, we arranged to meet downtown when we went out.

"I go to the Church of the New Faith now," she said suddenly.

"On Main Street?"

She nodded. "Oh, Pete, you don't know what it's done for me. After what happened with us I felt so low. I was just blue, from sunup until sundown. I'm not saying this to make you feel bad. But I couldn't shake it off. Nothing interested me anymore. Then I went to church. It changed my life, nothing has ever been the same for me since."

Now the floodgates were open and she began telling me about her church and how wonderful it was. There had never been a church like it. It was a new church for a new time, and it didn't have any of the old junk in it that ordinary churches had.

"I want you to meet Reverend Jim," Rena said. "He's the most incredible man! Wait until you hear him speak the Word of God. He's amazing."

"Is he for real?" I asked, remembering what Casey had said about the Reverend reminding him of a used car salesman.

"Oh God yes," said Rena. "He's as real as can be. He means every word he says, and better than that, he lives them. Will you come to church with me sometime, Pete?"

"I never even went to a regular church."

"This isn't like a regular church. This is much better than a regular church. We sing songs, and we learn about God and how He's really here and part of our lives. We—well, you should come and see for yourself."

We were on her street by now and we stood on the corner with the cars from Pacific Coast Highway whizzing past. The old bait store where my father used to buy his hooks and lines was closed, with the neon sign that said "Live Bait" shut off and not blinking like it did during the day.

"Will you come?" Rena asked again.

She looked so pretty and so earnest standing there in front of me, just close enough, the rose I'd given her in her hair, that there was no way I could refuse.

She clapped her hands together happily, then hugged me.

"Oh, praise God!" she cried. "I'm so glad. Pete, I'm glad we found each other again."

"Me too," I said.

We parted, with me promising to call her soon and tell her exactly when I'd come with her to church. She said anytime was okay, since she went just about every night of the week, and every night there were hymns, prayer meetings, and sermons by the Reverend. I was kind of curious to meet this Reverend, since Rena raved about him so.

And I was awfully glad to have seen her. I went home happier than I'd been in a long time, I had the kind of jump up and down feeling that comes when you've fallen in love. I scampered about, hearing the music of "The Russian Dance" in my head and thinking I could leap and fly in a way that would leave gravity behind. I took the crystal out of my pocket. Once again it seemed to be glowing, giving off a light all its own, although when I shut the light out to be sure that was what it was really doing it stopped, there was no light coming from it at all. And yet I'd been so sure.

Well, I said to it, one thing I have to say, you certainly did bring me luck.

Chapter 11

The Birthday Party

"Pete! Will you come here a minute, please?"

I heaved a sigh, and headed (reluctantly) for the living room. Whenever I came home I always came in through the back gate and went straight to my room and closed the door so I didn't have to see anybody.

"Pete!" my mother repeated liltingly. "Where are you?"

"I'm coming," I replied.

"Pete!" she cried again.

"Here I am, what do you want?" I said, going to the living room. I saw her sitting on the couch by the window, looking out at the garden. Darren was lying beside her, his head in her lap. She was twirling his hair with her fingers and stroking his cheeks, smiling in her sly-silly manner, lots of makeup on her face.

"Have a seat," she invited when I came into the living room. I sat down, noticing the newspaper stacked neatly on the coffee table and her glasses on top of it, along with her cigarettes and lighter. She hated her glasses, hated to wear them and only did when no one was around— she said they made her look old and she did not want to look old. Together it all seemed to create a gulf between us, a barrier just as real as the Great Wall of China, there seemed to be a thousand miles from where I sat over to where she was stroking Darren and whispering to him. I waited for her to say what was on her mind so I could leave but she was in no hurry, she sat twirling my brother's hair and saying things to him in baby talk. He would goo-goo gaga back at her and he refused to look in my direction, but kept his face averted from me the way he usually did.

"What is it?" I asked my mother again. I didn't want to linger around here. I had promised Rena I would go to her church with her tonight.

"What is it?" I repeated, throwing my voice across the Great Wall. "What do you want, Mother?"

At last she said, "Your brother wants to tell you something." She looked down at Darren. "Don't you, Funny-Bunny?"

He didn't say anything but turned his face up so she could kiss him on the mouth. She giggled after she did that, then looked at me quickly.

"You're jealous, aren't you?"

"What?"

"Yes, you are. I can tell. You're jealous, I know."

"I thought you wanted to tell me something."

She smiled. "Tell," she said to Darren. "Tell big brother."

"I'm sorry," he said reluctantly, not looking my way.

I held my hands up impatiently. "What's he trying to say?"

He wouldn't say it but buried his face in my mother's lap.

"Tell him," she coaxed, but he still couldn't manage it.

"He's sorry for what happened that day," she explained.

"What day?"

"The day he accidentally killed that little bird," she said. "He's sorry. Aren't you, my baby-baby?"

He nodded from down there.

"And now," my mother said, smiling at me, "it's your turn."

"My turn?"

"Yes. You can say you're sorry too."

"What have I got to be sorry about?"

"For what you did to him, of course, hitting him in the chest and throwing that water can at him. You shouldn't have done that to him, you know. He's awfully young, and something like that traumatizes him so, he's so sensitive. And affectionate too, he's an affectionate child. So you can just say you're sorry too," she said in a sugary tone.

I noticed, from the clock on the mantle over the fireplace, that it was time for me to be going. My mother was looking at me expectantly. Darren was looking up now, his lower lip curled poutishly, my mother stroking his hair with her long red nails.

"I'm not sorry," I said, from where I sat, a thousand miles away from them. "I'm not sorry and besides, it wasn't any accident, he killed that little bird on purpose."

The smile disappeared. "Now, Pete," she said, from way over there. "You do not need to start getting nasty. Especially after he was big enough to apologize to you. He would never do anything like that deliberately, he isn't that kind of a child. Are you, my baby?"

"No, Mama," he said.

"So you apologize now," she said to me.

I just shook my head and stood up.

"Pete," she said warningly.

I turned to go.

"Now you listen to me," she called. "You say you're sorry to your brother. You say you're sorry to him right now! Come back here! You come back here and say you're sorry to your brother or your father is going to hear about this!"

She kept on yelling but I didn't stop or turn around. I kept on going, out the back door, past my oak tree and the tall towering eucalyptus. I went by my van, parked in the alley, but I didn't get into it because I felt like walking, there was so much energy and restlessness inside.

I went out, looking at what I knew. I knew these trees and the cracked sidewalks, the pebbly alleys and the hedges and the neatly trimmed lawns. Thoughts came racing into my mind like always: What is time, what is God, what is your soul, why does my father hate me, why is my mother the way she is, what happens to a person when they die?

I kept on, looking at what I knew. Sometimes when I got up in the morning it felt to me like the whole world was being born all over again, and I would go outside and look at all this that was so familiar to me, and it would be as if I was seeing it again for the first time.

But my sanity was saved. That was the thing. I no longer felt I was going mad. The crystal Casey gave me, that I now carried in my pocket all the time, had indeed brought me luck, it had saved me. That and the horoscope, for since I had the crystal I hadn't had any more nightmares, and it seemed to me the two were working together. I was sleeping better, I felt safer, with that up there, almost as if Casey had invested it with some power to keep the demons and the bad luck away.

I looked at my watch and noticed I still had some time before I was due to meet Rena, so I walked along Pacific Coast Highway past the old brick school on 12th Street where I'd gone to grammar school, past the playing fields and the old bleachers where the kids played Little League with their parents watching and clapping and predicting how their son was on his way to being the next Mickey Mantle. I headed toward the far end of town. These are my streets, I thought, I know them, and part of me will always be here. I want to break away from here, and go with Tom to look for exotic places and adventures, but part of me will always belong here, will always be here, a little self that will never die, but will always be walking to the old school, stopping to steal an apple off a tree or play in a vacant lot. That little self will live forever, and the world is filled with these streets and these small selves that don't know about murder and people with their throats cut and fathers who beat them up and mothers who run around in their slips, and I wished I didn't know about these things either but at least I'm not going crazy anymore and I've put all that stuff behind me.

That was a great relief to me. I wondered if that was what crazy people felt like all the time. Maybe that was how poor old Deacon felt. Best not to think about him. I hadn't been thinking about him so much lately and I didn't want to start again now.

I went in through the back door without knocking, as I sometimes did, going into the kitchen. I heard an unfamiliar voice, a female voice, coming from the living room, and then Sleazy Mary came in, holding a plate in one hand and a pair of empty wine glass in the other. "Oh, hello Pete," she said, and went over to the sink and began washing some dishes and stacking them neatly in a dish drainer. She was in her mid-twenties, although she looked older, as if she had been used hard and put away dirty, as the saying goes. She would have been pretty if not for a sharp-shape to her upper lip that reminded you of the beak of a bird, an impression accentuated by a pointed-billed cap she usually wore. She plied her trade around town, charging whoever was interested for sex but just as often not charging anything, or else going through with it with a promise of payment later.

There were many times when I saw her and was tempted, but I never had the nerve to follow through. Tom, who knew more about this than I did, always said it was a bad idea, that I might catch something and be sorry for a long time afterwards. Everyone said she had gonorrhea and had given it to several people—that's where her nickname originated—and the rumor mill had it that she was cured of it now.

So I was tempted and repulsed at the same time, and this held true for Horrible Helen, who was a few years younger than Mary and less attractive. They both hung out in Ocean Avenue Park, and they were friends one day and hated each other the next, falling out over men or money. More than once they'd had hair-pulling-fingernail-scratching fights in the park while a lot of people stood around watching and laughing. They would shun each other for weeks after that and then one day they were friendly again.

Casey was sitting by himself in the living room playing his guitar. There was a cake on the old stove, the kind of cake you buy pre-packaged in the supermarket and is so sugary it never tastes as good as you expect it to. The candles had burned down and there were little puddles of wax on the frosting. A paper bag filled with empty cans of Budweiser sat near the door, waiting to be taken out to the garbage. Taurus now realized I had come in and gave a bark, then got up from beside Casey's rocking chair and came running over to say hello.

"Hey!" Casey cried. "Whyn't you tell me you were here?"

"Want some cake, Pete?" Mary asked.

"What's the celebration?" There was a bottle of wine of the table beside Casey and a small glass next to the bottle. "Is it your birthday, Casey?"

Mary smiled when I said this and I wondered if it could be *her* birthday. She poured a small amount of wine for me. "I have to go," she said.

"Did I interrupt something? Don't go just because of me."

"No, no," she said, patting me on the hand. "I was leaving anyway," and she went out the back door the same way I had come in.

"Man, I'm glad to see you," Casey said. "Glad you came by. You can help me celebrate."

"Celebrate what, Case?"

Casey smiled again, shook his head, and drank some more wine. He scratched at the place where his ear used to be, scratching at it carefully with his fingers. He said the strangest thing about it was that it felt like he still had an ear there sometimes.

There was a slight warmth in my pocket. I took my crystal out and looked at it. Once again it appeared to be glowing, giving off a light of its own. Or was it? It was a peek-a-boo kind of light, there one moment, gone the next. I was beginning to feel like the boy who cried wolf—I kept thinking it glowed that way, but whenever I was about to show it to anyone or believe it myself, it was gone. But here it was again, like an omen or a warning sign, and then the glow died out, faded away. What was it trying to tell me?

"One of the great failings of the human race," Casey said, "Is its short memory. How quickly people forget. You ever notice how fast something is forgotten? We have no sense of the past, of yesterday, we're always so into today. Especially us Americans. World War II is ancient history already. World War I is so far back no one even thinks about it anymore. You wait, in a few years Vietnam will be consigned to the same category. A few big shots are remembered but even they are forgotten in time, people don't know what they were really like, they make them into martyrs, like the Kennedys or Abe Lincoln or Martin Luther King. But most of us won't be remembered at all. How long is it since he died? Six weeks? Seven weeks? I don't recall exactly."

"You mean it's Deacon's birthday?" I gasped.

"You know what I notice?" Casey went on. "It's like he was never even here. Gone without a trace. He lived a long time in this town, and no one gives a damn. Ain't it a great life?"

Casey shifted about in his rocking chair. "I got up this morning thinking of him. I remembered how we used to take our scooters up to Big Sur and Mammoth Mountain, and I realized it was his birthday. Only one other person remembered, and that was Mary. Good old Mary. She has a good heart. She knew Deacon years ago too, before he lost his mind. Will we remember next year? Probably not. So here's to old Deacon, kid, wherever he is now."

Casey raised his glass and I did the same, and we drank to Deacon. My hand shook as I did it, but I don't think Casey noticed.

"If he is up there," Casey said, "he's probably sad. Sad nobody remembers him. I know I'd be sad, if I was him, and nobody remembered me. But nobody will." He sighed. "Wouldn't you be sad?"

"Yeah," I agreed. "Pretty damn sad."

Seven weeks, Casey had said. Funny how it seemed like so much longer. Like years. And then, too, it seemed like yesterday, closer even than yesterday, like it happened five minutes ago. But I hadn't thought of it in a while. I thought that like Tom I had succeeded in putting it behind me, like a snake shedding its old skin. But Casey's talking about Deacon brought it back again. Wasn't there anyplace I could go where I wouldn't be reminded of this? My heart raced a little faster, there was an unpleasant feeling in my stomach that always came when this subject was brought up. I drank more wine. Wine usually deadened those feelings. That was what wine was good for, to deaden feelings that you didn't want to have.

It was all behind me now, I thought. I no longer was part of it. I had left it in the dust.

I spied a medallion hanging from the back of Casey's rocking chair, and to change the subject I pointed to it.

"Hey, Case, what's that?"

"This?" He turned, and held it up for me to see. "I meant to show this to you. I found it at the beach the other day."

"What is it?"

"Take a close look."

I saw, now, that it was a pentagram.

"Whereabouts did you find it?" I asked.

"At the jetty, why do you ask?"

"Just curious."

"Funny thing," he said. "Or, I should say, it's not funny at all. There's something evil going on."

"Evil?"

"I was out walking yesterday morning," he said, suddenly deeply earnest, "over by the jetty, and I thought I saw bloodstains on one of the rocks. I went over to take a look and between the rocks I found a dead cat."

"A dead cat?" I parroted. "Why I--"

"What?" he asked, but I shook my head and indicated I wanted him to go on.

"Yes," he said. "A dead cat. A black cat. It had been mutilated, tortured to death."

"No," I said.

"Yes. And on some of the rocks there were some signs, drawn in--"

"Red?" I asked.

"Yeah, why?"

"Nothing. Go on."

"Pentagrams," he said. "And this," he held the medallion, "was lying in the sand, somebody dropped it there."

"What does it mean?" I asked, remembering the dead animals I'd found, and the weird markings on the rocks.

"That cat was sacrificed," Casey declared. "Somebody is doing a Black Mass at the jetty at night."

"No," I said again.

"Yes," he insisted.

"Who could be doing it?"

Casey rocked and rocked in his chair. "Well, goddamnit, Pete, you're a pretty smart boy, smarter than most."

"Not them," I said, with a sudden flash of clarity.

"Who else? That big guy with the pilot's glasses. The others, they're his familiars."

"Tell me again what familiars are."

"Evil spirits. Usually they're in the form of animals. But they can be people too."

And you weren't even in the old plant that night, I thought. "You think Dave is the devil?"

"Familiars are usually found around either the Evil One himself or somebody who's sold his soul to the Evil One. I think Dave sold his soul."

But I had seen the dead animals, and I had seen the markings on the rocks. Maybe I didn't want to know about it. That was the way to do it, wasn't it? Stay drunk or stoned all the time, and not think about anything. I got little Panama Red from my pocket, took some for myself and then gave it to Casey.

"You look a little dressed up," Casey observed, smoking. "Going out?"

"I'm meeting somebody."

Casey nodded approvingly. "That's it. Live it up. You never know what tomorrow will bring."

"You smell that?" I asked Casey.

"I don't smell anything."

An unpleasant smell was in the room now, the smell of a sewer, or when it's red tide and all the dead fish are in the water. I sniffed a couple of times. Casey's house normally had a smell to it, because he had trouble getting around and couldn't keep it clean. Maybe he hadn't dumped his trash, or something was dead nearby.

The smell got stronger. "Can't you smell that?" I asked.

"Smell what?"

"Like something's dead."

"I got some incense going."

"This isn't incense."

Casey shrugged. "This is pretty good," he said. "Where'd you get it?"

"Tom gets it. Say, that smell is strong. It's all around, everywhere."

Casey frowned, and settled back into his chair again. The smell was overpowering now, yet he seemed unaware of it. My heart was beating faster again, and I felt the hair on the back of my neck rising.

On the other side of the living room, around and behind Casey, there was an open window, with the late afternoon sun streaming through. Suddenly there was a breeze, the curtains blew about wildly, flopping and straining like to fish hooked through the gills. A seagull squawked as it flew past, and a cloud went in front of the sun. One of the candles Casey kept burning twenty-four hours a day suddenly went from yellow to blue. And then I was certain I'd gone insane, stark raving mad, the only place for me was the funny farm now, the padded cell, electric shocks and the straight jacket and the men in the white suits and butterfly nets.

He looked exactly the way he looked the night he was murdered, when Tom and I saw him lying there. His throat was cut from ear to ear, the blood was black and dried all around. He wore the same tattered clothes and I saw the slash marks on his chest where they'd tortured him. His face was like a skull's face, and grinned purposefully at me, just grinning calmly.

Deacon came in through the open window and sat down, looking right at me. There was a roaring in my head, as if a train was going through it, my ears rang from the noise. I stared, open-mouthed, at Casey, waiting for him to see it, but he didn't see anything, he just sat there smoking and drinking as if everything was all right.

"What do you want?" I said to Deacon, who didn't answer, but just kept staring at me.

"Huh?" said Casey, looking over at me.

"How did you get here?" I demanded, my voice rising and taking on a shrill quality.

"What?" Casey asked.

My reason was fast slipping away. There he was, just as big as life. So this is what total madness looks like, the dead just walk in and join birthday parties.

"What is it?" Casey asked.

"What do you want?" I cried. "Why are you here?"

I did my best to struggle against the madness and hysteria but it was getting the better of me fast, it was riding like a wave, getting stronger.

"What?" Casey said, looking concerned now.

"Why don't you just get the hell out of here?" I yelled.

"Who?"

"Him!"

"Who, for God's sake?"

"Him! Can't you see?"

"See what?"

"Can't you see him?" I screamed, losing all control now. "He's right there, right there, look at him why don't you?"

"Look at who?"

"Why are you doing this to me?" I yelled.

"I'm not doing anything to you."

"I didn't have a thing to do with it!" I hollered.

"Didn't have anything to do with what? Pete, what's the matter with you? Are you okay?"

"'Course I'm okay, you're the one who's not okay, can't you see?"

"See what, for God's sake?"

"Him!"

I stood up and pointed.

"Who?"

I was practically hyperventilating now. I thought I would faint, standing there, so great was my terror, with the blood pounding in my ears.

Deacon rose from his chair now, and I thought, with the greatest possible horror, he was coming for me. "No!" I bellowed in terror. "Get away!" I turned and ran for the door, leaving Casey behind, for he had gotten up from his rocker and was coming towards me, wanting to calm me down. But there was no calming me, not now, and nothing in the world could have kept me in that room. I bolted out the door and across the porch, almost falling on the small set of wooden steps, then ran through the yard and didn't bother with the gate but leaped over the white picket fence and came down on the other side. I heard Casey calling after me from the doorway but I hit the sidewalk running and didn't look back. I ran along the street thinking Deacon was right behind me. He'd come for me, I knew that, he'd come to take me to the dead place with him, he was lonely there, maybe he wanted company. But why was he coming for me, why didn't the dumb bastard go after Karlovitch and Waldo or Dave and Larry?

I kept on running. I ran along Marina Drive and along Electric Avenue. I ran along the old train tracks that were still in place but no trains ran on them anymore. They cut right through the center of town and I could remember, when I was small, that the trains really did run on these tracks. I would take pennies and nickels sometimes when I had them, and lay them on the tracks and wait until after a train had gone by. The pennies especially flattened out; they were almost like paper after the train had rolled over them. The nickels weren't so much fun and besides you could, in those days, buy something for a nickel. You could make a phone call for a nickel. You could buy a candy bar, like a Baby Ruth or a Butterfinger, for a nickel, or a whole pack of baseball cards with a flat slab of pink bubble gum inside. Just a few years ago I'd had baseball cards of all the great players, Don Drysdale, Sandy Koufax, Willie Mays, Mickey Mantle, Roger Maris from the year he hit sixty one homers and broke Babe Ruth's record. But I didn't have them anymore. I had lost interest in all that, I couldn't even tell you what I'd done with those cards, I wasn't even sure who won the World Series this year. Funny how stuff like that could mean so much to you for a while and then just a short time later mean nothing at all. And things changed so fast, that was funny too. Nowadays you couldn't buy anything for a nickel. Just a few years ago I could go to the movies on Saturday afternoon and it only cost a quarter to get in, and a whole box of popcorn was only a quarter also. I used to go in there and stay all day, over at the old Bay Theatre. I'd seen some great movies there too: *The Time Machine, Journey to the Center of the Earth, 20,000 Leagues Under the Sea, Darby O'Gill and the Little People,* but I'd been frightened when the banshee came.

At last I stopped running. I stopped running because I couldn't run anymore. I walked, panting, taking in huge gulps of air. At last I dared look back. There wasn't anybody. The street was empty.

Maybe I was guilty too. Maybe that was why Deacon had come. I hadn't done anything, no. That was the good and the bad of it. I hadn't done anything. But what to call it, what was I guilty of? I was guilty of knowing the truth and not telling it. I was guilty of standing by and doing nothing while another person was murdered. What kind of crime was that, did they send people to prison for it, like to Folsom or Soledad? Would they put me away for that? No, what happened was worse, the dead came to birthday parties for the dead, and they chased you, and you feared you were insane just when you thought you were getting better.

There are two ways to see this, I thought, and they both stink. One: What I saw was real, and Deacon's ghost is really out there, and he's going to haunt me and follow me and come into my room some night and do God-knows-what to me. Two: There is no ghost, and I just imagined that I saw Deacon. And if that is it, then I know this: When people begin to see things like that, they put them away in padded cells with no exit, they medicate them with thorazine and stellazine and if that doesn't work they give them electro-shock therapy and perform lobotomies on them so they just sit in a corner and smile at the wall for the rest of their lives.

My God, I thought in agony, what is happening to me? And what is going to happen to me? I've gone crazy, does it get worse from here? Maybe I'll see Deacon everyplace I go from here on. And people will notice this crazy guy Pete talking to himself, talking to people who aren't there.

I pulled myself together as best I could. I lit a cigarette and wished I had a drink. It was time for me to go and meet Rena, in fact I was late. Oh God, I thought, I hope nothing else happens tonight. I hope I don't see Deacon over there.

Chapter 12

The Light of the World

I did my best to look normal and cheerful when I found Rena waiting for me in front of the church on Main Street.

"I'm so glad to see you, Pete," she said. "I've been praying you would come. This is going to change your life, I can just feel it, can't you?"

She held my hand in both of hers, and that felt good. Her hands were warm, and comforting to me. We stood in the crowd that was gathering there, waiting for the church to open and the services to begin.

"They have services every night?" I asked Rena.

"Every night," she smiled.

"And are there always so many people?"

"Sometimes more," she said proudly. "Often more. More people are hearing the Word every day."

She looked awfully pretty, standing there, smelling as she always did of rose petals and violets. I stood a bit closer to her, and wished we were alone so she could hold me. She greeted many of the people who were gathered there, and introduced me to them. I shook their hands but I was so worked up I couldn't have recalled their names, I just went through the motions mechanically, all the while glancing to the side and over my shoulder.

"Are you expecting someone?" Rena smiled.

"Hmm? Oh no."

"Then why do you keep looking around?"

"I don't know, maybe I'm a little nervous."

"Well, don't be," she laughed. "There's nothing to be nervous about here. You're in God's house."

"Is that why you come here?"

"I've come home."

"Home?"

"Home to God. And there's something else too. You know you're going to live for a while, and then you're going to die. It isn't really a very long time that you're alive. And when you're getting ready to die, and you look back on your life, you're going to wonder what it was all for, what did it mean. I want to do something that matters."

"How do you know what matters?"

"This matters," she said, looking around at the people gathered. "Helping people matters. Feeding people who are hungry matters. Helping people that are addicted to heroin get their life back together—that matters. I look at my mother sometimes. She goes to work, she comes home, she has a drink or two, she goes to bed. Is that living?"

"What about old Spiro?" I asked.

"He's worse than ever. He stays at home and drinks all day. I pray for him."

She told me about some of the things the Reverend and the church did, helping people who needed help. She didn't talk much more about her home life but I got the idea she went to the church all the time so she wouldn't have to be at home. Listening to her talk, and seeing once again how her face glowed when she mentioned the Reverend and how much she admired him, I felt a twinge of jealousy.

Well, I thought, what did you expect? Did you think she would just wait for you the rest of her life? You dumped her, remember?

"You look pale," Rena observed. "You feeling all right?"

"Why," I said, "I'm fine, just fine, never better in my life."

What a liar, I thought.

We went through a door that had a sign above it proclaiming that all who entered were welcome, for this was the house of God. There were more notices, too, proclaiming the times for Bible study classes and prayer meetings, as well as the times when the free food was given out. We went down some steps and into a big room where there weren't any chairs to sit on, just a worn carpet, and everyone sat on the floor. There was a podium, and a large picture of Jesus as the Good Sheppard, and a cross. Inside everyone was silent. Rena quieted too. She sat cross-legged next to me and took out a pocket-sized green book and opened it. Looking over her shoulder I saw it was a book of the Psalms, the Proverbs, and the New Testament. As more people came in and sat down I saw that a lot of them had these books, and they opened them and began reading silently just as Rena was. No one talked above an occasional whisper. I saw that those people who weren't reading the little Bible-books were sitting with their eyes closed, as if in deep communion or meditation.

Pretty soon the room was almost full. I knew there were a lot of people who said New Faith Church was a hangout for deadbeats, dropouts, drug addicts, hippies, and other undesirables, and that it should be closed and the Reverend run out of town on a rail. And a lot of the people were like that—they were hippies, street people, junkies or ex-junkies trying to stay clean. Rena told me how the Reverend helped them all. He helped the junkies to get off drugs, helped the alcoholics to sober up, he collected surplus food from grocery stores and restaurants to give to the real down-and-outers. Some he found jobs for. He told the streetwalkers to start loving themselves and stop abusing themselves. These are the cast-offs and the lonely, I thought, the scattered and the shattered and they come here because no one wants them and they have no place left to go.

But I didn't know if it was the place for me or not. I didn't know if there was any place for me at all. This was a crazy world and it was hard to find your bearings in it. I didn't feel like I belonged anywhere. I felt like a stranger in the world.

By-and-by a bearded man who was dressed in rough but neat clothing and who sat in front facing the congregation began to clap his hands. All the little Bible-books were put away and everyone else began to clap too. Then the bearded fellow began to sing. He sang *"What The World Needs Now Is Love,"* and everyone took it up, following him, and in a moment all the people there were singing. Their voices rang out and rose joyously toward the rafters above and I sang with them, clapping my hands too.

"What the world needs now is love, sweet love…"

What the world needs now is love, they all sang, it was the only thing there was just too little of. I liked singing and clapping this way. So what if I was crazy and saw dead people walking about? It didn't seem to matter so much now.

When that song was over we sang *"Michael Row the Boat Ashore,"* *"Where Have All the Flowers Gone,"* and *"Amazing Grace."* We sang some others, too, that sounded like hymns, that I'd never heard before. But I liked the singing, and felt better for having done it.

Then the silence came back again, more intensely than ever, an almost sacred quiet. Rena sat with her hands in her lap, a look of deep contentment on her face, as if she had gone to a place she liked very much, a place she was happy and safe in. Her eyes were shut and her body moved just slightly as she breathed, her shoulders rising and falling.

Then the Reverend Jim Feather came in. He just came right in from the back of the room. No one announced his presence, but everyone knew he was there. Every eye popped open, and they all waited, holding their breaths, their attention riveted on him.

He was about thirty years old, with long black hair and a neatly trimmed black beard. He wore sandals, jeans, and a white top embroidered with silver studs along the sleeves. But I was taken by more than his appearance. There was a force radiating from him. I felt it at once. I had never felt anything like it before. It was like an aura all around him, and it projected outward, so that it touched every person in the room. He didn't smile, but you got the feeling he was smiling at you—in fact, as time went on and I got to know him, I realized he almost never smiled, but you always *thought* he was, for some reason. I felt, as he stood up there, that he was looking right at me, that he had picked me out, among all those people, to look at, to speak to, to welcome, and it wasn't until later I understood everyone else in the room felt that way.

Even though there wasn't any microphone, his voice jumped right out at you, as if projected from a stage. It was a wonderful voice, deep and strong; he had no doubts about what he had to say, and there was a reassurance there, it gave you faith when you listened to it. He also had a slight twang to his speech; it took me a minute to place it because it was there one second and gone the next. But after a while I recognized it: It was the same Kentucky twang my father had.

The Reverend began by saying God loves everybody. I had heard people say that before but it never truly registered with me until then. God loves everybody. That, as I took it, included me. Now I liked that idea even if I didn't understand what God was. God loves me, I said to myself. I sang this to myself several times: God loves me. God loves me. God loves me. Now that's nice. I like that. God. G-O-D. I didn't know who He was but it was nice that he loved everybody. But then it occurred to me that if God loves everybody then that meant He also loved the likes of Waldo and Karlovitch, and Dave and Larry too. That took some of the wind out of my sails. Later, after I had gotten to know the Reverend, I asked him about that, how he would feel about having Waldo and Karlovitch in church. I didn't include Dave and Larry, because that was too much of a stretch, but I'd known Waldo all my life.

"God loves us all," was his answer.

I had to hand it to a God who could love those guys. That was a feat their mothers weren't even capable of performing. But then, the Reverend wasn't in the old power plant that night either.

The Reverend talked for about an hour. Sometimes he blasted forth with thunder and lightning, and sometimes it was all sweetness and sunshine. He was stern, when he talked about sin, and had this look on his face that was downright scary, and he said how bad it was to sin and how the Judgment Day would come for each of us, and when it did we'd have to answer for what we'd done with our lives. Then he would change over, and talk about how much God loved each one of us, and how He loved the whole world and all that was in it.

He kept calling the audience his brothers and sisters. "Brothers and sisters," he would say, "do not ever doubt the Fatherhood of God and the Brotherhood of man." And sitting there, I felt that he meant it, that he really did regard the rest of us as his brothers and sisters. I had never heard anybody speak that way before.

"Brothers and sisters, God is in everything," said the Reverend from his pulpit. "If you look hard enough you can see the Light of God in the flowers and the trees and the bugs that crawl on the ground and fly in the air. God is in the most distant stars and in the suns, He's in the farthest reaches of the universe. There is no place we can go where God is not. His watchful loving eyes are upon us always. We cannot flee from Him because He is always there with us. Everything we do is written in that Holy Book He keeps at the base of His throne. I have seen the dew on the fleece, and I have seen the blood of the lamb, and the Psalmist says, 'Yea, the darkness hideth not from thee; but the night shineth as the day: the darkness and the light are both alike to thee...'"

Mostly I enjoyed the sermon. And I sat there trying *not* to like the Reverend, because of what Casey had said about him and because Rena seemed to like him so much. But hard as I tried not to, I did like him, I liked what he said and how he said it.

But there was one part I didn't like. He began talking about what was hidden coming to light and how there could be no secrets at all, and everything that was buried was coming up.

"Oh Earth, cover not my blood/And let my cry find no resting place/Even now, behold my witness is in heaven/And he that vouches for me is on high."

This made me uncomfortable. The more he went on about it the worse I got, and I wished I hadn't come here at all. Everyplace I went today I was getting hit with the same thing. I tried to stop listening but the words came anyway, and by the time he neared the end I was miserable and thinking of walking out even if it would hurt Rena's feelings. But then the Reverend got off this hidden-in-the-darkness-jazz and began to talk about how the light of Jesus is in all of us and how what we need to do is let it shine through and we'll all be born again of the spirit. Now this caught my attention and I began to think about that. I liked that idea. To be born again and start all over, with all the bad things I'd done and seen washed away and behind me. The more he went on about it the more it seemed I did feel something. It wasn't like anything I'd ever felt before. It was sort of like when I'd felt the crystal glowing, but this time the glow was coming from inside of me.

I looked at Rena sitting next to me. She was listening raptly to the Reverend's words, and I recalled how she'd said it was so great to help people, to help the bums and the freaks and the other assorted weirdoes that came here. I had rolled that one off when she said it but now I had a sudden and wild urge to do exactly that. To help people. To do something good. Something that mattered in some way.

While the Reverend talked and Rena sat beside me I felt I was being bathed in a light, a holy white light that totally surrounded me like a mother's arms. Was this the light the Reverend kept speaking of? I couldn't say, but it was a wonderful light and a wonderful feeling. It got brighter and as it engulfed me I felt I was being cleansed, all the bad things I had ever done were being washed away. An old self was gone and a new one, bright and clean and pure, untainted by the past, was emerging like a butterfly out of its cocoon.

I wanted to leap up, and shout this great news to everyone there, for it seemed important to share it. But I waited until the Reverend was done, hard as that was, and in the deep silence that followed I reached over to touch Rena on the shoulder. She had been holding her hands in front of her in prayer but when she turned to look at me and saw the change that had taken place she dropped her hands and let out a cry of joy.

"Oh, praise God!" she cried. "My prayers had been heard!"

She grabbed me by the hand and together we made our way through the now-standing congregation, going through the people like a plow in a field of yellow wheat. Rena led the way as we beat a path to the pulpit and knelt down, our hands still clasped tightly together.

"Oh Reverend Jim," she cried rapturously, "please baptize him right now! He's seen the light of the Lord!"

Reverend Jim took one look at me and said a "Hallelujah!" designed to make the chandeliers ring. A lot of people yelled "Praise the Lord!" and put their hands together in prayer and thanksgiving. Others fell down to the knees.

"What is your name, Brother?" the Reverend Jim asked me, and when I told him he cried "Hallelujah!" again. Then he got out some Holy Water, which he said he'd gotten right out of the River Jordan, and splashed it on my head to anoint me. Then he rubbed it into my hair, all the while praising God and thanking Him for His miracles and wonders which took place right before our eyes everyday. Then he produced one of those little green Bible-books and a pen, and opened it to the front where it said to write your name, for today was the day I had decided to receive Jesus as my savior. I wrote my name in there and signed, too, and wrote in the date, and the Reverend said another "Hallelujah!" and quoted, "'Behold, I stand at the door and knock; if any man hear my voice, and open the door, I will come in to him.'" I had been kneeling with my head bowed, but now I looked up, and saw that his eyes blazed like a deep and dark fire.

There was a chorus of "Hallelujahs!" now, and a lot of "Praise the Lords!" also. Rena and I stood up. She hugged me and the Reverend shook my hand and called me "Brother." He said he was thrilled to the depths of his soul about this, and it sounded to me like he meant it. All the other members of the congregation came up to me also, the men shaking hands with me, the women hugging me, welcoming me to the flock. The men thumped me on the back and called me "Brother" like the Reverend did. Some of the girls and the women cried. They all said this was the holiest of times, when a person came to the Lord, one of the holiest times there was. I looked the Reverend in the eye once more, and he smiled and shook my hand again. I liked him, and before Rena and I left the church I thanked him for what he'd done for me.

"I didn't do anything," he said. "I am only the instrument of the Lord."

•　　•　　•

Rena and I walked out the back way and down the alley behind Main Street. She said everyone always went out the front way and she wanted to be alone and quiet. I offered to walk her home.

"That would be wonderful," she said.

We walked for a few minutes in silence, me still feeling the effect of what had just happened. It was like that light was still around me, and outside, in the coolness of the night, it was stronger now, shielding me from the darkness. I looked up at the moon shining down, and felt its light joining with the holy light that was surrounding me.

"I'll never forget this," Rena said, as we walked in the darkness of the alley and saw our shadows passing over the rough surface. "Not as long as I live."

"Never is a long time," I commented.

"I won't forget," she declared. "I don't think you will either. Will you?"

"I have a long memory."

"So do I. I remember you in the first grade."

"I remember you then too."

"Do you? One time, when we were at the old school on 12th Street, I was hanging upside down from the monkey bars, and you said, 'Teacher, teacher, I declare, I see someone's underwear!' I was so embarrassed I thought I would die."

"You should have been embarrassed," I said, "because they had a big hole in them."

"They did not!"

"Oh yes they did."

"They probably did," she admitted ruefully.

"Do you remember what happened next?" I asked her.

"No, what was it?"

"You got down off the bars, took a rock and heaved it at me."

"Did it hit you?"

"Yes, right here. It hurt, too."

"Where was it?" she asked, stopping and looking at me. I pointed to my chest and she placed her hand on the spot where the rock had hit me, so long ago. Rena's hand was smooth, with long fingers, and she had a small ring on the third finger of her right hand which glinted just a bit in the moonlight. "There," she said, her fingers moving over my heart. "Is that better now?"

"Yes," I said. "I guess that was when you first touched my heart."

"Did it really?"

I took her hand and held it in both of mine now, holding it like a little lost bird. "Would you like it if I told you I love you, and I think I always have? Part of this heart of mine will always belong to you, no matter where I go or you go. That rock you threw all those years ago left its mark. Here, there's something I want you to have." I took off my necklace, the one Casey had given me with the Runestone Sowelu on it, and placed it around her neck. "You don't have to feel obligated to wear it," I went on, "unless you want to. But I want you to have it, because it's the most precious gift I could give to anyone right now."

Tears were flowing down her round smooth cheeks, one after the other, like drops of wax falling from a burning candle. Her shoulders trembled and she let the tears fall, not bothering to wipe them away. She took the ring she wore from her finger and taking my left hand, tried to put it on me. But my fingers were too big, except for the very last one, and with some effort she got it over the knuckles. "There," she said, "at least I have something to give you back. It isn't much."

"It's everything," I said, looking at the ordinary gold-colored ring with an aqua-blue stone on it. "It's the color of the ocean."

"I couldn't ask for anything more than this, ever," she said, hugging me tightly now. Her cheeks were still wet and left little marks of moisture on my shirt. The she dried her eyes and we walked the rest of the way to her house, holding hands still and not saying much. We stopped a few doors down from her house and said goodnight.

"I have to go in, I'm late as it is," she whispered, "but I want you to know I'll keep this always. Forever," she said.

"Forever," I repeated.

I kissed her goodnight and watched her go up the street and then to her door and inside. I went on to my house, three streets over, feeling light as a feather again. I must have imagined all that, I thought, thinking of what I had seen (or hadn't seen) at Casey's house. I went in the way I always did, through the back gate in the alley and in the back door. There were weeds growing against the fence, creeping up the old peeling paint, and my father, when he changed the oil in the cars, would dump the old oil there in a futile effort to kill the weeds. It never seemed to work, just made the weeds turn black for a time and then they were back again. I went in through the old squeaky gate, which hung crookedly on its hinges, and through the moonlit backyard, giving a glance at my oak tree as I went by, noting that while it didn't seem to have grown at all it was still alive and healthy. Then there was a screeching sounds and I saw two cats fighting near what was left of the old incinerator. In the moonlight the incinerator looked like a relic leftover from some time long past, with its crumbling sides and the iron door that hung, half-open, as if waiting for the final decision on its fate to be made.

My parents' bedroom was on the other side of the house, the new side, and this way I didn't disturb them when I went in. I saw a crack on the wall of the older section, where my room was, and took in a wheelbarrow and some sacks of concrete that hadn't been there when I left earlier today. My father, I recalled, had been saying that the foundation of the house needed some shoring up, and he was planning on doing some repair work on it this coming Saturday. My room was off by itself, which suited me. I could sit up late if I felt like it, playing my stereo softly or reading. Since my father wouldn't budge from this house, my mother, after a lot of nagging and pestering, had gotten him to put an addition on it. The kitchen was enlarged, a den and another bedroom and bathroom were added on. She had wanted a maid, too, since a lot of her friends at the Women's Club had maids, but once again the old man wouldn't yield and so she didn't get her way that time. My mother had sulked, spoiledly, over that one for several weeks.

I went in quietly as I could, not wanting to wake them. I went into my room happy and thinking about what had happened tonight. I put the ring Rena had given me in my Rune bag, so I would always know where it was, and kept thinking about the Light. That light that had washed over me had been beautiful and wonderful and I wished I could see it again, experience it once more. I was safe in that light. It had radiated love, real love, a strong and powerful and everlasting love. I wished I had been able to be in that light longer and lying there in my bed, I did my best to get it back. I tried and tried but it wouldn't come. I shut my eyes and tried calling for it, concentrating, but to no avail.

The little green book was across my chest and I wondered about the light. Would I ever get it back? It seemed familiar, somehow, but then I thought that can't be. But it was familiar, all the same, as though I knew where that light came from and where it went, and where it would take me if I followed it.

My door opened and Laurie-Anne came in. Damn! I'd forgotten to lock it. She came right in and sat on my bed, wearing one of her see-through nightgowns. Her hair was down and she didn't have any makeup on. She sat looking at me and smiling, just looking at me, crossing her bare legs and staring. "Hi," she said finally.

"What is it?" I asked.

"Nothing," she said, smiling still.

"What do you want?"

"I just wanted to tell my boy goodnight," she said, getting closer to me. "Can't your mother kiss you goodnight?" She leaned down to kiss me, but it wasn't a motherly kiss, she allowed her lips to linger too long beside mine. I pulled away, and she reached out to stroke my cheek. "Can't your mother come in and see if her boy is all right?"

I moved away and said, "Well, you can see I'm all right." I waited for her to leave but she didn't go anywhere. She just sat there, staring at me.

"I want to go to sleep now, Mother," I said at last.

She didn't say anything for a moment or two. Then she giggled. "Do you get scared at night?" she asked. "Do you ever have nightmares, and need your mother to come in and tell you it's going to be all right?"

"No."

"Don't you ever want to sleep with your mother, so you don't get scared?"

"No."

"Why are you so mean?" she asked. "You're never nice to me. Why can't you be nice to your mother? I just want to be nice to you. Won't you let me be nice to you? You've gotten so grown up, such a handsome boy, my boy, so grown up and so handsome." She turned and laid down beside me. "Can't I just lay here with you for a while? I want to lay here with you." She moved to put her head on my shoulder. I took in the unmistakable smell of gin. "Let's just be comfortable. We can, you know. It's all right."

"Don't," I said. "Stop it." By now she was lying full-length beside me, and I rolled so that she fell off the edge of the bed awkwardly.

"Damn you!" she said, furious now. "All I want is to be nice to you. You shouldn't be so mean to someone who loves you."

"Will you just get out of here?" I said. "Just get out of my room."

"What is this?" she said, spotting my little Bible-book and picking it up, like plucking a rose she had taken a sudden interest in. "Presented by the New Faith Church!" she exclaimed. "Where did you get this? You've never gone there, have you?"

"Something wrong with that?"

"Why," she said, holding the book tightly, "you are not to go there, ever! They use drugs in that place, they have sex orgies there! You are not to go there ever again!"

"You're crazy," I said, reaching for the book she held, but she moved it out of my reach.

"Millie Nash was telling everyone at Women's Club. She's heard all about it. That is a terrible place and the city is going to close it down. This town is for decent people, not people like them. Now, you are not to go there ever again, do you understand me?"

"Please give me my book back, Mother," I said, but she held onto it even tighter and wouldn't give it up.

"Not until you promise," she said.

I sat up, and took it away from her. "Give it here," I said, and she struggled for a moment, twisting and not wanting to give it up so that I had to peel and pry her fingers away from it.

"Now you listen to me," she said, shaking her finger, standing up furiously. "You either promise me right now, this minute, that you'll never set foot in that place ever again or else I'm going to go and get your father. Your father will make you promise, you wait and see."

"Go ahead," I said. "I don't care."

"You'll be sorry!" she vowed.

She stormed out and I locked the door behind her, turning the old-fashioned hook-like key in the lock, for the house had been built in 1939, when they still had locks with keyholes in them you could peep through. I didn't think she would really go and get my father up. She often threatened to do that but she almost never did. No doubt he had gone to bed drunk an hour or two ago and getting him up wouldn't be easy, nothing short of a hydrogen bomb going off would do it once he fell into bed. And if she did get him up he would be feeling awful and there was no telling what he'd do, he might turn on her, or Darren, just as easy as me. I opened my book and looked at the front again. I'd signed my name and written the date in there, saying that on this day, Thursday, November 7, 1968, I had accepted the Lord into my life. In a couple of weeks it would be Thanksgiving, and then Christmas would be coming soon after that. All the houses would be decorated with Christmas lights and nativity scenes in the front yards. That was a big thing around here, there was always a competition as to who had the most lights or the most detailed nativity. When I was small I looked forward to Christmas, I would count off the days on the calendar until it came, but the last few years it had lost the excitement it once had, it didn't seem like such a big deal anymore.

There was something like an explosion outside my door. It rocked on its hinges, it bent at the top. Something was smashing against it. "Open up! Open this door, goddamn it, open it right now!"

The pounding kept on until I got up and opened the door. George burst through, smelling of vodka and wearing his pajamas, his eyes wild and angry.

"What the hell is going on in here?" he yelled. "What are you doing to your mother?"

"I didn't do anything to her."

"You giving her trouble again?"

"No," I replied with some dignity. "She was giving me trouble, if you want to know the truth."

"Don't you talk about your mother that way," he snarled, and I braced myself for the blow that usually followed about now, the sharp two-knuckled blow to the arm or the open-handed whack to the side of the head. But he just let out a gasp of rage and then his eyes, bleary with drink, focused on the wall above my bed.

"What the hell is this?" he roared, staggering closer. He stared uneasily at my horoscope, blinking his eyes as if trying to focus them. He stared at the round wheels within wheels, at the little astrological symbols Casey had drawn in the different houses of the zodiac. He gaped, unsure of what to make of this, and then his face twisted with rage. "I told you once, I told you a thousand times I won't have any of the kind of hippie crap in the house!" Before I could stop him he tore it off the wall and ripped it apart, destroying it beyond any hope of putting it back together. I cried out as if it was my own flesh being torn, then stood in the center of my room, staring at the pieces, which he threw contemptuously to the floor. "You better just smarten up!" he yelled. "You better wise up or I'll really give you something to yell about!" And then he was gone, out the door and back to his room on the other side of the house.

I locked the door and put out the light and sat on my bed holding the pieces of the drawing in my hand, crying in a way I hadn't cried in years. I bawled, letting the tears fall freely, feeling all the pain I felt inside come bubbling out. I didn't cry loudly but just cried with silent, wracking sobs. There was no way to put the destroyed pieces back together, they were mutilated beyond repair, but I held them a long time anyway as if they had a healing power that could help me get over the hurt I felt, and I never did throw them away but kept them in a folder in my desk. At last I lay back in my bed and closed my eyes and tried to get that light to come again. It still wouldn't come, and I lay there in the dark, still clutching those torn pieces of paper and my Bible-book to me, and then at last something like the light did return, not like had been in the church but part of it, and I felt better. Then in the midst of it I thought of Deacon, and with that came the knowledge, the undisputed knowing, that I could never truly be in the light until that was taken care of.

But I didn't have any idea how I would take care of it

Chapter 13

In Church

"Have you gone completely crazy?" asked Tom.

"I don't think so."

"It can't be true," he insisted. "You *must* be crazy."

"I don't feel crazy," I said. "In fact, I feel like I've been crazy all my life and I'm now starting to get sane."

Tom stood staring at me, shaking his big blond head back and forth. Outside the rain came pounding down, an especially heavy rain that rattled the roof of the office. A leak had appeared near the corner and water oozed through it when it rained hardest, dripping down onto the floor until somebody put a bucket there to catch it.

"I've got it," he said, as if he had found an answer he had been seeking for years. "It's for love. It has to be."

"It isn't that," I said. "I swear it isn't that."

"It's gotta be," he maintained. "What else could it be?"

As Tom stood in the center of the room lamenting the door opened and Denny came in. At the same time a big cabin cruiser went past, sending a powerful wave in its wake.

"Denny," said Tom, as if Denny represented his last and best hope. "You gotta do something. Kick this guy, or shake him, but do something that will bring him back to his senses."

"Why, what's the matter with him?" Denny asked.

"He's going to church, he's got religion!" Tom cried.

"I don't believe it," Denny said.

"It's true," Tom affirmed.

"You mean that freaky church on Main Street, where all the bums and the whores and the junkies go?"

"That's the one," said Tom. "He says he saw some kind of a light in there the other night."

"What sort of a light was it, Pete?" Denny asked.

"He didn't see any light," Tom interrupted. "He's just temporarily off his rocker, that's all."

"Well," Denny said, "I don't know what you think I can do about it, Tom."

"Use your imagination, think of something!" Tom cried. "Bring him out of it!"

"He doesn't look any different," Denny said, peering at me intently.

"He's different on the inside, and that's where it counts the most," Tom declared.

"Say," Denny exclaimed, "I've got it! He's going there because that's where Rena goes, he's doing it to be with her."

"I already thought of that," Tom said disgustedly. "He says that isn't it."

"Is that it, Pete?" Denny asked.

"I can see Rena anytime, I don't need to go to church to do it."

"The chick hasn't been born who could ever get me into a church," Tom maintained.

"Let's smoke one," Denny suggested. "That'll clear out our brains and we can think of something to do about this."

"No," I said, holding up my hand. "I don't do that anymore. And you guys shouldn't either. It's badness to do that."

"See what I mean?" Tom said to Denny. "Next he'll be preaching to us."

"This *is* serious," Denny said. "You want some wine, Pete?"

"I don't drink anymore. And you shouldn't drink. That's also badness. Unholy."

"You see? You see?" said Tom.

"Say," said Denny, "what has gotten into you, Pete?"

"I just told you, he's got religion!" said Tom.

This was the start of my religious period, my time of going to church whenever I could and reading the Bible and praying a great deal. The Reverend said there was tremendous power in prayer and if you prayed hard enough all your wishes would come true. I prayed every night before I went to sleep and every morning when I got up. At night I prayed that I would be forgiven for my sins, for all the bad things I had done in my life, and when I thought about them it seemed like it was pretty long list.

That was just the start. And in the morning I prayed that God would be with me all day long, and I prayed that my father not be so mean to me when I went out to have my breakfast, for the Reverend had read to us, "Honor thy father and thy mother." I wanted to do that but it was pretty hard.

I also prayed for my nightmares to end, for after my father tore up the horoscope they came back again, in full force. It was as if Casey had invested that horoscope with some magical powers, for while it had been above my bed the nightmares had stopped, but now they were worse than ever. I woke up screaming, all covered with sweat, breathing hard and listening to all the rain drumming on the red bricks of the patio outside my window.

No one heard me, and for that I was grateful, glad I had been shunted off to the far side of the house. I would get up and wash the sweat from my face, then get back into bed. I did my best not to smoke anymore but sometimes I would get a cigarette out from the pack I had hidden under my bed alongside my Runes, and I would lay there smoking and listening to the rain.

I couldn't get back to sleep, so I would get the Runes out. This seemed a safe time to do that, the middle of the night. I laid them out, doing a Celtic cross or a three Rune spread, staring down at them, wondering what they were trying to say to me. One time I did think they were saying I would soon take a long journey and that turned out to be true. Other times I lay there staring up at the crack in the ceiling of my room, which seemed to be getting bigger with each passing day. I looked at the surfing posters I had on the walls, for I liked looking at them the same way Tom did, and at the books I had neatly arranged on a wooden bookcase: *The Grapes of Wrath, The Odyssey, The Iliad, The Call of the Wild,* and *Lord Jim.*

My face became haggard again, just like it had right after the murder. Bags and dark circles formed under my eyes. One morning George noticed how bad I looked.

"What's wrong with you?" he asked, regarding me from behind his newspaper. "You sick or something? You don't look good."

Something had changed since the night he destroyed my horoscope. I was less afraid of him than I used to be. Once I looked him in the eye and made him look away. Then I did it again. I felt stronger each time I did that and he seemed weaker. I could knock him down, I thought, looking at his bulging stomach and sagging chest. I practiced the karate moves Tom had taught me, diligently, day after day, and every day in P. E. class I did as many pull-ups and bar dips as I could. Then I thought of what the Reverend had told me, and said to myself I shouldn't be thinking this way, and I thought of how the Good Book said we should do good to those who did bad to us. But it was so damn hard to do when you really got down to it.

"I'm all right," I said sullenly. I looked past him at a worn spot on the carpet, which reminded me of the bald spot on the back of his head. Don't think that way, I thought. But I still wanted to knock him down.

"You sure?" he persisted, rubbing his temples. "You look terrible. Maybe you need to go to the doctor."

"I tell you I'm all right!" I barked, and looked him in the eye.

"He always looks like that!" Darren jeered from the other side of the table, sneering at me from behind boxes of Rice Krispies and Cheerios, his black eyebrows arching. "There's nothing the doctor can do to help him!" He made a face at me and stuck out his tongue. George saw it, and turned on him.

"Nobody asked you to butt in!" he roared. "You mind your own business, you damn sissy!"

Darren usually remained quiet when George was nearby, not wishing to draw his attention, because the kind of attention we got from him usually got took the form of a shout followed by a blow from hand or fist. And recently, when Darren had been caught stealing candy from a local store George had said, "You come here. I'm gonna give you a lickin'."

"But I don't want one!" Darren screeched. "Mama help! Mama don't let him! Don't let him do it!" Then George dragged Darren into the bedroom and closed the door and then gotten a belt and beat him until you could hear Darren screaming over on Catalina Island. Other times he came home drunk and taken the belt to him for being a sissy, saying all the while that *something* had to make a man of him. When George did speak to him Darren cringed away in terror, babbling in baby talk, and then would run and hide behind our mother, looking out fearfully.

Now Darren began to cry. He sobbed wrackingly, big tears rolling down his cheeks and leaving wet trails behind. "Knock it off!" George said warningly. Darren just cried harder. "I said knock it off! Stop it before I give you something to cry about!" Darren hung his head and covered his face, still weeping, and then George reached over and swatted him with his open hand. Darren howled, long and loud, like a dog howling when it hears a siren, then fled from the table. "Mama!" he called. "Mama!" George sat shaking his head.

"What kind of a kid is that?" he said. "Can't understand him when he talks. He plays with dolls. What's the matter with him?"

"What the hell are you asking me for?" I said sharply. "He's *your* kid."

He gave me an ugly look, and for a second I thought he might want to make something of this, but then Laurie-Anne came storming in from the kitchen, clad in her bathrobe, angrily shaking a pancake turner.

"Are you real proud of yourself?" she said. "He's in there crying his eyes out. What did you do to him this time?"

"Oh, for God's sake," George snorted disgustedly, and raised the shield of his newspaper up once more. "All you have to do is look at that kid and he starts crying. Isn't that right, Pete?" he said, turning my way as if he expected me to support him, the real men against the women and sissies. But I didn't say anything. I sat glaring at him, still thinking about how I could knock him down. From around the corner of the kitchen Darren peeped out, his eyes wide.

"Why must you always hurt him?" Laurie-Anne demanded, shaking the pancake turner up and down for added emphasis. "Why can't you ever be nice to him, the way a father should be to his son? Why can't anyone ever treat him decently? He never does anything wrong."

"He's a sissy!" George folded the newspaper in half and looked up at her angrily. "What kind of a man is he going to be?"

"He's a child!"

"He wouldn't last very long in the service!"

"Oh, you and your service can go to hell!"

"You've made him into a damn sissy, babying him all the time. He's gonna turn out *queer*, and you can thank yourself for that."

"I'd rather see him become a queer than see you keep on bullying him!"

I thought she might whack him across the face with the spatula, she was so angry. I sat, watching with a sort of gleefulness that comes when you watch two people you dislike get into a fight. But she didn't hit him. She yelled some more and he yelled back, and no one noticed as I left the table.

I went out the door, pulling on a jacket, for the weather had gotten even colder and it seemed to rain nearly every day that winter. The streets were wet and water was always running along in the gutters. Big puddles stood on sidewalks and in parking lots and they never seemed to get smaller even if the rain let up for a few days. But it always came back, the clouds would gather again in the sky, the blackness came, and the rain would begin once more.

I went to school, I went to work, and I went to church. That was my life. If I was working that day, I went to church as soon as I got off work, and stayed until eleven or midnight, sometimes later. I listened to the

Reverend's sermons, I went to prayer meetings and Bible study. I learned some of the Psalms, like the one that says, "The Lord is my shepherd, I shall not want," and another one, "The Lord is my light and my salvation; whom shall I fear?" I learned a little about Moses and the life of Jesus, which didn't do me any harm but a lot of good.

I went to be with Rena, and whenever I went to church I wore the ring she had given me, and she also wore the necklace I had given her. I went because I felt it was good for me, but I also went to spite my mother. Often when I came home she would be sitting up waiting for me. I would see her in the living room sitting with a reading light on, a book like *The Carpetbaggers* or *Valley of the Dolls* across her lap, wearing a robe with one of her see-through nightgowns on underneath, and she would glare sullenly at me when I came in. "Where have you been?" she would ask in a tone designed to create ice on Lake Tahoe. "At church," I would reply flippantly, and I got no small satisfaction out of the angry look that came onto her face. But she didn't try to stop me from going anymore, in spite of what she'd said about the sex orgies and dope fiends there. Instead she would shut off the light with an angry jerk of the hanging chain, and stalk away, and I would go off to my room and lock the door.

I prayed when I woke up after my nightmares, and I prayed whenever I thought of Deacon—especially when I thought of how I'd seen him at Casey's that time—and I prayed when I was frightened and sometimes after praying I didn't feel so frightened anymore. I prayed for my sanity, too, and hoped I would not go completely mad, for the idea of being crazy was scary to me too.

I think I went to church more than anything else because of that night in the old power plant. I went because I didn't want to think about it anymore, and going to church made it a little easier to bear what I knew. Sometimes I could go for an hour, two hours, a whole day, without thinking of what happened.

I stopped drinking, and I stopped smoking Panama Red. I tried hard not to masturbate but refraining from that wasn't so easy. After being with Rena for several hours and feeling the nearness of her close to me I would come home and get into my bed and it seemed I had no control over myself. The Reverend talked a lot about the sins of the flesh and how God had given these desires to us so we could overcome them and rise above them, and I tried and tried but I never could make it for very long. And I often thought of Carolyn, and how she was with all her clothes off, and that made it worse yet and there wasn't anything I could do about it, my flesh rose up like a geyser and demanded something be done.

Tom thought I had gone completely crazy, and said so often enough, but I didn't see him too much at this time. I was always at church and he spent a lot of his time with Tiffany—their affair was still going on, getting hotter and heavier every day, in fact—so we didn't see as much of each other as we used to. When we did he would say, "Are you still going to church?" and I would say "Yes," and he would shake his head like he still found it hard to believe.

I told a lot of this to the Reverend, and he was always sympathetic. "The path to God is the hardest path there is, Pete," he said. "This way is not the easy way, it is the hard way. Many are called and few are chosen, and narrow is the gate. You can be proud of yourself. Just about all of the old things that you're used to will fall away, the further along this road you go. Everyday it is a struggle. It starts all over again every morning when you wake up. You might lose everything—your friends, your parents, all that was part of your old life will be gone."

"Then what will be left?" I asked.

"God," he replied. "And then you'll discover you don't need anything else."

"Is that the way it is for you?" I asked.

"It's the only way for me."

I liked the Reverend in spite of myself. I had tried my best *not* to like him, but it didn't work out that way. He always made it a point to come over and shake my hand in a manly sort of fashion when I got to church, and say he was glad to see me. He asked how I was, and how things were at home, and how I was doing in school, and after a while my resistance broke down and I was won over. I didn't trust him at first and didn't want to open up with him, but after a while I did, for it's always nice to have someone to talk to, and I liked what he said, even if I didn't always understand it.

He said everyone was the same in the sight of God, rich or poor, black, white, yellow or brown. A junkie was just as precious to the Lord as the President of the United States—maybe even more so, because the junkie needed God more. One day I asked the Reverend how this could be.

He looked at me in that way he had to making you think he was smiling when he really wasn't. I don't know how he did it, but it made you feel good inside, it made you think he really cared, and that was rare enough in my experience. "We're all the Spirit made flesh," he said. "We're all made of the same clay, matter that wasn't anything until God breathed life into it. That what makes us all brothers and sisters, it makes the universe one."

"The universe," he told me another time, "is all one thing. It's God's creation, all of it, from right here where we are to the most distant star out in space. What is matter? Just atoms arranged in different ways and moving at different speeds. What is water? Two atoms of hydrogen and one of oxygen, right? Take away that one little atom of oxygen and you've got something different. God is what put that spark into it to make it move, to arrange it the way He wants it to be arranged, like a gigantic symphony, and He is the conductor."

I think what I liked best about the Reverend was the way he wasn't afraid to go right out into the streets for what he believed in. God was everywhere, he said. His job wasn't to stay holed up in any church, he had to take God's message to the people of the streets, the ones who needed it most. "This isn't a gospel for the dead, it's a gospel for the living," he would say. "It's for the real people and the real problems of life, that's what it was made for, that's what Christ came here to tell us."

So he would go to the park beside the pier, where the worst of the town rowdies and druggies hung out, a Bible in his hand, and preach the word of God. His faith gave him the courage to do this, and it did take guts to go there, for the toughs at the park didn't like being preached to. Sometimes the worst ones, like Waldo and Karlovitch, (and I always suspected Dave put them up to it) would heckle him and throw beer cans at him, and say he'd better get his holy ass back to church where it was safe. But the Reverend never got flustered or lost his equanimity. He said the doors of the church were open to everyone, and he had converted more than a few of these people.

At first I couldn't see the point of all this, especially when he came back from the park one day with a big gash in his head, the result of being hit with a 16 ounce can of Colt 45 malt liquor heaved at him by Waldo. He came into the church bleeding, holding one hand to his head, and giving thanks that he had been found worthy to receive a blow for the Lord. "I never would have thought Waldo could throw something that accurately," he said, while Rena and I dressed the wound and washed the blood away. "I saw him getting ready to throw it, but he was pretty far away, I never would have thought he could hit me from that distance. I know he's good with his fists, but I never knew he was so athletic."

"That Waldo is just plain vicious," Rena said, "and Karlovitch is even worse. Reverend Jim, I wish you wouldn't do this."

"Waldo used to pitch for the Little League team we were on together," I said, as Rena applied some Bactine to the wound.

"Was he any good?" asked the Reverend.

"Pretty darn good," I said. "He used to aim for the opposing batters' heads until the coach found out and made him stop. Are you sure you want him and Karlovitch in church?"

"God loves us all," he said.

"I'll bring him to church," I said, clenching my fists and turning to go. But he restrained me.

"The Apostles gave thanks after being beaten in the Lord's name," he said.

His mission was to take the word of God to the people of the streets, and nothing would deter him from that, not heckling or threats or getting hit in the head with a beer can. And it bore fruit, once in a while: Late at night there would be a scratching at the front door of the church, and there would be a rough-looking biker standing there shivering and looking hangdog, saying he was tired of this kind of life, and that he had come here looking for help.

That was when we gave thanks, happy to see another soul trying to come to God. They didn't always make it. Some just came for the night, and in the morning when they sobered up they were gone, back to their old ways. Some bounced back and forth like rubber balls. One day they were in church, singing hymns and hallelujahs, and the next day they were back at the park, smoking pot and cranking down speed.

The Reverend was always on call. Whenever somebody needed him he was there, no matter what time, day or night. These were his people, he said, his flock, and this was his mission. He was to take care of the ragged and the poor, the cast offs and the forgotten ones that nobody wanted. They had been given over into his care and nothing could make him forsake them, ever. People would come to him when their friends were about to commit suicide, or when they were freaked out on some bad lsd. He always went, saying his people were calling him. Nor did he ever lock the church. The doors were left open, day and night. The Reverend said it was God's house and you could not lock the doors to God's house. A few times people had broken in, and stolen things, but he still wouldn't lock the doors. I made sure I never left anything valuable there, because he said everything in the church belonged to God, it was all free so no one could actually steal any of it. A light was always left on, too, so that people knew they were welcome to come in anytime and pray or just be with God, and he slept downstairs and never locked his door either.

I went with him when he went on his house calls. That was when I saw the truly ugly side of life, the side people don't want to talk about and try to pretend doesn't exist in their town. I'll never forget what I saw: Kids that had been half-beaten to death, women puking and screaming from heroin withdrawals, alcoholics in the midst of delirium tremens.

Worst of all were the people strung out on crystal meth or MDA. They were hallucinating, seeing "meth monsters," they were in the midst of acute paranoia and they thought people were plotting to kill them or poison their food. Sometimes they wouldn't eat, and some were literally dying of starvation; I saw this, with my very own eyes. And it was even worse because I knew where they were getting the crystal meth and the MDA: Waldo and Karlovitch, and in the back ground was Dave, who gave them the bad stuff and told them to peddle it to whomever they could sell it to.

We helped some of these people, or I should say I helped the Reverend help them. Some of them got off the drugs altogether, started going to church and turned their lives around.

I told Rena I could understand why she found the church so rewarding. "It's like nothing else I've ever done meant anything," I said.

"All the rest seems so meaningless, doesn't it?" Rena replied. "My heart feels so full when I think of it. What does your heart feel like, Pete?"

"Sometimes it feels empty," I said, "and other times I don't know what is in there."

"Maybe you're afraid to look, and see."

"I might be."

"But maybe you won't always be," she said, laying her hand on my chest, the way she often did, covering my heart. I liked it when she did that, for she had to stand very close to me to do it, and I could smell her rose petals and violet scent and feel the nearness of her body. She was slender and rather tall, only two inches shorter than me, and I would look at the trim lines of her body and see the light glinting in her hair, and I felt my heart swelling up, I was so in love.

"I wish I knew what you have locked in there," she said, touching my chest once again.

"Maybe you already know."

"What? That you love me? Yes, but there's more, isn't there? I know there is. One day you'll open up, you must, you'll have to, everyone does."

There was a light that came into her eyes now when she spoke of the church and the Reverend. It had never been there before. It was like a joy that comes from deep within, something so special that her life at home, with her mother gone all the time and her drunken stepfather, could never touch. It was a joy that was all hers, and nothing, I thought, could ever take it away. I was glad for her, glad she had this. There were times when I thought I might be able to have it too, but they never lasted for long. Rena's heart was pure, she was pure, like snow that hasn't been walked on, but I wasn't.

As much as I liked the Reverend and came to admire the things he did I never gave myself entirely over to the church the way Rena did. I held a little bit back. I left myself a shred of doubt, an escape, the way a spider spins its web in three dimensions and always leaves itself a means of getting away.

I didn't know why I held back. There was something that told me to, a voice whispering in my ear—was it Pete speaking to me, telling me to watch out? One day when it was just the Reverend and me sorting clothes that had been donated to the church I asked, "Where you from, Reverend Jim?"

"Why, right here," he said cheerfully. "Right here in California. Same as you, right? We're rare birds, you and I, native Californians."

"No, *you're* not," I said boldly.

"What?" he replied, surprised. "What do you mean?"

Indeed, why did I say that? I'd heard him say before that he was a native Californian, but I knew he wasn't. I recognized a Kentucky twang in his voice. If you'd never heard it you wouldn't know what it was, but I knew.

"You weren't born in California," I declared, taking note of the astonished look on his face. "You have an accent just like the one my father has, and he came to California when he was nine years old."

"Where is your father from?"

"Kentucky. And you sound just like him, sometimes."

The Reverend laughed. The nonplussed look was gone from his face and he appeared as self-assured as always. "What an ear you've got, Pete. I can see why you're a writer. You're absolutely right. I'm from southern Kentucky, close to the Tennessee border. Is that where you're father comes from?"

"That's it," I said.

"I left there when I was sixteen," he admitted. "But I've been in California so long I always think of myself as a native. No harm in that, is there?" he said jovially, clapping me manfully on the shoulder.

"No," I said, "I guess not." I let it drop but it still troubled me. It didn't rest easy on my mind. It didn't seem like a big deal, but it stayed with me. Why would he lie about that? It wasn't anything, and yet it nagged at me—he had lied.

He had lied, and his laugh had a hollow ring to it when he admitted he'd been lying. It sounded forced, and phony, that laugh, and there was a voice in my mind that said: If he lied about that, maybe he lied about something else.

Some things didn't add up. He lectured everyone about the sins of the flesh but I saw the way he looked at some of the women in the church and I knew what he was thinking. I knew because I was thinking the same thing. Maybe he was struggling, the way I was struggling, every day. But I couldn't get free of that nagging doubt I had.

Rena and I were together all the time. We sat side by side during sermons, we went to prayer meetings and Bible study. We worked together giving out the free food every night. When we were finished I would walk her home, going slowly through the dark silent streets, sometimes in the rain, talking until it was quite late. Then she would go into her house, reluctantly, neither of us wanting to be separated from the other and neither of us wanting to go home. We held hands and hugged each other tightly, and we kissed and wanted to do more but that was all we did.

We felt the pull of temptation and desire. It was there, it was strong, sometimes so strong we could almost see it, and we could feel it all around us, a living thing, with us wherever we went.

One night in church, while we worked near the back entrance facing the alley, Rena said, "Sex out of marriage is a great sin. You know that, don't you, Pete?"

"I've heard that," I said, looking at her. I couldn't take my eyes away from her, and she raised one hand and touched the necklace I'd given her.

"And lusting in your heart is just as bad as actually doing it," she went on.

"I've heard that too."

"The Reverend says it's a great sin and we shouldn't do it," Rena declared.

"I know."

She stopped working altogether now. "I think of you whenever I touch this," she said. "And I touch it in my bed, when I'm lying there alone in the dark. And I'll wish you were there with me, that we were together that way."

"I wish it too," I said, my breath coming faster now.

"Am I committing a sin, Pete?" she asked.

"I guess you are. I guess we both are."

"Oh God," Rena said, her breasts heaving up and down now. "What are we going to do?"

"I don't know," I said, coming closer to her.

"Oh God," she breathed.

I took another step closer to her. "No," she said, holding up one hand weakly. "No, don't come near me right now, I'll turn to jelly if you do."

"I want to," I said.

"I do too," she said heavily. "I do too."

She melted into my arms now, and I held her. She was trembling all over. I kissed her, and we stood there with our hearts pounding. Her body was melting against mine, she was made of soft wax that I could mold and shape any way I wanted to.

Then she broke away from me. "No," she said. "No. We can't, we mustn't. Come with me. Pete, come, please."

She held my hand and went determinedly across the empty room downstairs to the altar, where we stood silently for a few moments. Then the Reverend came in, and when he saw us standing there, holding hands, our eyes wide and our hearts still pounding, he said, "What is troubling you two?"

"Reverend Jim," Rena said. "We need your help."

"Everyone says they need my help, but it's God's help they really need," he replied. "I am only the Lord's instrument. What is it?"

"We are afraid, Reverend," she said.

"Of what are you afraid, child?"

She didn't answer and he looked at us both keenly. At last I said, "We're afraid of committing a great sin."

Now he understood. "O, praise God!" he cried, lifting his face toward the ceiling and raising his hands reverentially. "Open my eyes, O Lord, that I may behold wondrous things! O thank God you've come to me! What faith and trust. I am humbled by you two. When God blesses a union between a man and a woman then it becomes a sacred things only He can take apart. But until He does this we all have to live with this daily struggle between the Spirit and the Flesh. Man is the Word made into matter and we must live up to that insofar as we can. I know how hard it is. God sees what you've done, you can be sure of that. Kneel down," he said, "and let us all pray together."

So the three of us knelt before the altar, and the Reverend clasped his hands together in front of him and prayed out loud. "Dearest Lord," he prayed, "help these two fine young people become strong enough in the faith to overcome temptation. There is no sin in their feelings for one another, for this kind of love is holy, and if it be thy will may they someday enjoy a life together blessed by You. But for now, Lord, please make them strong, and keep them from sin. Amen."

So we all prayed, and I felt better after. I felt proud of myself, too, proud that I hadn't given in to my feelings but had gone to the Reverend for help. He said he was proud of me as well.

"We all have a journey to make, Pete," he said. "Back to God, since we've strayed so far away from Him. It's a long journey, but it's a great one. Each time we do not sin, each time we overcome a temptation placed in our path, we've taken one more step on that journey."

"What happens when we aren't able to overcome it?" I asked. "What then?"

"Sometimes we slip and fall," he explained. "It happens. We are made of clay, so to speak, and sometimes the clay crumbles. I have people in my flock who won't touch booze or drugs for weeks, months, a year, some of them. And then for some reason they lose it all. They get drunk. They shoot up. Then they have to start all over. This is a daily struggle, Pete. But when we do slip, He is always there to pick us up. And then one day we complete our journey, and merge with Him once more.

"Rena's an awfully nice girl," he went on. "Pretty, too. Very pretty. I can understand why you feel the way you do about her. But you've got to be strong. She has all kinds of problems at home, she's in a very vulnerable place. If you were to go too far with her it would be very bad. But I can see that you genuinely care about her. For that I am grateful to the Lord, because that is exactly what she needs, someone who cares for her."

So I went on, and I was proud of my self-restraint. I felt kind of noble too, for I could see that Rena was ready, when I held her I could feel her need, and I always held back, keeping with the Reverend's words. That wasn't easy, but I felt good about myself afterwards. I thought about temptation and sin and how I had overcome it, and said to myself that I was doing well. But I was speaking too soon, or maybe the Lord had heard what I'd said and decided to test me and see if I really meant it, because it wasn't long after this the biggest temptation of all came my way, and all my self-restraint and noble feelings flew out the window. I had taken a few steps forward, but now I fell back, all the way past where I started.

Chapter 14

Carolyn

Main Street was all garland and tinsel from every lamppost, for it was the holiday season now and banners wished everyone peace and joy and a happy new year. Another year was ending, another journey of the earth around the sun completed. The earth kept spinning on its axis but why did it have to spin, what would happen it is just stopped? The sun stood still in the sky, it said in Joshua. What if everything in the universe came to a stop? The night we went into the old power plant Tom had said he wondered if the universe was in balance, everything hinging on everything else, a colossal balancing act—but what was it resting on? I looked up at the sun, that big rotating ball of cosmic fire, eternally burning, always trying to figure out who struck that first match. Where did that original spark come from? Who made it, and how did they do it? Was that what Pete was trying to tell me? Did he know the answer to the mystery of eternity? Two blackbirds flew overhead and landed on the roof of the office. A sleek, trim, blue-and-white cabin cruiser with the name "Swiss Pride" in bright letters on the hull came sliding up to the dock, the engine purring to a stop. A man came onto the deck and stood arrogantly on the bow, arms crossed, his gaze sweeping hotly over Denny and me. I was caught short, and stayed frozen where I was.

Denny and I had been sitting on the dock looking at the gray water and talking about how glad we would be when school let out for good in June, for we were both sick of high school. I had my ever-present little green Bible-book in my hand, open to the Acts of the Apostles. The water looked choppy and cold but we were happy to be outside, glad it wasn't raining now although more was expected to be coming anytime.

"Water looks cold, doesn't it?" Denny said. "Tom would surf in it. I wouldn't, but he would. Would you swim in this water, Pete?"

"Too cold for me," I said.

"Me too," he agreed. "I guess we better tie this one off."

We tied off the boat and I saw the man, and my heart froze. Then it began to beat like a drop hammer, because I saw, sitting on the deck in a director's chair, a scarf tied over her hair to protect it from the wind, someone I hadn't seen in a long time and didn't want to see again, and right then I wished I could run away, be somewhere else or be somebody else, cover my face with a mask or else grow proverbial wings and fly away.

When the boat was tied off the man leaped agilely onto the dock, tall, slim, well-built, with a square jaw and chiseled, handsome features on a brown face. His hair was black and wavy, stylishly cut over his ears, and he had a brightly colored scarf tied around his neck and he wore expensive-looking clothes.

"I am not just standing here because I like diz view or zomething!" he said arrogantly. "Giff the pump to me! Now! Can you not hear or whatever is your problem?"

I couldn't move, however. I was stuck fast, frozen, for all eternity on this dock, staring at the woman in the boat. She hadn't noticed me yet. She sat with a book on her lap, sitting there imperiously, her sunglasses giving her a mysterious look. Now I heard music coming from within the cabin of the boat, classical music I'd heard before, and then I remembered what it was, Seigfried's Rhine Journey, from Wagner.

Denny came to the rescue. He looked at me curiously, seeing that for some obscure private and perhaps insane reason of my own—for like Tom, he regarded me and my religious inclinations as somewhat mad—I couldn't, or wouldn't, move. He got the nozzle from the pump and gave it to the tall man.

"At last," he said loudly. "This is the slowest service I haff seen yet. Vhat is the matter with him? Is he afraid of working or zomething? Vhy does he not move like he should?"

These words broke the spell. I discovered I could, indeed, move again, I was not forever rooted to this spot. As Rudy climbed into the boat to fill up his tanks with gas I turned and looked right at the woman in the chair, who was shifting herself about, stretching so that her breasts rose and fell beneath the white sweater she had on. She saw me now and recognized me. She stood up, threw her head back and put her hands on her hips and laughed.

"Well! What a surprise! Whatever are you doing here?"

"This is where I work," I said stiffly.

"So it is," said Carolyn, smiling, but the smile looked like the smile you would see on the face of a cat when it spies a mouse. She came over to the edge of the boat and put her hands out. "Help me down," she said, and with my aid she clambered down off the boat and stood on the dock, holding my hand just a touch longer than she needed to and giving it a small and extra squeeze before letting go.

"I never thought to see you again," she declared.

"You said you didn't want to," I reminded. "That's what you said, remember?"

"Did I say that? And do you believe everything a woman tells you? You have a lot to learn, but as I recall, you pick it up fast. Do you think of me often?"

"No," I lied.

"Liar," she laughed. "I think of you often enough. Do you still have my book?"

"What book?"

"You remember, *Leaves of Grass.*"

"Yeah, somewhere, maybe, if I didn't lose it."

"Can you bring it to me? I could come here and get it. Will you be here tomorrow?"

"I'm here every day."

"Could you bring it over? To where the boat is tied up? That's where I'll be."

"What about him?" I said, glancing over at Rudy, who was standing on the deck watching and looking angry.

"Maybe he won't be there," she twittered. "Maybe if you were to bring it over tomorrow in the afternoon he wouldn't be there."

She stood on her tiptoes now, put her hands on my shoulders, and whispered the slip number in my ear. "Will you come?" she asked.

"Maybe I will."

"Come on," Rudy said loudly. He paid Denny for the gas and vaulted athletically back up onto the boat. "Come on," he repeated. "Carolyn, let's go from here."

I remembered something now, from a history class, some German words and I spoke them just loud enough. *"Raus,"* I said. *"Raus, Juden, raus."*

Rudy heard me. He straightened up to his full height, threw back his shoulders, and scowled furiously. "That isn't nice," Carolyn said, but she looked pleased, all the same, and smiled as she got back in the boat. Rudy helped her up onto the deck and she turned and waved as the boat pulled away from the dock.

"You know that woman?" Denny asked, coming over and speaking in an awed tone.

"Sort of."

"Wow," he said, letting out a low whistle. "How well do you know her? That husband or boyfriend of hers did not like you talking to her, that's for sure. You better watch out for that dude, he's gonna kick your ass first chance he gets. And he's a pretty big guy, too. But what a total asshole he is! He says, 'Giff me my change, you,' and 'Giff me de pump, hurry,' like I was his slave or something. What is he, German?"

"What else?"

"Now I see why we keep having wars with the Germans. That was pretty good, what you said to him, though, that got him, you ask me. But what's between you and that woman? That's what I want to know."

"Nothing," I said.

"Oh sure, sure," said Denny. "'Course there isn't. Does Tom know about it?"

"He can't know about something there isn't anything to know about."

Denny laughed again, knowingly, and didn't say anymore. And I didn't go to church that night. Instead I went home after work and rummaged about in my room. I went through a stack of books and notebooks in my closet until, at the very bottom, I found what I was looking for, the volume of Walt Whitman. Because of my bitterness at Carolyn I had put this book underneath all this debris but I knew exactly where it was. I got it out, wondering what would happen tomorrow when I took it back.

All my future, my fate, it seemed to me, was tied up with this book. Why I should think this I didn't know, but it did seem this way, like everything hinged on this slender volume. It was like a keystone holding back an avalanche. I had a sudden desire to throw it away, to toss it into the trash and let it go out with this week's garbage. Carolyn would forget about it, she would certainly never come looking for it. That way my last link with her would be gone. In that case, I asked myself, why did you keep it, why didn't you get rid of it long ago? I had said to myself many times I never wanted to see her again but now I wondered if that was true then why did I hang onto that book, the way a jilted lover holds onto an old ring, as a reminder of the good, the bad, and the bittersweet memories? Why did you keep it, why didn't you throw it away? All the while I pondered this and brooded over it there was a part of me that was thinking about what Carolyn and I used to do in her bed, how she felt when I touched her with the classical music going downstairs and the moonlight streaming in through the skylight.

I thought and thought about all I'd learned about sin and temptation. I thought of Rena—I loved her, and I felt so noble at keeping my hands off her. And I was so righteously indignant at Tom for what he was doing with Tiffany. Maybe I was worse—I surely couldn't say I was any better.

I kept on waking up during the night. When I did felt a kind of blackness all around me, a tunnel or a black hole nearby that was calling to me, wanting me to come into it. I didn't want to go, no, I wouldn't go into that blackness. WATCH OUT! said a voice from somewhere. Was it Pete speaking to me? Don't go in there, stay out. WATCH OUT!

But the blackness wouldn't go away, nor would the feeling that I had to go into it.

The next day, when it was quiet in the afternoon, I told Denny I was going for a walk.

"You going to see that woman that was here yesterday?" Denny asked eagerly.

"Only so I can return this book to her," I said. He raised his eyebrows. "That's all, see?" I insisted.

"Oh," he replied. "Okay. Sure it is. Of course it is. Why else would you go over there?"

"That's all there is," I maintained.

"I've heard about these women who like young guys, but this is the first time I've ever seen it myself," Denny said. "How did you happen to get that book from her?"

"She lent it to me, a long time ago."

"Oh," said Denny. "She just goes around lending books? To whoever happens to be nearby? Come on, Pete, why don't you admit it?"

"There isn't anything to admit."

"You lie, you think you might get some from her, that's what it is," Denny accused.

"Mind your own business, why don't you?"

"Okay, Pete, okay," he said. "I just wanted to know, that's all."

"Well don't."

I walked along the wooden docks, looking for the slip number Carolyn had given me yesterday, hearing my footsteps as they creaked along the wet wood, listening as the water lapped at the pilings below. I looked up at the sun, dim and hazy, because it was December now and the sun wasn't as bright and fierce as in the summer months. In fact Casey had told me that December 21 was the Winter Solstice, the longest night of the year. But I hadn't seen so much of Casey lately, he for sure thought I was crazy after that day at his house. He said the sun was a spark in infinity, we all were, everything. A row of palm trees swayed in the late afternoon breeze. A palm tree lived and died and then other palm trees took its place as if the old tree had never been there. And yet there was something that made that palm tree grow, some spark that set it in motion. Could it be that same spark that was inside the palm tree made the barnacles cling to the pilings underneath me? What was it, this spark, this light—yes, that was it, the light, where was it, how come I couldn't see it all the time? And if we all have that light within, we are all manifestations of it, then we are all alike, every single one of us. That made, I realized with sudden horror, Deacon the very same as me.

That thought jolted me but I put it out of my mind when I saw Carolyn sitting on the deck of the Swiss Pride. She wore sunglasses, had on a white scarf this time, tied around her red hair. An empty glass sat on the deck beside her and some Christmas carols blared from the cabin.

"Hello!" I called out, wondering what would happen next, half expecting Rudy to leap from out of nowhere and beat me to a pulp. Carolyn had told me many times of how strong he was, and of his jealousy and madness, saying he was more than capable of killing someone. This frightened me but it also gave what I was doing some added excitement, and a thrill ran through me as I came closer.

"Hi!" Carolyn closed the book she'd been reading and smiled at me. "I'm glad you came, for a while I was afraid you wouldn't. Can you stay and visit with me for a minute?"

"Where's the *fuhrer*?"

"He isn't here," she said vaguely. "I told you he might not be here when you came. Come inside?"

We went down some steps into the cramped space of the cabin.

"Here's your book," I said, handing the volume to her.

"Something to drink?" she asked.

"No."

"You have thought of me, sometimes, haven't you?" she asked.

"No," I said again.

She laughed. "Liar," she accused. "You think of me. I think of you."

"I try not to," I said sulkily.

Carolyn only laughed again, and in the cramped space of the cabin she put her arms around me and kissed me. I tried to pull away from her but she only laughed some more and kept on kissing me. "WATCH OUT!" said the voice. I could see the blackness, and everything was crumbling, all my faith and prayers, all of it gone, fallen into a morass of sin.

"You see?" said Carolyn, laughing still. "That didn't hurt, did it?"

She took my hand and guided it to her breast, closing her eyes. "Oh yes," she said softly, "oh yes," and then laughing again, she pushed me away teasingly. "Stop it," she said. "That's a wicked thing for a boy like you to be doing to me. Sure you won't have a drink?"

"I don't drink anymore," I said.

"Oh no?" she said. "So you've changed," she declared.

"Yes, I've changed."

"I've changed too. Don't I seem different to you?"

"No, not drastically."

"Well, I am," she declared. "Do you know how I've changed, want me to tell you? I live only for *me* now, only for what I want, for my pleasure, nothing else. I may want you today and not want you tomorrow, because everything is for *me*, I never give any thought to anybody else, I'm the whole universe, nothing outside of *me* matters. If you please me you can stay, if you don't you can leave. What do you think of that?"

I felt a swelling up inside of myself now, but the voice that had been saying WATCH OUT! was now telling me to run. Get out while the getting is good, it said, and I thought I had best heed its advice.

"Well?" Carolyn pressed softly. "What do you think?"

"About what?"

"My new philosophy of life," she purred, "the way I live now, what do you think of it?"

"I think it's awful," I said, "terrible," but it was hard for me to concentrate, she was standing so close to me, her body was touching mine, and mine was responding, even if I didn't want it to.

"It's only being honest. Most people wish they could be so honest, they just don't have the nerve."

"I have to get back," I said, for a great loneliness came into my heart now, and I had an image of Rena before me, and she was crying, and I was slipping into the blackness.

"Already? But you just arrived, you said you could stay a minute."

"I did, a minute's up, it's over, time flies, sometimes."

"Don't go yet," she said silkily, putting her hands on my shoulders. "Stay a while."

"What for?"

I had my little green Bible-book in my pocket and I touched it, to give me strength. But before I could leave the cabin door swung open and Rudy stood there, staring balefully, his arms crossed.

In the close quarters of the boat there was a screaming silence.

At last Carolyn spoke. Before she did I saw her face. There was a look on it, as if to say, Oh yes, I like this.

"Rudy," she said, "this is—I didn't get a chance to introduce you yesterday, this is—"

Her voice trailed off and stopped and the silence returned.

"Rudy," Carolyn said. "I hope you aren't going to embarrass me."

He still wouldn't speak but just stood there menacingly, tall, his long aristocratic face very European and becoming red with outrage.

"I asked him to come over," Carolyn said. "He returned this book to me, see?"

She held the Walt Whitman book up for him to see but he wouldn't look at it.

"You," he said to me, speaking at last in a voice boiling with suppressed fury, "get out."

"Okay," I said, looking at those big hands of his, hands that were smooth and unlined from never having to work with them, made for holding a sculptor's mallet or an artist's brush, but strong all the same, they could choke the life out of somebody if he ever decided to put them to that kind of use. "Sure. It's your boat."

"Yes it is my boat. Now get out. You think you can make fun of me?

Think again. Get out of here or I give you a beating you don't forget soon, you understand?"

"Yes," I said. "I understand."

"So go," he said, standing to one side of the door.

"Okay," I agreed.

"Move," he said.

"You bet," I said, moving. "It's cool, see?"

"It's also cool that you never come back here!"

"Sure," I said.

Now Carolyn suddenly began pulling at my sleeve.

"Sit down, Pete," she said. "You do not have to leave."

"Oh yes he does too haff to leave!" Rudy roared, hurting everyone's ears. "I kill him if I catch him here again."

"He's my guest," Carolyn said defiantly. "I invited him."

"Yes, you invited him. And for what do you invite him?"

"I invited him because I wanted to invite him!"

There was a fine time after that. They screamed at each and carried on, forgetting me completely, and I made my way up onto the deck. Then I heard Carolyn's voice behind me.

"Come back sometime," she called.

But Rudy was right behind her, shaking his fist.

"Stay away from her," he warned. "Else I come and fix you good."

I could hear them yelling at each other as I headed back toward the gas dock on the other side of the Marina.

Perhaps it was the element of danger that made me go back. I kept telling myself that I wouldn't go, and I got my book out and read some of the Psalms and prayed for strength but it came to nothing, I went back, again and again. Maybe there was nothing in the world that could have kept me from going back.

Carolyn warned me, over and over, of the danger I was in. Rudy hated my guts and was determined to beat the living daylights out of me. He was mad, she said, or nearly so, with a Germanic streak of violence. But he wasn't there when I went over, and he never caught us together again. His business called for him to drive up to Los Angeles just about every day, leaving Carolyn behind on the boat, although once in a while she went with him. Mostly, though, she stayed behind, working on her manuscript, (she was writing a novel, about a girl growing up in a small town in Massachusetts in the 1940s) for she had a small desk and a portable typewriter set up in the cabin. Rudy's business had something to do with some trusts, she said vaguely, adding that she didn't fully understand it. She only knew his money came from his family in Europe, in the form of bonds and stocks and different trust funds, and he went to the Gold Exchange on Wilshire Boulevard to change Deutschemarks over to Swiss Francs and then over to U.S. Dollars, a complicated process but one he understood well enough so he got the most for his money. He bought gold, too, Krugerands from South Africa.

"So what are you doing here?" I asked Carolyn.

She explained they were getting ready to go on a long ocean voyage. They had loaded the Swiss Pride up with everything they needed and as soon as Rudy had all his business affairs in order they were going to sail up and down the California coast. They would go to Avalon Harbor, over on Catalina Island, then sail north, to the Channel Islands off Santa Barbara. From there they were going to continue up the coast all the way to the Oregon border, then double back, going south again. They would go past Los Angeles and then down by San Diego and into the warm waters off Mexico, past Tijuana, Ensenada, all the way south to Cabo San Lucas. After that they might set sail for the South Pacific, Hawaii, Tahiti, and the Fiji Islands.

"When are you going to do all this?"

"Soon," she said, folding the map. "As soon as he gets all his business taken care of."

There was no skylight on the boat like there was in her townhouse but there was a stereo, an eight-track, and she would play the same Beethoven and Mozart and Wagner she had played when we were together before. Usually she would be waiting for me on the deck, sitting outside in the chair, the scarf tied over her hair to protect it from the wind. But sometimes she was below decks, in the cabin, wearing only her white silk robe with Chinese lettering on it, or else she would be undressed already and lying under the blankets, waiting for me. She would become aroused while she waited, and would masturbate, and would be excited already when I came, and so there weren't any preliminaries, we got right to it, our bodies thrashing together on the flat bed beneath the bulkhead when Rudy wasn't there, frantically grabbing, holding, moaning. She would be naked and smelling of bath oil, and sometimes she would wrap her legs around my head, pleading with me to put my tongue into her, and when I did she would gasp and shudder. When I slid inside of her, for she was wet and wanting, she would cry. "Oh! God! Give it to me! All the way! Please!" Her breasts heaved, her body contracted as she reached the peak of her pleasure, seeking something intangible and undefined, something she might never discover no matter how many times she reached her climax in search of it, she always had to go looking for it again. And afterwards we lay there, covered in sweat, still naked, our bodies slippery with it, in the narrow confines of the boat.

The she would laugh, and disengaging herself from me, she turned and rolled over, smoking. She toyed with the crystal around my neck. "Why do you wear this all the time? You never take it off."

"It brings me luck," I explained, "and keeps away evil influences."

"It didn't keep me away from you, did it?" she laughed,

"Are you evil?"

She only laughed again, and stretched herself like a cat does. "I don't believe in good or evil anymore," she said. "I only believe in pure lust and pleasure. There is no sin, how can there be? There's only me and what I want. You remember how bad I used to feel, when we were together before? I don't feel that way anymore. It makes life a lot easier."

When she talked I couldn't help but think of what the Reverend Jim had said about the spiritual way being the hardest way. He was right about that, I thought, and after being with Carolyn a few times I decided I didn't want to walk that hard path anymore. Her way was a lot easier and more fun too. You didn't always have to be worrying about sin and having to restrain yourself all the time. For a while when I went over there to see her I took my Bible-book with me, placing it in the pocket of my pants, but after the third or was it the fourth time I left it behind, left it on the desk of the office in the boat house. I would have a drink with Carolyn, slugging down some of her gin or one of her vodka gimlets, and she would be lying on the bed smiling in that cat-like self-satisfied way of hers. When my conscience chided me, reminding me of Rena and the church, I told it to shut up, and I was happier that way.

But what about the Light, it would say? Have you forgotten the Light?

No, I haven't forgotten the Light.

You'll never see the Light again.

(For the Light is the Power and the Glory, It said.)

(For you are the Light of the World, It said.)

(And the Kingdom Eternal, It said.)

Outside it was raining again, and I could hear the drops hitting the deck and the roof of the cabin, and for me the blackness was waiting. And that ghost of Deacon was still out there too, waiting for me, searching, and I had to make sure he didn't find me.

Chapter 15

Tom

Tom's guardians, Neal and Marianne, left for work early every day and did not get back until the evening hours, both of them possessing high-powered (and high-paying) jobs that demanded a great deal of their time. On weekends they liked going to parties in Newport Beach or Yorba Linda, or meeting people and drinking with them in one of the upscale watering holes in Irvine or Anaheim Hills or one of the other growing cities in Orange County where the *nouveau rich* were gathering in those days, so Neal could shake hands and slap shoulders and remind people that he intended to run for Congress in this district in two years and it would be a good idea if they voted for him. They did not come home until past the witching hour and when they did they were barely able to make it from the garage upstairs to their bedroom, and as often as not one or the other did not go upstairs at all but remained on the first floor and slept in the living room on the big leather couch. When Tom and I got up in the morning, either to go surfing or to work, we would creep past one of them snoring in an alcoholic haze as we headed out the door and into the archway._

All this suited Tom, because it left him free to do more or less as he pleased, and it suited me as well, for I spent the night there as often as I could after I stopped going to church.

Denny liked to come over too, so he could have a smoke or a drink and then leave to go on a date with Tiffany. Sometimes he brought Tiffany over with him, and there was a fine time then, because when Tiffany had smoked a little of Tom's Panama Red or swilled down several glasses of whisky the tender restraints that normally governed her behavior flew out the window like Peter Pan setting off for never-never land, and there was no telling what she might do or say.

One Saturday night we were upstairs in Tom's room, listening to the Beatles' new opus, *The White Album*, when Tom suddenly said, "Want to see something unbelievable? Turn off the lights."

Tom's room had a small balcony that overlooked the backyard, and when all four of us had crowded out there we saw ground lights illuminating all the flowers that Marianne grew: The yard was filled to bursting with flowers of all kinds, yellow flowers, red flowers, purple flowers, white and pink flowers. There were flowers in big clay pots, flowers in boxes of wood, flowers growing out of the ground in tiers that went to the back fence. Seen this way, they formed panoply of colors like a kaleidoscope or a Renaissance painting. She had won prizes for her flowers, Tom explained, and she loved adding new touches to the yard. On Saturdays and Sundays she would be out there digging and transplanting and watering, wearing green gloves, with a straw hat on her head and a smile on her face, something you didn't see on her very often.

"Why does she grow those ugly-looking plants that you see when you come in the door?" Denny asked.

"You mean the bitterweeds?"

"Whatever they are."

"She's not a happy person," Tom said.

"Can I have another drink, Tommy?" Tiffany asked.

"OK, but just a little," said Tom. "Neal suspects me of stealing his liquor so I have to be careful." He poured her some more whisky, then went over to his stereo and turned the album over.

"You don't need to be careful," Tiffany said, looking at him. "Why do people have to be careful? What's the point? You're always so careful about everything."

"You have to be careful," Tom replied.

"You should stop being so careful," Tiffany maintained.

Tiffany drank her whisky and looked at Tom in a way that made me wonder how Denny couldn't see what was going on. Tom looked at her quickly and then looked away. From the stereo we could hear: *"Blackbird singing in the dead of the night/Take these broken wings/And learn to fly/All your life."*

"What makes people happy?" asked Denny.

"Being in love," Tiffany said, looking at Tom again.

"Amen," said Denny, looking at Tiffany.

"Riding the waves," Tom said.

"Is anybody happy?" I asked. "I mean, really happy? Anybody, anywhere?"

"I wonder about that," Denny said. "I mean, look at how short life is. Look at us. How long do people live? Seventy, eighty years? That means we've all lived about one-fourth of the time we're going to live already. Maybe more. Think about that."

"This kind of talk is depressing," said Tiffany. She was dressed as she usually did, in a black dress and wearing the silver necklace Denny had given her. Her little pewter cross glinted in the light.

"Think about it," Denny persisted. "Look at that guy who killed himself a couple of months ago, Deacon. Poor drunken bastard. He just couldn't stand it anymore, and then he killed himself."

"Now you're really being depressing," said Tiffany. "He's better off dead."

"I mean, think about the poor guy," Denny continued. "He must have felt he had nothing to live for, no hope, nothing. It's sad, isn't it Pete? You knew him for a long time. Why do you think he did it?"

"How would I know?"

"He was your friend, wasn't he? When we were little kids you were at his house all the time. He thought a lot of you. I remember he said to me once, 'Keep your eye on that Pete, he'll really amount to something someday.' That's what he said."

"He wasn't my friend," I said sharply. "He was just an old bum who slept in the alley with the stray cats and a bottle of wine. I didn't know him any better than anybody else."

"Okay," Denny said, blinking his eyes and looking at me curiously. "We should go," he said to Tiffany.

"I don't want to go," Tiffany said. "I want to stay here."

"But we have to. We promised we'd go to that party."

"It's so boring. A party some friends of your parents are giving. Give me a break."

"Come on, honey," Denny said. "Please."

"Big fucking deal. They only invited us so they can say, 'This is our son and his girlfriend.' Showing us off like a couple of plastic dolls. I hate it."

"Come on, Tiff, it won't be so bad."

"Why don't you tell the truth? You want to take me someplace and fuck me."

"You shouldn't talk that way in front of people."

"Why don't you fuck me right here? I'm sure they would like to watch."

"You're drunk," Denny said.

"What about it, guys?" Tiffany said. "You want to watch?"

"Please don't talk like that," Denny pleaded.

"Maybe they would like to join in. We could have an orgy."

"We've gotta go," Denny insisted. "I shouldn't have let you drink that whisky." Even in the low light I could see how red his face had become.

"In the back of his car," Tiffany said. "He always wants to fuck in the back of his car. What do you think that's like for me? I never feel anything. I just pretend."

"See you guys later," Denny said, dragging Tiffany out the door.

"Goodbye Tommy," Tiffany called. We heard them go out the front door and then heard Denny's car start up. Tom quickly poured himself another drink and tossed it down.

"This is getting out of hand," he said, in the tone of someone who has just had a narrow escape from something he never thought would be dangerous in the first place.

"What's the matter?" I asked. "Did all that make you a little nervous?"

"I better put this back," he said, holding up the bottle of Jack Daniels, "before Neal gets home and notices it's not there."

Tom would get a rollaway bed out of the hall closet for me to sleep on and we'd lay there for hours, long into the night, talking, the lights out and flickering psychedelic candles burning and showing all different colors. Tom always slept with the window open, he craved fresh air and kept the window cracked even when it rained. Tonight it was clear and there was no rain, which made him happy. Tom's blond head averted toward the open window while he looked at the stars and tried, sometimes, to count them. He said that was a good way to fall asleep if you had insomnia, which he sometimes did, lay there and try to count all the stars on a clear night. Better than counting sheep anytime, he would say.

"You know what a quasar is?" he asked. "It's a humungous explosion way out in space, more powerful than the sun. I read about it. A huge release of energy. Sometimes when I look out into the sky at night I wonder what it would be like to see something like that." He turned back toward me. "I'm so glad you aren't going to that church anymore," he said. "I was afraid you were turning into a Holy Joe. What made you change, how come you stopped going?"

"I don't know, I just didn't feel right about it," I explained, not telling him the truth, that it was because of Carolyn and what I was doing with her.

"What happened? You stop believing?"

"Yeah, I still believe."

"Then what about Rena?"

That rang a bell in my heart and I said, "I don't want to talk about Rena."

"Okay," he said. "I can dig that. But who knows, maybe it's not permanent. Maybe you and her will get together again sometime, you can't ever tell what will happen in the future. Every end is a new start. Anybody could see you and her are crazy about each other. I'm kind of envious of you, in a way."

"What do you mean?"

"Love. I don't think I've ever felt it. I think I'm in love all the time but it never lasts. I'll be with them and go to bed with them but then I'll notice somebody else, and that's the end of it."

"What about Tiffany?"

"That's something altogether different," he said. "I can't explain it. It's like she's cast a spell on me or something. I can't seem to break it off like I usually do. I want to, but I can't. At first it was like somebody else has something and you want to play with it, you know what I mean? But now it's different. Maybe it's because I'm so unhappy, living this way, and I need something to hold on to."

"This doesn't seem so bad," I said. "Living here, I mean."

"You don't know them," he said. "They can't stand each other. Why do people stay married to someone they can't stand? I've slept with girls I didn't like too much, but I wouldn't marry one. I can't figure it out but there are lots of things in this world that don't make any sense to me. I can't even figure out why I do things, half the time, so how can I figure out other people? Still, sometimes I wish I knew. Here's two people who have it all, but they're not happy. I mean look at this place, look at all they've got, and then look at them. I've seen people with nothing but the clothes on their backs happier than they are. Doesn't make any sense to me but then nobody asked me to figure it out either."

I dozed off and a while later—I noticed the clock by his bed said it was past midnight—he nudged me with his hand. "Wake up," he said impishly. "Be ready for anything."

The front door slammed shut as Neal and Marianne came into the house. We heard angry voices downstairs. "You bastard! I saw what you were doing with that floozy!" Marianne shouted.

"Ha," said Tom. "She caught him again."

"What's it all about?" I asked.

"Did you get her phone number?" Marianne yelled.

"That Neal can't keep his hands off other women," Tom explained.

"You cheating bastard!" Marianne's angry voice echoed up the stairs.

Neal, Tom said, taking on a conspiratorial tone, would disappear when he and Marianne were at one of these *soirees* they loved to go to and she would find him in the midst of a passionate embrace with the wife of the host or in a dark corner groping an attractive divorcee. There would be a blowup the size of a mushroom cloud after that and for a week they didn't speak to each other and the atmosphere in the house would feel like the inside of a walk-in freezer, and one of them slept downstairs on the couch until the ice finally cracked and they made up and the cycle began once more. Fuel was added to the fire because Marianne suspected him of having one or two women on the side that he visited after a long day at his law office. It had been going on since right after they got married.

We heard Marianne come up the stairs and go into her bedroom, slamming the door in a way designed to make the pictures bounce on the walls. Neal stayed downstairs. All was quiet for a time, and then Tom said, "Hey. You hear that?"

I listened. At first I didn't hear anything.

"She isn't happy," I said, for it was Marianne crying.

"I never heard that before," Tom observed. He sat up and lit a candle, then lay back, looking at the ceiling. "What a life. I don't know if I can stand it here till next June. It seems like it's so far off. I don't know why I go to school. Do you think I ever learn anything? I never learn anything. Look at this." He reached under his bed and brought out a paperback copy of *The Great Gatsby.* "You ever read this? You probably have. I have to read it for this English class I'm in. I can't get anything out of it. What's with these people? They get no fun out of life. Most people are miserable, I think, because they don't do what they really *want* to do."

Tom was going good now. He sat up in bed and flipped contemptuously through the pages of the book, to show what he thought of Gatsby and Daisy and all the rest, F. Scott Fitzgerald and Zelda too, then tossed the book back under his bed. All was quiet, except for an occasional car in the distance. He slept in only his boxer shorts and the powerful muscles of his chest and stomach stood out in hard ridges. He was still deeply tan even though it was mid-winter; it was, I often thought enviously, as though he just had to take his shirt off and he got browner than anybody else, and he stayed that way until summer came again when he got *really* dark. It was the same with his physique; he didn't have to do anything for those muscles, they were just there naturally, just like they were on a tiger or a mountain lion. In P.E. class he could do more pull-ups, more pushups, more bar-dips than anybody else, he set records climbing the ropes and in agility drills.

"I promised everybody I'd finish school," he said. "I keep wishing I hadn't, though, but maybe it's a good thing, maybe if I hadn't promised I'd have run off by now. I'm trying to stand it, but it's not easy, going to school, sitting in those boring classes. Why are we alive, do you think?"

"I've been trying to figure that out for a long time," I said. "I'm no closer to the answer now than I ever was."

"There must be a reason," Tom declared. "I just know there is."

"You mean like each of us has a destiny?"

"Yeah, that's it, destiny. What are we destined for?"

"I've wondered about that. Why were we born here, and not someplace else? Why are we who we are, and not some other person? Is it all by chance or is there something behind it that has it all figured out?"

"God, you mean," Tom declared. "Didn't you find out any of those answers when you were going to church?"

"No," I said, still watching the shadows of the candles, "no, I didn't get any of the answers, just more questions."

"Do you think it was our destiny to see what happened that night?" he asked in a somber tone. "Do you think we were meant to see that?"

"I've thought about it a lot," I said.

"So have I. I've thought about it and thought about it. Why did we go in there that night, and why did *they*? And when I see those freaks, Dave and Larry, and then those morons. Waldo and Karlovitch, and I know they did it, it really gets to me."

"I know this much," said Tom, settling back into his bed, "when we cross that graduation line in June I'm gonna give a whoop of joy, then I'm gonna dance a jig right there on the spot. I'm gonna boogie on out and you'll never see me in a damn school again as long as I live."

He turned over onto this back and lay with his hands behind his head, looking through the window at the stars.

The following Friday night as they prepared to go out Neal and Marianne came into the kitchen where Tom and I sat. The chill between them was so strong that you could feel the temperature in the room decline by several degrees as soon as they entered. The Christmas tree lights blinked on and off. Bing Crosby sang from the big stereo cabinet. Marianne fixed herself a drink, then went over and changed the album to The Nutcracker. The Dance of the Sugar Plum Fairies began playing. She fastened long dangling earrings on and, smelling strongly of perfume, asked us how school was.

"Only a few months left," she observed, "and you'll both have high school behind you."

"Hallelujah," said Tom.

"I hope you are not as lackadaisical about school as Tom is."

"I get by, but that's about all."

"He's putting you on," Tom interjected. "He gets A's in everything."

"Do you know where you'll go to college yet?"

"No," I said.

"He's doing it again," said Tom. "He's going to UCLA."

"Are you?"

"Yes," I admitted.

"What will you do after you finish college?"

"I was thinking I might join the Peace Corps."

There was a sputtering sound from the bar. Neal looked as if he had just heard someone say they were planning on going to Moscow and study at the Che Guevera Institute.

"Now you're definitely putting us on," he said. "Why in the world would you want to do that?"

"Seems like a good thing to do," I said.

"And what about after that?" Neal pressed. "When you're finished saving the world, what then?"

"I'm not sure but I've thought about teaching."

Another horrified look. "There's no *money* in teaching," Neal said. "You want a real profession, one that *pays*."

"Money isn't everything."

Neal looked the way a true believer must look when he encounters an atheist. "I blame a lot of what's wrong with this country on the teachers," he said. "They don't teach our children properly, but fill them with a lot of liberal, idealistic nonsense that makes them feel it's incumbent upon them to go out and change the world, and rebel against authority. I firmly believe in the old saying, 'Those who can, do, and those who can't, teach.' We are seeing the results of all this liberalism in the so-called counter-culture and in campus unrest in some of our finest institutions of higher learning all over the country. It has to be stopped."

"Save the speech for when you run for Congress," said Marianne, waving her hand about impatiently.

"Our young people are being taught the wrong values," Neal went on. "Why, the finest men our country has ever produced—Andrew Carnegie, John D. Rockefeller, J.P. Morgan—the men who made America great—now those were men with the right values: Hard work, saving money, telling the truth."

"You are such a bore tonight," Marianne declared, finishing her drink. She went over to the bar and fixed herself another.

"All right if we have a drink, Auntie?" Tom asked.

"You're not going anyplace, are you?" Marianne said. "Don't call me Auntie. Only one," she allowed, "and not too strong. You might be right," she said to me. "Money isn't everything. It's important to try and do something you enjoy doing. If I had it to do over again I think I would have studied something else, and not gone into what I've gone into." She had a business degree from Long Beach State and worked for an accounting firm in Irvine.

Tom got the bottle of Beefeater's and poured a drink for himself and one for me. "What would you have studied?" he asked.

"Art," she replied. "Art history. I always liked that."

Neal nearly choked on his drink.

"Art!" he sputtered. "If there is anything this country doesn't need it's any more art or any more artists. Subversive, most of it. Useless, all of it."

"Cheers," said Tom, holding out his drink. "Here's to art, and more of it."

"This is high culture talking," Marianne said. "He wouldn't know Picasso from Pillsbury pudding."

"I may not know much about that artsy-stuff," Neal said. "I may not know a Picasso from a pipe organ. But I know some things. I know that we have to set a good example for our young people. I know we have to have good values and morals. I know that we have to have a strong work ethic. I know that we have to have the will to stop communism overseas before we have to stop it over here in our own backyard." He finished his drink and immediately poured himself another.

"You're already a bore. You don't need to be obnoxious too."

"We need to kill all them commie rats," said Tom, pretending like he held a gun in his hand.

Neal had been on the Angels Beach City Council, and was chairman of the local Republican Party. He had worked for Nixon in this past election. His reward for this would be his running for Congress in two years, when the incumbent retired and the seat he had held for years would be up for grabs.

"You don't want to be one of those people that go around fighting for the oppressed and the downtrodden," Neal said. "If you look closely, you'll see there's a good reason why the so-called 'underprivileged' are where they are. Most of them are just lazy. They could get jobs. They just don't want to. No, you should study something useful. Like law."

"That way you could be like him," Marianne said. "I imagine you like that idea." She finished her drink and went to get her coat, saying it was time for them to leave. She went out, leaving the scent of her perfume behind, her necklaces and earrings tinkling.

"Too bad he didn't get elected to Congress this year," Tom said when they were gone. "Then they would have been off to Washington and I would be here all alone. Alone meaning not with them."

"They'd just make you go with them," I said.

"No chance you would ever get me to Washington. Can't surf there. Wanna get drunk?"

"Oh, hell yes."

Tom played bartender, fixing us another gin-and-tonic from Neal and Marianne's well-stocked liquor cabinet. "Yeah, let's get drunk," he said. "Let's get drunk tonight and forget all our troubles. Rena's at church tonight, Tiffany's with Denny, so what else can we do? I'll drown my sorrows. Get drunk and cry into my booze."

"Because of Tiffany?" I asked.

"Tiffany who?"

"Go on, you mentioned her, not me. Is it bothering you that she's not with you but is with Denny tonight?"

He grinned slyly, out of the side of his mouth and didn't answer but took a drink. Could it be, I wondered, that he really cares about her? Who is using whom here?

"Know what I want to do?" he asked.

The lights seemed to flicker just a bit as I replied.

"What?" I said.

"Go to Mexico. Baja."

"Hell," I said. "You've been to Mexico."

"Mostly only to Tijuana, to visit the whorehouses, and then to Rosarita Beach, to surf. I went as far as Ensenada exactly one time. But listen. I want to show you something."

He got a Hammond World Atlas from a tall wooden bookcase.

"Look," he said, setting his drink aside. "The other night I was thumbing through this, looking at maps of all the places I'd like to go. I started to look at this." He showed me the page that had Mexico and Baja California on it.

"I read up on it," he went on. "Parts of it are still pretty wild and unsettled. But there's a highway that runs all the way south, all the way to right here." He pointed with his finger to the very tip of the Peninsula. "Here," he said, tapping the page, "to Cabo San Lucas. I hear that place is crazy. Think of it. Only a few people have ever done it, Pete, driven the length of the Baja Peninsula and back."

"Probably the others didn't live to tell about it," I said.

"Want to go?" Tom asked excitedly.

"No!"

"Why not?"

"Why do you want to go so bad? You want to run away from something? Is it Tiffany? So that's it."

"That isn't it!"

"Listen Tom," I said, "do you remember what happened the *last* time you wanted to go someplace?"

"You don't need to mention that," he said, looking a little crestfallen. "This isn't the same."

"Besides," I said, "I thought you wanted to set sail for the islands when school is out."

"I do. But I thought, this is something that's right here, it's only a hundred miles from here to the border, we could go anytime. It'd be a blast. We could take your van, pack it with everything we need, and take our boards. The surfing is hot down there. We could camp out alongside the roads. And things are cheap, it wouldn't cost much. You got money?"

"I've been saving all the money I make at the dock," I admitted. "I don't have anything to spend it on."

"Me too. When you want to go?"

"I never said I wanted to go at all."

"Maybe like when school is out? Promise me, Pete. Because listen, if I have something like that to look forward to, maybe I can stand it till June. If not, I might not make it."

I didn't promise I'd go, but I didn't say I wouldn't, either, and like the journey into the old power plant, this is another one I often wished I'd never taken. But it would be some time before we went, a few more cups had to be filled, before we could go

Chapter 16

The Man Who Was Always Right

An awful loneliness clung to me all the time now. I couldn't shake it. I didn't feel good when I left Carolyn. I went back again and again but I hated myself, after, for what I was doing, and I felt a desolation that nothing could take away. I missed Rena. I would go and sit on the dock and stare at the water, and sometimes it had a strange effect on me, there were times when I thought it spoke to me. I would sit and watch the rain come down, watch as it hit the water, steady, rhythmatic, drumming away, making little bb shots on the surface. I watched the turbulence of the water and the white caps on the ends of the small rising waves. A cigarette burned in the ashtray and I listened as hard as I could, trying to decipher what the sea was saying to me.

Because it occurred to me one night that there was a Great Message for me to hear. There was a Revelation, a Deep Knowing, for me and me alone. But I didn't know what it was. I listened and listened but I couldn't get it. I listened and listened but I didn't know what it was. But I knew it was important, it was the Great Knowledge, and I wanted to hear it.

I listened to the waves and the choppy water lapping and rustling about, and I listened as the fog rolled in, covering everything like paint. An eerie stillness came over everything then and I thought if I listened hard enough then I could hear the message. And maybe that was the message I was waiting for, the one that would put everything back in balance. I went to the beach, sometimes, and stood on the jetty where Tom and I had crossed that fatal night to go into the old power plant. I would listen, thinking I was so tantalizingly close to hearing it sometimes but I never did get it, and once when it began to rain I didn't move but stayed right there and got soaked to the skin because I was so certain that if I stayed there a little longer I would hear.

All the rain got me down. It seemed to never stop. In the afternoon I sat in the office at the dock with the chair leaning back against the wall, my feet off the floor, my arms crossed. I seemed to doze as I listened to the rain. It was light rain, not hard and heavy like it often was, and it had a soothing effect on me, I dozed but didn't go all the way to sleep. I was certain I heard voices. They were not in the room but outside, and while I could hear them plainly I could not make out what they were saying. Was it Pete trying to speak to me? No, there was more than one, and they were like a radio, muffled and indistinct. And I was absolutely sure they were speaking to me, they had the Revelation, the Great Knowledge, that I so wanted to know. Was it Pete talking to me, trying to tell me something?

Now the voices came closer. I was not afraid of them, even though they became louder now, and they spoke directly into my ear. But I still could not understand the words, and I sat up with a start, shouting.

My feet hit the floor with a crash. I looked about, shaken, as Tom came through the door, soaking wet.

"What's the matter?" he asked, standing in the doorway, dripping. "You look like you just saw a ghost."

"Worse than that," I said, "Why, the weirdest thing just happened to me," I went on, feeling at a loss to explain it. "It was like I was asleep, somebody was here—"

"Man, you were asleep," Tom stated.

"No, I wasn't," I insisted. "It may have seemed like it but I was—"

"I saw you," he said. "When I came past the window I saw you sitting there. You were fast asleep. Your mouth was wide open—you're lucky a fly didn't land in there and take up knitting."

I rubbed my face with my hand. "Maybe it was a dream at that," I admitted. "Sure didn't seem like it, though. So where you been? As if I didn't know."

Tom slumped into a chair opposite me, sighing. He always had this look after he'd been with Tiffany--the look of a guilty man who knows what he is doing is wrong but is going to keep on doing it anyway. Probably I had the same look after I'd been with Carolyn. And I thought I was so holy. I didn't feel so holy now. Tom's hair was wet and plastered down on his head, and some drops of water had congealed around the tops of his ears like bubbles.

"What was this dream you were having?" he asked.

"Somebody was trying to talk to me," I said lamely. "But I couldn't understand what they were saying."

Tom waited, as if he expected more. "Is that all?" he asked at last. "I was hoping for something exciting. I'll have to tell you about some of my dreams, sometime. They'll blow your mind. Sometimes I think I'm crazy, because of these dreams. I feel crazy, sometimes. Do you ever feel crazy, Pete?"

"Only all the time."

"I feel crazy because of what's happening," he said.

"You mean about Tiffany?"

"I thought this would've been over a long time ago," he said. "But I can't seem to break it off. I keep saying to myself, 'This is the last time, you're gonna tell her, no more,' but I can't bring myself to do it.

"You know what I wish? I wish I could run away. Just split this scene altogether. That seems like a real good solution to the problems I'm facing—don't face them. Run away. Leave it all behind. I've been doing that all my life, why should I change now? Remember the other night when we were talking about going to Baja? Let's go, let's do that. The life I'm living seems so fake to me, Pete. And the mess I'm in is just getting worse and worse. Well, you warned me that it might get sticky, but would

I listen? How can a guy listen when he thinks with his dick instead of his head? Ever since—ever since—that night—nothing's been the same. I can't explain it. It's like the world isn't the same anymore. But I do wish I could just take my surfboard and hit the road. Want to go with me? I don't think I want to go unless you go with me. We walked into that dark tunnel together, so our lives are intertwined, we gotta walk this road side by side, it wouldn't be any good otherwise."

He leaned back tiredly, as if worn out from his exertions with Tiffany. "Don't mind me," he said. "I'm feeling low. Maybe it's all this rain."

He was silent after that. He had come to relieve me, and so I told him goodbye and went out into the wet cold air, leaving him to wrestle with his conscience. Puddles lay all around, shimmering in the light. The rain let up, unexpectedly, and I splashed across the parking lot with the darkness growing quickly. But I did not go home. I was still uneasy. I didn't believe I had really been asleep. I'd had dreams that seemed real before. This was more like when I was at Casey's house and I'd seen Deacon's ghost. Maybe I was crazy again. It seemed like I hadn't been so crazy when I was going to church all the time, I had a firm hold on something then. I didn't have anything to hold onto anymore, that was what was the matter. I hadn't gone to church since this business with Carolyn started. I carried it inside of me and couldn't even tell anyone.

I missed Rena, too. I thought of how she laughed, and how happy she was at the church, and how we went out to help people together, taking the food and clothes to people who only had rags, and how she said she wanted to join the Peace Corps. I was lonely for that goodness, but I was going the other way now, my cup of badness was going to be filled this time.

I sat in my van for a long time, just sat there staring at the ocean. It became dark all around me and the evening star came out, twinkling down as if it too had a message for me, some vital information to impart. I recalled Tom's metaphor about the clock and the universe and I thought maybe the whole cosmos could speak to you if only you knew how to listen. Perhaps there was a way to tune in, maybe that light I had seen was some kind of universal, cosmic force that ran through everybody and everything, and if there was a means to open yourself up to it, like tuning a radio in to the right frequency, you could learn all it had to tell you.

But those voices had seemed so real. What was it they wanted to tell me? I wished I could have heard, have understood them. Maybe they were telling me to go away, like Tom said, to run off, leave all this behind. What would it be like, I wondered, looking at the ocean again, to sail over to Hawaii. Tom wants to do that in June, maybe I'll go with him after all. Why not, there isn't anything to hold me here anymore. Denny has his whole future planned out, I haven't planned anything. I'm just living day by day now. But Denny's whole world could come crashing down any second now, and then where will all his plans be, all his ideas will be shut down pretty quick, won't they? What will he do then? What would I do? Now the desire to go someplace I had never been before, someplace totally new, and start all over again, welled up inside of me and I told myself I would do that, and soon, I would travel and discover the world and see new places and people and not just look at them on television.

But you'll still be the same inside, a voice said, you can't run away from yourself. No matter where you go you'll take the same stuff with you, you can't leave it behind.

Now I didn't want to be alone anymore. But I didn't want to be with anybody, either. I just wanted to be a face in the crowd, anonymous, so I wouldn't feel so lonesome. I drove through the wet, silent streets, the tires of my van making the familiar whooshing sound as they cut through the water, stopped near the pier and got out. The rain and dampness had scattered the toughs who usually hung out at the park and I was just as glad, I didn't feel like encountering anybody like my old buddies Waldo and Karlovitch right now. But a walk on the pier appealed to me, and so I sauntered out there, pulling my black navy peacoat a little tighter.

I went part of the way out and leaned on the railing, looking directly out at the ocean, which was very dark and seemed to be getting ready to become rough, like a turbine cranking up and getting ready to run. The waves were getting higher, and choppier, and I could feel the pier shake as they hit the pilings. Looking at the black water made me think of the

Blackness, and I felt a shiver inside when I thought of it, hoping I wouldn't see it again.

I felt a chill on the back of my neck, and involuntarily I turned around, as if I feared somebody was sneaking up on me. Through the gathering darkness I saw a tall dark figure wearing a brown leather jacket, moving along deliberately, gracefully, the way a large predator moves, his whole body in harmony, long arms swinging, light, lean, and quick. The light from the lamps above glinted off his clear aviator style glasses, and I had a terrible feeling that Death was very close to me now.

"Well, well," he said, spotting me, coming over and standing beside me. He loomed above like a tall tree, speaking in his strangely high voice. "What do you know? To think I've found you here all alone, and without your shadow, Surfer Joe. Tsk, tsk. Opportunity beckons."

Oh Lord, I thought, bring back Rudy, he only wants to beat the hell out of me. This is Dave the murderer, the guy who cuts peoples' throats for fun. He smiled down at me, lighting a cigarette. His eyes blazed red in the darkness, whether from drugs or just what was burning inside of him I couldn't tell, but they blazed away, lit by some internal fire.

"I heard you've become holy, that you go to that church with all the freaks," he said. "Is it true?"

"No," I said, shaking my head vigorously, "no, it isn't true, I'm not religious, and I'm not holy."

"That's a relief," Dave said. He gave me one of his cigarettes, the black, jasmine-scented cigarettes that he smoked. I hesitated before I lit it. "Don't worry," he said. "It's just plain old tobacco. These are Russian cigarettes. Hard to find. Go ahead, try it. Good, isn't it?"

"It is good," I admitted. I took another drag and felt dizzy. "I used to go to the church, but I don't anymore, I gave it up."

"That's a good thing," said Dave. "Nothing good will ever come of that church or any other church. I know about churches. Love your fellow man and it is better to give than to receive. What crap. When I want something I take it. You wait for somebody to give anything to you and you'll be waiting when you're old and in your wheelchair."

He spoke rapidly, the words falling out of his mouth like bullets. I felt a mist was rising, a black mist that started to cover everything, like fog, hanging wetly over me. I was standing in blackness, like the blackness of the tunnel that night Tom and I had gone into the old power plant. The moon and stars were gone. Dave's eyes, those eyes of deadly nightshade, beamed out of this black mist, glowing with an unholy redness. I looked around for help. The pier was deserted; there were no fishermen or lonely gawkers like there usually were.

It was more than fear; it was terror. The blackness came from Dave, it was radiating off him just as surely as the Light I'd seen that night. So this is where the Blackness comes from, I thought wildly, from inside of yourself. Dave is all blackness, he's given himself completely over to it, just like Carolyn and her living only for her lusts and sin, he is all blackness inside and out.

I couldn't take my eyes away from him. I stared at him and he didn't look human anymore. His face was the face of a skull, smiling malevolently at me; it was the face of Death. Death had come for me the way he had come that night for Deacon. I felt it as certainly as I would have felt a surge of electricity. I wanted to run, but I felt paralyzed, rooted to this spot.

Dave fixed his eyes on me, and this time I couldn't look away. They were like the black tunnel, and when I looked into them I went deeper and deeper inside, Dave and I were descending together, we were going down, further and further, he was leading me. And just like I knew where the white light would lead to if I followed it far enough I knew where the black tunnel went. I wanted to run but I couldn't, I couldn't budge an inch. My will was being taken away from me. And I stared into those eyes and I saw in there everything I ever wanted, I could have it all, and more, if only I followed them all the way to the end and had the nerve to look at what was there. It reached out and caught me, drawing me in like a rip tide will draw you in, shining like a black light, wicked and malevolent but promising too.

This is the Blackness, I thought, it comes from me, just like the Light does. Just like I had the Light, I also have the Dark. And I knew suddenly that Waldo and Karlovitch had followed this darkness all the way, they had gone to the end and now they belonged to Dave, they were his, just like Casey had said.

"What is it?" asked Dave. "Did I say something?"

"What?"

"You looked a little weird there, are you stoned?"

"No, I'm not stoned."

"Want to get that way?" He took out a joint and lit it, then gave it to me. I smoked it, still shaken. "You know the difference between right and wrong?" he asked. "I'll tell you what it is. Right is what I want, and wrong is what you want. When I want something it's mine, I figure out a way to get it, but it's already mine because I thought of it. That makes life a lot simpler. That means I'm always right. I always win. I can't lose. Ever. *I'm* what counts. Nobody else. That's why I love the hippies. They want to give everything away. Give it to me, I'll take it. I'm gonna be so rich one day it'll blow your mind, richer than Onassis or J. Paul Getty, I'll rule the world, can you dig it?"

"From dealing drugs," I said.

"There's no better way."

"From people's pain and misery," I made bold to say.

"It's *their* pain, it's *their* misery," he said. "And it's their choice, too."

I thought of the people I had seen when I'd been at the church, people suffering and freaked out from the drugs that came from Dave.

"How can you live with yourself?" I asked.

"You may think, as I did once, that this world has a moral center, that there are such things as good and evil, right and wrong. That's just bullshit. Want to go for a ride with me?"

"In your Porsche?"

"We can go over to my place after. I'd like to get you stoned and take advantage of you. Want to go?"

"I'll go for a ride."

"But the other doesn't interest you? Maybe you'll change your mind. Don't knock it until you've tried it. If you ever do I hope I'm there to advise you." He smiled and his big white teeth showed.

He looked about quickly, and seeing there was no one around, reached into his pocket and took out a small mirror, the kind women carry for a quick make-up job, and dumped a quantity of white powder on it. He inhaled about half of it through a piece of straw, and offered the other half to me.

"Want some?"

"What is it?" I asked, doubtfully.

"China White," he said. "The best in the world. Try it."

I snorted half of it through one nostril and the rest through the other. It burned going down, as if I'd inhaled powdered fire. But almost immediately I felt a surge going through me, an invigorating rush of power. My teeth tingled. Everything seemed crystal-clear, there was no longer anything to be afraid of or to worry about. I smiled at Dave. He smiled back wickedly.

"Feels good, doesn't it?"

"I never felt anything like it."

"Ready to go for a ride?"

"Sure!" I felt like I was ready for anything.

We walked off the pier and over to where his Porsche was parked. It was stark red, a custom, cherry-red that leaped out at you. Inside was all paneling and velour, with deep comfortable leather seat.

"Fasten your seat belt," Dave advised.

The engine roared to life, throbbing and hammering smoothly. Dave threw a quick glance backward over his shoulder and the Porsche tore away from the curb as if pushed by a giant hand, tires screeching. Dave cut through town, going along Ocean Avenue to Electric, heedless of other traffic, taking corners so that I was tossed back and forth in my seat. When we got to Pacific Coast Highway Dave lashed the gearshift and the car shot forward like a projectile, going north, up the highway, toward Long Beach. He indicated the eight-track stereo and to a case filled with tapes. "Put on something you like," he said, speaking over the rush of the wind and the roar of the engine. I opened the case and took out the Rolling Stones.

"Good choice!" Dave commented. "I love the Stones. I love Mick Jagger. He's a friend of mine, you know."

"Oh bullshit," I scoffed.

"He is," Dave insisted. "I sold him some of my China White once."

I watched the speedometer rise steadily: Sixty miles an hour, seventy, eighty, ninety. Lights whizzed past us, Dave tore in and out of traffic.

"Aren't you worried about cops?"

"No fuckin' cop ever stops me," he replied.

"Where we going?"

He didn't answer but kept on zinging in and out of traffic.

"*I was born in a cross-fire hurricane/And I howled at my ma in the driving rain,*" Mick Jagger sang.

We kept going up Pacific Coast Highway, past Long Beach State and the Veteran's Hospital on Bellflower Boulevard. Dave sang and clapped his hands to the music. "*But it's all right now, in fact it's a gas,*" he sang. "*I'm jumpin' jack flash/It's a gas gas gas!*"

"You've never been to The Pike, have you?" he asked.

"I love The Pike," I said.

There was more traffic now and Dave had to slow down. I got the feeling he regarded all the other people on the road as having no business there, they were in *his* way, and they'd better get out of it. He became more and more animated, whether from the China White or his own natural personality I wasn't sure, but he talked and talked, asking how I was enjoying the ride, going on compulsively. "Here," he said, reaching over with a long arm and taking out another tape, "Put this on. It's my theme song."

It was the Stones again, "Sympathy for the Devil."

"*Please allow me to introduce myself/I'm a man of wealth and taste/I've been around for a long long year/Stole many a man's soul and faith.*"

"Mick Jagger's my idol," Dave said. "Want to know why? Because he doesn't give a fuck what anybody thinks of him. He does what he wants, lives the way he wants to live. He sleeps with men and he sleeps with women, and he doesn't care who knows about it. God," he said, looking over the windshield of his car, "God, it's a great time to be young. When was there ever a time like this? Know what I mean? There hasn't been a time like this for a thousand years and won't be for a thousand years more."

He drove into downtown Long Beach now, turning off Pacific Coast Highway near Atlantic Avenue and heading toward the ocean. We passed through a section of ramshackled old houses and fleabag hotels, vacant lots with high tumbleweeds growing in them and knots of people standing on street corners drinking wine from bottles in paper bags. Prostitutes walked the streets, and pimps in gaudy costumes stood about.

Dave took a sharp left turn and then a right onto Atlantic Avenue, which runs parallel with the ocean. Like Main Street in Angels Beach, the street lights were decorated with tinsel and garland and Christmas lights, and there were blinking lights wrapped around the palm trees that ran along the side that was closest to the beach. People walked to and fro on the sidewalk. We passed the old Long Beach Auditorium and the Rainbow Pier that circled it. Ahead of us I saw the Cyclone Racer and the Ferris Wheel, sticking up in the night sky and lit with bright lights of all different colors, and when we were almost directly in front of the entrance to the Pike, Dave whipped the Porsche into a small parking space on a dark side street.

"I got some business to do here," he said.

We walked across the busy boulevard, amidst much horn-honking and cars stopping, crossed the sidewalk, then went down the broad concrete stairs and up to the entrance to The Pike, going beneath the big neon sign that read, "Enter The Walk Of A Thousand Lights." Above the sign was an electronic face that kept changing from a clown with a big red nose to a devil with big black eyes. Dave smiled when he saw that. From within I could hear the screams of the people riding the Cyclone Racer, and I could hear the music blasting from the rides and the arcades and the Ferris Wheel.

The Pike was known as the Coney Island of the West, part Disneyland, part carnival. There were bars, tattoo parlors, shooting galleries, pinball games, booths where you could throw a softball at milk bottles made of lead and win a stuffed animal, and fortune tellers. There was a big, brightly-lit ferris wheel that turned against the night sky. The Pike's main street, which was called "The Walk Of A Thousand Lights," had a freak show where you could see Zuzu the Monkey Girl and Madame Kostova letting her pet snake wrap itself all around her body. There was Wing's Chinese Arcade, a Ripley's Believe It Or Not exhibit, a funhouse, and a merry-go-round. Drunks staggered about aimlessly. Barkers in panama hats and vests called out to the people passing by. Sailors from the different ships that had put into Long Beach walked around in small groups, eyeballing the whores. There were more of the colorfully dressed pimps, wearing big broad-brimmed hats with white feathers poking out of them.

"You ever ride the Cyclone Racer?" Dave asked.

"Damn right I have," I lied.

The Cyclone Racer was a wooden roller coaster built in 1915, famous by then as the last of its kind and the scariest roller coaster in the world. You could hear its wooden frame creaking as the cars raced over it and it seemed only a matter of time before something gave way and the cars full of brave riders went plunging straight down 100 feet into the ocean. I'd never had the nerve to ride it, but I'd always wanted to.

We walked into the midst of all this, Dave swaggering as if it all belonged to him. "Why don't you go ride the merry go round?" Dave suggested. Something in his tone told me I should do as he said, so I went over just as the ride was starting, paid my money, and got on. The carousel started, turning slowly with the music, that same old merry go round music that is the same everywhere, the horses moving slowly up and down. I kept my eyes on Dave, for I sensed something was about to happen. Sure enough, a few seconds later a tall slender black woman approached him from out of the crowd, holding out her hand to him to get his attention. At first I thought she was a prostitute, making advances at him, for she was dressed like one, in a black mini skirt and boots, but then I realized they weren't strangers. She was accompanied, I now realized, by a white man. He and Dave touched in a familiar manner, beyond an ordinary shaking of hands. He was small, and fidgety-looking, with bleached curly hair and a squarish jaw, and like Dave, he wore a leather jacket and long boots that came up past his knees. As the carousel rolled past Dave suddenly turned and pointed my way. He gestured several times with his long finger, as if wanting to be sure his listeners understood something. Then the carousel went on around and I couldn't see them anymore.

The ride came to a halt and I got off, uncertain of what I should do next. Then I felt a hand slip through my arm.

"Hi there." It was the black woman, the one I'd seen Dave with. "Let's get on the Ferris wheel, want to?" she purred, stroking my arm. "You and I, wouldn't you like to go up there with me?"

"Where's Dave?"

"He and Roger went somewhere, but they'll be back. Come on, let's go, honey."

Roger, I took it, was the little guy with the bleached out hair.

"What's your name?"

"Pete. What's your name?"

She only laughed. "You don't need to know my name." I bought two tickets for the Ferris wheel and we got on, getting into one of the cars and the attendant closed us in. "Now you're trapped in here with me, white boy," she said, still laughing and clutching my arm. Her nails were long and shiny, like a cat's claws, and her breath smelled strongly of alcohol. Her eyes had the same blazing look to them Dave's had, and I thought suddenly mine must have that look too, that look of fire, lit by the China White.

"What's going on?" I asked.

She smiled again, wickedly. "Haven't you figured it out yet?"

"No, what is it?"

She only laughed again.

There was a jolt and the Ferris wheel moved up, then stopped. It jolted and moved again, and we were at the crest, looking down on the Pike below us and the harbor, spreading out beyond. The lights of the city blinked and flared. The air was colder up here. The lights seemed to go on forever. "What is it, this thing broken down or something?"

"What's the matter, don't you like the view, honey? Or does the company bother you?"

"Why won't you tell me your name?"

"Maybe I don't have a name."

"Everybody's got a name."

"What does it mean to you, my name? What does it mean to you, the name of this nigger girl? What am I to you, except somebody you'd like to fuck? Shawntel, I'm Shawntel, you want to be my boyfriend? I'm not a whore, you think I'm a whore? Some men call me Shawntel from hell, you want to know why?"

"Why?"

She laughed again and took hold of my hand. She stroked it lightly with her long nails, up and down, up and down, slowly. "There now, does that feel good or what?" she asked. Her white teeth showed and she looked like a cat. Her teeth seemed pointed, as if sharpened deliberately, so that if she bit you she would take out a good sized hunk of your skin. Her hair was straight and had a kind of shine in the dark. Then she raised my hand to her lips and rubbed her lips on it. She took one of my fingers and put it into her mouth, mouthing it, in and out, saying, "Oh, oh," and shuddering, biting my finger lightly, then harder, just enough to begin to hurt. Then she put it out of her mouth and her hands went to my belt buckle. "You ever had your cock sucked?" she asked. I said yes. "Did you like it?" she went on, unbuttoning and unzipping all the while. "Do you know what it's like, to be in hell?" she asked. "I'll tell you, white boy, I'll tell you what it's like. It isn't all bad, no no, it isn't. It's pleasure like you can't stand, it's sweetness and ecstasy that becomes an agony of delight. That's what you can find in here," she said, indicating her body, writhing about now, "in here, in here, if you're game for it, if you have the nerve to go there, honey, if you have the nerve."

This is all madness, I thought, I have to be dreaming. Her lips went onto me and I realized, as I shuddered in exquisite pleasure, that this was no dream. Shawntel's head bobbed up and down, and once she looked up at me with those wild eyes.

"There," she said, "there, that's what it is, where it's at, that's the pain and the pleasure," she said, and I tried reaching for her, but even in the narrowness of the car she was elusive, I couldn't get hold of her, she slipped through my fingers like water. "Did you like it? Did you?" she asked.

"Yes," I said. "Yes."

I wanted more, but the Ferris wheel began to turn now, and she held me off easily. "Enjoy the ride now, enjoy the ride now," she said. "Sometime I'll let you touch me, but not now, not tonight, you've had enough for tonight."

"No, no, do it again, do it again."

When the ride was over she kissed me on the mouth and disappeared. I couldn't see where she went. Had I imagined the whole thing? Now, my pants were sticky and wet, telling me otherwise, it had all been real enough. But where was she? What was going on? There was no sign of her, nor of Dave either.

There was a shooting gallery nearby and I walked over to it.

I paid a quarter to fire at some ducks going along in a row. There was a loud banging and reverberation whenever I hit one. The ducks fell over, one after the other, but I didn't hit enough of them to win a prize.

When I was finished I was about to pay another quarter and try again but then I saw Dave standing nearby.

"We're all done here," he said. "Let's move."

I followed along and when we'd gone back up the concrete steps and across the broad street to his car he smirked and looked around. Then he started the engine and we shot off down the highway.

"How did you like Shawntel?" he asked.

"Fine."

"You want to be with her again?"

"Oh, hell yes."

"It can happen, it can happen," he said. "It can be arranged. I can arrange it. I can arrange anything. Whatever you want, I can get it for you." He kept looking around, out the window and in the rear-view mirror. He kept doing that all the way back to Angels Beach, and when we got there he drove down 11th Street, where his house was. When he got out of his car he looked all around one more time, then held out his hand. "Give it to me," he said.

I stared at him, uncomprehendingly.

"Shawntel gave you something to give to me," he said.

"No."

"Look in your pocket," Dave said, "your jacket pocket."

I put my hand in there and to my surprise brought back a small white paper package. Well, that was sure one on me. I never noticed a thing.

"You had a fortune in your pocket, and you didn't even know it, did you? That's how life goes, we never know what we've got till it's gone. Normally I don't like to do business that way but tonight there wasn't any choice, I was afraid somebody might be watching me. Here," he went on, handing me a bill. "That's what you get for holding that for me."

I held the bill in my hands. "Wow," I said.

"Easiest hundred dollars you ever made, right? And that's nothing compared to what you could make. I take care of the people who do things for me. I know how to treat people right. But if somebody crosses me, look out, better for them to have never been born." He turned on his heel. "Speaking of which," he said, as two figures came lumbering out of the fog. "Just look at what's coming," he said.

I stiffened, involuntarily, as Waldo and Karlovitch appeared. They scowled when the recognized me. "Hey, what's he doing here?" Waldo said, gesturing my way.

"Keep quiet, you moronic hulk," Dave said sharply. "Keep your mind on what you have to do, that way you may be able to accomplish it without screwing anything up." The three of them went into a brief huddle and then Waldo and Karlovitch turned and went back off into the fog. "Good riddance," said Dave. "Fools. There might be a total of 100 IQ points between the two of them and that's on a good day. Come inside."

There was a waist-high picket fence in front of his house and a walkway with grass on either side. An eagle made of plaster-of-Paris and painted black spread its wings above the mailbox. There was a big window in the front, and inside there was fancy leather furniture and psychedelic posters on the walls. A huge, expensive-looking stereo dominated the room. There was also a bookcase, but I couldn't see the titles, for when Dave flipped on the lights all was just red and fluorescent, so I couldn't see clearly enough to read them.

"Sit down and relax," Dave said genially. "Want something to drink? How about a little wine?" He took off his leather jacket and walked into the kitchen. When he came back he handed me a glass of red wine and then put on the stereo, tuning it to an underground FM station.

"That Shawntel," he said, "she can suck the chrome right off a bumper, with those thick lips of hers. You found that out, did you? She's really all right, for a nigger. I don't generally have any use for niggers, they're lazy for the most part, just like I don't have any use for queers, they're disturbed. Shawntel's all right. She does what I tell her to do. That's the secret, if you want to get along with me, do what I tell you. Then there's no arguments, and everything goes exactly the way it should. And you know what the best part is? You don't have to do any thinking, nor make any decisions. You just do what I say." He drank some wine, lit a cigarette, his eyes still glowing. "So," he said, "what do you think of my place?"

"Far out," I said, looking around, "great. Must be nice to live in."

"Yeah, me and Larry share it."

"Where is Larry?"

Dave shrugged. "Who knows? We're here all alone. He may not even come back tonight. In a while I'll show you the rest of the place. I've got a fountain out back. I love it here, it's quiet and peaceful. Sometimes I have to go to Mexico on business, I've even gone to Panama and Columbia. But I always look forward to coming back here. How'd you like to come with me? To Mexico, I mean? I'll pay your way. You ever been there?"

"No. I speak Spanish, though."

"How so?"

"School. I've had it for four years."

"Then we definitely have to go sometime," Dave declared.

"Okay," I shrugged, "sure, I'll go."

Dave smiled again and refilled my glass. "How do you like it?"

"It's good."

"Here, have some more, we might as well finish off the bottle, it's an excellent vintage." He sloshed some more wine until my glass was full, then poured the rest into his own. "Drink up, drink up," he said. "I've got plenty more. I love good wine. Good wine is like good love—rare. You ever been in love?"

"I've been in love."

He looked at me narrowly. "I imagine your experiences up until now have all been with teeny-boppers who are either virgins or who just lost their maidenhood, who might let you put your hand into their pants if it's your lucky night. There's more to it than that, you'll find." He drank from his glass and then stood up. "Come with me," he said. "I'll show you my fountains and garden."

We went down some steps into his backyard. He threw a switch and some dim lights came on. I heard a gentle swoosh of water from some fountains that were set up back there, and then the sound of water running. We passed a statue of a man and boy embracing. A statue of an angel poured water into one of the fountains. Lights flashed among the plants. "Nice, isn't it?" Dave said. "I spent a lot of money fixing this up, getting it the way I wanted it. If you're going to live, live well, I say. Get what you want, don't settle for anything less."

He put his arm over my shoulders and I felt a shudder. He kills, a voice said, he kills people and leaves their bodies lying in pools of their own blood. And yet his touch wasn't entirely unpleasant, I had a sudden urge to put my arm around him, to touch him back, thinking that my reaching out to him wouldn't be unwelcome, but no, that's what he's waiting for. Horror shot through me. What was I? A queer?

"What do you want?" Dave asked. "Everybody wants something. What is it you want? What's your dream? You can have it all."

"How?"

"I can show you. Be like me. I'll be a millionaire before I turn thirty. How old do you think I am?"

"Twenty-five?"

"Close. Twenty-six my last birthday. At least, in this life. Sometimes I think I've lived twenty or thirty lifetimes prior to this one, and this one is just a continuation of all the others. So I might be a thousand, two thousand years old. When I have enough money you know what I'll do? I'll buy an island in the Caribbean, and build a castle on it, and I'll be king of that castle and that island. Everyone will have to do what I tell them there. Let's go back inside," he suggested. "It's getting chilly out here."

He showed me around the rest of the house, pointing out this and that. He indicated some paintings on the walls, mostly all nudes, saying that artwork was a sound investment. "This stuff will be worth a fortune someday," he predicted. "I go to openings a lot, and buy if I see anything there I think worthwhile. Have you ever been to an opening of an artist's work? No? Then we must go sometime, I think you would enjoy it."

I espied a pair of *nunchakus* hung on a wall. "You know what those are?" Dave asked.

"I've seen them," I said. "Are you into karate? Tom is too."

"I thought all he could do is surf," said Dave.

"He's been teaching me."

"Has he now? Show me your stance."

I got into a forward stance. "Now do a reverse punch, said Dave." I did, and he said, "Not bad. Now try it this way." And he showed me how, keeping his fist vertical instead of turned sideways, and I could feel the increase in power. "See the difference?" said Dave. "If somebody is foolish enough to come at you like that, leading with their right, do an upward block and then reverse-punch them in the gut—he's gonna back off, believe me."

He stepped into a closet and brought out a pad similar to the ones football players use to practice their blocks on, only this one had a handle in the back. He held it up in front of him. "Now hit this," he said. I did it, doing it the way he had shown me, and after several tries succeeded in making him move backwards a step. "Good," he praised. "Pretty damn good. Keep practicing that and you'll be able to knock anyone down."

"Show me what you can do," I said.

He grinned just a bit and handed me the pad, then hit it quickly with chopping motions of either hand. After that he demonstrated a few moves of a *kata*.

"Here's one I really like," he said. "I'd love to do this to someone. Grab me by the collar."

I took him by the collar with both hands and with astonishing quickness he brought both his arms up, breaking the hold I had on him, and then brought his head forward, like a snake striking, using his forehead like a battering ram. He stopped less than a quarter-inch from my face, and if he hadn't he would have smashed my nose like a run-over beer can.

"Incredible," I said.

"You could do it if somebody came at you from the left," Dave said, showing me, "or the right," he went on, moving from the other side. "Just step in and throw your neck forward, and aim. With a little practice you'll be amazed at how well it would work."

"Now try this," he said, and executed a simultaneous movement with both fists.

"What was that?"

"One of my favorite moves. It's called the double punch. Try it."

I tried it. "Wow," I said. "What that would do."

"If you do it right it will certainly adjust somebody's attitude right fast," Dave said. 'I've seen it knock over some pretty strong men." He demonstrated a similar move, only with one arm above the other rather than side by side. "Same idea," he said. "Only it's harder to execute. It's called a U-punch. Kicks are better. I prefer to kick somebody if I have to, rather than dirty my hands in a fist fight." He demonstrated several kicks, which, with his long legs seemed to come from far away and connect as if they were bolts of lightning coming down from the sky.

"Now let's spar a little," he said, and jabbed at me with his left, not nearly as fast as he could, had he wanted to, and I jabbed back. "Come at me harder," he said. "Really try to hit me." I did, and he either blocked everything I did or else just dodged to one side or the other. Then, without warning, he threw his arms up, palms forward. "Stop! Stop!" He grimaced as if in pain. "I just pulled a muscle in my back." I stopped, dropping my hands, and as soon as I did he spun around with incredible speed, his elbow stopping less than an inch from my chin.

"You see?" he cried. "You see? That's one of the oldest tricks in the book. Fall for it and you'll get killed. Don't ever let up, don't ever show mercy. Those things are for suckers."

When we came to his bedroom Dave paused, standing in the open doorway.

"This is where I sleep," he said. "And fuck."

He put his arm around me again, squeezing my shoulder with his hand. I felt his strength when he did that, an unnatural strength, born perhaps of the drugs he took, or else from madness. "You're a nice boy, Pete," he said. "I like you. Do you know what that means? I wouldn't say that to just anybody. Most people bore me to death. But I like you. I think you and I could be good friends. What do you say? I'm a good person to have as your friend." He touched me in an affectionate manner, similar to the touch had exchanged earlier with the guy at the Pike. I felt, as I had felt on the pier, that I was in the presence of Death, that a large, predatory animal was descending on me, and that if I didn't do something I was going to be devoured in an unholy way. Dave's eyes were glowing behind the clear glasses, resembling the intense beams put out by a searchlight or a lighthouse. "Are you afraid?" he asked softly. "Don't be. I wouldn't hurt you. I want to be your friend, your special friend. Just relax."

His gaze was mesmeric. He had a hold of me just as surely as if he'd had a rope. I felt paralyzed, unable to move, as he came closer.

Then I said "Don't," breaking free. It was like throwing myself through a wall.

"What's the matter?" he asked.

"I gotta go," I said lamely.

Dave arched his eyebrows. "So soon?"

"It's late. I have school tomorrow."

I was afraid of what he might do and I backed away cautiously, noting with unease his large hands and the unnatural strength I'd felt in them. "I've enjoyed our evening together," he said. "Perhaps you'll come again?"

"Yeah," I said. "Maybe."

He walked me to the door and shook hands. Once I was passed the gate I breathed a little easier, and I turned. Dave was standing on the porch, looking after me. He was all red and black, standing there, outlined by the red fiery lights that came from within his house.

Chapter 17

Rena In The Rain

I was at the jetty, staring out at the ocean and listening to the waves, when I saw Rena again.

It looked to me like the rain was about to start again and I told myself I had better go soon, because I had stood there and gotten soaked enough times and I couldn't see any reason to do it again. It was dark and I didn't want to stay there all night. Would winter last forever and would this rain ever stop? From my vantage point on the rock I saw someone approaching, walking across the sand, dressed in jeans and a dark pullover sweater, her hair bouncing as she made her way.

I hadn't seen her in a long time and as much as I'd missed her I felt my heart begin to race, for I was ashamed of myself. There hadn't even been any breaking up this time, no explanation, no reason, nothing—I'd just stopped seeing her. I didn't feel right about it, and I wanted to say something, but with each passing day that became harder and harder.

She saw me now and her expression didn't change. She kept on coming and then stopped at the base of the rocks and stood with her hands on her hips, looking up at me, smiling, but without her usual sunniness, it was a sad smile that I'd never seen on her before.

"I'm glad the rain has stopped," she said from down there. "I needed to come here, I wanted to--it was like I had no other place to go." I noticed that the necklace I had given her was dangling from her neck, the sign of Sowleu, and I felt good about that, glad she was still wearing it.

She extended her hand. "Help me up," she asked, and when she was standing beside me she said, "I wanted to come and listen to the waves for a while, and feel the wind against my face. That's why I'm glad it's not raining. Do you think it'll rain? It's not going to rain, is it, Pete?" Her gaze went to the rocks, stretching out into the water in a curved line.

"How come you're not in church?" I asked. "That's where you always are, this time of day."

"I love the waves," she said. "I'm so grateful that I've grown up here, by the ocean, so I can listen to the waves and see them whenever I want to. Wouldn't it be awful to be away from them? If you lived someplace like Kansas or Nebraska where there wasn't any ocean? I think that would be awful. We're lucky. Those people, they don't have an ocean, think of what they're missing out on. Those poor people."

She turned toward me now. "I'm so glad you're here," she declared. "I was hoping you would be but you never know. I guess I came looking for you. Where have you been?"

I was hoping she wouldn't ask that. "Working," I said. "I have to work all the time now."

"That's not true," she said, "and even if it was, you could have called me, you could have done *something*. I miss you."

"I miss you too."

"I'm scared," she said suddenly. "Please hold me, Pete, I'm having a fear attack." I held her and I could feel her heart pounding wildly, like a runaway train. There was a sudden blast of wind and the loud crash of a wave; some of the spray landed on us.

"What is it?" I said. "What's the matter?"

"Don't talk," she pleaded. "Just hold onto me, and don't talk don't say anything."

Another wave crashed, sounding like an explosion. The rocks

trembled underneath us. "It's like the world is coming apart all around me," she said, "but as long as you hold me it's all right. Where have you been, Pete? You left me there, and now see what's happened? It wouldn't be like this if you'd stayed with me."

"What happened?" I asked.

"My knees are weak," she said. "My insides feel like jelly."

"Mine too."

"Sometimes," Rena said, "sometimes I feel like we've known each other forever. Do you ever feel that?"

"Yeah."

"So it doesn't matter, does it? Whatever you've done or what you've been doing, it doesn't matter, we're here now and we've always been here, the past and the future and the present are all the same, all happening at the same time, aren't they? There isn't any yesterday, and no tomorrow either. Kiss me. Kiss me right now."

The waves were pounding and crashing a few feet away while we stood there kissing on the rock in the moonlight. "Oh," Rena said. "Oh! Oh! Don't, don't kiss me that way, not like that, don't do it."

And I whispered, "Why not?"

"It's scary," she said. "It's scary, but I like it. You make me feel things I never felt before."

But I kissed her again, and she said, "I'll faint, I might faint."

The wind blasted again, and there was more spray landing on us. Then there were more drops, smaller ones, hitting us both.

"It's starting to rain," I said. Rena showed no signs of having heard me. The rain began to come down harder. She held me, tighter and tighter, squeezing me.

"Rena," I said, "let's get to some shelter," but she paid me no heed. The rain was coming down harder and harder now.

"We're getting soaked!" I nearly shouted.

"I don't care!" she shouted back. "I don't care! I want to hold onto you forever, don't make me let go!"

The rain fell harder, and the driving wind blew the drops onto us so the stung like small insects. "Do you want to get drowned?" I yelled.

"I don't care!" she shouted again, stubbornly. "I don't. I want to stay here like this forever."

"We can't stay here like this, we have to go."

"Oh, all right!" she cried.

Then, just as suddenly and inexplicably, she released her hold and fled. She made her way quickly over the rocks and jumped down from the far side, disappearing from my view while I stood there, looking on astonishedly.

"Rena!" I called. "Rena, wait!"

But my voice was lost in the wind and the rain.

The rain was pouring down now, whipping against my face. My hair was soaked. The half moon that had been out was long gone, covered by the black clouds that had been there all winter. The sea was whipping around violently. Where had she gone? I went over the rocks to the edge where she had jumped off but I saw nothing. The rain was coming down in blasts.

The path sloped downward, toward the bay. Above me was a flash of lightning, but no thunder, and it outlined the old plant looming above on its hill, sitting there massively behind the fence, like a castle surrounded by a moat. The glassy water of the bay stretched out ahead of me, and in the dim light I could see the currents going one way and then another. I went down the path, the same path Tom and I had gone on. But there was no sign of Rena, only the darkness.

My hair was soaked and plastered to my head. I was wet all the way to the skin. Nearby the sea was pounding and crashing the shoreline. I was about to give it up and go back the way I'd came; maybe the whole thing was a hallucination. Then I saw a slim figure sitting forlornly on a narrow strip of sand near the water's edge.

She was sitting with her knees drawn up and rocking slightly, looking out at the rain falling on the bay. She did not look up when I came near but just kept on sitting there that way, rocking on the sand.

"Are you gonna sit here like this all night?" I said, having to shout over the wind. "Come on, what's the matter with you, Rena?"

She didn't move or respond but just continued to sit, staring, her face set unhappily. Her hair and sweater were both soaked.

"Come on," I repeated.

She didn't move and so I said, "Oh, the hell with it," and started to walk away.

"Pete?"

"What?"

"Are there sting rays in there?" she asked, pointing at the bay.

"So they say."

"If I jump in, will one sting me? That's what I want."

"Why the hell do you want that?"

"Do you die, from a sting ray?" she asked. "What happens, do you die from the sting or do you drown?"

"You talk crazy."

"It's not crazy to want to die, is it?"

"Come on," I said. "Let's go."

She came with me, unprotesting now, and I led her back up the trail along the path and over the rocks to the beach, the wind and the rain pounding us all the while. She didn't speak a word until we were all the way across the sand and on First Street, sitting inside my van, out of the driving rain. It kept on, however, with its nonstop assault, we could hear it hitting the roof, pinging and thumping. I offered to drive her home.

"Isn't there someplace else we can go?"

For a moment I was at a loss and thought we could just sit here a while. Rena sat in the seat beside me, the water running down her face in rivulets, her hair tangled and soaked and matted. My wet clothes clung to me unpleasantly.

Now I had an idea. I looked at my watch. The dock would be closed, and Tom who had the closing shift would be gone by now. Rena sat still, making no effort to wipe away any of the water and staring straight ahead, looking out the window at the rain that pounded on the glass windshield and then ran off down the front.

"It's like the end of the world," she said. "All this rain. Maybe it's the second Flood, that's what some people say. This is more rain than there's ever been here before. Why is that, why is it raining so much *now*? Maybe it's Judgment Day. God is going to divide the world into the Good People and the Bad People. What happens to all this water, where does it go, and what will happen if all places that are supposed to store it fill up? What would happen then? I know what side God will put me on when He makes that Final Judgment even though I don't mean to be bad."

"You aren't bad," I said, noting, in the glare of the headlights, the small rivers of water running along both sides of the street. "You aren't bad, Rena. You're one of the best people I know."

"No," she insisted.

"I'm the one who's bad," I said.

"You don't know," she said cryptically. "You don't know the bad things I've done. Only God knows."

I drove across the bridge over the San Gabriel River and then over Marina Drive to the dock. When we were inside I made some coffee, and turned on the electric floor heater. The coils inside glowed red, and some heat began to rise.

"Stand over that," I advised. "You can dry off a little bit that way."

The coffee seemed to bring her out of her stupor. She drank it, holding the cup in her hand and standing over the heater, sighing.

I went into the other room, the one with the bed, noting that the coarse wool army-type blankets were all askew and thought Tom and Tiffany were probably lying there not long ago, and then I detected Tiffany's trademark smell of Chanel No. 5.

I found two white terrycloth robes in the closet, took them out, quickly removed my wet clothes and put one of the robes on.

"Here," I said, going back into the other room. "It stinks some, but if you want, you can put this one and let your clothes dry."

"I don't feel like being soaked any longer," Rena said, and she went into the bathroom, closing the door behind her. While she was gone I smoked a cigarette and looked idly out at the rain spattering the windows and the lights of the Marina and of Long Beach. When Rena came out she had her clothes in her arms in a bundle.

"This feels better," she said. She had brushed her hair back so that some of the knots and tangles were gone and it lay wetly over her ears in straight lines. "All this rain," she said, looking out the window into the blackness of the night, "will it ever stop?"

We watched the rain in silence for a few minutes and then she turned and went over to the sink. "More coffee?" she asked. I stood nearby and shook my head, unable to take my eyes away from the knot tied across her flat stomach and from the rising-swelling breasts above. All I have to do is give a yank, I thought, and everything is laid bare.

Perhaps she was reading my thoughts, or maybe they were showing plainly on my face, for she set her cup aside now and turned to me, standing erect, close to me, her eyes closed and her mouth halfway open.

I kissed her, just as I had kissed her on the beach in the rain, and her mouth was like soft, sweet honey. I was inflamed, all on fire. Her arms were about my neck and with a scooping motion I lifted her and carried her like a bride into the back room.

"Oh," she said, "this is it, isn't it? The moment, the one you wait for all your life."

I thought I would burst, explode. I laid her on the little bed and she was malleable, willing to be shaped and bent in my hands any way I wanted, like clay. I reached inside her robe and touched her; she let out a small cry of pleasure, and her body shook and trembled.

I had pictured this scene with Rena so many times, I had written it in the pages of my mind over and over so that now, when it was within my grasp, the Supreme Moment had arrived, I had trouble believing it was real and not a dream. For nearly a year now I had waited for this. We had gone together since last year, and had come close several times but always stopped short, sometimes coming tantalizingly close; many times we had made each other come with our rubbing and touching, and had spent hours kissing and petting, with me fumbling for her buttons and zippers, and, as time went on, able to remove first one piece of clothing and then another, like a long drawn out strip-poker game, each time getting a step closer to my eventual destination, taking the Big Prize of her virginity. And now, with her supine and yielding to my passion and caresses, willing to let me at long last, I was caught up in the most unwelcome way with a burst of conscience. Her robe slipped off her shoulders and she was naked in the darkness, sighing, her body arching just slightly with her want. I touched her again. Could I take advantage of her now? Did I want to do something that might cause her more grief?

"Pete," she murmured, "Pete, what is it, where are you?"

"I'm here."

"Come here, come to me, now, oh please now."

"Maybe we shouldn't..."

"We should, we should."

"Maybe not."

Her eyes opened now and she looked at me hard. "Come on," she said.

"I can't."

"What's the matter?"

"Nothing's the matter, I just don't think we should right now."

"Don't be silly."

"I'm not."

She saw now that I was serious and she pulled the robe back up about her shoulders.

"So you don't want me either," she said.

"It isn't that."

"What is it then?"

"It just wouldn't be right, right now."

"Oh, perfect," she said.

And then she covered her face with her hands and began to cry. She bawled and sobbed and carried on, then got up and went into the other room and put her still wet clothes back on. When she came out, she demanded angrily that I take her home right then.

She refused to speak a word all the way back to her house but sat so she was turned away from me, looking out the side window with her back my way, her hands tightly folded in her lap.

"Rena," I said. "Don't go like this."

She turned and looked at me sadly, and opened her mouth as if to say something soft. Then her anger came back, and she took off the necklace I had given her, the one with the Runestone_Sowleu on it, and flung it at me. "Here," she said, "take this back, I don't want it anymore."

"Rena," I said.

"Oh," she said, "just forget it."

She opened the door and went out, running across the walkway all the way to the door and then going inside.

Out of the spark shall come the inferno, and out of the darkness will come the children, dressed in white and wearing wings that flutter weakly as they reach for the sun.

Chapter 18

On the Dock

There was a letup in the rain soon after that. The fog lifted, the sun came out and shone brightly. I took a chair from the office and sat in the sunshine, letting it flow all over me, as if it had some power to heal, to take away all the doubt and confusion I felt inside. I sat, serenely, my eyes closed, dozing a little and feeling as I always did the gentle rock from the water and listening to the lapping of the waves on the barnacle-covered pilings, and felt, for a moment at least, something that resembled peace. I heard a seagull squawk high above me, then an angry shout that seemed at first to come from far away.

I opened my eyes lazily, and beheld, with a sudden and quickening sense of alarm, Rudy's big bulk raging down the gangplank. His fists were clenched and his face, so handsome and chiseled and square-jawed, was set into long angry lines. He gave a loud animal cry of rage and sprang like a tiger. I saw the danger coming, but he was so quick I barely had time to stand up and wasn't able to even start to duck my head or raise my hands before one of his fists crashed jarringly into my eye. As the eye immediately began to swell and throb he turned into an octopus, he grew a hundred arms, belting me in the stomach and the mouth at the same time, and I experienced the salty taste of my own blood.

"What the hell do you think you're doing?" Denny yelled bravely from the door of the office. "Stop it and get out of here, you Nazi bastard!"

"Hah!" Rudy yelled back righteously, standing over me and swinging his fists, for the last blow had spun me about and I'd gone down onto the wet gray wood of the dock. "This is vhat he gets! For doing the things he is doing!"

"I'll call the police!" Denny threatened, still in the doorway and ready to retreat inside and slam and lock the door if Rudy decided to come after *him*.

"Go ahead and call them, see if I care anyway!"

I thought that somehow I must get up. The dock was unsteady beneath me, my legs weren't working properly, but I had to get up. Rudy saw me struggling to my feet and he let out a joyous whoop, rushing at me again, his big fists flailing. We grappled, then he got me in a headlock, and started dragging me toward the edge of the dock.

"Now I throw you in the vater, let the sharks eat you, you dirty dirty bastard!" he cried. Blood was rushing to my head as his arm squeezed into the side of my neck. I could hear Denny yelling "Get him, Pete! Hit him back!" and I saw that in another second or two I was going to be heaved ignominiously into that cold choppy water, and somehow I had to get free.

I reached up and around with my left hand, making a claw of my fingers, and coming down over Rudy's long aristocratic nose hooked him and pulled hard as I could. He cried out in surprise, his head going back, and I twisted loose. At the same time I struck out, open-handed, hitting him the way Tom had shown me. I saw blood and kept on hitting. Rudy went backward, and fell over a small pile of wooden boxes, then crashed into the wall of the office, going down and staying there, bleeding badly, holding his hands out in front of him.

"All right!" Denny whooped. "Way to go, Pete! You showed him! That's the way! Get up and fight, you big bastard! Hit him again, Pete!

Kick his ass. Yee-haw!" He swung his fists and cavorted about, jumping up and down.

But I had no desire to hit him again and Rudy had no desire to get up and fight. I sat down on one of the barrels, my lips cut and bleeding, my eye throbbing and nearly swollen shut. Rudy stayed where he was, blood flowing steadily from his nose. From inside the office came the sound of the radio Denny had been listening to playing a song by the Beach Boys: *"Wouldn't it be nice if we were older/And we wouldn't have to wait so long/And wouldn't it be nice to live together/In the kind of world where we belong."*

For a moment no one spoke. Rudy and I sat there bleeding. Denny looked first at me, then at Rudy, his mouth open. Then Rudy croaked, "All I vant is for you to stay away from her."

"Well, he doesn't have to stay away from anybody!" Denny cried. "He can see her if he wants to. Right, Pete?"

"Oh, shut up," Rudy said, his hand still to his nose. "I am not talking to you. This has nothing to do with you only him, see? And I am no Nazi. I was only a small boy when that happened and I didn't know nothing about it, so please do not call me that anymore. He would you like it if people call you names for something that happened when you were a little kid?" He scooped more blood away, then asked, "Do you have some tissues or anything? This is getting all over me."

"There's some paper towels inside," Denny offered. "Tilt your head back, that'll help stop the blood."

He went in the office and came back a second later with his hands full of wet paper towels. He gave some to me and the rest of Rudy, who wiped his face off and then applied them to his nose, which was by now badly swollen. I dabbed at my mouth, looking curiously at the blood that came away.

"She was saying all dese things," Rudy said. "Saying how you are so much better with her than me, for she has a tongue of burning coals, that woman. At last I could stand it no more, and I say, 'I will go over there and teach that boy a lesson,' and so I came here looking for you. But I know the fault is not yours. It is her, and I think I have had enough. I think I will go back home to Europe soon, for that is where I belong. California is a crazy place, with many crazy people, and if I stay here I will become crazy like they are."

"You want a beer?" Denny offered.

"Yes, I vould like a beer."

Denny got three bottles of beer from the refrigerator and we sat and drank them, Rudy and I still nursing our wounds.

"Women are nothing but a great deal of trouble for men," Rudy declared. "This one has caused me only misery since I met her, even though she is very beautiful and I have always liked American women. From now on I think I go only to prostitutes. I do not think I will ever have one living with me again but will only live alone."

"Well, I don't know about anybody else, but I know one thing about me," Denny said smugly. "I'm acquainted with one really lucky guy and that man is me. You know why? Because I am hooked up with one of the best girls alive. Tiffany's her name. Want to see her picture?" Without waiting for an answer Denny dug into his wallet and showed a toothie-blond snapshot of Tiffany, the one he liked best and showed most often to people, the one of Tiffany standing sexily in her backyard, hands on her hips and her body thrust forward. "See what I mean?" Denny asked. "That's her."

"She is lovely," Rudy admitted, looking at the picture critically. "That is very lucky for you. She is a nice girl, you say?"

"Oh, the nicest," said Denny, and I did my best not to choke on the beer I was drinking.

"You are going to marry her?" asked Rudy.

"Oh, hell yes," said Denny. "I love her, with all my heart."

"Well, good luck," Rudy said. "I hope it will all work out for you the way it should. I have never seen too many happy marriages myself but they do happen sometimes, I think. Screw them but do not marry them, that is going to be my motto concerning women from now on."

He drank the rest of his beer with gusto, smacking his lips. "There is nothing like beer," he said. "I think beer will fix everything." He stood up, then put out his hand. "We should shake hands now, don't you think?

I think we are even and none of those hard feelings, yes?"

"Okay," I said, and he and I shook hands. Denny stepped forward and shook hands too, and then Rudy went off, back up the gangplank, still holding one of the bloody towels to his nose.

"That's the greatest thing I ever saw in my life," Denny declared, wringing my hand like he never wanted to let it go. "I can't wait till Tom hears about this. He won't believe it! Is he ever gonna be pissed he didn't see it, man did he ever miss out! God, I'm proud of you, Pete. You really whipped his ass. I never would have thought you could do it."

"You didn't?"

"Oh, hell no. Although it's really too bad you and him had to fight, because he's actually a pretty nice guy, once you get to know him." He took a step away and eyeballed me knowingly. "Who did you think you were fooling, Pete? It was just like I said, wasn't it? About you and that woman with the red hair? I knew it all along, I had that one scoped out, didn't I? 'Oh no,' you used to say, 'I'm just taking this book over there to her, I'm only going over there to read poetry, all we did was sit and talk.' What a liar you are!"

"Mind your own business, I told you," I said, speaking out of my swollen mouth, which was by now, like my eye, becoming very tender.

"Okay," he grinned. "Okay, I will. But just tell me this: Are you going to keep on seeing her?"

"I don't know," I replied, touching my eye gently. "I really don't know."

Overhead a seagull squawked, and a cloud was passing in front of the sun.

"Wait till Tom hears about this," said Denny.

•   •   •

Tom's reaction was one thing—what my father thought was another.

"Look at you!" he snarled.

He had just gotten home from work and appeared to be in his usual unhappy mood. He rubbed his temples with both hands, glaring at me.

"When are you going to learn you can't settle everything with your fists?" he roared.

"Yeah," Darren put in. "When will you learn?"

"Going around fighting like a kid," George said, bringing his hands up and rubbing them together in the old familiar washing motion. "When are you going to grow up?"

"When will you grow up?" Darren echoed.

"This guy hit me first!" I said defensively.

"You probably asked for it!" George declared. We were standing in the center of the living room. "You smart ass. You wouldn't last long in the service," he declared, "you're such a damn misfit and smart ass. Don't you know," he bellowed, "you're going to have to live in society? You and that stupid surfboard."

"Society," I said. "You and your society. What's it ever done for anybody? It stinks, your society, and so do you, you leave a stench wherever you go."

His face turned red and his eyes bulged in their sockets. "You apologize for that!" he screamed.

I didn't say anything but just shook my head. But all the while I was looking him in the eye.

"You apologize!" he yelled again.

"No," I said.

He swung wildly, hitting me like he usually did with a two-knuckle blow to my upper arm. "Apologize!" he screamed insanely, and hit me again.

"Go to hell," I said, still looking him in the eye.

He roared incoherently, his face wild, and hit me another time.

There was silence for a moment. We stood staring at each other, George standing with his chest heaving, almost out of breath, almost hyperventilating.

Then I said, "Fuck yourself. And fuck your society too, it should be buried in a garbage dump, and you with it."

The scream that followed this was scarcely human. He swung wildly, his arm arcing in a long roundhouse. I blocked it, the way I had been practicing, with an upward block that knocked his arm back. This hurt him, I could see from the look on his face, but the surprise was even greater. He swung again, and again I blocked it. I smiled at him and he swung with the other arm and I blocked that one too. For an instant we stared at each other. Then I shoved him. He moved backwards and I shoved him again. Then I took him by the collar and pushed him back until he hit the wall. I heard Laurie-Ann let out a screech as some of her prized china fell from a shelf onto the floor, crashing and bouncing, and she stood with her hands to her face.

George screamed again and grabbed for me with both hands, as if he meant to get me by the throat. I stepped into him, throwing my arms up and out, knocking his aside, then struck with my forehead the way Dave had shown me. George went backward again, crying out in pain and hitting the wall once more, even harder this time, and I hit his unprotected, soft stomach with reverse punch. He crumbled over and went down. I heard another screech from Laurie-Ann, and then from the corner of my eye I saw her smile.

George glared up at me, his face twisted with hate, as if to say, "All right, I'm licked. So what?"

"Why do you hate me?" I yelled. "Who was Pete?"

"What?"

"Who was Pete?" I repeated.

"He was my friend..."

"What happened to him? How did he die?"

He didn't answer so I grabbed him and shook him as hard as I could. "How did he die?"

"We were on advance patrol...Ran into some North Koreans... surprised us..."

"When? What day was it?"

"I don't remember..."

"Yes you do! It was the day I was born, wasn't it? Wasn't it?"

"Yes..."

"How did he die?"

"I tried to save him..."

"You're a liar! He saved you! You ran and he saved you! That's why you hate me, isn't it? It's true, isn't it? Isn't it?"

I was so hysterical by this point that I didn't know what I was doing. I had taken him by the collar again, stood him up, and was slamming him against the wall, over and over, all the while screaming "Isn't it?" All his resistance had faded away like a match burning down, he had no strength left.

I might have done him some serious injury, or even killed him at his point, but then a picture came into my mind. I saw another face now, the face of a younger man, not one red and bloated from drink but happy, laughing, coming home from work and scooping me up over his shoulder and carrying me around, saying, "What have I got here? A sack of potatoes, that's what this is, an old sack of potatoes." I had laughed and he had laughed and everybody was happy. What had happened, what had gone wrong? Where did that little boy go? Where had that young and happy man gone? Why had things changed? Too bad they were all gone, those people we used to be.

Abruptly I let him go. "A sack of potatoes," I said. It just came out.

"What?"

"Nothing," I said. Then he remembered. I could see it on his face. He knew what I meant.

"You," he said, and it was the last shovelful of dirt on the grave. "You."

"Yeah, me," I said back to him, sneering. "And you too."

So at last I knew the truth—Pete had saved his life, Pete deserved the award for bravery that George had taken the credit for. In some twisted way he had tried to extirpate his guilt by naming me after his friend. But every time he saw me he was reminded of what had happened and of what he had done, and so he had, in an equally twisted fashion, taken his guilt and shame out on me, hoping, perhaps, that he could escape from it that way. He had lived a lie, and the lie, like the ripples that come when a rock is dropped in clear water, had reached out and engulfed all those around him, muddying their lives just as he had muddied his own. There are some lies you just can't escape from, and the truth will follow you no matter how far you run or how deep you try to bury it.

Chapter 19

Over-Wound

I stayed away as long as I could, I didn't want to go home. I worked late and then stayed at the dock, wanting at all costs to avoid seeing my father anymore.

I went in my usual way, through the back gate, parking my van in the alley. Even in the moonlight I could see my oak tree and I looked at it like I always did, saying to myself, "Yes, it is growing, you just can't see it," but wishing all the same that it would grow faster. I wanted to see it sprout leaves, and sturdy limbs that hung out to the alley, I wanted to see its trunk thicken and get bigger and bigger until you couldn't get your arms all the way around it. Its roots would go deep into the ground so that it was almost permanent on this spot, the way a tall building's foundations are strong and securely laid. Nearby it, next to the fence, even though I couldn't see it in the dark, was the grave of the baby bird. The markers, the small twigs, were still there, sticking up out of the damp, leaf-covered ground, only noticeable if you were looking for them. I also saw where George had been working to shore up the house's sagging foundations, for the wheelbarrow was still sitting there, along with a shovel and hoe and some half-empty bags of concrete and sand.

When I went inside I saw with some relief that George wasn't around. Darren wasn't home either. Laurie-Ann sat in front of the television getting drunk. She didn't drink as much as George did, as a general rule, but tonight she was really putting it away. She was sitting in her chair smoking and drinking, wearing one of her low-cut tops and short skirts, looking sullen, drinking steadily and determinedly, as if she were drinking to get revenge on someone.

"Where is everybody?" I asked.

Her features when she answered, were all drawn into an angry-frozen expression behind all the makeup she had on. "Where is who?" she replied sullenly.

"Oh," I said, "the other people who live here. Dad, and the other guy, my brother, Darren, I think his name is."

She snorted, drank from her glass of gin, and lit another cigarette from the one she was smoking.

"Your brother," she pronounced, "is spending the night at Gary Doolittle's."

"I guess that's a good place for him to spend the night," I said, "if he's going to spend the night anywhere."

"What do you mean by that?" she asked.

"Nothing."

"Oh yes, you did."

"No. I didn't mean anything."

"I think you did!" she almost yelled. Then she settled back in her chair, staring vacantly at the television.

"And Dad? Where is Dad?"

"Huh?" she replied.

"Dad?" I persisted. "You remember him, don't you? Comes here to sleep here every night."

"Oh," she said. "Your father. You want to know where your father is, don't you?"

"That's the general idea."

"He isn't here."

"Do tell," I said.

"He," she stated, "has gone away."

"Where did he go? Can you tell me or is it a state secret?"

"Hunting," she spat. "He went on a hunting trip. With some of the boys. You know. The ones he goes to the bars with. He came home. Got his rifle. Then left. That's all. He won't be home for a few days. After all, it's the holiday season. Now do you unnerstan'? Where your father is? He isn't here, is he?"

"I guess not."

"So now you unnerstan'," she said again, taking another drink. The bottle, I saw, which had been nearly full the last time I saw it was a long ways down. "You can see now, can't you see?"

"Sure," I said.

She took another drink and stared, red-eyed, at me. "He isn't here," she said once more. "He just left. And I'm sitting here. Right here. He just left me here. Twenty-two years of this," she declared, as if that was a revelation from on high. "Twenty-two years I've had this. Tha's a long time, isn't it?"

"I guess it is."

"Too goddamn long. One of these days I'll show him. I didn't have to marry him, I had plenty of other offers. I was doing him a favor, now look at what he does to me. Don't you think I'll show him?"

She sat, mumbling drunkenly to herself, saying she was going to teach him a lesson one day and it wouldn't be too goddamn long, either.

"You want a drink?" she asked me.

"No."

"It's okay, you can have a drink with me. Go ahead and smoke, too. I know you smoke, you don't need to hide it from me, I can smell it in your bedroom and I can see the pack in your pocket right now, so there's no sense in pretending. I don't care. You're almost a man now. You're getting to be so grown up. I know you don't like your poor, old mother too much but you could have a drink with her, couldn't you?"

"No," I said again. "I think I'll go to bed now."

"You don't want to sit here and keep your poor old mother company, do you?" she said. She reached over and held my hand, girlishly, but I took my hand away.

"What's a matter?" she asked. "I'm your mother. Isn't it all right for your poor old mother to pat her little boy on the hand? Your poor, old mother," she said again, as if it were a line from scripture. She drank some more and looked right at me, her eyes dull with drink. "You were so tiny, I held you when you were so tiny, so little, and now you're so big, and you don't like your poor, old mother."

"I'm tired," I said.

"I'm old," she went on. "No one likes me because I'm old. Only Darren, 'cause he's my baby. But he won't always. No, he'll grow up and forget about me just like you."

"I'm going to bed," I told her.

"Tired of your poor old mother's company?"

"No," I said. "Just tired."

I went to my room, closing the door and being careful to lock it, and lay down on my bed. I looked up at the crack in the ceiling, for it looked as if it was getting bigger everyday. I felt the soreness now that seemed to be all over me, from Rudy and my father, every part of me hurt. Maybe I should have taken that drink. That always seemed to ease the pain. Get drunk and block it out and by tomorrow it won't seem so bad. That was the way to do it, that was the way they did it, wasn't it? Just get drunk and forget about it, that was the way.

I picked up my little green Bible-book, the one I hardly ever looked at anymore. Too bad I'd left all that behind. Too bad I'd lost the light. It was a bad thing to lose the light, what were you to do then? Where was I to go, where was I to turn? I didn't know. I was lost. I am lost, I said to myself, and inside I felt very empty.

Just then there was a knock on my door.

"What?" I called from my bed.

"Can I come in?"

"You want something, Mother?"

"Lemme in, I want to ask you something."

Reluctantly I unlocked the door and she came in, seating herself on the edge of my bed. She swayed, as if she had trouble sitting up without assistance, and began patting my feet affectionately. Then she took my toes in her fingers and began playing with them, saying, "This little piggy went to market, this little piggy stayed home," squeezing and shaking them, her breasts flouncing all around wildly.

"What is it you want?" I asked, drawing my feet away.

"Oh, I don't know, exactly," she slurred, reaching determinedly for my feet once again. "I don't wanna bother you," she said.

"Well, what is it?" I asked.

She didn't answer. She had hold of my feet again and started to play with them once more.

"Mother," I said, "you said you wanted something."

"Huh?" she said. "Oh. Yes. I just wondered. I wondered about that girl you used to go with, what was her name, Rena. The one you went to the prom with last year. How come you never see her anymore? Did she break up with you? Or did you break up with her?"

"You came in here now to ask me that?"

"Do you see her anymore? I just wondered. What happened? Because I just want to know."

"No," I said, hoping she would leave. "I don't see her anymore."

But she didn't leave. She remained on my bed, just sitting there and not leaving.

"Don't you have any other girlfriends?" she asked after a while of sitting there and not leaving.

"Why do you want to know that now?"

"Do you?" she persisted.

"No."

"Not even one? Ho-ho. I wish I were younger and not so old. You know why? Then I could be your girlfriend. Wouldn't you like that? I'll bet you would like that. Then I could show your father something. I could be your girlfriend and you could take me to the Senior Prom and the Homecoming Dance, and we could have lots of fun together. Couldn't we? Because boys are supposed to think their mothers are beautiful, and take them dancing, and do everything for them, but you won't do that, any of that, not with me, not you, oh no."

Now she fell over, flopping down on the bed beside me. I waited for her to get up but she didn't move, she stayed there, and I could hear her breathing beside me. I thought she had passed out, she didn't move for so long. Now this is just great, I thought. What am I going to do if she stays here all night? But then she stirred, and I could tell she was awake still. She reached over and took my hand and pulled it over to her. I pulled away, and said, "Don't."

"But I want you to touch me," she giggled.

"Will you just leave?"

"I want to stay here with you," she said plaintively. "It's okay for me to be in here with you. I'm your mother. It's okay. Here. I'll show you." She turned over so she was facing me now, and made as if to get under the blankets with me.

"Let me in," she said, giggling again.

"Mother," I said, "go on, I want to go to sleep now, I'm tired. I want you to get out of my bedroom now."

"Why? I'm not doing anything wrong. I'm your mother. It's all right for me to be in here with my boy."

She tried to put her arms around me. I pushed at her, but I was afraid if I pushed too hard she would fall onto the floor and hurt herself.

"I just want to see how my boy is, that's all," she said, giggling. "I just want to see how he is." She reached under the blankets now, her hand creeping down like a spider descending.

"Don't!" I yelled, pushing at her again. "Stop it!"

She sat up, chuckling and swaying back and forth. "Ha-ha-ha! I know you really want me to touch you, you just won't admit it."

"Get out," I said.

She only laughed and stayed where she was. "I won't go," she said. "I won't. Not till you tell me. Not till I see, not till you let me see," she said. "I want to know," she went on, her voice trailing off. "Have you ever," she said, and paused. "What I mean," she said, and paused again. "What I want to know," she said, and paused. "This is it," she said. "What I want to know, is, is, is my boy a virgin still? Is he? I only want to know."

I covered my face with the blanket. "Get out!" I yelled. "Go away, please, just go away now, Mother."

She laughed and got up at last, and as soon as she was gone I locked the door, vowing not to open it again no matter what. I heard her go down the hallway and back to the den to fix herself another drink. A few minutes passed by in silence. I hoped she would pass out. But just when I thought I could relax she was at my door again. She knocked, and when I didn't answer she tried the knob. Finding it locked, she began knocking once more.

"Are you in there?" she yelled. "This is your mother! You open this door right now! Do you hear me? You open this door! I want to talk to you! Open it up or I'll get your father!"

When I wouldn't open the door or answer her she began to pound, so that the door buckled and jolted. She gave this up after a short time, though, and kept on yelling.

"Open this door! You open it right now! Do you know what your father is going to do to you when he hears about this? Are you ever going to be sorry when I tell him, oh, you just wait! You'll be sorry.

"All right," she said after this had gone on for about ten minutes and she was out of breath. "If that's the way you want it, all right. I'm going to tell your father about this.

"You don't fool me," she called. "You want to see your mother naked. I know you do. I'm taking my clothes off now. Won't you open the door and see that? Come on, look at your mother. Don't you want to see your mother this way?"

She began pounding and hitting at the door again, and in between hits she described each article of clothing as she took it off. "I'm taking off my skirt now," she said, "don't you want to see? Now I'm taking off my bra, do you want to see my titties?" Then she became angry again, and once more began to beat on the door, demanding I let her in. "You open up! I want to talk to you! Open this door!"

I don't know how long this went on. I lay in my bed, smoking one cigarette after another, staring at the ceiling. She would pound on the door and then stop for a few minutes, and just when I thought she had given up or maybe passed out she would start up again, pounding and kicking at the door. She became hysterical, going on and on.

Finally, mercifully, she went away. I heard her unsteady footsteps on the old wooden floor of this part of the house. Then I heard her talking on the telephone, speaking in loud, drunken tones. I couldn't make out what she was saying but a look at the clock told me it was past midnight and a funny time to be calling anybody. I lay in my bed feeling scared and not knowing what to do. The talking stopped, but I didn't dare go out and see what was going on. I kept hoping she would pass out, but I'd hear her walking around.

When another hour had gone by I opened my door and peeped out. The house was all dark, every light was shut off. Good, I thought. She laid down and crashed, finally. But who the hell was she talking to? Just then the phone rang, startling the hell out of me. A light popped on in the living room and I saw she had been sitting on the couch. She answered on the first ring and spoke quietly this time before hanging up, unaware that I was nearby. She rose, went to her room, and emerged wearing a coat and high heels. She clomped drunkenly down the hallway and went out the back door. I heard, in the stillness of the night, the garage door open, and her El Dorado start up. She didn't bother to warm it but backed out of the garage right away. The engine died, once, and she restarted it, and I heard it lurch away down the alley.

When I was certain she was gone I went to the liquor cabinet and poured myself a drink of scotch, thinking it would help calm my nerves and maybe now I could get some sleep. But it wasn't any use. I couldn't sleep. I went back to bed and lay there the rest of the night, just dozing sometimes, seeing it become eventually lighter outside and watching as the sun came up. My mother didn't come back. At last I rolled out of bed, feeling like I'd been through a war, about as over-wound as I could be, fixed myself some coffee and realized it was Saturday, and I had to be at work at seven am and work all day long.

•   •   •

I couldn't go home, no, the thought of going home made me feel sick inside. When I got off work in the afternoon I went, aimlessly, downtown and walked out on the pier. The wind was blowing, a cold raw wind that picked up speed when it hit the water and then blew up, burning the skin of my face. I buried my hands in the pockets of my black navy peacoat and turned my back to the wind, listening to the waves crashing. The water was gray, with dirty white caps on it.

There weren't many people on the pier but I noticed a figure nearby, clad like me in a heavy jacket and wearing a ski cap, leaning on the railing and looking at the water. She noticed me at the same time I saw her, gave a start and a double take, and came right over.

"Oh!" she said. "Pete! Your face! What happened to you?"

"Doesn't matter," I said. I hadn't seen Rena since that night she'd acted so strangely on the beach and had thrown my Sowelu necklace at me. "I'm glad to see you. Where've you been?"

"Look what I found," she said, standing before me now. "I was going through some stuff today and I found it. Look." She handed over a picture, a three by five snapshot, which I held in my hands and looked at carefully.

"Do you remember?" she asked.

"Sure, 'course I remember, who couldn't remember that?"

She didn't look the same now as she had then, for this picture was taken last year when she and I had gone to the prom together, and she was dressed in a formal gown and smiling, her hair all expensively done up. The light was out of her eyes, the light that sunny light that had always been there before, it was gone now, just as surely as a bulb shutting down it wasn't there.

And the boy I saw in the picture didn't have much to do with the guy holding the photo. He was smiling as if he didn't have a care in the world, standing there all black-tied and uncomfortable in these formal clothes but still happy. This isn't me, I said to myself, or if it is it is a part of me that is long gone.

"It seems like so long ago, doesn't it?" Rena asked.

"Ages ago," I agreed.

"I've been looking all over for you," Rena said. "I kept calling your house but there's never anybody there. Once I got your mother but she sounded so drunk she didn't make any sense when she talked."

"She's on a bender," I said. "Why have you been looking for me?"

"There's something I have to tell you."

"What is it?"

"I did such a stupid thing," she said, "when I got mad and gave that necklace back to you. I've cried so many times because I wish I hadn't done that."

"That's something that can be fixed, easy enough," I said, unfastening the hook that was around my neck and placing it on hers. She was very grateful for this, and thanked me over and over, feeling the smooth Runestone with her fingers.

"Oh, I'm so glad," she said, "so glad to have this back. Will you always be my friend, Pete?"

"I told you that a long time ago."

"No matter what?" she pressed.

"Yeah, sure."

"Oh," she said with sudden anguish, "it isn't fair of me to ask you that. Not fair at all, because you don't know."

"What don't I know?"

"You said you love me--do you still?"

"Yes," I said. "I told you that night at the church that part of this—" I pointed to my heart--"will always be yours, as much of it as you want to claim."

Rena's nose ran and she sniffed and wiped at it with her fingers. She looked at me, then past me, out at the rough choppy water.

"You remember that night in the rain?" she asked. She fingered the Runestone nervously, still looking past me at the water, the wind blowing in her face. She tugged the edges of her cap, pulling it down lower. "I wanted to tell you a story that night, but I couldn't bring myself to do it. So I'm going to tell you now and if you don't want to be my friend after, and if you don't love me after, I'll understand, Pete, I will understand."

I felt a kind of vague dread welling up inside, an anxiety in my stomach, something telling me that maybe I didn't want to hear this. But I was going to hear it no matter what, Fate was holding me fast to this spot, and sometimes there are things you can't walk away from.

"For a long time," she began, "I don't really know how long, there's been this problem with my stepfather."

"What sort of a problem?"

"He keeps on touching me in places where he shouldn't touch me—he grabs my breasts, he tries to touch me down here. He always pretended he was playing, or tickling me, but I knew after a while that it wasn't playing. And then he started to go further, and got bolder.

"And it always happens when my mother isn't home. He never does it when she's there. And for the past year or so she's been working at the Captain's Inn at the Marina, working late, sometimes she isn't home until two or three in the morning. I'd go to bed and Spiro would get drunk and come into my bedroom. It was awful, there's no lock on my door. He would come in there and I'd have to fight him off. One night he ripped my nightgown, just tore it, and I told my mother it got caught on something and that's how it ripped."

"Why don't you tell her what the bastard is doing?" I said.

"I tried," she said. "I tried and tried, Pete. But she would never listen. I couldn't bring myself to tell her directly until about three months ago. Spiro got real drunk one night and came in my room and I couldn't fight him off. He kept grabbing me and finally he got my nightgown off and threw me on the bed..."

"Oh God," I said.

"He didn't really rape me," Rena said. "He got on top of me and humped on me until he came in his pants. So I told, I told my mother."

"What did she do?"

"She slapped me. She slapped me and said it was a lie. She said if anything happened it was my fault, I was probably acting like a slut, and she said didn't want to hear about it anymore.

"So I decided the only thing to do was never be home with him. That's when I started to go to church all the time, and stay late, so I wouldn't have to be home. That gave me some place to go. You see, he always gets so drunk he passes out by midnight or one o'clock, so it was safe then. So I went to church and stayed there, and by the time I got home he was always asleep and wouldn't bother me."

"Pretty smart," I said, feeling some relief now, thinking this is bad but not that bad, I was afraid it might be a lot worse. But then I looked into Rena's pretty eyes and realized there was more to come.

"That's one of the reasons I loved the church so much," she said. "That, and because I liked what we did there. Oh, Pete, I was so happy when we were there together, how come you stopped coming? None of this would have happened if you'd been there."

"What wouldn't have happened?" I asked, the dread welling up inside of me once more.

"Do you know what it's like to feel trapped, like there's no escape? That's how I felt. At the church. I was alone there, after you stopped coming, with him, with him, and he would ask me what was wrong, because I was crying all the time. He started to hold me, and say to me things were going to be all right. I told it all to him, about you, about Spiro, my mother, everything, and he said for me not to cry.

"Then one night," she went on, and her face looked as if all the feeling had been drained out of it, "one night he started holding me differently."

"Who did?"

"He held me differently, and he started kissing me--"

"My God," I said.

"...And he said, he said, he wished I could stay there all night."

I stared at her now, all the dread I felt inside cracking open, like a tumor, all the poison flowing out.

"So what happened?" I said at last, but I already knew, and then there was a voice inside saying, "You don't want to know."

"I was frozen," Rena said. "I never in a million years would have thought Reverend Jim felt that way. I looked up to him, I thought he was the greatest man I ever met. I thought it must be a nightmare. Have you ever had that happen to you, Pete, something so bad, so unbelievable, that you say to yourself, 'This can't be real, I'm going to wake up any moment now?' That's what I felt. Oh, wait, Pete, don't turn away, I've got to tell you everything now," she pleaded, tugging at me, and I realized that unconsciously I had turned sideways, maybe to try and block out the rest, what I knew was coming next, letting the wind roar in my ears. "I have to finish," she said. "I've got to now, since I've started. And then I'm done. And then when I'm done, if you never want to see me again I'll understand, it'll be ok, see?"

"Okay," I said numbly. "All right. Go ahead."

"Can't you guess the rest?" she asked.

"Yes, I can guess."

"But do you see how it is?" she said, suddenly pleading. "Do you see why I had to let him do it? I didn't want to lose the church. I had no place else to go, I didn't want to go home, I couldn't go home. So it was him or Spiro, and I chose him. Do you have any idea what that's like, to feel trapped that way?"

"So," I said, still numb, "is it still going on?"

"I can't do anything about it," Rena said, in a wooden tone. I felt that she was shutting off her emotions, or trying to, but they kept coming back, in surges, wracking her. "It's like I'm his slave. When he comes for me, when he touches me, I fall to pieces inside, I say to myself, "No, not again," but I can't stop it, I can't. And I don't feel anything after that, it's like I become a robot, and it's really very interesting because I notice now that I go someplace else, it's like I'm not there, I black out, sort of.

"He says I'm sent by Satan, that I'm a temptation he has to overcome. Sometimes I believe it myself, even though in my heart I don't really think it's true, but I do blame myself, I hate myself, sometimes, for all of this. I really do, and I'll wish I was dead and sometimes I say I'm going to kill myself, but I haven't done it or tried it yet."

We were quiet now. The numb feeling passed and a sick feeling grew and I felt it was overwhelming me. I wanted to cry, and I wanted to scream in agony too. I feared I might explode if I heard anymore.

"Well," Rena said at last, "that's the story. What do you think of it?" Her face was set and she didn't look at me but looked out at the water, he face round with the ski cap on her head. "Well, Pete, what do you think?"

she said again.

"That night," I said, "that night in the rain--"

"That was a very bad night, I think I would have killed myself if you hadn't been there," she said. "Some nights are worse than others." She smiled sadly. "It's really some story, isn't it? Too bad they never write books or make movies out of stories like that. I'm caught in a trap, I'm like a fly in a spider's web. Wasn't there a song, by Elvis Presley, called that? How did it go, I can't remember. 'I'm caught in a trap, I can't walk out.' Wasn't that how it went? I wish I could remember the rest of the words because—"

"Oh for Christ's sake shut up!" I yelled.

"Do you want this back?" she asked, holding out the Sowelu necklace.

I didn't answer but looked away, at the cold water below.

"Do you?" Rena persisted. "Do you want it back, Pete? I wouldn't blame you if you did. You wouldn't want somebody like me to have it. You could find somebody nice to give it to, somebody who isn't like me."

"No," I said, "no, I want you to keep it. I still have the ring you gave me."

I held up the aqua ring she had given me. Rena and I both stared at it. Then all her control cracked and the tears burst forth. "I have to go," she said. "I have to go to the church—to him! Goodbye, Pete. I'll never forget you."

I couldn't bring myself to say goodbye and I just kept watching her as she turned away and went the way she'd come, toward Main Street. I watched her go, watched her walking alongside the cold metal railing of the pier and then descending down the stairs that go to the beach, out of sight, and then I turned away.

I felt like a circuit pushed all the way to overload. I was all churned up inside, as if there was a typhoon going on in there, but I didn't know how to let it out. All my capacitors and diodes were ready to explode, they couldn't stand anymore. One more straw, I thought, and the camel's back will break.

I walked, blindly in the wind, my hands unfeelingly skimming the round metal railing as I walked and kept walking until I came to the very end of the pier and stood looking at the endless expanse of water. The pier shook underneath me when a wave lashed the pilings. I looked out for Catalina but there was no sign of it, the day was too cloudy and overcast. I stood beneath a lamppost, watching the declining sun and the choppy water. In less than an hour it would be dark.

Now I noticed my hands were gripping the railing so hard my knuckles were white, and when I let go there were imprints and rust on my palms. I straightened my fingers painfully, for they were cold and red from the raw wind. I wished, right then, I could scream, just scream as loud as I could, scream in pain and let out all the agony I felt. Below me the water swirled about the pilings, swirling gray and white, looking dirty as well as cold, and the wind kept whipping at my face. I dug out a cigarette and lit it, wishing I had a drink, a drink of anything, I didn't care what. I'll get drunk tonight, I promised myself, good and drunk, I'll get lying down stinking drunk, wait and see, that's what I'll do, I'll show them, I'll show them all.

Up above me a seagull squawked, and I saw it perched regally on a lamppost. Did a seagull feel anything like I was feeling? Now I wished I could cry, but I couldn't do that either, and I kept staring down at the water. Each wave seemed to beckon to me, the white caps were like pillows to, calling me to come and lie down on them. The pier rocked slightly again from the agitation of the water. What would happen if the pier collapsed? It's old, been here many years, what if it all just fell apart? What if everything fell apart? Everything in the whole world? What if the world itself fell apart? Wouldn't that be a shame. Wouldn't that just be a shame. You keep hoping things will get better but the truth is they just keep on getting worse. They all lie, you can't trust any of them. So what is the good in any of it? Being alive is hard, it hurts, it's pain after pain after pain...Below me the water bubbled, like the liquid in a witch's cauldron.

Above me the seagull let out another loud squawk. I didn't look up. He squawked again. When I looked he left his perch on the rounded part of the lamppost and floated effortlessly on an air current, just spreading his wings and letting himself go. The wind carried him nowhere in a gentle fashion, and he squawked once more, looking right at me now, going in circles, small and easy, around and around, all the while looking right at me, as if he wanted to be sure I understood. He made this circle four or five times, and I never took my eye off him because I knew that he, like the voices I heard sometimes, was trying to tell me something important. Then he flapped his wings in long, languid motions, and flew off to join a big flock of seagulls high above.

I heard a voice behind me, calling my name. I saw Tom coming toward me. He was smiling, but I could tell from his stride he wasn't a whole lot happier than I was.

"Beautiful," he said, surveying my battle scars diligently. "Beautiful! I've never seen a better shiner than that. Wow! Denny told me about it but I thought he had to be exaggerating. That German dude really busted you one, didn't he? But Denny says you kicked his ass. And just think, you had that squeeze going with that lady with the red hair all this time and you never told me. How come you never told me about it, Pete? I never knew you liked older women."

"I just couldn't," I said. "I didn't think you'd believe me. There were times when I couldn't believe it myself."

"You can't get much realer than this," he said, with a sober examination of my wounds. "But if you want to dance you gotta pay the fucking piper. One way or another, you gotta pay. I know. That's philosophy. I read it in a book once."

"When did you ever read a book?"

"I read plenty of books," he insisted.

"What brings you out here?" I asked.

"Oh, man," he said, shaking his head and leaning both elbows on the railing. "It's cold out here," he observed. "Too damn cold. What are you trying to do? Freeze yourself? What a life this is," he declared. "This is some fucking life, you know that?"

"It sucks," I agreed. "It really sucks, from one end to the other."

Tom looked about quickly. There weren't many people on the pier and those that were there were mostly fishing and looking morosely at the water. Tom reached into the pocket of his jacket and produced a dark pint bottle. "This'll warm us up," he smiled. "I liberated it from Neal's liquor cabinet today when he wasn't looking. Can you believe the bastard's been locking it up lately? He thinks I steal from it."

"Now why in the hell would he think that?" I said, thankfully taking a drink. Just what I need, I thought gratefully, and the fiery liquid burned going down, burning away some of the pain I felt.

"Just because a bottle is missing once in a while," Tom said unreasonably. "That's no reason for him not to trust me. He can't prove I steal from it. He just thinks I do, but he can't prove it."

"Doesn't he count and measure everything?" I asked, drinking again. "That's what my mother does."

"Sure he does," Tom said stubbornly. "But does that prove it?"

"Oh, for God's sake," I said. "Gimme another drink."

"Okay, one more to take the chill off and that's it, we'll save this because it's good stuff. Nothing but the best for Uncle Neal, you know."

He took another drink and put the flat bottle back into his jacket. He looked mystically out at the ocean, gray and choppy as it was, as if he could see all the way to the end of it. "I keep asking myself why I'm here," he said.

"You mean, why you're alive?"

"No. I have asked myself that, plenty of times, but I what I mean is, why am I here, in this town, living with those two plastic fakes? I can't stand it, Pete, I really can't. So I keep on asking myself, what I am doing here? Why am I doing this? So I can graduate from high school next June? What the hell do I care about that? I don't plan on going to any damn college. You can have all that college bullshit. There's a whole world out there, man, and I want to see it. I want to see all those places we've talked about--Hawaii, Fiji, Australia, New Zealand. What's that book you tell me about sometimes, where the guy goes all over the Greek islands, trying to get home?"

"Oh," I said. "*The Odyssey.*"

"Yeah, that's the one. I'd like to see all those places. I want to see the whole world. Instead, what am I doing? Sitting here on my ass. And for what?"

He slowed down now, and took a breath. "I was with that cunt Tiffany earlier," he confessed. "I keep saying I'll never see her again and I always do. You know what she says today? She wants us to run away together. I told her no way. You know what she says to that? She says she's gonna tell Denny everything. That really shook me up, Pete. I wouldn't want to face that. Can you imagine what he'd feel like? Can you imagine what he'd say? Think of how his face would be, with those big eyes of his looking right at me. I've seen that face enough times in my dreams, Pete, I don't want to see it in real life. This got way, way out of control. I made a big mistake, I played with fire, and now I'm paying for it. I'm at the end of my chain, Pete, I can't stand it anymore, all of it, any of it."

Today I felt the same way he did, and so I didn't try to talk him out of it the way I usually did. Standing on the pier, with the cold wind howling and the sun going down, thinking of everything that happened, I said,

"You know what? I think you're right."

"You do?"

"Oh, hell yes. I feel the same way. Who needs this crap, day in and day out? I'm sick of it too. Let's do something."

"Like what?"

"Whatever you want to do. Let's run away!"

"Where'll we go?"

"I don't care! Someplace, anyplace! Let's just go, and the hell with everything else!"

"Okay," Tom said, getting caught up in the idea too. "All right. Yeah! To hell with all of them!"

"To hell with them all!" I shouted.

"Let's have a drink on it!" Tom proposed, and he got out his bottle again. We both drank, coughing as we did so.

"But what," Tom asked, holding the bottle in one hand and wiping his mouth with the other, "are we really gonna do?"

"Who cares, anyway?" I said. "How 'bout we just get into my van and follow the front end for a while, how does that sound?"

"Sounds great."

"You always wanted to go to Baja, so let's go to Baja."

"To Baja!" Tom cried.

"Lemme have another drink," I said.

"You're getting to be a regular alcoholic," Tom observed, giving over the bottle.

"That's right," I said, taking a drink. "I'm an alcoholic, you bet your ass I am!"

"Me too," said Tom. "I'm an alcoholic too. I'm gonna be a happy alcoholic. If there's anything I don't want, it's any of these miserable fucking alcoholics around. Have one more for the road?"

"Sure," I said, starting to feel the liquor working its way into me, starting to feel good at last, the pain easing a little now.

"I'm sick of that bitch Tiffany," said Tom. "I told her I'm not gonna see her anymore."

"That's good," I said. "It's about time."

"She said she's gonna kill herself. Think she will?"

"No. People who say they will don't ever really."

"That's what I figured," said Tom gratefully. "But I'm glad to hear you say it."

He put the bottle back into his jacket and then took in a deep breath, his chest swelling. "Look what I found."

I took the small object he handed me and looked at it in the dim light. "The magic circle!" I whooped. "You found it."

"I told you it wasn't really lost."

"Now we can take it with us."

"Are you ready?" asked Tom.

"You're damn right!"

"Then let's go!" Tom said proudly, giving a last glance at the setting sun. "You know what this is, don't you? Goodbye old way, hello new day!"

We walked off together, heading toward the front of the pier and a new life. I put my hand into my pocket and felt my fingers close on something. When I took it out I saw it was the picture from last year's prom. I looked at it again for a moment, looked at the girl in the picture whom I loved then and still loved even now. Where had she gone, where had we both gone? I crumbled the picture up and threw it over the side, watching at it fell down to the water and floated for a few moments before sinking slowly and disappearing.

"What was that?" asked Tom.

"Something that doesn't matter anymore," I told him.

Chapter 20

Kekaha

"Man, ain't this the life?" asked Tom.

"It is," I agreed. "The best."

We ended up in Laguna Beach, which is far off but not as far off as the moon, and had settled into a place called Kekaha to live. Nobody knew we were there, as far as we could tell; nobody would think to look for us there, if anybody was looking for us. We were far enough away so that all the things troubling us seemed a comfortable ways back, out of reach, and couldn't touch us anymore. We felt safe, and the longer we stayed there the safer we felt.

"You couldn't get me to go back to any of that," Tom went on. "Would you? I wouldn't, not for anything."

"Me either," I agreed.

There was a massive granite boulder out in the back of Kekaha and we were sitting there, along with Anjanette, our new friend whom we had just met, smoking and enjoying the stillness of the afternoon.

"What about you, sis?" Tom asked Anjanette. "Would you go back to what you came from?"

"You mean to a copper-mining town in Arizona and a husband that used to beat the holy hell out of me?" she replied. "There's nothing for me to go back to. I do miss my little girl sometimes, though."

"You'll see her again," Tom predicted.

"I wish I was so sure. How can you be so sure?"

"Sometime you can just know things.

"If I had known," I said, "how great it is to be free of all that, I would have run away a long time ago."

"It's fun being a runaway, isn't it?" said Tom.

"Oh, hell yes."

"I told you. I knew. That's because I was a runaway before, so I knew how it was. We're all three runaways, aren't we?"

"I guess I was afraid, until I tried it," I said.

"Once you've done the thing you're afraid of," Anjanette said, "and you find out it isn't so bad after all, you've taken a big step toward liberation."

We met Anjanette when we arrived at Kekaha and right away she became as close to us as we were with each other. She said we had all known each other in our past lives, probably we had been brothers and sister, and we had come together now, in this place and time, to complete some unfinished business we had with each other, some karma that had to be worked out. In just a few days it was as if we had known each other all our lives.

Kekaha. Tom loved it there. He said he'd never been happier in his life. He said the only thing that would make him happier was a ticket to Hawaii. But he said that could wait, he was sure he'd be going there soon enough. And it was like we were in Hawaii, for Kekaha is a Hawaiian word that means "The Place," and the man who owned it, The Professor, and his adopted son Duke, were both Hawaiians. Tom was overjoyed when he learned this, and said it was an omen, it meant he would be in the Islands before long. He went to town and bought himself a cheap watch and set it on Hawaiian time, which is two hours behind California time. So if you asked him what time it was and it was one in the afternoon he would say it was eleven in the morning, a fact which got a lot of people confused until they learned not to ask Tom for the time. He said he could practically feel those giant waves at Waimea Bay underneath him now, and he could see those Hawaiian girls in their grass skirts and their asses shaking. "I go to sleep thinking about them," he said. "I can see them, doing their dances."

"And if you're lucky," I said, "You might even have a wet dream about them."

"Sometimes I do," he confessed.

Everyday he rose early, put on his wetsuit, (for it was still wintertime and the water was cold) took his longboard and went down to the beach and put in a couple of hours surfing. For Laguna Beach had some great spots, like Wood's Cove, that not everybody knew about, and the surfing there was fine. It would still be dark out, and I'd hear him wake up and begin moving around, for we shared a room on the third floor of the place, an old Victorian style mansion a lot like Casey's house, and he'd say, "Come on, Pete, let's go catch some waves." I'd sit up in my bed, (which was only a mattress on the floor) light a cigarette, and maybe I'd go with him and maybe I wouldn't. But either way, I was happy too.

Kekaha sat in a green valley in the hills behind Laguna Beach. To get there you went up Laguna Canyon Road off Pacific Coast Highway a few miles and then turned off onto a side street, going back into the hills until the pavement ended. There was a dirt road that went by some evergreens and old shacks, and some cow pastures that actually had cows in them (at night we could hear them mooing as they made their way along the trail back toward the barn) and then there was a sign that said "Private Road" and you followed it to where it ended at the big brown Victorian mansion with peeling paint, gingerbread eaves and pillars in the front.

The van was filled with our stuff, all the stuff we'd brought with us when we ran away. What do you take along when you run away from home? Our surfboards were attached to the roof, held there securely on the racks, and we'd each brought some assorted items, clothes mostly, for it's not easy to know what to take when you leave home and have no intention of ever returning again. I was happy to go, there didn't seem to be anything else for me to do, but I still felt desolate inside when I thought about everything. For I had looked one last time at my house and my room, and when you do that you can't help but think of all the good things and the good times, like Christmas when you're small and you still believe in Santa Claus coming down the chimney, and birthday cakes, and how fresh and fine every new day once felt, and how the summer twilights would seem to last forever when my father was outside cutting the grass on a Saturday afternoon. So I snuck around—my mother was passed out and didn't hear me for once—and got my few things. I got up under my bed and took my Runes, for I thought it would be good to have them along. I also went into the kitchen and took the extra set of keys to my van, reaching into the bottom drawer by the sink to do it.

I took one last look at everything as I went out through the backyard. I said goodbye, silently, to my oak tree, hoping it would be able to go on without me tending to it. Then I was gone, out the back gate like a thief in the night, and nobody saw the few tears I shed as I went.

•   •   •

We had planned on lighting out for Baja. But we didn't go there right then. The first few nights we stayed in some crash pads along the coast, for there were a lot of them in those days, places where you could go and stay overnight a for a few days if you needed to. But along the way we heard about Kekaha, or I should say Tom did, and as soon as he heard about it he said it had to be the place he wanted to go, anyplace with a name like that, and run by Hawaiians, had to be the place for him. So Kekaha was where we went, and we were both happy we did.

We explored the tide pools along the Laguna coastline, looking in the caves and at the rock formations, Tom moving lithely, sure-footedly, jumping from rock to rock with ease.

"Man," he would say, "I wish we'd run away a long time ago, Pete. I've never been so happy."

"Me either," I said.

255

"It's because I found the magic circle," Tom declared. "That's when things turned around for us."

"You never should have lost it in the first place," I said reprovingly.

We had money, too. We both had the money we'd made while working at the gas dock, and when we set out we decided to pool our cash and put me in charge of it, since Tom was careless about things like that. So I put it all into an old sock and kept it under my mattress in our room. There was a lot of cash in there, and you didn't have to pay any rent at Kekaha, only work a few hours everyday in exchange for your room and board. So that way our money remained there for us, which was a good thing, for we would need it, later on.

There were rules at Kekaha. It was not a place where anything goes. But the rules were pretty basic, like don't hurt anybody else and treat your neighbor like your brother or sister. Every once in a while somebody would come along who wouldn't respect the rules, and Duke would put them out. But that didn't happen too often. You had to do your work, and you had to be on time when the food was served, or else you didn't get to eat. Duke gave out the work assignments everyday and he made sure you did what you were supposed to do. Tom and I figured it was a fair enough deal. There were some big gardens in the back, where the fruit trees and vegetables grew, and we spent a lot of time out there, hoeing and weeding. We also fixed and painted things, hammering down boards that had come loose on the davenport, sanding and painting around the windows, repairing some leaking pipes. It wasn't very hard work, and the rest of the time was your own. When we had nothing else to do we practiced karate, and I showed Tom the moves Dave had shown me, giving special attention to the one I'd used to knock my father down. He didn't seem as impressed with them as I was, but he learned them quickly, and we practiced them together, in a clearing behind the house.

You could stay there as long as you wanted, provided you obeyed the rules and did your work. Some people came and only stayed one night. Others stayed longer and then moved on. There were some, like Anjanette, who were more or less permanent residents. She had been there more than a year.

We only ate two times a day at Kekaha. That was the Professor's idea. He said most people ate too much and people didn't need three meals a day, only two. So there was a big breakfast served at mid-morning and then dinner in the late afternoon. Duke generally gave the kitchen work to the girls and women on the theory that women had more experience with it and could do a better job, and the men usually did the heavier work, although Tom and I spent plenty of time washing dishes, since everyone had to take their turn.

The food was mostly vegetarian, which neither of us liked at first. After a while we got used to it. The Professor said red meat had too much fat in it and wasn't good for you, and besides, you took in all the karma of the dead animal when you ate its flesh. Sometimes the meat eaters like Tom and me would raise a cry of protest, and so we would have hamburgers, but not very often. Sometimes there was fish or chicken. Eggs were all right to eat, and they came right out of the henhouse next to the garden. There was brown rice, and a lot of beans, black beans and red beans, which the Professor said had more protein in them than meat, and there were also some yellow beans from India called dahl, which were made into a kind of gravy and served with the rice. We also ate a lot of potatoes, and brown bread, which was baked right there in the big kitchen on the huge old iron stove, but never anything made with white flour or white sugar, because that was bad for you too.

Most people realized that a few hours' work each day was a small price to pay for room and board too. Tom and I worked in the garden, we chipped old paint and repainted parts of the house, inside and out, and had a good time doing it. We built ladders and made a scaffold for reaching the higher parts of the house, which Duke said we would paint if the rain ever stopped long enough. It was fun, and we liked working together. We sawed wood for the big fireplace in the living room where everybody gathered at night, split it and stacked it outside, dug up stumps of dead trees and hauled them away, then came back and filled in the holes with dirt.

So we settled into life there, and liked it, and tried not to think about what we'd left behind. I bought a wire bound theme book to use as a journal, and began to write in it everyday, writing about the people who were there and sometimes about what I felt, too, although I tried to avoid confronting my feelings if I could, since they made me hurt so bad inside.

When I sat by myself on the rock in the back—Anjanette had named it "Meditation Rock," saying it was a good place to come and meditate—with my journal on my lap, I saw in front of me two big eyes pleading, as if out of the darkness. And I heard bright laughter, too, and I saw a young girl who was very happy because she was doing something she believed in doing, and I was beside her, sorting clothes to give to people who had only rags to wear, or preparing to take food to people who had only garbage to eat. And we were walking along the beach holding hands, or playing like children on the rocks of the jetty. When I thought about her I became all crawly inside, especially when I imagined her with the Reverend Jim. Sometimes when those feelings became too strong tears would run out of my eyes, but I wiped them away and told myself I had to go on with things, that I couldn't spend my life thinking about what was behind me.

Tom knew all about it, for I had told him, when we left. He was outraged, and suggested we go back and beat the hell out of the Reverend. I said that wouldn't do any good, since there was still her stepfather to contend with. Tom said we might kidnap her, and take her away from all of them, but we decided to drop the idea.

I told Anjanette about it too, for one day she saw me weeping and asked what was wrong. "I've never seen you cry before, what's the matter?" she asked. So I told her, and her face became oblong with a mixture of sympathy and anger as I talked. "Oh God," she said. "That poor girl! I hope she's able to escape from those people someday, and that your heart doesn't hurt so bad. Maybe you'll see her again, don't despair. No one knows what will happen tomorrow."

I wrote all this down in my journal, writing earnestly on Meditation Rock or else upstairs in our room, and then hid the journal under my mattress, right next to our money. This was an old habit, I suppose, left over from home, because of the way my mother always snooped through my things. I filled in page after page, carefully dating each one, writing with a Bic pen I brought with me.

I wrote a lot about the Professor, too, the man who owned Kekaha, and about Duke, his adopted son. The Professor was an elfish little fellow, and I never learned what his real name was. I might as well tell you about him now. Everybody just called him "The Professor," and said he was crazy.

He was crazy in a good way. He never hurt anybody. He went all about clad in the most outlandish costumes, green or bright red shorts, suspenders and derby hats, so that he really did look like an elf, since he was short and nearly as big around as he was tall and had ears so large they looked like they could pick up radio signals. He talked to himself or else talked to the long test tubes he carried with him, and he spent hours staring at them and the thick multi-colored liquids inside, watching as the oozed slowly from one end of the tube to the other and then crawling back again.

People made up all kinds of stories about him and it was impossible to find out which ones were true and which ones weren't. According to the most common story he came from a wealthy planter's family on Maui. But his calling was science, and he'd been a professor at Berkeley. There he had done germ warfare research, but his conscience got the better of him and he protested, loudly, and gotten booted out for his trouble. That was when he went crazy, and he had come here, to Laguna, and founded Kekaha. There was a laboratory in the basement of the house and he spent a lot of time in there, alone and doing God-knows-what sort of experiments, like a mad scientist out of a grade-B movie. The lab was the only place at Kekaha that was off-limits. It was kept locked all the time and only Duke had the key. That just made everyone all the more curious about it, and all the more determined to get in and see what was really there, but nobody ever did. The lab remained a mystery, although some people claimed to know what the Professor was doing in: usually the stories involved the creation of a new, super-powerful kind of LSD that would even blow Timothy Leary's mind. But nobody really knew.

One time I asked the Professor what was in the test tubes he carried about with him. He looked at me and smiled and then went to talking about emulsions, compounds, viscosity and the periodic table of the elements, but it was like he was speaking another language, I couldn't make anything out of it. So I asked him if I could smell them, which wasn't very smart, for the smell was of a very powerful chemical kind of odor that made me lightheaded for the rest of the day.

I wandered off, feeling dizzy and disoriented, and ran into Duke out in back by the garden.

"Hey Duke," I said, "what does the Professor have in those test tubes?"

"Hell, I don't know, Brother Pete," he replied. "It's all Greek to me. You look a little green around the gills. What happened, did you get a whiff of them?"

"Yeah," I admitted.

"My father always told me, Brother Pete, that curiosity killed the cat."

"Who was your father, Duke?"

"He was a soldier, spent his life in the Army, mostly in the Islands. I'm half black and half Hawaiian—the Hawaiian part comes from my mother."

Duke was so big, walking around in his Hawaiian shirts, and he had such a calming presence, that not many people acted up when he was around. When he was nearby people relaxed and were on their good behavior. Once in a while someone would come to Kekaha who was doped up and wanted to party all night, and if they wouldn't knock it off he would put them out. After a short while Tom and I found we could read him pretty well. His first warning came when he said, "What's the matter with you, you tired of living?" and that generally made people take notice—it was a signal that his patience was running out. After that there weren't any more chances or excuses, the violators had to leave. A few times Tom and I helped him throw out some drunks who had come and thought this was a free love pad, and they were so obnoxious we were tempted to smack them around, but Duke wouldn't have any of that. He said we had to forgive them, for they knew not what they did. "You tell 'em, you big black nigger!" one of the drunks, who was a safe distance away, shouted. But Duke didn't get mad or say anything back. He said what he always said, that everyone was made of the same clay, and had to be forgiven. I had tried that, and didn't often succeed, but I could see the feeling of it, and knew it was based on something good even if it wasn't always possible to do.

• • •

People came and went. There were runaways, like Tom and me, some of them a lot younger than we were, kids as little as fourteen sometimes. Two times the truant officer came around and we hid out with the rest of them, even though I was eighteen by now and Tom nineteen, and legally there was nothing they could do to us. But we didn't want anybody to know where we were, and so we hid, scattered with the other kids, and nobody got caught.

Other people came too: Vietnam Vets, people on the road, people going somewhere, people going nowhere. Some were bound for San Francisco, for the Haight-Ashbury, some were bound for Big Sur or the mountains around Santa Cruz. Some didn't know where they were going, they were just looking for someplace to go.

The green hills behind Laguna Beach were in those days filled with clusters of one room shacks and cabins and tents, where lived an assortment of freaks, dropouts and dope heads. The energy of the area seemed to draw them there. Some lived in small groups, and others all alone.

One of the loners was a rotund, bearded man whom everyone referred to as Whalebelly and even less kindly as "Porky." What his real name was I never knew. He lived alone in a rickety wooden shack tucked into a valley beside a hill and he really had an unusual belly—it stuck way out in front of him like a basketball and bounced up and down when he walked. And he actually did look a little like Porky Pig, for he had a round face and thick upturned lips that did make you think of a pig when you saw him, and I suspected he grew the beard to try and cover that up. He had been in the army in Vietnam and had gone mad because of it. He seemed to live on beer, for he started drinking as soon as he got up in the morning and kept at it all day, so that he absolutely reeked with the smell of barely and hops—when he was nearby it was easy to imagine you were in a brewery in Milwaukee. He never washed, but wore dirty clothes and had streaks of dirt on his hands and face.

He often came to Kekaha, coming in through the front gate and pausing long enough to throw a coin into the fountain in front, then stand there for a moment or two while he thought about the wish he had just made before coming onto the big wooden porch and stand there with his hat in his hand. "OK if I hang around for a while?" he would ask Duke.

"Just as long as you behave yourself, Brother," Duke would reply seriously.

"I won't bother no one," Whalebelly promised. "I swear to God I won't, Duke."

"I heard that before," Duke replied. "Keep an eye on him," he said to Tom and I. "Come and get me if he starts to act up."

"All I wanta do is hang around for a little while," Whalebelly said. "You don't know how lonesome I get, over there all by myself with no one to talk to."

At first neither Tom nor I could understand why Duke was reluctant to let Whalebelly hang out at Kekaha, because he never said much but appeared content to just sit on the floor or in a bean-bag chair and smile vacantly at whoever was nearby and wait for somebody to talk to him. "You're nice guys," he said to Tom and me one day. "Why don't you come over to my place and have a beer?" He glanced uneasily at Duke, who stood nearby.

"Oh no you don't," Duke said sternly. "You do not go over there." He looked narrowly at Whalebelly. "Brother Whale, you tired of living?"

"No sir," said Whalebelly quickly.

"You know better than that."

"I been havin' really bad nightmares lately, Duke," Whalebelly said another time. "I wake up scared and shaking all over. I don't want to be by myself. Please lemme spend the night here."

"You know what I said, Brother."

"Please Duke, gimme one more chance."

"No more chances, Brother Whale."

"Why don't you let the poor bastard stay here?" Tom asked.

"I let him stay here once. Never again."

"Why? What happened?"

"You don't want to know, Brother Tom, you really don't want to know."

Anjanette would sit and talk to him for hours sometimes, but Duke always made sure she was never alone with him, always insisting that one of us stay close by. "He's a lost soul," she said, "and he's in an awful lot of pain, I can see it in his eyes." Whalebelly was ever so grateful for this. "You don't have to talk to me," he would say to her. "I don't know why you would want to. I know I'm ugly, and I'm fat, and I stink too. But it's just that I get so lonesome, over there all by myself, no one to talk to. A fella can go crazy."

"I can see that you're lonesome," Anjanette said.

"I deserve to be lonely," Whalebelly said. "I deserve a lot worse than to just be lonely. You wouldn't want to talk to me if you knew what I did when I was over there in Nam. You'd spit on me, that's what you'd do, you'd tell me to get out."

"I wouldn't spit on you," Anjanette said. "I wouldn't tell you to get the hell out."

"Maybe you wouldn't at that," Whalebelly said gratefully. "You're an angel, Anjanette, or awful close to bein' one. I should go. I don't want to get on nobody's nerves."

"You're not getting on my nerves," Anjanette said.

"But I might hurt somebody."

"You won't hurt anybody. I know you wouldn't. You don't want to hurt anybody, do you?"

"No missy. I never wanted to hurt nobody. The only reason I ever hurt anybody over there is because they made me." A crafty look came onto his face. "Angel Angie, let's you and me go for a walk in the woods all by ourselves."

"I warned you about that, Brother Whale," Duke said. "You can go home now."

"I'm sorry," said Whalebelly. "I didn't mean it."

"Now!" said Duke, and Whalebelly slunk out with his head hanging.

All this made me more and more curious about him, and so one day when Duke wasn't around I talked Tom into going with me over to Whalebelly's cabin. We walked across the field and up the dirt road that curved around the hill and kept following it until we saw it in the distance. He greeted us with a smile on his porcine face, a beer in one hand and a Bowie knife in the other. "Come in, you guys. Good to see you. How 'bout a beer? Have a beer, have two beers, have three—drink all the beer you want. I'm so glad you come over to be with me." His walls were decorated with Playboy centerfolds and the famous poster of Raquel Welch from *One Million Years B.C.* We sat down on some wooden crates to drink our beer, Whalebelly sitting across from us in the only chair in the room, smiling and playing with the big Bowie knife. He kept stabbing it into a block of wood in front of him, stabbing into it and making little chips fly in the air, all the while smiling as he stabbed at that wood.

"I killed a guy with this over there," he said.

"A Viet Cong?" Tom asked.

"Oh hell no. A GI. He was in my squad."

"You killed one of your own guys?"

"You shoulda seen it," Whalebelly went on. "The way he bled. It was beautiful. Death is beautiful."

All the time he spoke he continued to hack away at that block of wood. I looked at the debris strewn on the floor—old issues of *Playboy* and other nudie magazines, torn newspapers, and heaps of empty beer cans. "Your friend, Anjanette, she's nice. She's one of the nicest people I ever met. She's like a angel. And you guys, you're great guys. Most people don't want to talk to me, but you guys always do, and Anjanette always does. That means a lot to me. I'm so lonesome. I feel like a outcast." He rubbed his face with his dirty hands.

"When I first seen you two, I thought you was queer," he said.

"Queer?"

"Yeah. The way you always hang out together, I thought for sure you was two queers. I thought, if I invite those two over for a beer, I'll have to say, 'two beers for two queers.'" He laughed loudly. "That's funny, ain't it?" He jabbed at the block of wood several times, and looked at us expectantly. "I mean, it's funny how I thought you two guys was queer. That's funny, ain't it?"

"I guess," said Tom.

"I thought, 'These guys might try to queer me.' You wouldn't try to queer me, would ya?"

Neither of us said anything and the smile left Whalebelly's face. He hacked at the block of wood as if he wanted to break it in half. "I was just tryin' to make a joke," he said. "I just thought it was funny that I took you two guys for queers. You don't have to get all huffy about it."

"I mean, shit," said Whalebelly. "I invite you two over to my place to have a beer and some friendly conversation, and then when I try to make a little joke you get cross with me." He glared at us, and felt the edge of his Bowie knife with his thumb. "You know, if you take and cut somebody with this, how much blood will come? Lots of blood, rivers of blood. Blood, blood, blood!"

"Want to see my critters?" he asked, smiling once more. "I got lots of critters, lemme show 'em to you." We followed him toward the back door of the cabin, stepping over the trash and going through a filthy kitchen and passing the open door of an equally dirty bathroom, then out the back where the rest of the flotsam of the man's life resided: an old Indian Scout motorcycle with the engine taken apart and the front wheel removed, an equally old Ford Ranchero pickup truck sitting on blocks with the hood raised and a couple of combination wrenches lying flat on the engine, and more of the ubiquitous empty beer cans.

"Look at this," said Whalebelly. He showed us a large glass cage wherein resided a boa constrictor, sleeping peacefully beside a gnarled chunk of driftwood. "That's Lyndon," he said. "I named him after President Johnson. He eats rats, mice, lizards—eats 'em alive. You oughta see it. It's beautiful. This here's General Westmoreland," he went on, showing us a much-smaller glass cage that had a floor of sand and a horned toad in it, the kind you can find in the Mojave Desert. He also had an iguana. "This is Nixon," he said. "He looks sorta like Nixon, don't he?" Another cage held a big green parrot that let out a sudden squawk at his approach. "This is Ho Chi Minh," Whalebelly said. "Don't put your finger in there," he went on warningly. "That beak of his is razor-sharp."

"I used to have a pet tarantula," said Tom.

"A tarantula! Wouldn't I love to have one of them! What did ya do with him?

"My guardian made me get rid of it."

"That's too bad," said Whalebelly sadly. "I wish I could have a rattlesnake. Or a black mamba. The most poisonous snake in the world. You get bit by one of them and you only got minutes to live."

We went back inside the shack. Whalebelly got us each another beer. "How 'bout I show ya my gun collection?" Going into his bedroom brought out an armload of weapons.

"None of these are loaded, are they?" asked Tom.

"Naw," said Whalebelly. He showed us an AK-47, which he said he had brought back from Vietnam, and a .45 automatic, then a .357 magnum and a 12 gauge pump-action shotgun.

"Whaddya think?" Whalebelly asked eagerly.

"Guns make me nervous," said Tom.

"I thought you'd like 'em," said Whalebelly, crestfallen. He put the guns away and then got out some pictures from Vietnam, snapshots of him and other G.I.s in Saigon, posing with Vietnamese prostitutes. "They got some knocked-out pussy over there," he said. "You ever fuck a slanty-eyed girl?"

"No," said Tom.

"You should try one some time, they're great. What about you?"

"I never have either," I admitted.

"You *ever* fuck a girl?"

"'Course he has," said Tom.

"You sure? You ain't puttin' me on now?"

"Nobody's putting you on," I said.

"'Cause you don't look like a guy whose fucked many girls."

"What about you?" I asked. "Have you been with a lot of girls?"

Whalebelly's face changed again. It fell. "I used to," he said. "I used to get lots of girls. Not no more. Ever since I come back from the Nam—it just ain't been the same. I don't feel like fuckin' 'em. All I want to do is hit 'em with little thin whips until they cry, or else take a dildo and put it in 'em and work it back and forth. But I can't find too many who'll let me do that." He looked at us expectantly. "You know any girls who'd let me do that?"

"You're sick," said Tom.

"What about Anjanette?" he asked.

"What about her?" said Tom.

"You ever fuck her?" Whalebelly asked.

"You are a sick, disgusting pervert," Tom said.

"I invite you to come over and have a friendly beer with me. You sit in my house and drink my beer and you don't even say thank you and then you start calling me names."

"Thanks for the beer, pervert," said Tom.

"Yeah, thanks for the beer, sicko," I added.

"Don't go," he said. "I'm sorry. I just want to be friends. I'm lonesome."

"No surprise," said Tom.

"Wouldja come back some time?"

"No!"

"Oh!" he wailed. "Please!"

"Duke is right not to let you hang around," said Tom. "You're worse than crazy."

We left Whalebelly standing disconsolately on his porch, his head hanging and leaning his fat body against a wooden post. "I'm sorry," he said over and over.

"Someday somebody's gonna kill you," Tom predicted.

"I wish they would," Whalebelly mourned. "I wish they would."

We didn't tell anyone about our adventure at Whalebelly's cabin and he didn't come around anymore. We didn't see him again until much later, after our trip to Baja.

•   •   •

Anjanette's eyes were always curious and alert, darting out from beneath blond bangs that came to her eyebrows. They were light blue, full of life and goodness. Her cheekbones were high and her lips rosy, and she smelled of patchouli oil, which she rubbed on herself after her shower every morning. She had fair skin that was also very soft and smooth to look at, and blonde hair like Tom and me. And there was a scar on her wrist, and one on her face, too, high on her cheek, a slashing kind of scar about an inch long.

From the start she seemed familiar to me, like a face I'd seen once in a dream. Sometimes I called her "Auntie," which delighted her, and Tom called her "Sis." She became a kind of older sister to Tom and I, and before we had been at Kekaha a week the three of us were inseparable.

Anjanette wanted to be an artist. She had a studio set up in an alcove on the highest floor of the house, where she painted with oils and water colors. Her room, which was right next to ours on the third floor, was filled with paintings she had done, and also with small clay sculptures she made. She drew, using a pencil, and made sketches of Tom and me on our surfboards and me writing in my journal. She also drew Tom and I together, walking on a hill, and did a sketch of all three of us on a pier, looking out at the waves with some black clouds in the background.

"Why are the black clouds there, Auntie?" I asked, for their presence bothered me. I thought this picture should be all sunny and warmth, a celebration of our friendship, and these clouds looked ominous and forbidding.

"I'm not sure," she replied. "They just came out, something told me to put them there. That's how it works, Pete, you create something and you don't know why, you just know it is supposed to be that way. Maybe later on I'll figure out the reason."

She had come to Laguna Beach because a lot of artists lived there. The main streets of town were lined with galleries and there were several art schools close by. Anjanette wanted to attend one of them, and sometimes I would see her studying the brochures of one of the different schools, figuring out the tuition and looking at the entrance requirements. But she never quite got up the nerve to apply to one of them. She made all kinds of excuses. She said her work wasn't good enough to get her in; she said she could never afford the tuition. But she kept looking at the brochures anyway, and kept on dreaming her dream.

Sometimes she went to the local library and checked out thick books with pictures of famous paintings in them: Impressionists, Expressionists, Dadaists, Cubists, Picasso, Degas, Matisse, Monet. She sat looking at them for hours, and when I sat, as I sometimes did, looking at them with her, she would tell me which ones she liked best and why. I told her about Rudy's creation of "The Inferno," and she wanted to know more about that and said she wished she could have seen it.

Anjanette did the Runes and the Tarot cards, she told fortunes and read palms. Sometimes she went to Main Beach in Laguna and set up a little stand where she charged people to tell them about their futures. She made some money doing this, money which she saved toward her tuition to one of the art schools she wanted to attend. She liked my crystal, too, and said it was very powerful. I told her how it glowed, sometimes, and that I never had told that to anyone before for fear they would think I was crazy. She said I wasn't crazy at all, it really did glow, only no one else could see it, that was all. That made me feel better, and I told her, nervously, about the voices I heard sometimes.

"What do they say?" she asked.

"I can never understand them. It's like a radio on the other side of a wall. I know it's there, but I can't really hear it."

Anjanette looked at me thoughtfully. "Do you ever *feel* them, like they were close to you?"

"Sometimes it's as if they were right beside me, speaking into my ear. But I still can't understand what they're saying."

"Why, I know what it is," Anjanette smiled brightly. "You're not crazy, Pete. Those are angels speaking to you."

"Angels? Are you sure?"

"I've heard about it before. They're on another plane of existence, that's all, we can't understand them. You're lucky. Not many people are so fortunate to have angels speak to them. It must be something real important that they want to tell you."

"I've always felt that," I said. "I've always felt it was important. Do you think I'll ever know what it is?"

"Oh yes," she said positively. "I know you will, I'm certain of it. Because they wouldn't be talking to you if it wasn't important."

"Why are you so sure?"

"Because they talked to me, once."

"What happened?"

"I'll tell you some other time."

"Promise?"

"Yes. It's about this," she said, pointing to the scar on her wrist, "and this," she went on, pointing now to the scar on her face. "Just remember there are lots of other worlds, coexisting with this one, all around us, all the time."

She showed me another trick, one time. She took my crystal and held it by its chain so that it dangled from her fingers. "Now watch," she said. "This is a way you can communicate with your deepest self." The crystal hung motionless and then, when Anjanette said, "Are you there?" it began to move in a side-to-side manner. I was astounded. "Are you doing that?" I asked. "Look at my fingers, are they moving?" she asked. I had to admit they weren't. The chain hung over her fingertips, there was no way she could be making it move. "Show Pete no," Anjanette instructed, and now the crystal began to move in a circular motion. Around and around it went, swinging in a circle that got bigger and faster as it moved. "What is doing that?" I asked.

"The inner self, the deepest self, the one that never sleeps but is always there, and knows everything. Here. You want to try?"

"What are you, a witch?" I asked, talking the crystal in my fingers.

"What if I was, wouldn't you like me anymore?"

"Sure I would."

I held the crystal until it stopped spinning and was motionless. "Are you there?" I asked, doing it just the way Anjanette had. For a few seconds nothing happened. Then it began to move, the same way it had when Anjanette held it, moving back and forth like a pendulum. "You can ask it anything," she said, "and it will tell you. Especially about yourself, because it knows everything about you."

She dressed in the baggiest and frumpiest kind of clothes, and did her best to look plain. She never wore any makeup. She never went out with anybody or had any boyfriends. Once, when I was upstairs in her studio, I asked her why.

"Maybe I don't like men," she replied, laughingly, from her easel, for she was busily working on a painting.

"No," I said. "That's not true, is it?"

She laughed again. "No," she assured me, "it's not. I'm celibate. Do you know what that is?"

"I think I do. But why would you want to be that way?"

"There's a good reason," she said. "Someday I'll tell you about it. But not now. It might make you sad."

Something touched my mind lightly right then and I realized it must have something to do with the scars on her wrist and face.

Anjanette, Tom and I went to the beach together, explored the tide pools and the caves, walked downtown, and became more attached to each other with each passing day. Tom, for once in his life, appeared to have no designs on her whatever. I couldn't say the same about myself. Underneath the frumpy clothes I knew there was something definitely worth seeing more of, and I often fantasized about what it must be like. But I kept those feelings hidden.

•   •   •

My hair grew longer and longer, until it covered my ears and came down past my collar, although Anjanette trimmed it for me so it never got too shaggy. Tom let his hair grow too, and it looked good on him, making him resemble a marauding Viking in a long ship.

Most of the time I was pretty carefree, although once in a while my conscience would go to work on me. It would say things like, "What's going to become of you now? Look at what you've done. You've gone and dropped out of high school, you won't graduate, let alone go to college like everybody else." But after a while this would pass, and I'd feel easy in my mind again. There was a wonderful sense of freedom in being away from all that. After a while I didn't see how I could ever go back to the way I used to live.

I really didn't miss anybody, except Rena. I found myself thinking of her all the time and there were many occasions when I was very close to calling her and telling her where I was, and asking her how she was doing. But I never did. I didn't really want to know how she was doing, since I knew already, and I didn't want to think about that because it made me feel all mushy inside. I thought of my mother and my father and my brother but I couldn't say I missed them. So there wasn't anything to go back to.

And a lot of the things I thought of and remembered were things I was just as happy to get shut of. I thought of my brother and I was real glad I wouldn't have to deal with him anymore. I remembered the way he'd killed the baby bird that started all the trouble. I didn't like him and he'd sure as hell never liked me, so it was just as well. Because there are some things you have to face even if you don't want to face them. And it wasn't too much fun to admit this to myself, because we are brought up to think we are supposed to love certain people, like the people in our families, and I figured there had to be something wrong with me if I didn't love mine. But then I found I could live with it. But I had cast everything aside, I wasn't like normal people anymore, and so I said to myself this was okay too. There were a lot of things I didn't want to think about and when they came into my mind I did my best to shut them out.

I spent more and more time with Anjanette. I'd sit in the alcove with her while she worked. Sometimes I'd sit there for hours, not saying anything, writing while she painted or drew. Or else we would talk and talk, telling each other everything we could think of telling. Other times she would spread the Tarot cards or the Runestones out in front of her, studying them. I told her about Carolyn, and about my family, too, and it made me feel better to talk about it.

She said all this was written in the stars long before any of us were born, just as Casey always said. It was all preordained. She loved magic and believed in it, and she believed in ghosts, fairies, nature spirits, and said there was a spirit in everything. I told her about Casey, and how he was into all that as well, and said I would like to introduce her to him someday. I told her about everything except Deacon's murder and seeing his ghost that time. Those were things I couldn't tell anybody.

She also believed in the power of evil. When she talked about that I thought of Dave, and what I'd seen that night I went to the Pike with him. Anjanette said the Devil was real, and she also believed in witches, vampires, and familiars. She said there was white and black magic, and that once she'd had the opportunity to learn the "old religion" from a witch, who had offered to teach her everything she knew.

"Why didn't you do it?" I asked.

"There's a darkness to everything. I didn't want any more darkness."

Sometimes we went walking in the green hills around Kekaha, walking along the cow paths and along trails in the fog. "What would happen?" she would ask, "If we, in this fog, walked out of our world and into another one? A secret world of fairies and dragons and black knights?" Some nights it was so quiet we could hear the surf pounding even though the beach was miles away. Ghostly sounds echoed along the cow paths. "Remember I told you I was a witch."

"Are you a witch?"

"Maybe."

"Go on, you're no witch."

"But I've seen the darkness," she said. "I was looking into a mirror once, and I didn't like what I saw. I didn't like the face that stared back at me, I didn't like who I was. This isn't me, I thought. I wanted to hurt myself, to punish myself, for what I had done."

"What had you done?"

"There was a razor blade nearby and I slashed my face with it." That explained the scar near her cheekbone, a thin scar, finer than a pencil line. "I watched the blood flow. It ran down my face. Very red. Onto my shirt, and I wondered, why go on living? Why not just end it, get it over with, be done with it all? So I took the razor and slashed my wrist, right there where you feel your pulse, and I watched the blood flow into the sink."

"But why, Anjanette, why?"

"I felt a great feeling of peace come over me," she said. "It was as if all my life played itself out before my eyes. And I had a kind of revelation. There is something in the flow of blood that does that to a person. It was like a primal flow, pulsing out of my wrist, watching my life ebb away like a candle burning down. Life doesn't end when your body dies. What is this body? It is something we walk around in, that's all. It was like I went to another place where I could see all this. It was as clear as anything ever was to me. And I knew I'd come back, and do it all again, one way or another."

"So you stopped the bleeding?"

"Just in time, I think, much longer and I would have been dead. I made a bargain with God. I told God I'd live. I also told Him that since sex was part of the way I'd abused myself, I couldn't have it anymore. I know that if I have it before I'm supposed to something terrible will happen to me. It will be like opening Pandora's box, if I ever violate this bargain I made with God. All the demons I'm holding back will come flying out."

So now I understood why she dressed the way she did, and why she went out of her way to keep men from noticing her. She'd made a bargain with God.

•   •   •

On the first floor of Kekaha was a big common room where people sat and talked or read from the numerous books and magazines that floated around the place. Nearby the common room was a library filled with books on all sorts of subjects: Some were from the Professor's past life as a scientist, volumes on organic chemistry and physics and molecular biology. But there were many others as well, philosophers like Plato and Aristotle, Saint Augustine, Jean-Paul Sartre. There were also a lot of travel books, describing various destinations in the world, from Europe to the Taj Mahal in India.

One day Tom noticed a travel book about Baja California.

"Just check this out," he said, and for the next several days that book was never out of his sight, and he kept pestering me by showing me pictures of the sights the peninsula had to offer. What excited him the most were the photographs of the long white beaches.

"Just imagine it," he kept saying. "Surfing there. It might be as good as the North Shore."

"I can sense what is coming," I said to Anjanette.

"I can see a journey in your near future," she laughed, "and I don't need the Runes or an astrology chart to do it."

"Want to come along with us?"

This took her by surprise. "Won't three be a crowd?"

"Not if it's us three."

"How long would we be gone?"

"A few weeks."

"All right. It'll be fun."

Maybe it all had to be that way, perhaps it was all written in the stars, as Casey always said, long before any of us were born.

Chapter 21

Baja

So we set off one fine morning early in 1969, on what would prove to be the journey of a lifetime.

The radio played and our spirits were high, and we went down Pacific Coast Highway through Dana Point, Capistrano Beach, San Clemente, and past Camp Pendleton, through Oceanside and past La Jolla toward San Diego. We took turns driving. When we got to the International Border at San Ysidro where there was a sign and an arrow that read "U.S." and pointed north and another arrow that pointed south and said "Mexico," Anjanette was at the wheel. It was midday and there were a lot of people crossing the border, going in a slow, steady stream. Some bored-looking Border Patrolmen stood about, waving people by. We had our tourist cards and Mexican Insurance for the van. The fellow at the gate paused when he saw us, then signaled us through without a word being said.

The change was immediate, we felt it at once. Back there was the United States, now we were in Mexico. Boys stood about hawking woven baskets, sombreros, belts, leather goods. There were stalls and tables set up along both sides of the road, with people holding up their wares and calling out in Spanish and accented English. A river of tourists went by, haggling, examining, sometimes buying, mostly just looking. The traffic moved slowly, creeping along, stopping and then moving again.

"Let's stop," I suggested.

"Let's get out of TJ first," said Tom. "We want to get away from the border."

"You brought the magic circle along, didn't you?"

"I wouldn't make a trip like this without it."

The traffic was creeping along. Ahead of us we saw a Mexican policeman, wearing a brown uniform, a gun on his hip, directing traffic. He would blow his whistle and wave, then hold up his hand and point to another line of traffic and signal them to go. There was a lot of traffic ahead of us and we could see all the cars swirling this way and that.

We were right beside the traffic cop now. He was, I saw, not much older than we were, with a swooping black moustache that gave him the look of a brigand.

"Try your Spanish out, Pete," Tom urged.

"You *se habla espanol*, don't you?"

"Yeah, but I want to hear yours. Mine I learned in the streets, you learned yours in school."

I leaned my head forward and out the window. *"Por favor,"* I said, *"ensemene el camina a Ensenada?"* (Will you show me the road to Ensenada?)

He smiled, amusedly, then pointed straight ahead. He gave a signal, *"Pasame,"* he said, and we went on, along *Paseo de Tijuana*.

The sidewalks were crowded with people, most of them American tourists. Mexican music blasted from the radios and stereos that were for sale. Anjanette drove slowly, carefully, so we could see as much as we could and keep up with the traffic also. Then we saw a sign that said "Ensenada" and Anjanette turned to the right and we went across *Avenida Padre Kino* and onto *Benito Juarez*, getting away from the downtown section. Now we saw some pasteboard houses and dogs prowling in search of a scrap of food. Some kids were playing on the dirt street. They waved gaily to us as we went by. They were all dressed in rags and they were just small kids. We saw another Ensenada sign and were getting out of the city by now. Pretty soon we were onto a highway, passing by shacks on either side, and in some places were came close to the ocean on our right, and in others the road swerved inland again. There were cactus and red colored flowers in some places. The ocean looked peaceful and inviting, rolling onto the white beach and going back out again. Tom said there was good surfing all over Baja.

Anjanette said she was tired of driving when we got to Rosarito Beach, so we changed and I began driving again. By now we were on the road to Ensenada and all around us was desert. The road stretched out ahead of us. There was almost no other traffic, just a lone car here and there. The hills rose up in the distance, and we passed through some small settlements that weren't even villages, just collections of huts and pasteboard houses, surrounded by forests of junked cars and other debris. Here and there was a horse to be seen, grazing. We spotted some fishing boats trolling past on the ocean. Turkey vultures rested on fence posts. We passed a man riding a donkey, with several other donkeys along with him, each loaded with bags of goods he was taking to market. We waved at him as we went past, and he waved back, smiling.

At a curio shop by the ocean we stopped and Anjanette and I each bought a leather *vaquero* hat, but Tom didn't buy anything. He said the further south we got the better deals we could get.

"This was a bargain at ten bucks," I said, putting the hat on. "How do I look?"

"Like an American boy wearing a Mexican hat," said Anjanette.

We passed *La Mision,* looking down at the spectacular coastline, and then swung upward to a plateau. Outside Ensenada we saw more fishing boats, and then we came to the town itself. We parked at San Miguel Beach, where we could camp right beside the water.

We parked next to a clump of palm trees. Beyond us was the ocean, and there was an island within swimming distance offshore. Tom said we could go surfing in the morning, if we felt like it, and he also said it would be fun to swim out to that island. But we were all hungry, and decided to walk into town and get something to eat.

We locked the van and headed up the embankment, crossing a long bridge. We passed a wagon where a man and his son sold fresh fruit, and we all bought some, apples, oranges, pineapple, mixed in a bowl and tasting like it came straight off the tree. Then we came to a wooden stand in the street where we could buy fried fish, and the fish was just as fresh as the fruit, deep fried and covered in vinegar. But after we ate the fish we were thirsty, and when we came to a restaurant we sat down at a table outside on the sidewalk beneath a thatched roof, sitting at a round table and feeling the warm twilight air.

"Ain't this great?" Tom said. "Anjanette, put your hat on, why don't you, so we can see what you look like in it."

She obliged, tying the draw string beneath her chin.

"What's the verdict?" she asked.

"You look wonderful," I said, and when I said it she looked at me and then looked away.

By and by a waiter came over.

"*Si?*" he asked politely. He had a white cloth over his arm.

"*Tres cervezas,*" Tom said.

"*Si senor, tres cervezas,*" the waiter repeated.

"Ain't this great?" Tom said again.

"Oh, hell yes," I agreed.

We sat drinking beer and munching from a basket of tortilla chips, dipping them in a bowl of salsa.

"Whose idea was it to come here?" I asked.

"Mine, if you recall," Tom said.

"Well," I said, saluting him with my beer, "that was one swell idea you had this time."

"Thank you," he said with a bow. "I don't mind taking credit when the credit is due me. This is just what we need."

We drank more beer and ate more chips and salsa. Darkness was coming but the air was warm and pleasant. We left *pesos* on the table for the waiter and went back to our camp.

"How far is it to where we're going?" Anjanette asked.

"Over a thousand miles."

"Wow."

But it was going to take us a long time to get there, and we weren't in any hurry. None of us had any pressing engagements back home. In the morning Tom and I went surfing, then swam out to the island. Anjanette watched us from the beach. We went into town for breakfast after we dried off, then got back onto the highway, going south.

The highway weaved back and forth, from the coast on the Pacific side all the way to the center of Baja and then back again. We preferred the coast, naturally, but when we had to go inland we saw some of the most amazing sights and countryside, more spectacular than we had ever imagined it could be.

Baja is divided into two parts, north and south, and the further south we went the more astonishing everything became, and often the going got harder and slower. In some places the roads weren't roads at all, but trails strewn with rocks and barely wide enough for the van to pass over, and there wasn't any choice but to go so slowly a snail made good time by comparison. We took turns driving, and stopped when we felt like it. We camped out at night on the long, beautiful beaches, lying in the open beside the van, Anjanette in the middle, Tom and I on either side, looking up at the stars.

The further south we ventured, the clearer the sky became. I never saw such a clear sky anywhere, and I never saw so many stars. It was a long way from the fogginess back home. Some nights we tried to count them, but always gave up, there were just too many. We saw whole clusters_of them, all grouped together and hanging there in the sky, and we wondered how far away they really were and if anybody would ever see them up close, and I remembered what Tom had said that night, about everything in the universe being in balance. We would lay there, a driftwood fire going, drinking red wine but not smoking anything, because we'd heard how strict the laws were in Mexico and if you got busted with so much as a seed on you they'd lock you up and you wouldn't see daylight again until the next century. We heard the coyotes howling mournfully at the moon, and listened to the surf crashing. Then a screech owl would let loose, and dogs would bark in the distance, and after that it got so quiet it seemed the whole world was asleep.

Sometimes there were strange desert sounds, like someone talking in the distance, and a crying-wailing sound. The wailing, we found out, was *La Llonora,* the lost spirit of the desert, a banshee-like creature that roams the southwest looking for souls to capture and carry away. She scared Anjanette one night. She woke me up—she was lying between Tom and I, as usual, and she pushed as my shoulder and whispered, "Pete, Pete, wake up! Do you hear that?" I lay there for a while listening and at last I heard it too, a long low cry that rose and fell, echoing over the cactus and the sagebrush before it died away. "I'm scared," Anjanette said. "Let me sleep closer to you." She scooted over until she was right beside me, and even though we were separated by the blankets I was aware all the rest of the night of her closeness to me.

There were also the lights, the strange desert lights that came right up out of the ground and danced about boisterously, then faded away even as *La Llonora's* cry faded away. They were balls of light, coming up out of the ground and then separating, becoming two shapes instead of one, moving all about, hovering, moving, stopping and hovering again. They were a bright white in color, and they gave off an aura that was bluish. Anjanette said they were ghost lights, for she'd heard about them, and said they wouldn't harm us. Some nights when I couldn't sleep I'd lay there and look at them, watch them as they moved. They bounced, like basketballs being dribbled, and then stopped moving altogether and faded from sight. "It's the spirits of the dead," Anjanette would say. "I can feel them all around us."

"Are you trying to scare me?" I whispered back.

"They're protecting us," she declared. "They won't let anything bad happen to us."

We were a *long* way from home, everything was so different here and everything we'd known was so far back. I thought about Rena, wondering how she was. I thought of my mother and father and wondered if I'd ever see them again and wondered what they'd say if they knew where I was. And what would everybody else say if they knew where we'd gone? I thought of Denny and Tiffany, and Casey Jones, and Neal and Marianne, and I wondered how they all were. Back in Angels Beach the kids Tom and I had known were still in school, sitting in classrooms and waiting for June when school would let out, and here we were, so far away from all of that. Then I thought, maybe I'll never go back, I like it so well here.

The weather was warm but not hot, and we went about in short sleeve shirts and shorts. Anjanette wore a halter top. When we needed to we stopped and swam to refresh ourselves, then we sat on the white sand and dried off in the sun, usually with no one else around as far as you could see. It was like we had this whole world to ourselves here. We swam without our clothes on sometimes, and Anjanette would frolic in the water like a sea goddess. She was really something to look at when you got beyond the baggy pants and the sweatshirts.

One morning the three of us swam out to a rock that was perhaps a quarter of a mile off shore. It jutted up out of the ocean in several tiers. We sat on one of the ledges that faced the shore for a few minutes, just letting the all-powerful, all-healing sun wash over us like a wave, listening as the surf hit the rock on the other side. Then Tom climbed up to the top, looking out at the Pacific.

"Hey," he cried, raising his arms out to either side like wings, "look at me. I feel as if I could just fly away from here." He stood there, silhouetted against the morning sun, and then he pointed excitedly. "Look at that!" he called. "Look! You have to see this!"

Now Anjanette and I saw it too—enormous shapes in the water, coming to the surface and then diving down so that the fan-like tails followed them like arrows. When they came to the surface they blew out huge spouts of water from the hole behind their heads, and frisked about with each other as if they were playing, like kids on a schoolyard.

"It's the grey whales," said Tom. "I read about them."

"Where are they going?" Anjanette asked.

"The Bering Sea. In the fall they migrate from there all the way down here, to Scammon's Lagoon in Baja, and the spring and early summer they start back again."

"They're huge."

"They get up to 50 feet long," said Tom. "And can weigh 40 tons. The old-time whalers used to call them Devilfish, because they fight like hell when they're being hunted."

Right at that moment one of the whales came up out of the ocean, the gigantic snout fairly exploding from the water, followed by the massive oblong body that had a strange gracefulness to it,_like a giant ballerina dancing.

"What a sight," said Anjanette. "Look! There's a small one."

A calf about one-fourth the size of its mother came to the surface now, its mother close by, protectively staying near.

We kept on heading south. The van was always filled with the scent of Anjanette's patchouli oil. We had our crystals, Runestones, Tarot cards, and the Magic Circle, and sometimes at night we would get them out and consult them. Anjanette looked at them carefully and from them we decided to avoid certain towns and not to travel on particular days. We usually did as the stones or the cards advised.

One night she got the Runes out while we sat at a table in restaurant south of Ensenada, on the Pacific side of the Peninsula. She began laying them out, one after the other, unmindful of the stares she drew from the people around us. By and by a woman came over and inquired as to what, exactly, these stones were, and when Anjanette told her she smiled and called them *"Piedras de palabras,"* the stones of words, and called Anjanette *"La Adivina,"* the Fortune Teller. So sometimes after that Anjanette told fortunes in the different places we went to.

We dressed like the natives more and more. I wore my vaquero hat, a white peasant top, a red sash, and sandals. Tom and Anjanette dressed the same way. We looked less and less like tourists, although since we all three had blond hair we couldn't pass for natives. Tom was already tan, he was always tan, even if never went out in the sun, (or so it seemed), but Anjanette and I got darker and darker the longer we were there and the more time we spent in the sun.

As much as we could we stayed near the ocean, so Tom and I could surf in the mornings and just because we liked being beside the sea. Sometimes the road ran inland, and we followed it because we had to, deeper into the desert country. But it was a beautiful desert, quiet and deserted, with huge patches of color thrown in against the brown and gray. Sometimes in the distance we saw green mountains sticking up into the sky, resembling domes, and we came upon fields of yellow flowers with clumps of green bushes growing here and there. We saw entire forests of date trees, just growing wild. Near the middle of the Peninsula we came upon a moonscape of craggy rocks and boulders strewn all about, with craters carved into the earth of solid rock. We stood there, looking at it, awestruck and silent at what we were seeing. Sometimes we climbed to the top of tall hills and stood looking out over the panorama surrounding us, and we saw islands of green off shore. The coast of Baja is dotted with islands on both sides, Pacific and Gulf as well. Some are so small they are more like rocks protruding out of the ocean, and others are much bigger. Some of the larger ones, on the Gulf side, have people living on them, people that have lived on these islands for hundreds, if not thousands, of years, living the same way they have always lived. They were very dark and much more Indian-looking than other Mexican people are, handsome and dignified and stoic. We watched the surf crashing against the rocks, smashing into them and then throwing white foam up into the air like a geyser, the water reaching upward as if it wanted to touch the sky, then falling back down.

We passed through Maeadero, Santa Tomas, San Vincente, Colonet, Camalu, and other places that had no names. We saw the ruins of missions built by the Spanish going as far back as the 1600s. After El Rosario the road went inland, to the spine of Baja, you may say. For a long time there wasn't anything, just the endless desert. We passed through the Laguna Chapala, a dry lake which marked our crossing of the 28th parallel, which divides Baja north and south, and we reached Santo Rosalio on the other side for our first look at the Gulf of California, also known as the Sea of Cortez.

•   •   •

It was a colossal country there, wild and primitive. Sometimes we went for days without seeing any people at all. We listened to the tape deck and sang with the music, for by now the radio was picking up only static. Other times we just listened to the awesome silence of the desert.

Some of the mountains ran as high as 10,000 feet, towering majestically in the distance, some looking like pyramids, others more like chimneys. There were giant *cordon* cactus that were more than 60 feet high and can weigh ten tons, and the towering *cirios*, tree-like plants that only grow in Baja. And there were the barrel cactus, whose meat you can chew to quench your thirst if you run out of water, and the *chirinola* cactus, which grows horizontally on the ground like a vine, and while the end dies the front stays alive and keeps growing. We saw the little pincushion cactus, which don't grow any higher than an inch and have red, ribbon-like flowers sprouting off them, and bojum trees where fierce-looking red-tailed hawks nest. In some places there were ironwood trees that live for hundreds of years. There were *ocotillos* (elephant trees), and the *cholla,* or jumping cactus, and prickly pear cactus, all growing amongst the rocks and the desert sand. We drove over mountains and hills, and came down off them into shallow valleys of white sand. Some of the people we saw lived in thatched huts, and had a horse or a broken down car outside. They waved as we went by.

On some of the beaches on the Pacific side were bones and even whole skeletons of whales that had come ashore and died. The water was so clear you could see right to the bottom, and we explored the tide pools and the rocks and sat and watched the sun go down in the late afternoon. The sunsets in Baja are breathtaking, with a red sky and red clouds exploding out over the ocean as far as you could see. We were awestruck by the majesty of it all, and by the fact that we were there alone. The waves would come lapping up on the beach and as the sun went down the wet sand would take on a silver color, and birds with long thin beaks would be all over it, poking down into the sand in search of sand crabs to eat.

In the San Felipe desert we saw wild burros running in packs. At night, camped by the van, we heard mountain lions howling in the distance. Tom caught an iguana, which he didn't keep but set free, and he also caught a tarantula, but didn't keep it either. He was going after a gila monster next, but we talked him out of it. We saw scorpions, hiding under rocks, and rattlesnakes, and learned that on one of the islands off Baja lives the world's only rattlesnake that doesn't rattle.

We saw the jungle near Rio Mulege, and we went by Scammon's Lagoon. Tom caught a green sea turtle on the beach one day, and ran around like a little kid at Christmas, he was so happy. He set it free soon after, but he was delighted to have seen it, saying he had never seen one like that before.

So we kept on heading south, weaving to and fro across the length of Baja, sleeping outside at night under the stars and the black sky and the white moon, only concerned about today and not thinking of tomorrow until it arrived. In the morning each new day seemed full of promise and hope, and I looked out at the long flat beaches and the white sand and the blue water touching it, and felt at times that we were the first people to ever walk on them and whatever we did was brand new and had never been done before. Each day I felt reborn, and I know Tom and Anjanette felt the same way. Life had started all over again, like new leaves growing on trees in the spring or flowers opening up when the rays of the sun fall on them. It was a new start, a new world, a new life.

Chapter 22

The Chubasco

Eventually we came to a wild and primitive stretch of beach some miles north of La Paz, on the Gulf side of the Peninsula, and set up camp there. We had all agreed we were tired of driving and wanted to camp for a few days.

Anjanette had heard about an old mission nearby at San Javier, and cave paintings that weren't far away, and she was dying to see them both. She had picked up a little of the language as we traveled, enough to make herself understood, and people had told her about these sights, exciting her curiosity. Both were within walking distance of our camp, she said excitedly one morning, and she wanted Tom and I to come with her.

We had set up our camp alongside a bluff facing the sea. At night we would build a fire and sit around it, looking up at the stars and drinking wine, and then go to sleep as the fire went low, the way we always did, listening to the soft sounds of the small waves. At night we'd hear the different birds of the desert talking, as well as a coyote crying out its mournful song in the darkness.

We had a tarp set up, and chairs and a small camp table, all centered around the fire. Our surfboards lay out to one side. Various other items were spread out here and there. We explored the tide pools, dove into the beautiful clear water from the rocks. Sometimes Tom would climb higher and higher on the side of the cliff before he dove off, looking as if he'd been doing this all his life, climbing lithely, all tan and muscular, and then off he would go, leaping out away from the rocks as if given an extra push, settling gracefully into a swan dive that took him *kersplat* into the water, barely breaking the surface. A second later his blond head would protrude, his hair plastered down, and he would wave at us and swim to shore. Show off, I would say to myself, because while I dove from the lower cliffs I was afraid to go as high as he did and dive, and so I said to myself that he was showboating, as he had a tendency to do sometimes, like when he did spinners while surfing or hunkered down into a picture-perfect *Quasimodo*.

So we set out, walking inland, and the further we got from the beach the more desert-like the terrain became. We went along an old rocky road that was lined with cactus and sagebrush, and was used by travelers of all sorts: We saw tire tracks, the imprints of horses and mules, as well as footprints. As we got closer to the village we became aware of people around us. A head would pop up out of the brush and disappear, or we would go by a shack with a horse corral beside it.

The church was outside the village, sitting there all by itself, and when we got there we stood looking at it.

"Just imagine," Anjanette cried. "It's over 200 years old. Look at the style."

"What style?" Tom asked. "It just looks like an old church made of rock."

"Haven't you noticed anything about all the missions we've seen?" Anjanette said impatiently. "Look at the architecture."

"What about it?"

"You can't see the difference?"

"No."

"This was one of the first missions built here, and it's done in the Moorish style, like in Toledo or Seville."

"Toledo, you mean in Ohio?"

"No, in Spain."

"Ohio's not in Spain."

"Oh, for God's sakes!"

"I can see the difference," I said. "It looks sort of Arabian."

"What are you talking about?" said Tom. "You mean there were A-rabs here? I thought you said it was Spaniards who built this."

"Yes," Anjanette cried, "It looks kind of like a mosque, doesn't it? You can see the Arab influence. From when there were Moors in Spain."

"Moors," said Tom. "A-rabs. Next you'll be telling me A-rabs built the mission in San Juan Capistrano."

"Tom, you are such a lowbrow," said Anjanette.

We walked all around the mission, looking at the old, crumbling walls and the tall domes, Anjanette and I admiring it, Tom looking bored. Anjanette grabbed my arm and squeezed it excitedly as she quoted from the guidebook, telling me how this was the only original California mission that was still intact. She wore shorts and her blond hair cascaded down her back. She also had on sandals and like me, wore her vaquero hat against the sun.

We had to walk through the village to get to the cave paintings. There was a fountain in the village square with a Madonna and child in the center that bubbled merrily away, and the people glanced curiously at us as we went by but otherwise paid us little heed; tourists were not that much of a rarity in San Javier.

An Indian girl walked past us several times. She wore a long blue and white print dress and she walked barefoot over the sand and rocks of the street. She passed us once, disappeared, reappeared, went by us again, not looking our way until the third time, when she and Tom locked eyes. She went on ahead of us as we went out of town and along the trail toward where the paintings were. Tom followed her with his eyes. Before she turned to go off down a side trail she turned and smiled invitingly at him.

"You two go on," he said. "I'll catch up with you later."

"But we're going to see the cave paintings," Anjanette protested.

"I just saw something more interesting than a cave painting. You go see the paintings, I'll meet you back here."

"Where will you be?"

"I'll be around."

"Wait," said Anjanette. "These people may not take kindly to white boys messing with their women. Wear this. It'll keep you safe." She gave him an amulet. "Take it, please, Tom, so I don't worry."

Tom had seen enough to know that Anjanette's charms and spells weren't to be taken lightly, so he put the amulet around his neck. It was silver in color and shaped like a heart. (Anjanette always carried a ready supply of charms, amulets, and potions of one kind or another with her.) Then he laughed, raffishly, gave us a thumbs up, and set out down the trail with his cocky insolent walk, going the same way the Indian girl had gone.

"What are you so worried about?" I asked Anjanette.

"I just have a feeling—you two are both so reckless sometimes."

"We've been good this trip, most of the time."

We kept on going along a road, through some open country, up a hill and over it, then down and up again. We came to a cluster of rocks jutting out the side of a hill and climbed toward the mouth of a cave. We stood on the rocks and saw the first paintings. They were painted starkly on the underside of some huge boulders. They were just there, and they came leaping out at you, paintings of deer and of people, stick-like and flat, but in bright colors, more reds of varying hues than anything else. Some figures of people were painted in black, overlaid on the figures of animals.

Then we went inside the cave. The mouth opened up and we stood in a huge, round chamber, with curving walls that went up toward a flat ceiling, and faded back into an endless gloom of black. I immediately thought of the tunnel that led into the old power plant, and wondered if this was going to lead me into a similar kind of dilemma. Then Anjanette turned on the flashlight she had brought with her, and shined it on the walls.

These weren't like the rock paintings, but more of a mural that covered both sides of the wall and parts of the ceiling and ran back into the cave for over 500 feet. There were more paintings of animals, deer with prominent horns running, as if trying to escape from something, for their forelegs were raised up and their mouths slightly open, giving an impression of being frightened. In many places the paintings were laid over one another. There were strange markings that looked almost like eyes, and more animals, some peaceful, others fleeing. But most spectacular were the people, done in black, most of them standing with their arms reaching upward, as if in prayer or beseeching their gods for a blessing.

We walked deeper into the cave, and saw more of the mural, the flashlight revealing it in chunks, like a slowly running silent movie: Now the people-figures were in red, and like the ones that came before them their arms were upraised, but their posture was different, there was more of a feeling of movement. "What are they doing?" I asked.

"They're dancing," Anjanette declared. She handed me the flashlight and stepped closer, not touching them, but holding both her hands out with the palms turned toward the paintings as if they were going to transmit some energy or knowledge to her, osmotically. "They're dancing," she repeated. "Aren't they beautiful? This is The Cave of the Dancers."

There were more figures of deer and sheep, and a mountain goat with a face that was partially red and partially black. Then, by itself, was another drawing of a person, only he had his arms upraised in a gesture of surrender, and his body was shot full of arrows.

"What do you think he did?" Anjanette asked. "Was he a murderer who was punished? Or was he an enemy they killed?"

"Maybe he's a sacrifice," I said. "When did these get painted?"

"I remember reading about them in one of my art books," said Anjanette. "They worked on them for generation after generation. They could go back 7,000 years."

7,000 years, I thought. I tried to imagine these people, living here 7,000 years ago, hunting and fishing and procreating, and coming all the way in here to paint these figures on the walls of a cave, with only torches for light, leaving them for future generations to look at and wonder about. What had they been like, those people? Were they anything like us? Did they love, did they hate, did they kiss their children good-night after telling them a story? They lived, they died, others came after them to live and die too, all part of the ongoing cycle of birth, life, death, returning to whatever it was we came from.

"They're sort of like the cave paintings in Altamira, Spain," said Anjanette, peering at them intently through the gloom, "or the ones in Lascaux, France. "Those are 16,000 years old. I read about them in my art books."

There were pictures of hunters going after bison and deer with spears and arrows, and others of people fishing with long poles. The very last one was of a person by himself, arms upraised like the others but moving in the opposite direction and looking away, searchingly. "What's he doing?" I asked.

"He's looking for something."

"Like a new road to follow?" I wondered. "A new direction in life."

"What were they thinking?" Anjanette said. "Were they wanting to leave this behind, so people in the future would know they were here? Perhaps they wanted to leave something behind, so they would be remembered. Do you think we'll be remembered, Pete? Does it matter, what we do? Will anybody remember us? Just imagine," she went on, speaking in the darkness, for we had come to the end of the cave now, "those Indians 7,000 years ago, painting in here, trying to contact their gods. You can feel their presence still, can't you? Put out the light for a moment, Pete, let's commune with them." I put out the light and Anjanette and I held hands in the darkness. She wanted to contact the spirits of the Old Indians but as we stood there close together I was having other thoughts and feelings that I couldn't keep back. I knew I shouldn't be having them, not about her, but I was, they were real, like a beast I'd kept locked up that had found a way out. Our hands were joined and there was a surge of powerful energy between them, as if a circuit had been opened. She must have been feeling it too because she abruptly said, "Let's go now," and let go of my hand.

We went back to the village, Anjanette talking excitedly about the paintings and the spirits of the Indians. But when we reached the fountain there was no sign of Tom.

"I might have known," Anjanette said.

We walked all around the main street of the village, looking in shops and cafes. The Indians were going to and fro and paid us no special heed. We came back to the fountain with the Madonna and child in the center and stood there, looking about. Anjanette suddenly looked tired from the long walk and she sat on the fountain's edge, put her hand into the water and rubbed some on her face. A small boy approached us.

"Your name Pete?"

"Maybe."

"You want this," he said, holding up a folded piece of paper.

"No," I said automatically. "Go away. Shoo."

"You better take it, Pete," said Anjanette.

I reached for it but the boy said, "Cost you a buck."

I offered him a peso but he wouldn't take it. "I said a buck," he insisted.

I gave him a dollar bill and he skipped away happily. "What's it say?" Anjanette asked.

"'Greetings to my two favorite compadres,'" I read. "'I haven't made it all the way yet but it looks good so far. Go on without me, I'm invited for dinner. Don't do anything you wouldn't want me to know about. Tomboy the Great.'"

"I guess we might as well keep on walking," I said.

We kept walking, back toward the beach where we were camped, going along the rocky road. There were some red flowers blooming, and birds flying overhead. "When it comes to girls, Tom has the magic touch," I said. "It even works here."

"You sound jealous," Anjanette observed.

"I am not," I protested. "I just wish I knew what it is."

A rabbit came alongside us out of the brush, tearing along crazily, even for a rabbit, running first one way and then another, frantic. He was followed by a huge flock of birds in the air, flying unusually high and fast, going straight north. They flew above us, row after row, all of them following the lead bird, strung out behind that one symmetrically in a long V-formation. Where were they going? And why were they in such a hurry?

I felt a change in the air now, and a change over the land as well. The sun got dimmer, like a light bulb getting less electricity fed to it. There was a gust of wind that blew intensely for a moment and then died away as if it had never been there. I sensed the animals stirring in the brush all around us. There was an uneasiness, as if they were frightened en masse—the snakes, the rabbits, the coyotes, the wild dogs of the desert and the cats too, the pumas and the lynx, all preparing to take cover. We came upon a rise now and I could see the sea from there. Far out in the distance over the horizon there was a dark line of clouds. They were arranged in a strange line across the sky, with some that seemed to drop straight down to the water.

We weren't far from camp now, and I felt, irrationally, that we should hurry. When we reached the bottom of the hill there was another blast of wind, very powerful this time, which blew our hair back and caught us by surprise. Anjanette's hat blew off and rolled along the trail for a ways. She ran to get it. Off to our left was a group of Indian shacks, and as we passed them the men were outside, frantically tossing ropes over their thatched roofs and driving stakes of re-bar into the ground with a 16-pound sledgehammer. They would attach the ropes to the stakes and pull them tight. They didn't glance at us as we went by but kept on working. A horse tethered nearby whinnied and kicked. In the distance I heard a wave crash and while at first I paid it no real attention it came to me that this was the Cortez and the waves didn't crash that way here.

I cupped my hands and called over to the Indians. "*Hola! Que paso?*"

The man swinging the sledge hammer paused only long enough to reply in a few terse words before going back to his work.

"What did he say?" asked Anjanette.

"Oh shit," I said.

"What's the matter?"

"Come on!" I yelled, taking her by the hand so I could pull her along. "Run for your life!"

"What is it?" she demanded, running along beside me, one hand holding her hat so it wouldn't blow off again.

"A *chubasco* is about to hit! We've gotta get back to the van and get under cover right now!"

Another blast of wind hit us, more powerful than the last one, and lasting longer, a sustained blast that blew sand in our eyes and pelted us with pebbles that smacked our arms and bare legs like small stinging insects. On foot, it now seemed a million miles back over to where the van was parked. The sheet of wind that had hit us died away, only to be followed by another and then another, slowing us down to a crawl, for we were walking directly into it.

Now there was a scream of thunder overhead, a roar like a cannon going off. We winced involuntarily, then kept going, shielding our eyes with our hands. "We're going to get blown away!" Anjanette cried, but we kept going, slowly, steadily, over some rocks, cutting across a patch of sand by the road, and finally, just as the rain hit, down the embankment by the beach where the van was parked. All was lit up by a pitchfork of lightning out over the water, followed by another clap of thunder. The normally placid Cortez was jumping and raging, with blazing white caps and rolling waves. The gear we had left out by the van was all being blown away. But we had, by sheer luck, parked close to the embankment, and so the van itself was somewhat shielded from the wind. The first few drops of rain, the trickle that precedes a deluge, hit us now, and so did the real wind, for what had come before was just a warm-up, because as I opened the side door of the van so Anjanette could get in first there came a blast of wind that blew the tarp we had set up from its moorings. It broke loose, as if being yanked by a giant hand, first one corner, then the other right after it, then the third. The last one held for a moment and then it too gave way, and the canvas blew off down the beach and out of sight.

"Come on Pete, get in, forget the stuff!" Anjanette yelled. I hopped in and slid the door shut behind me, then sat down next to Anjanette. The van rocked back and forth from the wind.

"'Come on in, I'll give you shelter from the storm,'" Anjanette said, quoting Bob Dylan. "Will the van turn over?" she asked fearfully.

There was a drumming of rain on the roof, more and more, growing steadily until it became a roar. "No," I said. "We're right next to the rocks and the back of the van is to the wind. Our boards and all our stuff outside will get blown to hell, though. Nothing we can do about it. Wow!" I continued. "Have you ever seen anything like it in your life?"

"Never," she said, "never in my life." She grabbed my arm and held it tightly, clutching as if it were a line through to her as she was about to drown. "I can't think of the last time I was this scared, either, Pete. God! I'm so glad you're here with me. I don't think I would have made it back here without you. And what if we'd been five minutes later? We might be dead! Oh! And Tom! What if he didn't get undercover?"

"He must have," I said. "What a day he picked to go looking for romance. I hope he was inside her house, and not under a *boojum* tree somewhere. Don't worry. Tom's a survivor. He'll be okay. One thing about a *chubasco*, they don't last too long."

"They don't?"

"No. They just blow everything to hell and move on."

"Well now that's good to know," Anjanette said gratefully, but right about then there was a crash of lightning exploding as it hit the ground. It sounded like it was not five feel away from the van and while it scared me to death—and I did my best not to let that show—Anjanette nearly jumped out of her skin. She cried out and grabbed me once more, holding me even tighter this time, as if I was her first and last hope, and that if she held onto me she might either be saved from dying here, on this remote beach on this forgotten peninsula, who would want to die here at all, or else, if she had to die, she wouldn't die alone but would take me with her, we would go into the Great Unknown together. She had said, more than once, in her semi-mystical caballistic moments, that death was nothing to fear. It was, after all, only the death of the body, and the body wasn't anything, only dust to dust and ashes to ashes. I realized then that it is one thing to talk about that, you might even believe it, but it is another to really do it, to not be scared out of your mind when lightning is crashing all around you.

Anjanette held onto me, in fact she was right up against me now, saying "Oh! Oh! Oh!" in her fear. I could smell her patchouli oil and felt her breast against my arm. It was growing darker and darker outside as the storm came directly overhead. "God, look at that," she said. "It's black outside. There is no sun. I just realized I'm afraid to die, Pete. I want to live. I'm glad you were here with me."

"We're not going to die," I said.

"Promise?"

"Sure."

"I'm glad anyway. Are you afraid to die?"

"I never thought about it." But that wasn't true. Of course I was afraid. Wasn't everybody? But what was I really afraid of? Dying, and not being able to do all the things I wanted to do? And what were those, and what did it matter anyway? If you were dead you wouldn't care.

"I guess you think I'm silly," Anjanette said.

"Silly? Why?"

"Oh, I always talk about charms and amulets and spells, and then when there's a little storm and lightning I get scared I'm going to die. Oh!" she cried when more lightning crashed. "I'm sorry," she said, rubbing at her face with her hand. "This psyches me out."

"You've got your cross to protect you," I said. "I hope it will reach out and protect me too."

"Oh it will," Anjanette said positively. "The Egyptians believed the ankh was a symbol of life and immortality. Do you think life is everlasting, Pete?"

"It must be."

"This is a wonderful life-experience," she went on, sitting with her knees drawn up and her arms clasped around them. "Traveling with you and Tom this way. I love both of you. No matter what happens, anyplace, anywhere I go, I'll never forget this and what it means to me. This trip is like an epic journey out of a book. Wow. Is it ever dark out there. Listen to that rain. Why do they call it a *chubasco*, what does it mean?"

"It's a storm native to these parts. Most everyplace in the world has storms and winds that make people crazy. Wind does strange things to people. In Europe they have what they call a *foehn* wind, and doctors say blood won't clot normally when its blowing. There is also the *sirocco* of the Mediterranean. Suicide goes up when a *sirocco* is blowing, so does depression."

"That's fascinating," Anjanette said. "How do you know all this?"

"I read a lot. Everybody says I read too much."

"What do you like to read?"

"Oh, everything, anything. It drives people crazy."

"Why does it drive people crazy?"

"It bothers them."

"Like who?"

"My father always said I read too much. He said I always had my nose in some stupid book."

"Most people wished their kids read more."

"Not him. I was going to kill him. I wanted to. I almost did, once. But I couldn't bring myself to do it so I left home instead. I don't know what will become of me now. And you know what? I don't care."

"Lots of people want to kill their fathers," Anjanette said. "I never wanted to kill mine, but I did want to kill my mother lots of times. Why is it we always want to kill the people who are closest to us? I don't know, except that the people we love are the ones who can hurt us the most, and we expect things from them.

"We're all runaways, you, me, Tom. We're all on the run from something. But whenever you run to, you take that thing you're running from along with you, it goes with you and follows you no matter how far you run or where you run to. I don't know what it is you and Tom are running from, but there is something."

Sometimes when Anjanette was doing the Tarot or the Runes there was an expression that came onto her face, a serious, focused expression that made her resemble a different person. She looked older, and wise; I always thought of how she said she was once a Druid priestess. Now she produced the Runes from her among her things. Her long white fingers plunged inside the red bag and I heard the familiar clink of the stones. "Ah," she said, drawing out the Rune Perthro and holding it up for me to see. "You know this one, don't you?"

"Sure. It means a mystery, a hidden matter."

"Something hidden that is going to come to light," she said. "You and Tom are hiding something. But you won't be able to hide it forever. Sooner or later you'll have to bring it out and face it. You can't run all your life. I know that. Do you want to tell me what it is?"

"You're barking up the wrong tree, Anjanette. There isn't anything."

"Oh yes there is."

"No there isn't. What could there be? Two surfer boys like us."

There was another clap of thunder outside. The van rocked back and forth violently from an especially powerful blast of wind. Rain was hitting the sides of the van as well as the roof in a steady staccato. "Hold on," I said, "this is like a roller coaster ride." The blast died away but there were more coming as the storm reached its climax.

"Anjanette," I said, "I figured out why you dress the way you do, back in the States."

"Why?"

"You'd never have any peace, if people saw how beautiful you really are. Talk about hiding something."

"Oh, I am not," she said, but she looked pleased, all the same.

Our hands were beside one another on the floor of the van and they moved at the same time, as if moving under a volition all their own, coming together and holding on. Our fingers intertwined. Anjanette's hand was soft and felt very nice to the touch, and holding it made a thrill run through me. We were sitting there looking right at each other. I saw every line and contour of her face, saw the light colored eyebrows and the fair hair on her upper cheekbones that was all but invisible. Her eyes were deep blue, like a calm sea, and were bottomless, like the universe. I thought, right then, looking into them, that I was looking into a tunnel that led directly into infinity. Where would this take me, where would I go if I went in there? And what would I find on the other side? There was a promise of some sort here, but a warning too--don't go, it was saying. Once again, as if some force other than our own wills were acting upon us, our mouths came together and we kissed deeply and long. We didn't break apart until there was another clap of thunder outside. We were both out of breath, and looking at each other.

At last Anjanette said, "You shouldn't have done that, Pete."

And I said, "I know."

She said, "You shouldn't have."

"I'm sorry."

"You know what would happen if—I told you all about it."

"I know," I said. "I'm sorry. It's just that—"

We kissed again, longer this time, continuing until we were immersed in it, this kiss felt like it could go on forever, and I felt I would burst inside.

"Don't, Pete, don't," she said.

Anjanette pushed at me, half—heartedly, then dissolved liquidly into my arms again. "Don't—don't," she kept saying. "You can't—you can't—don't you see—don't you—"

By this time we were on the floor of the van, stretched out amidst the clutter of boxes and scattered items of varying size and shape that we carried back there: Food, clothes, transistor radios, plates and other dishes of plastic, the kind you take when you go camping. Another blast of wind shook the van. "I want you, I want you," she whispered to me, "but we can't—you know we can't—"

I was on her by now, but we were still dressed, clawing at each other, holding tightly. I felt her body stiffening, then trembling, as I moved on her. We moved together, in a cadence of pleasure and want. Anjanette shuddered, just as I was shuddering and rocking, faster and faster, until it came to an end right when there was another clap of thunder outside.

Afterward we lay there listening to the rain. It seemed the storm was passing, for there was less thunder now, and what we heard was moving further away. Then I laughed a little bit. I couldn't help it.

"What are you laughing about?" Anjanette demanded. "This is not funny, it is not something to laugh about."

"My pants are all sticky and wet," I said. "It's like I had a wet dream. I haven't had one for a long time. Only this time I was awake."

Anjanette laughed some too, and she patted my cheek affectionately.

"You know this can't ever happen again," she said.

Now I became worried. "You don't think that what you said would happen is going to happen, do you? Because of this?"

"No, I guess not. Because we didn't really do it. But it might have happened. We came awfully close. And it can't happen again, Pete. You understand, don't you?"

I said I understood, and when she asked me to promise I promised, and she looked at me real hard to see if I meant it. She was satisfied with what she saw, because she sat up and began to rearrange her clothes, a tug here, a yank there, then got a brush and began to swipe at her hair with it.

"What would Tom say?" she asked. "If he knew about this? How would he feel, what would he say?"

What would Tom say? I hadn't thought of that. What *would* Tom say? He'd be crushed, naturally, and he would feel betrayed. Somehow the idea didn't bother me that much. In fact it was all I could do to keep from laughing out loud when I thought about it, laughing with sheer delight. For it seemed to me that I had, at long last, stolen a march on him, I had gotten someplace before he did, I had beaten him at something. Name one thing Tom couldn't do better than me. When it came to surfing I wasn't even in his league. He scampered around the cliffs here, diving off them like a native, and when he saw a girl he wanted he just went right up and talked to her like there was no doubt in his mind that she would be absolutely delighted at the whole idea. And ninety-nine times out of one hundred, they were. And he could deny it all he wanted to, there was no way I'd ever believe he didn't want Anjanette just as bad as I did. All that sister-brother talk was as bogus as the earth being flat. He'd do it, too. If things had been reversed and he'd been here alone with Anjanette he'd have done the same thing, you couldn't tell me anything different, not after what he'd done with Tiffany back in the States. The guy would fuck anything that would hold still for him. What was it he always said, a stiff dick had no conscience? His more than any other had no conscience. I had beaten him to it, that was all, and even if I hadn't gotten in all the way it was the next best thing. It was payback, in a way, for what he had done with Tiffany.

But in the hours and days that followed, as we cleaned up after the storm and headed south toward La Paz (Tom had weathered the storm just fine, in the loving arms of the Indian girl and within the four solid walls of her home) I experienced all sorts of conflicting feelings. My elation faded, and I felt guilty, thinking I had betrayed both Tom and Anjanette. What if we had really gone all the way, what would happen to her then? I wouldn't have cared, not right then while it was happening. Then, when I thought of how good Anjanette felt in my arms I longed for her again, and would have given anything to have those moments back.

And a few times I thought Tom gave me a strange glance here and there, as if he knew or at least suspected that something had happened. He never said anything about it. But I thought he had to suspect, anybody would. But maybe I was imagining things.

Anjanette and I had a secret now, something we had shared, only us. I'd catch her looking at me and I'd look back. She would look away before Tom noticed anything, and I would feel something like satisfaction inside. She preferred me to him. That was a good feeling, all the more so when I thought of how the girls always ran over me to get to Tom.

A lot of our stuff had gotten blown away with the chubasco, but we didn't lose anything of great value. We cleaned up our camp, found whatever we could, tied our boards back on the roof of the van, and went on to La Paz.

Chapter 23

The Promenade

I was in one of those Hemingwayesque bars of driftwood logs and bamboo and fisherman's netting thrown over the top and on the windows that dot the coastline on the Cortez side of Baja, when I met Ray.

"Hey boy," he said from the table where he sat alone, an empty beer bottle in front of him. "Buy me a beer and I'll tell your fortune for you."

"I don't need anybody to tell my fortune," I said. "I've got this." I took my crystal from my pocket. "But I'll buy you a beer."

The gnarled face lit up and he came over to sit beside me at the bar.

"Good to see another *norteamericano*," he said. "Not many get down this way."

His face was grizzled and lined from the wind, his hair was white, and his hands were calloused and bent. A fisherman, I assumed.

"How long you been in La Paz?" he asked.

"Just got here."

"You like it?"

"Oh, hell yes."

"I love it here," the old fellow said. "I wouldn't live anywhere else in the world, and I wouldn't be anything else in the world. I'm the happiest man on earth, boy, what do you think about that?"

"What are you?" I asked. "A fisherman?"

"Why, hell, boy, I'm something a lot more than a fisherman. I'm a *vagabundo del mar.*"

"So you're one of the *vagabundos,*" I said. I had heard about them all the way from the start of our journey. Everybody seemed to know of them, but few people claimed to have actually met one.

"You're damn right," he said. "My name's Ray, Ray Harris. Been out here since '53."

"What does a *vagabundo* do?"

"Do?" he parroted. "Do? It isn't about *doing*, it's about *being,* see? It's a way of life. It's about what's in here," he said, pointing at his heart.

The *vagabundos* were a secret brotherhood, he explained, dedicated to helping people in need. You could find them all over the Sea of Cortez, men who lived by the water in huts, not owning much more than a dugout canoe and a harpoon. But if a boater got into trouble, he could count on a *vagabundo* coming to help him. If a tourist got shipwrecked on one of the many islands that criss-cross the Cortez, a *vagabundo* would come to the rescue. *Vagabundos* had been known to even go to the Isle of Tiburon, a place nobody else would set foot, if somebody needed help. "You've heard about that, I suppose," he asked, and I told him I had, and that I'd even seen some Seri Indians, who were supposed to be cannibals. He nodded appreciatively. "And we never ask a penny for what we do," he said proudly. "We're like the old Knights Templars, sworn to do good and live in poverty."

"It sounds like being a *vagabundo* is another way of being a bum."

"That isn't true," he bristled. "It was my destiny."

I bought him another beer and he relaxed. "I bet you're going to the Promenade tonight."

"What's the promenade?"

"Why," he said, "that's one of the best things about La Paz," and he laughed, and then winked. "There's five women for every man here. I swear it's no joke. The men are all out working in the fields, or else out on the fishing boats. So it's a tradition around here, on Thursday nights and Sunday nights all the unattached girls to the Promenade Square and try to meet men. If I was a young buck like you I sure as hell would go there."

I remembered that today was Thursday, and told myself it might be worth going over and taking a look.

"I have to go," I said, picking up my hat.

"Come on, buy me another beer."

"I gotta go."

"Don't forget," he called to me, "you have to seek your destiny. It'll come looking for you if you don't."

What was my destiny? I'd asked myself that enough times.

•   •   •

La Paz has a large wharf and Spanish-style *hacienda* houses. There were stores for tourists and some big hotels. I cantered along until I came back to the *malecon,* and then after hesitating a moment I began walking toward the Promenade Square. I didn't really believe what old Ray had said about there being more women than men here, but the idea was intriguing enough that I decided it was worth taking a look at.

And it turned out he was right—there were a lot more girls than men. The women were all on one side, and the men were lined up on the other. The women walked in a counter-clockwise direction, the men walked the other way, so the two groups formed parallel lines, going past each other slowly and deliberately. The girls would smile demurely and then look away, covering their faces sometimes, the men pausing when things looked promising. But no words were exchanged. It was all done in the most electric kind of silence. The men wore embroidered vests, white shirts and tight pants, the women had on long dresses and lace, with combs in their hair.

I joined in. No one took any special notice of my presence, even though I was the only *norteamericano* there. The longer this went on the better I liked it. I shuffled along, smiling at the girls, and some of them smiled back and one in particular flashed her black eyes at me, and I was beginning to wonder what the next step was, how do you get from here to the saying hello what's-your-name part, and a breeze blew in nicely from the ocean and I heard the rumble of the waves, and then I spotted Anjanette nearby. She waved eagerly to me, and so I left the Promenade line and went over to her.

"Are you having any luck?" she asked, smiling.

"I just got started. *Quien sabe?*"

"Tom sent me to find you," Anjanette explained. "There's a party at the Hotel Los Cocos we've been invited to. A bunch of Americans he met. I think he's flirting with one of the girls. Do you want to go?"

"I don't mind."

"If you want to stay here, it's okay. It looks to me like you were doing all right."

"No," I said, "a party sounds fine. I can't seem to figure out how to get to step two here, anyway."

Anjanette and I walked along the tree-lined waterfront, feeling the wind blowing in off the bay. Some ships sat in the harbor, waiting to be unloaded. We went down a narrow quiet street and toward the lobby of a big, old, grand-looking hotel, the kind only the richest tourists would stay in. It was built in the same Spanish-Arabian style as the missions we had seen.

"Isn't this town wonderful?" Anjanette asked as we went in past the main desk and onto the terrace in the back. "I love it here."

"Me too."

"Pete, you and Tom are the best friends I ever had," Anjanette declared suddenly. "I've never been happier in my life, since I met you two."

"That's the truth," I said. "We're the best of friends, aren't we?"

A band was playing in the corner. There was a dance floor and people were dancing to a cha-cha-cha kind of beat. There was a constant sound of glasses clinking and white-jacketed waiters hurried along with their trays full of drinks and bottles. The guests seemed to all be Americans. As we came in I noticed something scurrying in a corner and saw that it was a large cockroach. "Ugh," I said, pointing it out to Anjanette. "They grow big here, don't they?"

"You wouldn't think you would see one in a place like this."

"Hey! Over here! Pete, Anjanette!" Tom called, standing up and waving to us. He was sitting with a group of Americans. Several tables had been pushed together to accommodate them all. They made places for Anjanette and I and we sat down with them.

They were a very collegiate-looking crowd and it turned out that was exactly what they were, a group of students and two professors from Duke University in North Carolina. They had been in southern Mexico, the man who was obviously the one in charge explained, doing some anthropological field work, but they had finished earlier than planned and had taken the ferry from Mazatlan over here to La Paz, "Just so we can say we did it."

His name was Professor McLeod, and he stood up courteously and offered to shake hands with us both, speaking in a melodious southern accent. He wore a tweed jacket with patches on the elbows. He introduced us to the lady on his left, a scholarly-looking woman who was the other professor, and then to the rest of the students, boys and girls who all looked very far from home. One, a tall, pale, reedy fellow named Randall, greeted us with a bright smile that did not extend to his burning gray eyes. He didn't shake hands but instead said, "May God bless you always." When his strange eyes lighted on Anjanette they lingered, looking her up and down. "God bless you," he repeated.

Tom was already drunk. He and a black-haired girl named Sheila sat talking by themselves at the far end of the table.

"I understand you've driven all the way here." Professor McLeod said. "That's supposed to be almost impossible to do, so I am told. You're quite a group of adventurers. Where are you bound for from here?"

"Cabo San Lucas," I said.

"I've heard about Cabo," he said. He produced a pipe and began trying to light it. He put a match to it over and over, drew, then tapped it. "A small fishing village, right at the end of the Peninsula. John Steinbeck visited there during his journey to the Sea of Cortez in 1940.

Why do you want to go there?"

"To complete our journey," I said. "When we set out, from San Ysidro, we said we were going to drive all the way to the end of the Peninsula."

"Quite an accomplishment," said the Professor. "You form an interesting little group. You seem very attached to one another. Where do you live, may I ask?"

Anjanette and I told him a little about Kekaha, which he said he would like to visit sometime. "Communal life," he mused. "Very interesting. How long are you going to stay in Baja?"

"I like it here so much," I said, drinking a margarita, "that I may never go back."

"You want to dance?" Randall asked Anjanette abruptly.

"All right," she said, but she didn't look too thrilled about it.

"What prompted you to go on this adventure?" the Professor asked. "What is your motivation?"

"I'm not sure," I said. "Maybe so we could just say we had done it."

"That doesn't seem like a very good reason to me," said the Professor, trying once again to light his pipe. "But I suppose, in this day and age, it's as good as any other."

I drank some more, then looked at Anjanette dancing with Randall. "I might stay here and become a *vagabundo del mar*."

"A what?"

"A gypsy of the sea," I said, and told him about Ray and the secret brotherhood of the *vagabundos*.

"How utterly fascinating," said Professor McLeod. "I never heard of them before. I would love to meet one. How many of these people did this fellow say there were?"

"I don't think anybody knows, but Ray said he thought there were around one hundred of them."

"And do you think he was sincere when he said he was the happiest man in the world?"

I looked up, because the song had ended and Anjanette and Randall had come back to the table.

"Who claims to be the happiest man in the world?" Randall asked. He sat down and picked up his drink, and I saw that his hands were trembling and that his fingernails were bitten and ragged-looking. He saw that I noticed, and hid his hands under the table.

"A fellow Pete here met earlier in the day, a sea-going gypsy who has renounced the material life," the Professor explained.

"He couldn't be," Randall declared, smiling. "True happiness only comes when you have taken the Lord into your heart."

"How do you know he hasn't?" I asked.

"Hasn't what?"

"Taken the Lord into his heart?"

"Has he?"

"I asked you first."

"Randall is our resident religious person," Professor McLeod broke in. "He speaks with all the fire of a newly-won convert, which in fact, he is."

"It's true, I only found the Lord recently," Randall said. "After years of sin and debauchery I was born again. I know now the only way to salvation and grace is through the mercy of our beloved Lord, Jesus Christ. There is no other way. Hell-fire awaits everyone else. I escaped hell-fire," he said smugly. "I now have a personal and intimate relationship with Jesus Christ, our Lord. And it is only when you have that, that you can find real peace, true happiness."

"Randall is giving up his studies in anthropology to study for the ministry," Professor McLeod said.

"The pagan idolatry and heathen idol-worship we saw in Yucatan was very good for me," Randall said. "It shows me how much of the Lord's work remains to be done. I also saw proof of His mighty vengeance. He destroyed those people because of their wicked ways, just like he destroyed Sodom and Gomorrah, just as he will destroy anyone who doesn't believe in him. I saw that just as surely as I can see Anjanette's lovely face." He smiled and raised his glass to her in a salute.

"Yes, well, that's one possible explanation," said Professor McLeod, "but certainly not the only one."

"It is the only one," Randall said inflexibly. "You can never doubt the great works of the Lord."

"What do you know about the Lord?" I said.

Randall smiled. "We Christians know that His way is the only way. We know that there are billions of people who will perish, horribly, when Judgment Day comes, because they do not know Him."

"You sound like that makes you happy," I said.

"On the contrary," he said. "It makes me very sad. I spend a great deal of my time grieving for them, the pagans, the Jews, the Buddhists, all those who aren't Christians, for they will all die at the hand of our Master. It saddens me to know that they could escape this fate, if only they would take Him into their hearts."

"So you're saying that anyone who doesn't believe the way you do is doomed?" I asked him.

"It isn't what I believe. It's what God believes. He rejects Jews, because they do not believe in our Lord Jesus. He rejects Hindus, because they believe in many gods." He finished his drink and signaled the waiter for another.

"Why can't people worship God in their own way?"

Randall smiled again. "In the Bible it says very plainly, 'I am a jealous God, and you shall have no other gods before me.' There is only one way to worship Him. There is only one way to love Him. There is only one way to interpret His holy words. All the other ways are the ways of damnation, and will lead to hell. The Bible says so."

"So you believe everything in the Bible?" I asked.

"Every single thing. The Bible says it, I believe it, that settles it. I believe God created man in His own image, and that He created the world in six days, and that on the seventh day, He rested."

"Why would God need to rest?" I asked.

The smile disappeared only to be replaced by a scowl. "You need to read the Bible more," he said.

Anjanette nudged me with her elbow.

"Let's go and dance," she said.

"I don't think I've ever danced with you before," she said. "And I wanted to get you away from that weird guy. What do you think of this party?"

"Boring, so far."

"I think so too. We're only here because Tom has the hots for that college girl. Think he'll get anywhere with her?"

I glanced over at her. "She looks like a prude."

"You can't judge a book by its cover, remember," Anjanette smiled. "She's all covered up, hiding herself. Those are just the ones who are doing it the most."

"I don't like that guy," I said.

"You mean Randall?"

"Yeah, the weirdo."

"He's weirder than you think," said Anjanette. "All the time I was dancing with him he just kept talking about how holy he is, but all he did was paw me, you know, grabbing my ass, trying to get a cheap feel. That's how holy he is."

"I think I'll go over there," I said, "and bust him one on his holy nose."

"Oh, please don't do that!" Anjanette pleaded. "I'd feel terrible. There's no need for it."

"All right," I said. "But I still don't like the guy. Don't dance with him anymore, ok?"

"Let's stay here in Baja forever, you, me, Tom. Want to?"

"Count me in."

Anjanette, like always, had her Runestones with her, and when we got back to the table she began to lay them out. Everyone watched with interest although they were all quick to say they did not believe in anything like this.

"Are you a fortuneteller, by profession?" Professor McLeod asked, his pipe in his mouth.

"No. I was a whore once, though," and let the words hang in the air like a gust of black smoke. There was a sudden silence at our part of the table.

I polished off the rest of my margarita and poured myself some more. "You pick the greatest times to decide to be a stand-up comedian," I said to her, *sotto voce*.

"This party needs to be livened up," she whispered back.

"Was that a serious statement?" asked Professor McLeod.

"Yes," came the reply.

"When you say—whore," said the lady professor, and from the way she said "whore" I got the impression she had never spoken the word publicly before, "do you mean whore as in—" She stopped, as if unable to finish the sentence.

"I mean," said Anjanette, "whore as in prostitute. Whore as in hooker." She went on laying out the Runes.

Again there was an uncomfortable silence. I drank more of the margarita and as it went to work on me I had all I could do to keep from laughing. Across from me Randall sat, and I saw his hands clench as if he was trying to squeeze something. Then Professor McLeod asked, nervously, "Is that how you all met, by chance?"

"Oh no," Anjanette said.

He looked relieved. "And I take it you don't—practice—that occupation any longer?"

"No," Anjanette said. "I'm retired."

A sense of relief came into the general atmosphere now. Everyone relaxed. Professor McLeod's pipe had gone out and he set about relighting it.

"These Runes," he said, "appear to be a form of divination. Similar to the I Ching or the Oracle at Delphi."

"They are tools of the devil," Randall declared.

"You find divination all over the world," said Professor McLeod.

"Those stones are evil," Randall said. "They should be destroyed."

"They are no more evil than tossing a coin to determine a dispute is evil," said the Professor.

"They're demonic," said Randall. "The devil's work."

He began to pound the table and point at Anjanette.

"You are a whore, a witch, an abomination," he said.

"Take it easy, my boy," said Professor McLeod to Randall, laying a hand on his shoulder. "It looks to me like you've had a little too much to drink."

"The Lord your God *hates* people who use charms and engage in witchcraft," Randall stated wildly. "The Bible says, 'Thou shalt not suffer a witch to live.' Witch! Whore! Abomination!"

He emphasized each line by pounding on the table. He was standing by now, and glasses and cups were falling over as he flailed about.

"Randall," Professor McLeod said uneasily, "I think you'd better go to bed."

"You'll burn in hell, you're evil," Randall said to Anjanette.

She drew back in her chair, frightened, and there was a scream and Randall dove across the table, hands outstretched like hooks.

Glasses, plates, silverware all went crashing to the floor. There were screams of dismay. "For the love of God I must kill this witch!" Randall shouted.

The table went over, knocking me sideways, and landed on top of me, pinning me to the floor. To my horror, I saw Randall's hands close over Anjanette's soft neck, the thumbs digging in. Her windpipe was being crushed. She gurgled feeble choking sounds and beat impotently at him, trying to get him off her, but to no avail.

I untangled myself from my chair and pushed the table off, just as Tom arrived. He began hitting Randall in the face. Over and over Tom's powerful fist smashed into Randall's nose, and then his mouth. Blood streamed and flowed down his neck and then onto his shirt. More blows followed, the blood was gushing now, and still he held onto Anjanette's throat. At last I grabbed one of Randall's hands with both of mine and Tom did the same thing. We twisted and pried and finally broke the terrible hold. Anjanette coughed and choked, holding her hands to her bruised throat, her face pale, tears flowing out of her eyes. Randall thrashed and struggled and screamed, spittle from his mouth mingling with his freely flowing blood. I hit him several times in the body, and Tom hit his face. He seemed to feel nothing, not the smashed nose, not the blows to the mouth that turned his lips into swollen tatters of meat. He thrashed about like a wild beast, and I had to hold on with both hands to keep him from getting loose.

"Get a hammerlock on the son-of-a-bitch," Tom cried, but I wasn't able to bend his arm and neither was Tom. Then, with a superhuman effort, Randall broke the hold I had on him and pulled loose from Tom. In a second he was gone, running through the crowd and out of sight.

I was all for going after him, but Tom stopped me. "Let the bastard go for now, let's see how Anjanette's doing," and we went to her. She was sitting up now, still choking horribly, and when we got there she began to cry.

"How is it, babe?" Tom asked.

"Why did he do that?" she asked weakly, barely able to speak, sounding as if she were speaking through a tube. "What did I do to him? I was only looking at my Runes."

"He's a fucking lunatic," said Tom. "If I see that guy again I'm gonna kill him."

The two professors were horrified, and kept saying how sorry they were. "He hasn't been the same since he went to a revivalist meeting a few months ago and came back saying he had been touched by the hand of God," said Professor McLeod.

"What the hell did you bring him along for, if you knew he was a nut case?" asked Tom.

"I thought he was harmless," said Professor McLeod weakly.

"Well, he isn't," said Tom. "And if I see him again I'll show him a few things."

This was the end of the party, and we went back to the hostel we were staying in, considerably shaken up and almost sober from the commotion. We gathered up Anjanette's Runes from the floor and walked back through the quiet streets, Anjanette still sobbing and hurting, Tom saying over and over what he'd do to Randall if he ever caught up with him again.

"It's my fault," he said. "It was my idea to go to this party. I'm sorry, Anjanette."

"It isn't your fault," she said. She was unable, for nearly a week after this, to speak normally. There were some terrible bruises on her throat, purple blotches from Randall's fingers.

She couldn't sleep that night, and she said the next morning that whenever she closed her eyes she saw him coming at her again. For the next several days, until the bruises went away, she wore a scarf about her neck, in order to hide them, and many times after I saw her looking at them, as if she wondered if she could wipe them away somehow. It took a long time for them to fade

Chapter 24

Cabo San Lucas

We reached Cabo San Lucas the next day.

It was just a village in those days, although there were some swanky hotels for wealthy tourists outside of town, close to a small airport. There was one main street that was made of dirt. There were shops and cafes along both sides of the street, with side streets going in both directions as well. From either end of town you could make your way to the water.

The first day we got there we stood on the Cabo San Lucas Ferry, where a ship had just docked from Puerto Vallarta. This was where Mexico's Highway 1 came to an end, and we were 1059 miles from where we had started back in San Ysidro.

There was a beach near Land's End, and we used to go there, for this was the very end of the Baja Peninsula. There were some tall, stately rocks known as the Friars which jutted out of the sea, and they formed a trail that went into the ocean like stepping stones and then abruptly came to an end. You could sit right there and watch the rocks peter out and see the place where California comes to an end, and where the Pacific Ocean and the Sea of Cortez come together. Nearby, all alone, stood another tall rock, called the Bishop, looking down frowningly on all this, with the waves swirling all around and the sea dropping off sharply to great depths just a few feet away.

The beaches we had seen so far were beautiful enough, but the Cabo San Lucas beaches took your breath away. They stretched out endlessly, long cords of unblemished sand that was white like snow, laying there in contrast to the deep blue of the sea. There were tall cliffs and caves to explore, and we watched whales spout as they rounded the cape. In the distance the 6,000 foot peaks of the Sierra de la Victoria rose up majestically. In the surrounding countryside were trees and thatched huts, and fields of sugar cane, dates, bananas, papayas, and mangoes.

We took a room at a hostel near the beach. Usually we went for a swim first thing, to wake us up. Sometimes we spent the day together and other times we went our separate ways. Tom would surf and explore the tide pools, Anjanette went for long walks on the beach, and I would wander through town. I had found a coffee shop I liked, Don Pepe's it was called, and I would sit on the second floor balcony and drink espresso or the rich, thick *cafe* they serve there, watching the people as they went by and writing in my journal. Some mornings I got up early, earlier than Tom, got into my van and drove to a deserted point on the eastern side of the cape, and watched the sun come up. There was a cafe that opened early, catering to the fishermen who went out with the morning tide, and I would get a big styrofoam cup of "*cafe con leche pero no sukla, por favor,*" (coffee with milk but no sugar, please,") and watch the spectacular sunrise. I would go down among the rocks on the bluffs, and sit, my back against a boulder in the half-light, listening to the surf come in and out far below me, and sip at my coffee. Then, on the far horizon over the water, would come the first light of the sun, a red glow, growing larger and larger with each passing second, spreading its long light over the smooth peaceful surface of the sea. I would rise and greet the sun, spreading my arms out in the sign of Sowelu. And in my mind I wanted to play the drum roll to *Also Sprach Zarathustra*, which Carolyn had played so many times when we were in her bed, because it seemed like every time the sun rose it was a triumph, a new beginning, the darkness was being vanquished and the light emerged victorious. Because every end is a new beginning, the world was being born again and I was being reborn with it. It was like witnessing a birth, to see the sun rise higher and higher in the sky, as if struggling to emerge from the night, like a butterfly struggling out of its cocoon, and then there it was, in all its glory, spreading its light over the world again. Far below me I heard the elephant seals bark, as if applauding the new day, and out in the ocean manta rays leaped from the water. The waves crashed harder, just that one time, as if they were cannons being fired in salutation.

And at night sometimes I would head out in the other direction, taking the road out of town and going to some cliffs that faced the Pacific side of the Cape, and here I'd look at the sun going down. And if the sun rising was like a birth, then the sunset was like a death. The sun was a white ball, dropping lower and lower on the horizon, turning blood red the lower down it went, until it touched the water. The round edges became more defined, and it assumed a bright red clarity, a shining disk of fire in the sky. It dropped lower and lower, and then was gone just as surely as if it had never been there. What is death, I wondered, what is life? How does life go into a body, what puts it there? Does the sun give life? And if it does, who put that sun up there in the first place, what made it begin to shine on the first morning the world began? Where did life come from? Once when I was sitting at my table in the coffee shop in the village a yellow wasp, of which there are many in Baja, slow and bumbling, came buzzing too close to me and so I swatted it, knocking the life out of it right there in front of me. I stared at it after. Its transparent wings were folded and quiet now, all four of them (wasps have four wings, I learned) and its legs no longer moved. I looked at the three parts of its body, and prodded it with the end of my pen, turning it over. Its body was stripped with small black lines, its antennae hooked sharply outward. One moment life and been inside it, now that life was gone. Now it was just dead matter, and was sorry I killed it. For a long time I sat staring at the wasp, wondering if I could somehow put the life back in. But that didn't work, and I realized, if I hadn't known it before, that there was no putting the life back into something once it was taken out.

• • •

In the morning I thought of life, in the evening of death. Two times now death had touched me, first Brian, and then Deacon. And I felt responsible for them both. I could have stopped Brian from going into the old plant that time, and maybe there was some way I could have stopped those guys from killing Deacon. Two deaths had been laid on me, and there was one thing more hanging over me, something I still had to do, and yet I lacked the courage to do it.

Sometimes when I sat I wondered about the very first sunrise. I wished I had been there to see it. And I thought of how the sun has been doing this everyday for billions of years. And the ocean, rolling in and out like that, forever—everything just seemed right, in harmony, as I sat like that, all was happening just as it was supposed to.

But sitting there reflecting that way it came to me that I wasn't right inside, there was still something wrong. I had run away, hoping, believing, I could leave all the bad stuff behind. But I understood, more and more, that you can't run away, it comes with you, it always does. A terrible wrong had been done, and I wouldn't be right inside until I had set it right.

This came to me little by little, in bits and pieces, because I had pressed all this down very far and it kept on coming back to the surface during these morning meditations of mine. I remembered those visions I'd had of Deacon's head covered with spiders and when I looked out at the ocean I realized he was still out there suffering like that, out on some ethereal plane that I couldn't see but which was real all the same, and his torment would go on until I did what I had to do. I felt I was caught in an awful trap. I knew what I had to do—I had to go back to Angels Beach and tell the police that it was Dave and Larry who killed Deacon. For a while I thought of sending a letter, but then I realized that wouldn't do any good. No, I had to go and do it in person, and take the consequences. This was bad enough, for as Tom had said Dave and Larry would no doubt kill me, but just as bad was that I had sworn a sacred oath to Tom that I would never tell. Not only that, but if I told I'd have to say that Tom was there too, and drag him into it. So there I was, caught in a trap, and I couldn't see any way out of it.

• • •

Tom and I went surfing almost every morning. The weather here was warmer than it was in the States, in fact it was downright hot and getting hotter everyday, up near 100 degrees sometimes, and so we didn't need wetsuits even in the early morning because the water here was warm too. Sometimes I liked watching him better than I liked surfing, because he was a spectacular sight to see out there on his board. He came winging down a wave dramatically, locked in and doing a spinner or the Quasimodo. I'd come in after a few rides and just sit on the beach, watching.

And there was nobody else surfing here. The place was undiscovered. He'd come in and sit next to me on the beach, his hair plastered to his head, and say in an almost reverential tone how great it was to be here.

• • •

It wasn't long before the locals were used to us. They saw that we weren't ordinary tourists; plainly, we had come to stay for a while. Soon they had created names of their own for us: Tom was "*el hombre del mar*," the man of the sea, while Anjanette was "*la muchacha dorea*," the golden girl. I was known as "*el escritor*," the writer, because they saw me sitting pensively on the veranda of the coffee house writing in my journal everyday. Life seemed so peaceful that I thought often of a song that seemed made for how we lived here:

"Slow down, you move too fast/You got to make the morning last
Just kicking down the cobblestones/Looking for fun and feeling groovy."

Sometimes when I was sitting at the cafe in the village I'd see a golden head that seemed to have a halo around it moving gracefully through the people on the street, and Anjanette would come up the stairs, her sketchbook in hand, and join me at my table. She became more beautiful everyday. She would show me what she had drawn, and I would read to her what I had written. "You write like I draw," she said.

She drew the sea, and the rocks, and the people. She drew men in *sombreros,* working in the fields with their machetes, or the fishermen at their boats. She would get up early sometimes and go to the docks and watch them as they prepared to go out with the morning tide, watch as they geared up their boats, loading their lines and their bait, and then she would some back in the afternoon when they returned with their catches and take a look at them then too. Huge waves would be crashing in the background, the boats would be tossed about on the sea like leaves. "Remember the storm, back near La Paz?" she asked once. "How could I forget that?" I replied. "Well, look at this," she said, and showed me a sketch she had begun, titled, of course, "*Chubasco.*" It was of a van and two people caught in a storm, with everything flying about everywhere and the two people struggling to get to safety. I looked at the people in the drawing. It wasn't exactly me and her, but there was a resemblance there very definitely.

She had taken one of her crystals that had hung from her alcove and brought it with her to Baja. It hung from her neck the way mine did and she wore it for the same reason, for luck. It flashed in the sun and she said if she looked in it long enough she could see things in there, answers to questions came to her that way, and she saw things she wanted to paint or draw.

The bruises on her neck faded in time, and so did the memory of what happened, although she still cried out in her sleep sometimes and woke up, saying she had been dreaming about it. But she didn't harbor any hatred for Randall. She said we should pray for him instead. I never prayed for him and I don't think Tom did either. I still prayed, though. I prayed that those bad things I still felt inside would be taken away, be released, the way Tom had released the wasp Pepsis that day, that they be turned loose in the air. But I didn't always pray. When I got scared I believed, and then I prayed, but when I didn't feel scared I didn't believe. I thought of that phony Reverend Jim and Rena and how I'd been taken in by that Church, and I said to myself I wouldn't ever pray again as long as I lived, but that didn't last. I had brought my Bible-book along with me, and once in a while I would open it up, and read to myself from the Psalms or the New Testament. Sometimes I wrote little essays in my journal about what I thought it all meant, what God was and what Jesus' life had been all about. Then I'd be embarrassed, and I'd put the book away, and wouldn't think of any of that for a while.

One day Anjanette showed me another drawing she'd made. "Here are the children, here," she said, for it was of a scene at the beach, "and here are the fishermen about to set off in their boats. See the old men? They are seeing the past, this is what they used to do, while the children are seeing the future, what they will be doing someday. This is their life, what they were born into, and it's there one day and then it passes on like a candle burning out. That's why you have to grab it while you can, because you only have a short time in the sun."

"Is this our time in the sun?" I asked.

"Yes, this is our day," she replied. "Get all you can from it, because it won't come again."

"What comes after?" I asked. "What came before? Do you know? Can anybody know? I always wondered how the universe could go on forever. What's at the end of forever?"

"This is like a dream, all of it," Anjanette said. She looked out at the street below. "Maybe it's all a dream, life, I mean. We just dream the whole thing, and when we die we just wake up from it. 'Life is but a dream,' remember that?"

"But who's dreaming it? God?" I asked. "All that stuff is way up the clouds. Sometimes I like it better down on earth. Don't you ever wish for somebody to hold you, to love you, to pat you on the head and tell you how beautiful you are?"

She looked at me for a long time. "Oh yes," she said finally. "Very much. You don't know how much, Pete."

"Maybe I do know."

"No one can know. How can you really know what's in somebody else's heart?"

"Maybe you can. I think I know what's in yours..."

"No you don't, you can't, and I want you to stop talking like this."

"Why?"

"Just don't."

"All right, I won't. But you can't escape from it so easy."

"But I can still escape. And I can still do what I have to do."

"We all have to do that," I said.

Chapter 25

Robert

We were in the little cantina called Paco's Place on the far side of the village, sitting at a wooden table drinking beer. Anjanette had her Runestones laid out in a Celtic Cross and was peering at them intently. A man—an American by the look of him—walking by paused, looked at them, then looked at us. "Do you read palms too?" he asked Anjanette.

We all tensed, remembering what had happened in La Paz. "What's it to you?" Tom shot back.

"I had my palm read by a woman, years ago, who claimed to be a gypsy," the man replied. "I didn't believe it so much at the time but everything she said came true. I always wished I could find her again. Do you mind if I join you? I came down here by myself from L.A. and I'm so sick of talking to these rich tourist-types at the hotel. Boring! You're the first real-looking people I've seen since I got here. I'm Robert," he said, eagerly offering his hand to each of us. "So tell me," he said to Anjanette, "do you read palms?"

"I'm better at the Tarot and the Runes."

"So these are the Runes. I've read about them. Are they any good?"

"Try them and see," Anjanette offered.

He asked some questions and Anjanette answered them by digging into the Rune bag and telling him what each of the glyphs represented. Robert was plainly impressed by what turned up.

"Are you a gypsy?" he asked Anjanette.

"Do I look like a gypsy?" she countered.

"You look like an angel, and you are one of the most beautiful women I've come across in a long time. I'll give you one hundred dollars for a longer reading, if you'll do it now."

Anjanette looked uncertainly at Tom and I. We looked Robert over. He was around thirty-five, on the short side, slightly built and fragile-looking. His small hands, which he placed on the table, appeared soft and weak—hands that would break if shaken too hard. He wore a black shirt, open at the collar, tight-fitting white pants and shoes, all of which looked as if they cost a lot when he purchased them at Orbach's or Sach's Fifth Avenue back in the States. He smiled at us, then raised his hands and held them up and open in a reassuring manner.

"Just don't go anywhere," said Tom.

Robert and Anjanette went off to a table in the corner of the room. Tom frowned, drank his beer, and kept throwing sidelong glances toward where Robert and Anjanette were sitting.

"What's bugging you?" I asked.

"There's something about that guy," he said.

"He's harmless," I said.

"He's up to something," Tom declared. "Did you notice his hands?"

"Girl's hands," I said. "So what?"

"He's up to something," Tom repeated.

When Robert and Anjanette came back a half-hour later Robert was smiling happily.

"I'm absolutely astonished," he said, "at what these little stones know. I can't figure out how they work, but they work. I'd like to buy you all a drink."

He ordered margaritas for everyone. "I'm so happy to meet you," he said. "It gets lonely, being here all by yourself."

"So why'd you come here then?" Tom asked.

"Since my wife left me I really don't have anyone to go with," Robert said. "I was going to ask my secretary to come with me, but we decided her husband might object. He's rather a large man, and as you can see I'm not exactly Mr. Universe." He laughed, self-deprecatingly, and looked longingly at Anjanette. "I prefer to be called Robert, rather than Bob," he said. "An old habit, left over from my mother. She always called me Robert. I can hear her now, calling me in a sharp voice. 'Robert! Come here right now!' And I'd come, even though I knew I'd get boxed on the ears most of the time."

"What about your father?" I asked.

"I never knew my father. I was raised by my mother, who was very over-protective and possessive, as so many mothers are. But I don't expect you to be fascinated with my life story. It's the three of you that I'm intrigued with. You're the most interesting trio I've come across in a long time. What are you—runaways, dropouts? Are you on the run from the law? Are you brothers and sister? Do you have a plural marriage?"

We all laughed, spontaneously, at that, and then Tom said, "Guess."

"You're like apples from the same tree, so I would guess you were brothers and sister, but somehow I don't get that feeling," Robert said. "So I would say you have dropped out—a smart choice to make, these days. I'm thinking of doing it myself. I get so tired of the rat race in L.A. sometimes."

"So be like us," said Tom. "Leave it all behind you."

"I'd like to Tom, I really would. But it's not so easy. That's why I am so fascinated by the Runes. I have some tough business decisions to make soon, and they can give me some real insights."

"What is it you do?" I asked.

"I'm an architect, Pete. I design commercial property—offices, industrial centers, that sort of thing. The firm I work for is very successful but I've been thinking of branching out on my own."

"I thought you said you were thinking of dropping out?" I asked.

Robert laughed good naturedly. "I guess you can see I'm torn in two directions," he said. "Part of me wants to give it all up altogether, be like you, be free, and the other part of me wants to be in thick of things, competing, making money, being a success, whatever that is. And now, with my wife gone, my life has changed, I have an opportunity to do something new, something different. I want to be happy. That's what caught my attention about you three—you seem so happy, you have something intangible, something I don't have, something I've never had, and it's something that can't be bought."

"Not for any price," said Anjanette.

"Would you go out with me?" Robert asked. Once again all three of us laughed. "I'm sorry," said Robert. "I probably shouldn't have said that. It's just that—"

"I don't date," Anjanette said.

"I'd like all three of you to come to my hotel for dinner tonight," Robert said. "We could continue our party there. They have a bar, and a discothèque, and the finest cuisine in Mexico. We could have a great time." All three of us shook our heads, so he said, "Then how about tomorrow night? I'm staying at the Hotel San Cabo. I can send a cab for you."

The three of us exchanged glances. "I don't mind," I said. Anjanette nodded. Tom rolled his eyes. "Then it's settled," said Robert happily. "I know we'll have a great time."

• • •

"You know what I think?" Tom said. "I think that guy was just drunk and shooting off his mouth. He wanted to play the big shot to impress us, especially you, Anja. I'll bet he's forgotten all about this so-called invitation for dinner at this high-assed hotel of his, and we're getting all dressed up for nothing. 'Oh, my hotel has the finest cuisine in Mexico, just call me Robert, that's what mommy calls me.' Ha. He's some rich spoiled bastard who probably inherited all his money and doesn't know what to do with himself."

We were getting dressed, putting on our best clothes. I wore my vaquero hat and my red sash that swung from my side like a sword.

Anjanette wore a peasant top, jeans, and boots that came to her knees. She also put on some makeup and lipstick. We'd never seen her dress up so much before. Tom wore a polo shirt, and white trousers, and kept saying he didn't think there would be any cab.

"I think that guy was full of shit," he repeated. "I bet no cab shows up at all."

No one argued with him. I shaved and put on some Old Spice aftershave. But then, lo and behold, a cab did appear, a large red Ford Galaxy, driven by a small rotund fellow named Benny who never stopped smiling and said *Senor* Roberto had sent him from the Hotel Cabo, and were we ready to come now?

"How much did you say you wanted to bet?" Anjanette asked Tom.

We piled into the back seat. The hotel, Benny said, was seven miles out of town, close to the airport, and for our amusement he put on some loud, raucous Mexican music that reverberated in our ears. He swayed and bounced behind the wheel as he drove through town, heading toward the beach at *Puerto Chileno*, overlooking the Cortez.

"There's only one reason why this guy is inviting us here tonight," Tom said the cab made its way over the rutty roads. "He's hoping to get in your pants."

"Well, he won't succeed," Anjanette promised. "If that makes you feel any better."

"You sure about that, Anja?" Tom pressed, looking unconvinced.

"Of course," Anjanette said firmly, sounding as if she wanted to drop the subject. She stared out the window at the *Sierra de la Victoria*, her head turning softly on her white neck. Why was Tom so worried about this, I wondered, this in particular? I felt a sense of anticipation growing. In a while the hotel came into view, rising like a castle out of the ground, and Benny dropped us off in front of the long stone steps that led to the lobby. There was no need to give him anything, he assured us, for *Senor* Roberto had taken care of all that already.

We went through the hotel lobby. People were checking in and out, inquiring about flight times and future bookings. There was a sign with the exchange rate behind the desk, how much the peso was worth in dollars, in marks, in Swiss francs. Other people sat about, their luggage close by, waiting for a cab to the airport.

We made our way through to the bar, where Robert sat waiting for us, sitting by himself and drinking a margarita. He brightened when he saw us, rising to kiss Anjanette on the cheek, shaking hands with Tom and me. Once again I noticed his small hands and thin wrists. His handshake was weak, as if his hands held no strength in them at all. His head bobbed around on a thin neck.

"I'm so glad you came," he said, sounding grateful. "I was afraid you might not show—either you'd forgotten or changed your minds. Shall we have a drink?"

He ordered margaritas from the cocktail waitress, a young black-haired Mexican woman who wore a white top and black pants that were split in the sides from her ankles to her hips. She smiled and spoke in English with hardly an accent at all.

"Four margaritas," she said, writing with a pen on a pad.

Tom looked up at her, liked what he saw, smiled, and said, "*Deseo usted para mi novia.*"

"*Gracias,*" she laughed good naturedly. "*Pero tengo un novio.*"

"So," observed Robert, "you speak the language."

"So does Pete," Tom said.

"What did you say to her?" Anjanette asked. "As if I couldn't guess."

"O Lord, was there ever a man more misunderstood?" Tom intoned with injured innocence.

"What did he say, Pete?" Anjanette asked.

"He said he wished she was his sweetheart," I said. "She says she already has one."

"I say we toast our new friendship," Robert proposed, lifting his glass. "May it be everlasting."

We clinked our glasses and he said once again how glad he was we had come. "I'm so happy to meet the three of you," he said warmly. "Usually all I meet are these stuffy business types. Uptight. I like to get *loose* sometimes, you know what I mean? I like to let it all hang out, and *boogie* down. Some people hold it all in. Not me. I try to be as real as I can be. I like to be *hip*. I think I'm pretty hip, for a stuffy businessman. Don't you think I'm pretty hip?" he asked Tom.

"For an architect, you might be," said Tom.

"I would have been happier if you said yes, unequivocally, but I guess I can live with that," Robert said. "Good margaritas, don't you think?"

"They're all right, I suppose," Tom conceded. "I think I like the ones at Paco's better."

"I do yoga also," said Robert. "I'm something of a *yogi*, you might say. I've been doing it long before it became fashionable. I'm seeking *satori*. That's the state of spiritual enlightenment in Zen Buddhism."

"Anything you can't do?" Tom asked.

"Tom," Anjanette said warningly.

"How long you been here?" Tom asked Robert.

"This trip, a week now. Flew in from L.A. and spent a couple of days just unwinding. I swam, relaxed, and spent some time amongst these world-famous rock formations here, went to town a lot. When I go to a country I like to be with the real people, that's why I went to the cantina last night and had the good fortune to meet you all. When I go to Mexico I like to be with the Mexicans, not just the rich tourists or the upper classes. I've been to Tahiti, Bali, and Rio. I hope to go to many other places in my life."

Tom set his margarita down with a clank on the table. "I wouldn't call this," he said with a wide panoramic look around the luxurious bar we were sitting in, "being with the Mexicans."

"Then what would you call it, Tom?"

"I call it—traveling first class. And if I could, I might travel that way too. But I sure as hell wouldn't go around saying I'd been with the people of a place. Because I wouldn't have. The real people are out there," he gestured, "fishing in leaky old boats, and catching sharks from dugout canoes. I'll be you haven't seen any of them, not one time."

"I daresay," said Robert, from behind his margarita glass, "that you're right, Tom. The way to really see a place is the way you are doing it. Being right there, in the middle of it all. You have the freedom to do that, and the courage too. I envy you those qualities and I salute you for it."

He raised his glass, drained it, signaled for another. "I wish I had that freedom," he sighed, "and that courage as well."

"Well, what the hell's stopping you?" Tom demanded. "Is somebody holding a gun to your head, and telling you that you can't do any of the things we've done? You could do it too, if you wanted."

"You're partly right, Tom," Robert said. "But it isn't that easy."

"Sure it is," Tom insisted.

"It's that I have responsibilities."

"I thought you said your wife left you," Tom parried.

"Oh, it isn't that," said Robert. "It isn't that at all."

"Then what is it?" Tom asked. "What did she leave you for?"

"She didn't really leave me," Robert explained. "It was the other way around, you see. I didn't want to be married anymore. I no longer found my wife sexually attractive, so it wasn't a marriage any longer. I wanted my freedom. And I got it. I provided well enough for her. I have the money. I did her no wrong that way, I can tell you. But I still have responsibilities, all the same. I have my interests, my work, and I have to see to them."

"Sounds like a real drag," said Tom.

"Oh it is, Tom. You don't know how much I would like to be like you, free, and just go from place to place and not have any one with any holds on me. God, that would be wonderful. And to surf! I've always wanted to surf. What freedom that must be, riding the waves. Are you a good surfer, Tom?"

"He's one of the best," I said.

"Tell me," Robert said, "where are you all going from here?"

"We don't know," said Tom. "We might not go anywhere from here, we might just stay, we like it so much."

"Well, wherever you go, I'd love to go with you," said Robert. "I mean that. Say. Perhaps we could take the ferry over to Puerta Vallarta or Mazatlan, the four of us, and spend a few days there. Would you be interested in doing that?"

"It might be all right," Tom said unenthusiastically.

"I think I'd like that," said Anjanette.

"I think I would too," I said. "You can count me in."

"Splendid! Far out," said Robert.

We had more margaritas and then went into the dining room for dinner. Robert kept on saying that this was some of the best food to be had in Mexico, but he chatted away all through dinner, eating very little, his head bobbing about on his thin neck. He smiled a lot but seemed unable to look you in the eye. His eyes were small, narrow, and aqueous, darting all about. He was dressed in another expensive-looking outfit, this time a white shirt and black trousers.

"You live in L.A.?" I asked him.

"Actually I live in the Hollywood Hills, Pete," he told me. "I have a big house at the top of a crest and a wonderful view of Los Angeles at night. You should see the lights, they are fantastic! If and when you come back to the States you must come and visit me. We could have lots of fun together."

"Doing what?" Tom asked.

"Why, you name it, Tom," Robert said brightly. Dinner was over and we were drinking margaritas again. "Anything you three wanted to do, we can do. Have you spent much time in L.A.? There's Griffith Park, the Observatory, the Zoo, the museums--you name it, we could have a wonderful time."

"All that stuff sounds really *dead* to me," said Tom.

"Oh," said Robert. "Well. Perhaps Pete and Anjanette would like to."

"We do everything together," Tom declared.

"Really?" Robert looked at Tom with his watery eyes, raising his eyebrows. "*Everything?*"

"What do you mean?" Tom said dangerously.

"Nothing," said Robert quickly.

"I'd love some coffee right now," Anjanette said, and I saw her reach under the table and swat Tom on the leg.

"I guess I wouldn't mind some coffee either," he said.

I felt irritated with Tom. Where did he get off being so possessive with Anjanette tonight, and so obnoxious to Robert, who seemed to me a decent, lonely-rich fellow who was desperate to be friends? Robert's coming on to Anjanette was rather humorous and pathetic to me, so why did it bug Tom so badly?

"I hope," Robert said to Anjanette, "you brought the Runes with you tonight?"

"And the Tarot cards too," she smiled.

"Good. I'm looking forward to a reading later. Do you recall my asking last night about a business venture, and you drew the Rune of money and good fortune?"

"Yes, that was Fehu."

"Well, I called my office today, and this deal is coming off better than anyone hoped for. Those stones are phenomenal."

He smiled happily, then raised his glass in another salute to us. "Pretty soon they're going to have music in the disco," he said. "We can all go in there and dance if you like. The band is from the States. They have a light show, too, the kind that you see at Whiskey-A-Go-Go on the Sunset Strip. When you come to my house we can go there and have a blast. Does that sound like more fun than the zoo, Tom?"

"It might be fun at that," Tom allowed, smiling.

"You can all stay at my house," Robert said. "I have plenty of room. We'll have a glorious time. I have a Ferrari," he said. "Anyone ever drive a Ferrari?"

"A *Ferrari*?" asked Tom. "For real, you have a Ferrari?"

"Yes."

"Pinch me, I must be dreaming," said Tom. "What color is it?"

"Red."

"I've always dreamed of driving a red Ferrari."

"You ever ride in a Ferrari, Pete?" Robert asked.

"No," I said. "I do know somebody with a Porsche."

"A Porsche is not even in the same class as a Ferrari," said Tom.

I noticed, now, from the corner of my eye, a vaguely familiar sight, but one that stirred my mind like a spoon in a pot. A man was passing through the dining room on his way to the bar. He wore a tweed jacket with patches on the elbows, and he had an unlit pipe in his hand. His brows were knitted together, as if his mind were one hundred miles above the real world of earth, fire and water. I was on my second or third margarita—I was losing count—and I rubbed my forehead as if trying to get my brain cells to circulate faster. Turning to Tom, I said, "Isn't that Dr. McLeod, that we met in La Paz?"

Anjanette started visibly at the words "La Paz," and turned pale. Tom sat up straighter. He saw only Dr. McLeod's back. "Sure looks like him," he said. "Come on, let's check it out."

"Is *he* there?" Anjanette asked weakly.

"Stay here," Tom told her.

"What is it?" asked Robert. "Trouble?"

"It might be."

"Anything I can do?"

"Just stay here with Anjanette."

"Oh yes, delighted to do *that*."

We went through the dining room toward the bar, Tom hurrying ahead of me. I wouldn't have given much for Randall's chances if he did happen to be anywhere around.

We found Dr. McLeod sitting at the bar, engaged in what seemed to be his lifelong occupation of attempting to light his pipe. He put the flame to it, drew earnestly, then put the flame to it again. A vodka gimlet sat in front of him, and when he saw us his face lit up.

"The happy wanderers," he said. "I wondered if we might run into you here. You said Cabo was your next port-of-call."

"Is that Holy-Joe son-of-a-bitch Randall anyplace nearby?" Tom demanded.

"We haven't seen him since that dreadful night in La Paz."

Tom relaxed a little.

"Sit down, you two," Dr. McLeod invited. "And where is your lovely, fortune-telling companion?"

"She's in the dining room," I said. "I thought you all were taking the ferry back to Mazatlan, and then going home?"

"A change in plans. We did take the ferry over to Mazatlan," Dr. McLeod explained. "But when we arrived we found a message from the Department, saying they wanted more data from the *Chichen Itza* site. So it was back to Yucatan for us. We did some more work there and then returned to Mazatlan and decided to cross the Cortez one more time, this time in order to see Cabo. Don't you love it here? Have you spent much time in the village? Doesn't it seem like something out of Hemingway?"

"Who?" asked Tom.

"Are you staying here?" asked Dr. McLeod. "Is this your hotel?"

"We're having dinner here," I said. "And we were going to come and dance, as soon as the music starts."

"I must go and tell the others," said Dr. McLeod, finishing his drink. "We'll have a grand time. Shall we meet in half an hour?"

"We shall," said Tom, and Dr. McLeod hurried off, his pipe still in his hands, unlit.

•　　•　　•

A half hour later we were all together at a table in the discotheque. It was much like that night in La Paz, with several tables all pushed together end to end to make room for us all. We introduced Robert to Dr. McLeod and the Lady Professor, whose name, we found out, was Mary Ruth, and to the students.

Tom had gotten nowhere with Sheila in La Paz but he obviously thought it was worth a second effort, because he sat down beside her and they soon were as engrossed as they had been the last time they met. I found myself sitting beside a girl named Beth. I had noticed her in La Paz but couldn't recall her name and I didn't think she had spoken a word that night. She was quiet, sitting there wide-eyed, as if this was very exciting to her but she didn't know if she really wanted to participate or just watch from the sidelines.

The disco was three-quarters full. The people were mostly Americans, with some wealthy-looking Mexicans and people who looked like Europeans thrown in for good measure. There was a stage raised higher than the dance floor and not long after we arrived the lights went down but not all the way out, and the band members came on the stage and picked up their instruments and began tuning them up. "The music is going to start," said Robert. "This guy coming out is the MC. Wait until you hear these guys, Pete."

"How is everybody doing out there?" shouted the MC. When there wasn't much response he repeated, "I said, how is everybody doing out there? You ready to party tonight? You want to get it on?" Now there was a loud yell. "You ready to get down and dirty? Ladies and gentleman, boys and girls, the Hotel San Cabo is proud to present, from Los Angeles, California—." The name of the band was drowned out in the screaming that started when the lead singer took the microphone and the band started to play. The dance floor was light up all in white. A strobe light and a color wheel went to work. The dance floor went into a sort of perpetual motion, the dancers' every movement highlighted like an old silent movie. The light was a physical thing, and wasn't just light but more like water, you had to move through it as if you were in a river.

Tom and Sheila went off to dance right away. "Would you dance with me?" Robert asked Anjanette, and so they went off to dance too. The two professors also went to the dance floor, dancing stiffly but earnestly. The wide eyed girl, Beth, swayed slightly to the beat of the music, and then looked right at me. I saw there wasn't any getting out of it, so I said, "Would you like to dance?" and she still didn't speak but nodded, and we went out to the dance floor, stepping into the hazy-crazy blinking lights where the floor seemed to rise up off its moorings, and all the movements around were exaggerated and surreal, a mural that was alive and moving.

I guided Beth out to the center of the dance floor, near to where Tom, Sheila, Robert and Anjanette were dancing. She danced rigidly at first but loosened up after a while, moving about gracefully to the rhythm of the music.

"*Devil with a blue dress on…*" sang the band.

I looked at Anjanette, dancing with Robert. She smiled and waved. She was taller than Robert, and she danced with an easy grace that reminded me of Tom on his surfboard—easy and natural, as if a minimum of effort was involved. I looked at her swaying hips and thought of what had almost happened during the chubasco (I thought of that often) and then resentfully at Robert, who was, I had to admit, a pretty good dancer too.

"*Good golly Miss Molly…*" the band sang.

A great energy emanated from the stage, like a quasar exploding out in space and sending its force fulgurating through the universe. Everyone danced wildly, waving their arms and clapping their hands to the music.

I danced several more dances with Beth (although I was looking at Anjanette most of the time) while the band played *Ride My Seesaw* and *Gimme Some Lovin'* and *Jumpin' Jack Flash*. When the band went into the old Sam Cooke song, *Ain't It Peculiar*, Beth tugged at my sleeve.

"I'd like to sit this one out," she said with a melodious Southern accent.

"Oh," I said, as we made our way off the dance floor, "so you *can* talk."

"Of course I can talk."

"It's just that I never heard you say anything before."

"How old are you?" she asked.

"Twenty-one," I lied.

"You don't look twenty-one," she said skeptically. "Do you go to school?"

"I was going to UCLA," I lied, "but I dropped out so I could bum around."

"This is my first real trip away from home," said Beth. "I'm going to Europe next year."

"What are you going to do there?"

"See lots of things I've always wanted to see. Was your friend really a prostitute?"

"What do you care?"

"I'd like to talk to her about it. I think it's interesting."

In spite of the warmth of the place now I felt a sudden chill. It was like when you're sweating after a hard workout in the gym and you step outside and get hit by a blast of cold air. I felt chilled to the bone.

A tall lithe figure stood in front of me, staring, no, peering, at me. The figure was all black, with a long sleeved shirt that had billowing sleeves, like a pirate out of the 18th Century, ready to plunder the

Spanish Main. But this figure had no face. Instead, it was the face of a skull, a bare skull grinning down at me, the eyes sightless, a hole where the nose had been. And I knew this was Death. Death was close enough to touch me. Had he come to take me? Was he going to take me now, here, from this place? I didn't think it could be my time to die. I prepared to shout, to scream, to say it couldn't be my time yet, I had so much more to do, why, I hadn't even begun yet, I hadn't even started.

Now the death figure was gone. "Let's dance," I said to Beth, and without waiting for her to say yes I seized her by the arm and guided her back out onto the dancer floor, shaking and gyrating as the band played.

I kept dancing, as if by dancing I might get that image of death out of my mind. And it was gone, I no longer saw it, but it was replaced now by another one that was worse. I saw the face, the leonine handsome slightly effeminate face, the deadly nightshade eyes that were covered by the mirrored glasses. He was standing on the edge of the dance floor, tall, imperious, looking out at the people dancing as if he was the king and all this had been arranged for his entertainment. Then he disappeared, behind some people dancing. It can't be him, I thought, what would he be doing here?

But I couldn't get that face out of my mind. I had to prove that I was wrong. I was seeing things. A slower song came on—*Groovin',*— and my arms were full of Beth, who hummed to the music.

She clung tightly to me. "*Groovin' on a Sunday afternoon,*" she hummed. But I could think only of Anjanette, and when I looked at Beth's face I could see only Anjanette's regal one. When I smelled Beth's perfume I could only smell Anjanette's patchouli oil.

"Are you looking for somebody?" Beth asked.

"I thought I saw something."

"What?"

"A ghost I thought I left a long ways back."

"What are you talking about?"

"Never mind," I said, for now I saw him, standing there, looking right at me.

"Is that you?" asked Dave Myers.

I let Beth go and stood still. "What are you doing here?"

"I might ask you the same thing," said Dave, coming over to shake hands. "But, come to think of it, I did hear something about you and your friend having disappeared. I never would have dreamed you'd turn up in Cabo."

"Where's the rest of your friends, are they here too? Larry, Waldo, Karlovitch?"

"Larry's about somewhere. I wouldn't bring Waldo and Karlovitch here, they'd ruin the place. Anyway, Karlovitch has heard his country's call. Waldo is too stupid to talk about. Why don't you introduce me to your lovely companion?"

I introduced him to Beth. He bowed ceremoniously from the waist and kissed her hand. "A rose, by any other name, would smell as sweet," he said, his eyes wild and blazing. "May the goddess of love smile on you both tonight. Perhaps I'll run into you later," he said, and bowed once more, gave me a friendly tap on the shoulder, then vanished.

Before Beth had the chance to ask me anything about Dave, I grasped her hand and led her back onto the dance floor. The band was playing a medley of hard-driving rock songs and I danced wildly, crazily, spinning and capering like I had gone mad, perhaps there was something inside of me I was trying to get out, a demon I had to exorcise and the only way I could do it was by dancing. I danced faster and harder, whirling and twirling. Then, through the surreal strobe-light haze, I saw Anjanette, who smiled and waved to me. I moved over so I was dancing with Anjanette and Robert was dancing with Beth. I danced close enough to Anjanette so I could speak to her.

"I was worried," I said. "You were gone."

"Why were you worried?" she smiled.

"I don't know, I just was."

"I gave Robert a quick Rune reading," she said, speaking into my ear. "He gave me another hundred dollars. Pete, the guy must be *loaded*."

"Yeah, but what does he want? Look, there's Tom and Sheila."

I put my arm around Anjanette's shoulder and we went into a heel kicking dance, stepping forward, kicking out with our feet, then going backward, then coming forward again, all to the beat of the music. Then we separated, and joining hands, danced that way for a while. Then Tom and Sheila came in and joined us, as well as Beth and Robert, and we formed a circle, and danced that way, holding hands and coming together, like a flower's petals opening and closing back in upon itself. Then we all went one way and then back the other in a circle, formed a line, and people danced between the rows by themselves.

When we all split apart I danced over next to Tom. "Guess who's here?" I said.

"Who? That Holy Joe son-of-a-bitch?"

"No. Worse than that. You'll never believe it."

"Who?"

"Dave!"

"Dave?" Tom parroted. "You mean Dave-from-home-Dave? Dave-who-cuts-people's-throats-Dave?"

"That's the one," I affirmed.

"You're seeing things," said Tom.

"Oh yeah? Look over there, tell me what you see."

Dave was standing at the edge of the dance floor, tall and dapper, smoking and watching the action. When he saw us both looking his way he raised a hand, whether in greeting or imprecation I couldn't tell. He smiled.

"What the hell is he doing here?" Tom wondered.

"If only I knew..."

"You don't think he came looking for us, do you?"

"Couldn't be. Could it?"

I was still shaken by what I had seen, that image of Death. It was like a moment in time when I saw more than the eyes normally reveal. Maybe, I said wildly to myself, maybe I saw Dave as he really is, maybe what we usually see is an illusion, he is really Death. The idea shook me up. He'd taken Deacon, now he was dogging me. I looked again and saw Larry now, short, thickset, with a neck that a Brahma bull would envy, standing nearby. Death's helper, I thought.

I found I was dancing with Beth again. We joined a line of people and were boogying to *In the Midnight Hour*. The line snaked across the dance floor through the shattering of lights, and then, as if it had a mind of its own, it stopped, and the people formed two lines facing each other, and each couple danced through to the end, with everyone else clapping their hands and cheering them on. I looked and saw Tom and Anjanette talking to Dave. Dave was talking animatedly, and staring at Anjanette as if fascinated.

"I'm gonna wait till the midnight hour…"

The tempo got faster and faster, the energy on the dance floor got stronger and stronger, tuned up like a machine pushed to its highest possible speed. The strobe lights kept flashing and the color wheel rotated red, blue, white, yellow.

Now it slowed down, as if the machine would break if made to go any faster. "Now," said the lead singer, "it's time for a blast from the past!" Suddenly Anjanette was in front of me, with Robert in tow behind her. "Let's make a switch," she suggested. "I want to dance this one with you," as the band began playing *The Great Pretender*.

"Yes, I'm the great pretender
Pretending that I'm doing well
My need is such I pretend too much
I'm lonely but no one can tell"

"Oh Pete," said Anjanette, "isn't this wonderful? I can't believe how happy I am, being here with you and Tom. It's like we're in the midst of the best in life."

"Maybe we should stay here forever," I said.

"Do you really mean that?"

"I never meant anything more."

"Yes I'm the great pretender
Just laughin' and gay like a clown
I've played the game but to my real shame
You've left me to grieve all alone"

We were holding each other tighter and tighter, as if we never wanted to let go. Anjanette buried her head on my shoulder. "Hey, watch it you two," Tom said, dancing past with Sheila. "None of that hanky-panky stuff in here." He and Sheila went on by, lost in the crowd. Anjanette looked up at me, smiled, her lips slightly parted. I kissed her and she returned it, squeezing me even tighter. Then she broke it off.

"Don't," she said. "We can't. You know we can't."

"But it felt good," I said, looking around, trying to determine if Tom had seen what just happened. "You know it felt good."

"Too real is this feeling of make-believe

Too real when I feel what my heart can't conceal"

"We can't," Anjanette repeated.

"But it felt good," I persisted.

"Yes," she admitted, "It felt good. You're a bad boy, Pete. You think bad things."

We kissed again and held each other even tighter. *The Great Pretender* came to an end and the band announced they were taking a break. "Let's go sit down," I said.

We sat down near Robert and Beth and the two professors.

"It appears everyone is having a good time," said Robert.

"I am," I said. "Super. Wonderful."

"Aren't you glad you accepted my invitation?" said Robert smugly, then announced he was standing the whole table to drinks.

"Where did Tom and Sheila go?" Anjanette asked, looking around. They were nowhere to be seen.

"Three guesses on what they're doing," I said. "Out on the beach, most likely."

"You and Tom, you're both bad boys."

Everyone drank more margueritas. Even Anjanette appeared to be getting drunk now.

I looked over at Anjanette and smiled, then reached under the table to touch her hand. She squeezed mine back. People were paying their bills and leaving the bar; it was getting an emptied-out look as the evening came to an end.

"You know, I was thinking," said Robert, "why don't we, the three of us, go to my suite for a nightcap? Tom probably went for a walk with Sheila, and who knows when they'll return, eh? We can leave word for him here as to where we'll be. You're welcome to come along," he said to Beth.

"No thank you," said Beth. "I've got to get up early."

"Yes, we all do," said Dr. McLeod. "We're going back to La Paz tomorrow, and then once more across the Cortez. This has been quite an experience, I must say."

Robert insisted on getting what was left of the bill, and then he, Anjanette and I said goodnight and went through the door single file, out into the broad hallway past the lobby. The desk was still lit up, as if it never closed but had to be open and on call twenty four hours a day. People sat about the lobby just as they had when we arrived, only the faces were different faces now. A very overweight man who looked like an American emitted a blubbering snore as we went by while his wife, slim and snappily dressed, looked at him in disgust. The doorman opened the glass doors for us, and we went outside into the coolness of the night air, and heard the waves crashing on the beach, roaring, like hungry lions.

Chapter 26

The Black Pit

"What a beautiful night," Robert observed. We all stood still for a moment, letting the fresh air wash over us. It did feel good after the smoke-filled air of the disco. The full moon bathed us in its light, and beyond the moon the night sky looked like an ocean of stars. Robert gestured expansively at the fountain and the long tiled paths all around. "What I love about this place is the Mexicans don't build their hotels up and down the way we do. They spread them out." He pointed at the building, laid out in different levels. "I have an oceanfront suite," he said, gesturing down the pathway.

We went along the tile way, past well-cared for shrubs and cactus. Men dressed in vests and black pants hurried by, carrying trays with dishes on them. "Room service," Robert said. "Perhaps we can order something. Are you tired?" he asked us both. "I'm a night person. I sometimes forget other people go to bed earlier than I. If you are, I have something that will wake you up."

He winked and we went on down to his suite. As soon as we were inside he got on the phone and ordered a pitcher of margaritas. He then got a small, well-concealed bag from the depths of a massive leather suitcase. He produced a small hash pipe. "Want some?" he asked. "I always bring some with me."

We each had a few hits of hash while we waited for the margaritas. "Aren't you worried about getting busted at the airports?" I asked.

"Hum?" Robert said. He had barely heard me, for he was staring at Anjanette. She had sat down at a small couch by herself and was busily laying out the Tarot cards. "Oh," he said, still staring at her, "they rarely search your luggage when you travel first-class. Can you cast spells?" he asked Anjanette. "You've cast one on me," he sighed.

"Don't be silly," Anjanette said reprovingly. "You barely know me."

"Why is that so important?" Robert asked plaintively. "Don't you believe in love at first sight?"

Anjanette didn't answer but turned a card over, studying it.

"I'm not sure I believe in love at all," she said after a while, not looking up but still studying the Tarot cards, turning one over, studying it, then going on to another.

"Let's do a line," Robert suggested. "Want to? That'll pick us up, after all the booze and dancing." He got a small square mirror out, and a glass vial. From the vial he poured out some white powder, and using a razor blade he chopped the white powder until it was very fine and separated it into three equal lines. "This is good stuff, Pete," he said. "Good quality, expensive. Just what I need. Tom doesn't know what he's missing."

The suite was large, and lavish, befitting someone who travels first class wherever he goes. There were Mexican paintings on the walls, scenes of haciendas and Spanish-looking girls with fans in front of their faces and tiaras and bows in their hair. Two in particular caught Anjanette's attention. "Look at that," she said. "It's by Frida Kahlo. And that one's by Diego Rivera."

"Are they originals?" asked Robert.

"No, they're replicas. I've read about both of them."

"Who are they?"

"Famous Mexican painters. Great stuff. I wish I could do something like that."

We each inhaled a line of the white powder. It burned as it went down but once it got down I felt a rush of good feelings, of rejuvenation. My teeth tingled and so did my gonads. I suddenly wished I had tried harder with that girl, what was her name, I couldn't remember. I looked at Anjanette. Why was she always so familiar to me, like a face I had known in dreams all my life? Through the open windows we could hear the crashing of the sea.

"God, you're beautiful," Robert said to Anjanette.

"Oh, will you cut it out?" she replied.

"I can't help it," he said. "You've bewitched me. And you know, I'm supposed to fly home tomorrow, and the idea of going without you makes my blood chill. Perhaps you could fly back with me? There's always room in first class."

"I thought you said you were a yogi," Anjanette said reprovingly.

"Oh, I am," Robert said earnestly. "I'm actually a pretty highly advanced yogi, you know."

"I thought yogis transcended the body."

"I'm not that far along."

"Then you aren't really a yogi," she declared. "You just say you are."

"Yes, I am," he insisted. "I get up early every morning and practice."

"Bullshit," Anjanette said.

"Look," said Robert. "I'll show you, you'll see."

He got onto the floor now and began doing some odd stretchings and other contortions that appeared to me to be designed to torture a person and not bring them any closer to God. Robert grunted and groaned and moaned and thrashed all about, trying to touch his chin to his knee and so forth. After a while he stopped, and looked at us as if he wanted our approval more than anything in the world.

"There," he said. "You see? You see?" He spoke as if he had proved something beyond all argument.

"That doesn't look like yoga to me," said Anjanette. "It looks more like masochism."

Robert looked crestfallen. The margaritas arrived now and he took a drink. "Come back with me," he said again. "You too, Pete."

"I couldn't do that," Anjanette said.

"The times we could have," said Robert.

"Anyway," said Anjanette, "you'd be disappointed if I did go with you, Robert."

"Oh, I think not," he maintained.

"Oh yes you would."

"No," he said, holding one palm out like someone who wanted to hold up a heavy weight. "I feel so close to all three of you, it's as if I've known you all for a long time, I know what would happen, we'd all be very happy. I know it. You connect me with what is real, what's important. You don't know what it would mean to me, to have you all with me, back home."

"There are dark forces all around us tonight," Anjanette said. "It wouldn't take much to set them free."

"Let them come, I welcome them," Robert said. "With open arms I welcome them!"

"You don't know what you're saying," said Anjanette.

"I do, I do, I swear to God I do," Robert said. "Look, I'll get on my knees, if you want."

I felt like I was in a place where nothing mattered. The white powder was coursing through me, along with the hash and all the booze. I had never been to a place like this before. Nothing matters here. You can do anything, and it doesn't matter. I've seen Death, what if he takes me tonight while I sleep? Better to live while you can, before he comes for you. What would you do if you were told you only had six months to live?

"I'm seeking something higher," Anjanette said to Robert. "You want me to go back to the States with you and become your mistress, your bedpartner, isn't that right?"

"Well," said Robert, taken somewhat aback at her bluntness, "I wouldn't put it quite like that."

"What other way is there to put it, Robert?"

Robert didn't answer but sat there looking embarrassed.

"Isn't that right, Robert?" she asked again.

"Isn't it, Robert?" she asked.

It doesn't matter, I thought, sitting there smoking and looking, first at Anjanette, then at Robert. It doesn't matter at all, none of it makes one goddamn bit of difference. Nothing does.

"This isn't true, what you think," Robert said. "I like you, I like all of you. Please don't think that of me."

"What should we think of you, Robert?"

"Not that. Please not that."

"Robert. You don't even know me. You don't love me. What you love is this body. That's what you love. You want this, don't you, you want to put your cock in it, isn't that it?"

"No," Robert said in a small voice, "no, that isn't it, it's not like that, it's not what you think, not like that."

"Pete," Anjanette asked. "Do you believe him?"

"No," I said, and laughed.

"I wish I could tell you how I feel," said Robert. "I wish I could make you understand."

"I said you would be disappointed if I were to go back to the States with you, Robert, do you know why I said that? Pete knows why. I was a whore once, Robert. That's right. A whore. I sold my body for money. I let men pay me in exchange for using it the way they wanted to. But then one day I couldn't stand it anymore and so I slashed at my wrists with a razor blade, do you see the scar? And I stood watching the life pour out of me and down the drain and I felt the presence of an angel telling me not to do it. And I made a pact with that angel. I am seeking to go beyond the material plane, to ascend to something higher. And I swore, right then, that I would never let my body be violated again. And if I ever break that holy vow, then I can feel all the forces of darkness that gathered around me while I stood there dying will come loose, they'll take me to the blackest pits of hell. Do you understand, Robert?"

"O Lord," Robert said in a small voice.

"Do you?" she repeated.

I didn't laugh but I thought, it doesn't matter, none of it, and it's all very funny.

"I'm sorry," Robert said. "I didn't understand."

Anjanette finished her margarita. "I need some fresh air. I'm going for a walk on the beach."

"I'll go with you," Robert offered.

"I want to go by myself."

She walked out majestically, closing the door softly behind her. We could hear, in the quiet of the late night, her boots on the tile as she made her way toward the water.

"Wow," Robert said. "Wow oh wow oh wow oh wow. What a woman that is. What an incredible woman. My God."

He said he needed more white powder and so he got out his glass vial. We did another line. I felt I was being lifted out of myself, I wasn't myself anymore. I felt I was growing, changing, I could do anything. There was a beast inside and I wanted to let him out. I wanted to be bad, the darkness was near, and I wanted to go into the darkness.

"You are so lucky, Pete," Robert said. "To have friends like the friends you have. People who really care about you. I envy you. There really isn't anybody who cares about me."

"Really?" I asked, with no compassion at all. "Nobody?"

"Not a damn soul," he replied as if he expected me to cry.

"That's too fucking bad," I said brutally. "Why do you think that is?"

"I've always felt that way," he said slowly. "I've always felt that nobody cared about me, because I wasn't worth caring about. I feel worthless. I've always felt worthless. Useless. Like nothing I did matters."

"Why don't you do something about it then? Instead of feeling sorry for yourself."

"You're a wise young man, Pete."

"No I'm not," I said. "I'm not wise at all."

"I wish I could be like you, Pete," Robert went on. "Smart, good-looking, full of life. You really live, you and your friends. You're not afraid to take chances. Me, I'm afraid of everything. I never take any risks. I'm afraid of what will happen if it goes wrong. It's awful to be like that. Awful." He looked at me intensely. "There's so much I could learn from you. You could teach me how to live."

"Just do it," I said. "Stop whining about it and do it."

"Could I?" he replied. "Do you really think I could? I feel as if my meeting you has opened a new door for me. It's changing me, I'm being changed. You know something? I think I'm falling in love. You've been in love, haven't you, Pete?"

"Maybe."

"What happened?"

"I don't want to talk about it."

"Was she pretty?" Robert persisted.

"She was beautiful," I said.

"But what happened?" Robert repeated. "Tell me, I'd really like to know."

"I said I don't want to talk about it! Can't you hear?"

"O God," said Robert. "My head! My head feels like it's being shot from a cannon! Maybe I did too many lines. Do you think so? What is this feeling? She's so beautiful," he went on. "It's a funny thing, but I feel I can't live without her. Oh God! Will you look at that?"

Anjanette was standing in the moonlight on the beach, looking like a sea-goddess rising out of the sand. Her back was to us, and she stood at the water's edge, letting it lap over her feet. Robert stared at her worshipfully, and his breathing got harder and faster.

"Oh," he said, holding his head in his hands, "what shall I do? What shall I do?"

"You heard what she said," I told him.

"That's exactly what I mean," he moaned. "Exactly what I mean."

He sat on the floor rocking and moaning. "I'm so lonely," he said, "so lonely so lonely so lonely. Why doesn't anyone care about me? I'm not a bad person. "

The door opened and Anjanette came back in. Robert flung himself down on the floor at her feet, his hands clasped in front of him as if in prayer. "Look, Angel Anjanette," he cried, "on my knees I'll say it: Please come back with me, please! This is like a fire I can't put out, it's burning me up inside. You don't have to do a single thing, just come with me! Oh God, please make her come with me! You don't know what it would mean to me, you don't know you don't know."

He carried on like this for a while, sobbing and weeping and pleading. Once Anjanette looked over at me as if there was something she wanted me to do, but there wasn't anything I could do. At last Robert gave it up. He seemed to have forgotten I was there, and when he noticed me his face puffed out hopefully, and his eyes lit up a little, as if I was his last hope.

Then he stood, wiping his eyes.

"I'm sorry," he said. "I'm such a fool. I wish I wasn't such a fool. But I hurt so much inside. I just wish the hurt would go away, and there isn't anything that can make it go away."

Neither of us said anything. Outside we could hear the waves crashing on the beach.

"Sometimes I just wish I was dead," said Robert.

No one said anything to that. Outside the waves crashed even harder.

"If I was dead then I wouldn't bother anybody anymore," Robert said.

No one spoke.

"Nobody would care anyway, if I was dead," Robert went on. "No one's ever cared about me."

Silence filled the room.

"I'm sorry," Robert said after a while. "Maybe if you felt the way I do inside you would understand. I saw the three of you in the cantina and I felt the love you have for each other and I wished I could be part of it, that I could be one of you, and that you would accept me and care about me the way you do about each other, that's all I wanted."

There was another uncomfortable silence and then he said, "I'm so ashamed."

"Maybe we should go," I said at last.

"Oh no," Robert said. "Please don't do that. Don't leave. *I'll* go. I won't come back tonight. You can stay here, you don't want to ride back to the village this late."

I protested, and so did Anjanette, but there was no talking him out of it. Before we could do anything he was out the door and gone. His footsteps died away and Anjanette and I sat looking at each other.

"It's late," I said finally.

"Poor man," Anjanette said. "Do you think he'll be all right? He's so upset. Poor lonely man. Like everyone else in the world, he's lonely. Maybe we should go try to find him."

"No way," I said.

"Are you too drunk?"

"I think I am beyond drunk."

I was far, far out there, and I didn't feel like myself anymore. I was changing, transforming, I was turning into somebody else. A part of me was being released, a dark part, one I had always known was there but I had never seen. It was growing and getting stronger, rising like the lava of a volcano will rise, white hot and running fast. It was The Beast, The Darkness. Dave, I thought, it's Dave, that's what he is.

My eyes focused on Anjanette now. She sat in her chair, smoking, relaxed and smiling, her long hair in shimmering waves, her soft neck still distantly showing the effects of La Paz. I looked at her long legs and thought of the sea nymph I had seen frolicking in the water so many times. Pandora's box was open, and there was no way to close the lid.

Anjanette drank another margarita, tossing it off, saying that she too felt she had gone to a place of being past drunk, she was in a kind of twilight zone.

"I feel strange," she said. "All tightened up."

"Is it like tension, in your neck and shoulders?" I asked. She nodded and I rose unsteadily but meaningfully from my chair and went behind her.

"Oh," she cried, "that feels nice. That's great. I love being massaged. Say," she said, "that strange guy from back home Tom introduced me to tonight, do you know him too?"

"Who?"

"I can't remember his name--Tom said he's from Angels Beach."

"Dave," I said.

"Yes, that's it, Dave. Do you know him?"

"I know him."

"He's a creepy kind of person, isn't he?"

"He's worse than that."

"I got an awful feeling from him," she said.

"I'm not surprised."

I worked my fingers down to her shoulders, using my thumbs to knead and massage her the way a baker works dough, working steadily. After a few minutes I suggested she lay down so I could do her back, and she went cooperatively into the bedroom and fell face down on the bed. I massaged her back a while, and she lay emitting sounds of enjoyment. Then I gently rolled her over and began doing the front of her, her shoulders and chest muscles. Anjanette lay, eyes shut, a look of contentment on her face.

The lights were out; moonlight came in through the windows. I could hear the roll of the waves outside. Robert's belongings were strewn about the room, suitcases, smaller bags, an expensive-looking camera on the dresser. I allowed my fingers to work their way lower and lower onto Anjanette's body. Now they were moving over her breasts, and I felt them respond to my touch, they quivered, and she arched her back just slightly.

Her eyes came open and she looked at me. I was caressing her now, not massaging her anymore. I touched her sides and she arched her body once more.

"Maybe you shouldn't touch me like that, Pete," she said.

I kept on, though. She sighed, and then giggled, as if I were tickling her.

"Don't," she said languidly. "Pete, don't touch me that way, don't do it."

But it wasn't Pete she was talking to, not the one she knew. This was somebody else and he wasn't listening. My hands went to her shoulders, and then to caress her face and cheeks. She reached and held one of my hands in hers, saying, "Don't, don't," weakly, and the heat was out of control now, a fire was raging and there was only one way to put it out. "Don't look like that, Pete," she said. "You don't look like yourself when you look that way. Please," she was begging now, "please stop. Please don't."

But I felt the surge of dark power, all the darkness I had inside was coming out. In the dim light I saw her golden head move as she tried to sit up, but there was no escape for her, she couldn't resist the dark force. I swooped and captured her, the way an eagle will glide down to capture its prey, and my hands were like talons now, no longer gentle but predatory, bent on getting what they wanted. I caught her, she was like moist clay, I could bend her, move her, shape her in my hands as I pleased, make her into whatever I wanted her to be, like Pygmalion with Galatea.

I held her, stopping her in her tracks, kissing her. "No," she protested, "no, no, please," but there was no stopping this, it was a train set in motion, you might as well try to hold back the ocean. Her resistance crumbled in layers. I kissed her, and she kissed me back. We fell together onto the bed.

Her protests were only feeble whimperings now. Soon they ceased. Only once she looked at me, with a kind of horror, but I was far beyond caring about that. Our bodies conjoined. She was like deliciously yielding honey that enveloped me from head to foot. I had fallen headlong into a sea of wonder and joy, soft wax that smelled of patchouli oil and surrounded me with pleasure. I felt Anjanette reach her peak and heard her cry "Goddamn you!" as it burst forth, and then I did too, and after that I don't remember anything.

•   •   •

I woke up at daylight. Pushing, pushing, inside of me, hurting me, a pole. A pole at work, a stick. Confusion flooded me— where was I? There was someone behind me, holding me tightly, hands gripping my chest. Where was Anjanette? I felt a surge of horror—what had I done? Where did she go? And yet this pushing from behind wouldn't stop. Weak hands held me. I could, with small effort, break them loose, but I wasn't awake yet. I was being penetrated, and with a cry I broke free.

Robert's face greeted me.

"What the hell?" I mumbled, my head spinning and throbbing. "What the hell is this?"

He was smiling at me, searchingly, pleadingly. Then he reached for me. I was still in too much of a daze to resist. My temples pounded. But as his lips came near mine I twisted away, pushing him back, shuddering. He smiled, a weak, watery smile.

"I came in, I came back," he said, "and I saw you were alone," he smiled, panting the way a dog will pant, "and so I decided to join you. See."

I still did not completely understand what happened, but I was beginning to, and I drew away in loathing. I got out of the bed, wobbly on my feet, the room spinning all around me. Robert rose from the bed and came toward me, ridiculously naked, cave chested, pasty white skinned, hairless, pot bellied, but his penis erect and shaking.

"Please," he said, "please, just a little more, let me finish, that's all I want. I'll give you anything, anything, if you'll let me."

I hit him in the stomach and he doubled over gratefully, arms across himself. "Come back with me," he said. "I'll pay for everything. I'll give you whatever you want." I hit him again, this time in the face, bringing blood. He made no effort to fight back or protect himself, but just stood there as I hit him again and again, all the while smiling weakly, until the last punch drove him back and he fell on the floor next to the bed, his face bloody and dripping. "I deserve it," he mumbled through his broken lips. "This is just what I should get." I bent down and hit him one more time, smashing his nose, and this time blood spurted like a fountain. His pants were hung neatly over a nearby chair and I thought of him coming into the room, seeing me in the bed by myself, taking his clothes off and taking the time to hang his pants over the chair before he got into the bed with me. I seized his wallet and took a huge wad of bills from it, all American money, all fifties and hundreds. I fumbled around as fast as I could and found my own clothes, which had gotten scattered about during the night, put them on quickly and ran out the door, stuffing the money into my pocket, the blood still on my hands, Robert's blood, my blood, and Anjanette's blood too.

Chapter 27

Lost

When I got back to our room at the hostel I expected her to be there, and I had fine plans of apologizing, but I was alone. For a long time I sat, staring out the window, waiting for her to appear, half-convinced that she would, any moment, and then I could say all the things I wanted to say and make everything all right. The silence reflected the sense of emptiness I felt. Then at some point I went into the bathroom and noticed her things were gone, and with a mounting sense of fear I looked in her closet and saw that it had been cleaned out too. No trace of her remained except the lingering scent of her patchouli oil. Then I noticed a piece of paper on the small wooden kitchen table.

"Dear Pete," I read. "I'm going to go and pay my debt to God. It isn't your fault. A."

Early in the afternoon Tom appeared.

"Hey," he said, coming in through the door brightly, although looking a little tired at the same time. "That was some party last night. I had a blast, what about you? How did it go? Did you get anywhere with that Beth?"

"Who?"

"I'll take a wild guess that means no," said Tom. He walked into the bedroom, taking his shirt off as he went, then came back, pulling a clean one on over his head. "That Sheila is really something. Why didn't I meet any of these college chicks before? It's enough to make me want to continue my education. And a Southerner too, no less, that claims to be religious. 'Oh, I believe in God,' she says. "Sex out of marriage is wrong.' If this is what religion does to them I might even try it myself. Do you know something? My balls are actually sore and that's a first for me. I don't know how many times we went at it, I lost count. Talk about insatiable." He stopped talking for a moment and peered at me intently. "Hey," he said, "you all right? You look a little low. What happened, did you over-indulge last night? And where's Anjanette?"

"I don't know," I said.

He looked at me curiously, cocking his head to one side, then looked in Anjanette's room. "What's going on? Where's her stuff?"

"I don't know," I repeated.

"What the hell do you mean?"

"Just that—I don't know."

"This is weird," said Tom. He looked at me uncertainly, questioningly, hands on his hips. "What happened last night?"

"Nothing."

"What do you mean, nothing?"

"Just that—nothing."

"When did you see her last?"

"At the hotel. We went to Robert's room for a nightcap."

"You left her with Robert? That was a stupid thing to do. I might have known he'd be mixed up in this. We better go find her."

We drove out to the hotel, with my sense of anxiety growing all the while. The desk clerk told us he hadn't seen her.

Tom asked him about Robert.

"He checked out," the clerk said in his excellent English, and gestured toward his face. "He must have made someone angry—he had bruises all over."

"I wonder what happened to him?" Tom said.

"He probably got funny with the wrong guy," I said.

We saw Professor McLeod sitting by himself in the bar and went over to him. As always, he was engaged in trying to light his pipe. "Ah, the two happy adventurers," he smiled. "Come to see us off? We had a change in plans. We have to take a bus back to La Paz, and catch the ferry from there to Mazatlan, and then a bus will take us to Mexico City. We'll fly home from there. What about you two and your lovely friend? Still planning to stay here indefinitely? I must say, I envy the freedom you have to do that. To just pack up and leave everything behind and go on an adventure like this. That's really living life to the fullest. I wish I could spend more time with you two," he continued, "and learn more of your story. I'd like to include it in a book I'm writing. I'm calling it 'Random Thoughts,' modeled along the lines of Aurelius' *Meditations*. People could learn from your story, I think, yours and that of your friend. What happened with her? Why did she leave? And with those two?"

"What are you talking about?" Tom asked, frowning.

Professor McLeod paused in his musings and regarded his pipe intently. "I saw her get into a cab earlier today. A cab bound for the airport."

"Was she alone?" I asked.

"She was with these two Americans that were staying here, rather sinister-looking fellows, I must say. One tall, with these mirror-sunglasses on, the other short and squat like the proverbial Cretan bull. I wondered what she was doing with them."

"When was this?" Tom asked.

"A few hours ago. There aren't that many flights from that airport, so she may still be there."

We drove over the rocky road to the airport, making as good a time as we could, but when we got there we saw the only flight to Los Angeles had already taken off. Disconsolately, we went back to the hostel.

"What in the hell is going on?" Tom kept asking. "Why did she leave without saying a word? And with *them*! What could have happened?"

It was getting close to sunset by now and we wandered into the village to get something to eat, although I had no appetite at all, and ignored my food but just drank several glasses of wine. Tom didn't eat much either, and when we were done we walked down to the beach near the Bishop and looked at the sun going down and watched the waves come and go. There were times when the waves crashed on the beach like an explosion, hurling sprays of water into the air violently and then coming gently back down, almost floating, like feathers borne on the wind.

"You ever think about home?" Tom asked.

"Sometimes."

"I mean as in going home."

"I've been thinking I'd like to stay here forever. I've never been happier."

"There isn't much to go back to. And this—"he spread his arms expansively and pirouetted around in a complete 360 degree circle—"this has been like paradise. A dream. I wonder, sometimes, if it all isn't a dream, life, I mean."

"Like maybe we've done all this already, and we just keep living it over and over again."

"I felt that about you, I felt it about Anjanette, like I knew you already, I didn't even have to introduce myself." He paused, and looked out at the sun as it settled down over the ocean. "But what does it all mean? What is it all for? It has to mean something, there has to be a reason for all this."

"You remember the night we went into the old power plant, and you were talking about the universe being kept in balance? Maybe we are all just like parts in a machine, and when we come together we balance everything the way it is supposed to be, and if we split apart, before we're supposed to, it throws things off, puts them out of balance."

"Then her leaving puts things wrong," he declared. "There's a part taken out that shouldn't have been. Something's wrong. Something's unbalanced."

We went back to our room, for it was dark by then. I didn't sleep much that night, just tossed and turned, and whenever I closed my eyes I saw Anjanette's face coming at me. She was in deep pain, accusing me of betraying her and telling me I couldn't keep this to myself. Then, out of the other side of my mind would come a small voice telling me to say nothing, to just keep playing dumb. Tom would never find out what happened. Robert was long gone, and he certainly wouldn't want to reveal what had gone on.

Then that part of my brain shut down and I asked myself if I could live with two lies. I had one huge one that I was keeping hidden, how could I live with another? But what good would it do? Tom didn't need to know what I did. In time he would forget about it. We could go on here as we had been, no need for anything to change.

But in the morning when I got up I saw how empty the place seemed without here. That emptiness was like a reproach to me, reminding me of what I had done.

"Let's go surfing," Tom suggested.

We got our boards and took the van to the beach. The surfing wasn't good, the waves were small and didn't have much shape. We caught a few and then came up on the beach and sat in the sand.

"Beautiful morning, isn't it?" said Tom. "All the mornings here are so beautiful."

"Tom," I said. "There's something I gotta tell you."

"What?" he said, still looking out at the ocean.

"I know why she left."

"I miss her," he said. "I wish she'd come back. Think she will?"

"You remember what she said? About her making a pact with God, and what would happen if she ever broke it?"

He turned toward me now, his eyes frozen. "What are you saying?"

"You know what I'm saying."

He leaped to his feet. I stood up too.

"Are you saying—are you saying that you and her—"

"Yes," I told him.

"You're lying! It can't be. I don't believe it."

"It was my fault. I made her."

"No!" Tom screamed, a scream like that of a wounded animal. "No, you couldn't have!"

"I did. It was me. I did it."

"Goddamn you!" He came at me in a blurred motion. I hardly felt the blows. I went down on the sand, closing my eyes, expecting more to follow, but none did. When I opened them Tom was nowhere in sight. I had something clasped in my hand, and when I turned it over I discovered it was his St. Christopher medal, and I realized I must have pulled it loose from his neck in the struggle. His surfboard lay alongside mine in the morning sun, drops of water glistening on the lines that ran from one end to the other.

•   •   •

Two days later I was driving north, the same way we had come, only now I was alone and the countryside, which had seemed so full of life when we had come through it now seemed desolate, dry, as if its essence had been taken by the heat of incipient summer. At night I pulled over and slept in the back of the van, or else made a camp by myself on the beach, and sat by a little fire and listened to the waves breaking in the dark.

I kept going north, not hurrying, just going steadily, not sure where I was planning to end up, just going. I stayed on the Gulf side of the peninsula, and stopped sometimes and looked out at the water, and imagined old-time sailing ships that only had the wind to power them sailing into the Gulf from the Pacific, laden with treasure looted from the Spanish Main or else in pursuit of another ship, cannons firing and pirates in colorful clothes and eye patches lining her decks. Too bad there aren't any pirates anymore, I thought, maybe I could become one. Yes, a pirate. Wouldn't that be fun?

What am I going to do now, I kept thinking. What am I going to do now?

•   •   •

One day I stopped at a dark café with a tin roof and a few wooden tables inside. In the corner I saw a blond head looking at me through the

361

gloom, and saw that the body it was attached to was leaning back in a rickety chair comfortably, a beer on the table in front of him.

"It's about time you got here," Tom said. "What kept you?"

I couldn't hold back a whoop of joy. I rushed over and flung my arms around him.

"I knew you'd turn up sooner or later," he said. "You got my Christopher?"

"How'd you get here?" I asked.

"Thumbed," he said, "which gets a little hairy in this part of the world. Not that much traffic, other than guys on donkeys or driving tractors. Not easy to get a ride."

I couldn't hold it back any longer. I put my head down on the table and started weeping. "What have I done?" I kept saying. "What have I done?"

Tom didn't say too much, just sat there and let me get it out of my system. When I had finished and dried my eyes, he said, "You know what we have to do, don't you?"

I raised my head and looked at him.

"We have to go back. We have to find her."

"Of course," I said. "That's it. We have to. To make things right."

"It's our destiny," said Tom. "They've been tied together since we went into that black tunnel in the old power plant. Hers too. It's all tied together—I don't know how, or why, or how it works, but I know it's true."

"It won't be easy," I said. "We might both get killed."

"That could happen," he said, but then he dug into his pocket and took something out. "Don't forget we have this."

"All right!" I said. "The magic circle. I thought it was lost again."

"This isn't something you can lose," he said. "But I want you to take charge of it now. I'm always afraid I *will* lose it, and then what will happen to us both?" He peered at me intently for a moment, then stood up and tapped me lightly on the shoulder. "We better get started. How long will it take us to get from here back to the States?" He grinned. "Will your van make it?"

"'Course it'll make it. It got us here, didn't it?"

"Then let's get moving!"

We fairly jumped into the van and started driving north. We had 800 miles to go, all the way back to the States and then on to Kekaha.

She would be there, I thought. She has to be. I have to make this right. Things are out of balance, and they have to be put back the way they are supposed to be.

Chapter 28

Homecoming

There was an eerie feeling at Kekaha when we got there. It was a feeling of emptiness, of abandonment. There was nobody around. It was breakfast time but there was no one in the kitchen, no smell of food, no pots on the stove.

"This is strange," said Tom. "Where is everyone?"

We looked at each other, bleary-eyed, for we had been driving non-stop in order to get back as quickly as we could, and Kekaha seemed a natural place to go to first. We had paused only when we had to, agonizing as we went over the rocky roads that we'd had so much fun crossing when we had come down the Peninsula. We had often driven all night, only stopping when we were too tired to go any further. One time, in a village past Loreto, we were stranded for three days when the van broke down, the distributor cap had cracked. We waited, impatiently, for the part to arrive and we could get rolling again. Then we were off, going the same way we had come, not stopping too look at anything but going on with a deep sense of purpose. We came across at San Ysidro in the middle of the night, and were waved through by a sleepy-looking Border

Patrol agent, and were back in the U.S. at long last.

I had been praying all the time that we would find Anjanette at Kekaha. We had convinced ourselves, in fact, that in her hurt at what I had done she had accepted the plane ride back with Dave and Larry but then had gone home and would be waiting for us there. When we arrived we leaped out of the van, in spite of our fatigue, full of anticipation, and dashed into the house, going past the fountain and up the wooden steps.

No one seemed to be around. Our voices rang hollowly off the walls. There was a deserted feeling in the way the dishes were laying about, as if they hadn't been touched in days. Then a little boy, no more than three, came wandering into the kitchen. His face was dirty, and his hair was stringy and long. He looked up at us and said something neither of us could understand, and stood staring. A moment later his mother came in, a thin, pasty-faced girl of twenty, wearing a long paisley dress.

"Who the hell are you?" she demanded.

"We live here," Tom explained. "We've been gone—"

"Oh yes, to Mexico, I heard about you," she interrupted.

"Where is everybody?" I asked.

The girl picked the little boy up and held him with one bony arm. "Apple!" he sang.

"Apple!" she sang back in the same sing-song voice. "So I guess you haven't heard?" she asked us.

"No, heard what?"

"Apple!" the kid sang.

"Apple!" the girl sang back.

She jiggled him up and down playfully. Then she brushed a strand of long disheveled hair back from her forehead. "About the big bust," she said.

"What big bust?"

Now the kid began to cry. The girl put him in a high chair, got a jar of Gerber's baby food from the refrigerator, and began to feed him with a plastic spoon. "I'm Ginny," she explained. "This is Falcon. We just came here from Taos, New Mexico. We used to live on a communal farm there, a women's collective called Ariadne. They helped me a lot, specially after my boyfriend knocked me up and then dumped me, letting me stay there and all. But I always wanted to see California, so I came here and now I wish I hadn't, I don't think California's so great after all, not what I've seen of it."

Tom and I slumped down at the table. "You look tired," Ginny observed. "Want some coffee? I think I'll go back to New Mexico as soon as I can. Ariadne is all about women. It's run by women and it's for women only. I had this boyfriend—Steve's his name—he's the only guy I ever had sex with. He knocked me up and then left me high and dry, ran off with some slut. I hope she gives him the clap, I heard she gave it to somebody else. I didn't have no place to go, my mom and dad disowned me when they found out I was pregnant. So I went to Ariadne, and I was grateful for it." Her long hair flew around behind her as moved about.

"Tell us about this bust," I requested.

Ginny cleaned Falcon's face with the spoon. "A few weeks back," she said, "the cops came here, armed with shotguns and warrants, and busted the whole place. I guess it was some fucking scene. They found drugs, mostly pot, but some acid too. They broke up the Professor's lab, they thought he was making acid down there. Everybody got arrested, and taken to city jail."

"Were you here then?" asked Tom.

"No, I came after. I heard all about it, though."

"So where's Duke and the Professor?"

"They're in court this morning, some kind of preliminary appearance. Most everybody has gotten out on bail by now, but they all headed in different directions, figuring this place is too hot to hang around in anymore. Me and Falcon are the only ones here now. Duke and the Professor are going to be glad to see you. They've talked about you a lot."

"What about Anjanette?" I asked.

Ginny shook her head. "Never heard of her."

Now Falcon began to cry again. Ginny took him from the high chair, unceremoniously undid the buttons of her dress, and began breast-feeding him. "There, there, little one," she said. Tom and I went upstairs to our room.

It was just as we'd left it, all our stuff was there. Then we went next door to Anjanette's room, and were disheartened to discover she had been there. Her clothes were mostly gone, and all her personal things. Her artwork—her sketches, paintings, clay sculptures—were all neatly packed to one side.

We returned to the kitchen, both of us hungry, but there wasn't much food. We scrounged some cereal and bread, and ate in silence. Afterwards we went outside to sit on the porch, and a couple of hours later Duke and the Professor came home.

"Well, glory be," Duke said when he saw us. He and the Professor were both dressed in serious-looking suits, for their court appearance, Duke explained, and he came right over to shake our hands and thump us on the back. The Professor smiled and shook hands too, and babbled in a way that made no more sense than what Ginny's kid Falcon had said. Then he disappeared.

"He's gotta put his lab back together," Duke explained. "The cops smashed it during the bust."

The bust was all he talked about. "I thought I was back in Selma, Alabama, and it was 1965 all over again," he said. "I was sitting right here on the porch, taking a snooze, and all of a sudden this panzer division comes down on us, complete with dogs and bullhorns and shotguns.

"We got most of the charges thrown out," he went on, taking off his tie. "Only a few left now. The lawyer thinks we can beat those, even, but it will take some time and effort."

"You seen Anjanette?" I asked.

"I wanted to ask you about that," he said, frowning. "I have seen her. But it wasn't good, men, no, it wasn't good at all. Made me real uneasy. It was about a week ago. I was sitting right here, thinking about--what else-- all this legal crap, and this red Porsche pulls up in front. Out gets this tall white boy, real haughty-looking, wearing these clear-style glasses. With him is this blond woman. She's got on high heels, black stockings, and she's in a real short black dress. And she's all made up, red lipstick, lots of makeup and eye shadow.

"My first thought is, 'Here's a pimp with his prize whore.' I guess I've seen enough whores and pimps in my time to know what I'm talking about. But then they get closer, coming up the steps here, this guy with the glasses walking and looking like he owns the place, and I see the blond with him is Anjanette!"

"Oh God in Heaven," said Tom, and he looked down at the ground for a moment. I didn't say anything, but just felt sick inside.

"Well, my eyes about come out of my head," Duke continued. "I just couldn't believe what I was seeing. She has the coldest look on her face. Just cold, like ice, and she went on by me without saying a word. Not a single word. Like I wasn't even here. Almost like she didn't want me to see her.

"But I jumped up, and I said, 'Anjie, hello!' All she says back is, "Hi, Duke,' real cool, just like that, like nothing, really. I said, 'Where's Tom and Pete, didn't you bring those two rascals back with you?' 'No,' is all she said. 'I've come to get some of my things,' she says, and then she and this guy, who smirked at me, go upstairs. A while later they came out, and she's got some of her stuff packed. Then they took off.

"It sure didn't sit right with me," Duke went on. "I puzzled and puzzled over the whole thing. Something is wrong, I says to myself. It was like she was another person. And I didn't like seeing her dressed that way—she looked like a fancy whore. And there's something real disturbing about that guy she was with. Before she left I looked him in the eye, and what I saw shook me all the way to the bone. This guy belongs to the Devil, I said to myself, and I just knew that, I didn't even have to think about it. She's a good person, she should not be with a guy like him. Now what's going on, do you two know?"

We just shook our heads. There wasn't anything we could say. We unloaded our things from the van, and then drove to Angels Beach, thinking we might be able to pick up Anjanette's trail there.

• • •

I don't know why but I thought it might be different when I returned. In some ways I suppose it was similar to when I came out of the old power plant that night--I thought the world must have changed, but it hadn't, not in any way I could see. Now I was back from Baja, thinking I would find my hometown changed in some radical way only to discover it was just the same as I remembered it. It seemed I had been gone for years, but it really hadn't been that long at all.

We cruised slowly up and down Main Street, keeping a sharp eye out, not seeing anybody we knew or wanted to talk to. The same crowd was milling out in front of the New Faith Chapel, in fact it seemed bigger now than before. I looked to see if Rena was among them, but she was nowhere in sight.

We went over to where Dave and Larry lived on 11th Street, but there wasn't anybody there. Dave's red Porsche wasn't in the driveway, although the same black eagle still perched on the mailbox. The drapes of the big front window were drawn shut. We hung out there a while, waiting, but saw nothing, and finally gave it up and went over to see our old friend Casey.

•　　•　　•

He was ever so glad to see us, squeezing our hands painfully in his power-grip and whacking us on the back. "Where the hell you two been?" he demanded. "I heard you ran away from home, both of you."

"We did," said Tom. "But now we're back."

We went into his house and told him about our trek into Baja. "I've never even gone that far down there," he said. "Not all the way to Cabo. One time I went to San Felipe to fish. It sounds great. What made you come back?"

"We gotta find somebody," Tom said.

"Who?"

"Somebody important," said Tom. "Somebody real important."

We told him most of it, and Casey's eyes grew centered and purposeful. "I know exactly where you can find her," he said. "She's with Dave, and his orangutan brother."

"You've seen her?" Tom cried.

"Oh, hell yes."

"When?"

"Hell, just a day or two ago. I hate to tell you guys this, but she's peddlin' her ass all over town."

Tom and I looked at each other. Tom said, "Oh shit," very softly. I didn't say anything.

"It's a good thing you came by when you did," Casey said. "I gotta go away for a few days, up to 'Frisco, my mother isn't feeling too well. But here." He produced a key and gave it to me. "Take this. If you need a place to crash, or hang out, or to hide out in, feel free to come here and do it."

"Hell, Casey," I said. "We don't want to drag you into this."

"It sounds like this could get hairy," he replied. "You might need a place to go. You guys be careful."

We thanked him, and when we left it occurred to me there was something else I had to do while we were here.

"I gotta go over to where I used to live," I said.

"What the hell for?"

"I just do."

"I feel sick," said Tom. "Do you?" I nodded. "Drop me off at the dock, then," he went on. "I'll see if old Denny has heard anything that might be of use to us. You can pick me up there after you've done your thing."

I left him at the Marina and then drove back out Pacific Coast Highway and down 16th Street. I didn't go on the street itself but went down the alley and parked about four houses away. Then I got out and walked along. Everything looked the same from here. The old eucalyptus tree swayed in the breeze, the weeds were growing where they always did alongside the fence, and there were still oil spots where my father dumped the old oil from the cars when he changed it, thinking the oil would kill the weeds but never did, they always grew up again anyway. The same old trash cans were there, and the garage door was down. I saw the vacant lot next door, and thought of my room and all my things that were in there. For a while I got pretty choked up. I kept thinking of a song I heard once:

"Come along, won't you come along home now/Night is falling and the path is steep

Come along, won't you come along home now/Water's running and the river is deep."

I stood on one of the steel trash cans and looked over the fence. I popped my head over carefully, just in case anybody was there. But I didn't see anyone. I was glad to see that my oak tree was all right. I had feared that with me gone, my brother would make good on his threat to chop it down. But there it was, and it even looked as if it had grown some. Then I heard someone coming, and I pulled my head down and peeped through the big cracks in the fence.

My brother Darren came out of the garage and went over to the hose in the flower bed. He turned the water on, and filled the watering can. Then he came walking toward the far end of the yard, stopping at where my tree was planted, and poured water onto it. He poured it very conscientiously, just like I used to, making sure everything got enough moisture.

I put my head over the fence. "Hey, Ugly," I called. "What are you doing? Watering your stupid tree?"

The water can fell Darren's hand and he stared at me, wide-eyed, his black brows arching upward. "Pete!" he exclaimed. "Is it really you?"

"Sure!"

"Where you been?"

"Here and there."

"Mom and Dad been worried, Pete."

"Tell them I'm okay."

He looked sheepishly at the watering can. "There wasn't any reason to let it die," he explained. "It's been here so long. So I water it sometimes. I figured if you ever came back and it was dead, you'd be mad." He peered at me, with sudden concern. "You're not coming back, are you?" he asked. "To live, I mean?"

"No," I said. "I'm not coming back."

Relief flooded my brother's face like a light. "Mom and Dad's still the same," he said. "Dad's drunk all the time. They'll be happy to know you're okay, you been away so long."

I told him goodbye and jumped down off the trash can and went back to my van, not sure now why I had come here. Maybe it was just to make sure the oak tree was all right. I'll come back ten years from now, I told myself, and check on it again. But I also knew, deep down, that sometimes there isn't any going back home once you've gone away.

•   •   •

I drove out of the alley and onto Landing Avenue. As I passed by 14th Street I saw a familiar figure walking on the sidewalk. I honked the horn and stopped.

"Rena!" I called from the window.

She fairly flew into the van, crying and hugging me.

"Where are you going?" I asked her. "I'll give you a ride."

"Oh," she said, "I'm not going anywhere. I'm just walking. I don't have anywhere to go. Sometimes I walk for hours without stopping. Where've you been? I've been so lonesome since you left."

I told her a little about Kekaha. "Oh," she said. "It sounds wonderful. Can I please go there with you? Can you take me there?"

Rena was as pretty as ever, but I saw black circles under her eyes, as if she never got any sleep, and her face looked wan and used.

"I'll be going back in a few hours," I said. "You really want to go there?"

"Oh God yes," she said fervently. "More than you'll ever know. My mother isn't home. I could pack a few things and sneak out later. Will you take me there?"

"Meet me at Main and 12th Street," I said. "At ten."

She said she would, and we kissed and hugged and got out and walked away happily. The load in my heart felt a little less heavy now. To be with Rena again! I couldn't ask for anything more than that! Man, I wanted to sing, and dance too. This was good. This was wonderful!

I drove back over to the Marina, and went down the old familiar gangplank to the dock. There I found Tom, Denny, and Tiffany inside the office.

Denny came leaping over to shake hands. Tiffany was right behind him, hugging me. We all said how glad we were to see each other again. "Tom's been telling us about your adventures," Denny said. "I can't believe it, it's too much, even for you two."

We talked about that, about Baja and Laguna, for a few more minutes, and then Denny and Tiffany told us their Big News:

"We're engaged," they said.

This led to another round of hand-shaking and hugging, and then some wine was brought out and we drank to their happiness and wished them all the best. Denny looked like someone who's just been elected President. He beamed, and lit up a small cigar, not a big fat one but a smaller one with a white holder on the end. Tiffany looked more like a beach bunny than ever. She had her hair in donkey ears, with little red ribbons tied to either side. And she was all dressed in white--a white top, and white shorts, and her hair looked even more blond than I recalled.

"You're looking good, Tiffany," I said.

"Oh no, I don't," she said, obviously pleased at the compliment. "I lost all my tan over the winter, and I've just gotten so fat. I feel like an absolute whale."

The date for their marriage wasn't set yet.

"So if you guys ever need jobs, in between adventures, you can always have one with me," he promised. "Because I never forget who my friends are."

Tiffany sat placid as a flower while Denny said this, although an awfully guilty look passed across Tom's face. Tiffany finished her wine and set her glass down.

"I am so glad you two are back," she said. "Please don't ever go away again without at least telling us where you'll be." She came and kissed me lightly on the cheek and then did the same to Tom, a sisterly peck, saying she had to go now but wanted to see us again soon. Denny walked her outside, and through the window we saw them embrace passionately at the foot of the gangplank.

"So what are you guys gonna do?" Denny said when he came back inside. "About school, and all that?"

"Haven't really thought about it," I said.

We told him about Anjanette, and how we had come back to find her. He hadn't seen her, but said he would be on the lookout.

We stayed and talked for a while after that. Denny told us a lot of things that seemed very far removed from us, things about school and what was going on in town. It all seemed to have no bearing on what we'd been through. Then we said goodbye, and as we went out the door Denny called to us.

"Hey, you guys! No matter what happens, don't forget that we agreed to meet in 1988."

"We won't forget," I said.

When we got into the van Tom slammed the door disgustedly.

"That dumb shit!" he said. "He's going to marry that tramp! I can't believe it. What a fucking dummy. He had no sooner gone into the bathroom then she was trying to kiss me, and get me to say I'd meet her later."

"Are you going to?"

"Hell no! That slut!"

"We're going to have some company when we go home tonight," I said, and told him that Rena was coming back with us.

"Hey," said Tom. "That's good. That must make you happy. And it's a good thing for her, she can get out of that mess she's in."

It was dark by now, and we drove back into town. Once again we went to Dave and Larry's house. But we didn't have any luck. There was nobody there, although while we spied on the place we did see several people come to the door and knock, then go away when there wasn't any answer.

"Let's break in," said Tom. "Go through a window."

"That's too risky," I said. "And besides, what we want is Anjanette."

"What if she's in there, tied up or something?"

"I don't know, but I just don't think that's it."

We waited and waited, but saw nothing, and finally at ten we left and drove over to 12th Street to get Rena.

• • •

She was there, waiting for us, right where she said she would be. She looked very frightened, standing there, a couple of battered suitcases beside her, wearing a sweater. When she got into the back of the van with her stuff I saw in the dim light how pale she looked, and the hollowness of her face.

"Are you ready?" I asked her.

"Yes," she said. "I'm more than ready. I've been here for an hour. I was scared you wouldn't come. I'm just plain scared. Running away! I never thought I'd do it. But you both did, and survived."

"You will too," Tom predicted. "You'll like it where we're going."

That turned out to be true. Rena took to Kekaha right away. She and Ginny hit it off as soon as they met. They went to town together to buy food, and Rena would hold Ginny's kid Falcon on her lap, and play with him.

I was glad to have Rena there, and felt that at long last something was going right for me.

Two or three days went by. We were restless, wanting to get back onto Anjanette's trail. But we waited and while we did Rena and I spent a lot of time talking, out on Meditation Rock. She didn't want to be touched so I didn't touch her. She said she didn't know if she could ever have anyone touch her again. Outwardly she seemed the same but if anyone came too close to her or looked as if they were going to touch her recoiled away in horror.

She was terrified that the Reverend would find out where she was. "If he knew I was here he would come right over and do his best to talk me into going back."

"He better not come over here," I said.

"You don't know him," she said. "He'll do anything. I used to tell him I was going to run away, and he would say he'd follow me and find me. He thought he could make me do anything, because he had so much control over me."

"Well," I said, "It's over now."

"As if it could ever be over," she said. "It'll always be happening, in here."

She pointed to her heart. "I don't know if this will ever be fixed," she said sadly.

Tom had an idea at last. "Look," he said. "Let's go back to Angels Beach. If Dave and Larry aren't around, we can at least find their stooges, Waldo and Karlovitch, and maybe get something out of them."

"What if they don't want to tell us anything?" I asked.

"We can make them tell," Tom grimly. "We can ask them if they'd like to explain to the cops where they were one night last September."

At this I sat up straighter, and stared at him.

"Yeah, I know," he said. "We swore to never tell. But maybe we can find out something, if we threaten those two bastards hard enough."

So we drove back to Angels Beach, and this time we had a little more luck than before.

Once again we staked out Dave and Larry's house, and once again there was nothing doing there. We waited around and were about to give it up and try something else when Tom nudged me with his elbow and pointed to a black bowler hat with a peace sign on it coming up the street.

"There's your buddy," he said.

Waldo didn't see us. He came along with his familiar walk that was part lope and part strut, his thick shoulders just slightly rolling and his stolid face set in its usual sullen expression. His fists were always partly clenched, as if he was ready to hit someone. He went through the little gate and knocked at the door, then waited.

"I wonder where his pal Karlovitch is?" Tom wondered.

Waldo knocked again. Then he peered in the windows, and when he was certain no one was home he turned and went out toward Ocean Avenue.

"Let's follow him," said Tom. "See where the bastard goes."

We followed him on foot as he went down Ocean Avenue and across Main Street. He went all the way to Marina Drive, past the old power plant, and down the pathway next to the San Gabriel River. We followed at a distance, making sure he was in sight but not close enough to where he could see us, staying on the high road while he walked beside the rocks and the water. Finally he came to a lonely, isolated spot, and he waited there, sitting idly on a rock and smoking a cigarette in the springtime sun.

We stayed out of sight, watching and waiting. Tom grew impatient. "What the hell is the creep doing," he muttered. "He's just sitting there." But soon after Waldo had finished his cigarette and flipped the butt into the water we saw another figure approaching from the other direction. As it came closer and closer we saw that it had on jeans, a tight-fitting sweater, and a sharp-billed cap. Then we both gasped, and suppressed laughter.

"Sleazy Mary!" I giggled, happy to laugh, for I had so little to laugh at lately. It felt good to laugh, even at this, because from where we were we saw it all, not that we wanted to. Sleazy Mary and Waldo lay down amidst the rocks and the dirt. I won't tell everything they did—it was just sick, that's all, and I didn't watch the whole thing but turned my head away, covering my eyes, it was all so revolting, and Tom did the same.

At last this travesty was over, and Waldo gave Sleazy Mary some money. She went off the same way she'd come, happily counting her cash. A couple of minutes later Waldo came out from among the rocks, buttoning his pants, and his path brought him right to us. When he saw us standing there waiting for him he began to look pretty sick, the way someone will when they get caught doing something they don't want people to find out about.

"Well Cowabunga!" he cried. "I never thought to see you guys again." He grinned, sheepishly, knowing we must have seen what he'd just been doing with Sleazy Mary. We were blocking his path and looking grim, so he didn't try to get by us but bent his arms at the elbows. He knew we hadn't come to pay him a friendly visit.

"Okay," he said at last, "what d'you guys want with me?"

"Where's Dave and Larry?" Tom said determinedly.

A look of understanding flashed onto Waldo's face, then it vanished and he looked at us slyly.

"Just go over to their house and knock on the door," he said. "You know where they live, same as I do. Tell you what—next time I see 'em I'll tell 'em I seen ya."

He threw back his shoulders and made as if to march through us, but Tom pushed him back.

"Where the fuck are they?" he demanded.

"How the hell would I know?" Waldo countered.

"How about this, Waldo," Tom asked, twisting the name. "How about we tell everybody in town that we just saw you with Sleazy Mary."

"You wouldn't, would ya?" Waldo squeaked.

"You're goddamn right we will," I said.

Waldo swallowed hard. "Look you guys," he said pleadingly. "I can't tell you nothin'. You know what Dave would do to me if he ever found out I even *talked* to you?"

"We know," I said, "and we don't give a fuck. So come on, shit-for-brains, talk!"

"You always been an asshole, Pete," he snarled. "You always been one and you'll always be one. Bein' away hasn't changed you any. But just tell me one thing: Why do you want to find them? Since when is Dave and Larry such good friends of yours?"

"We're looking for a friend of ours," said Tom.

"Okay," said Waldo. "Now I got it. Everybody thinks I'm so fuckin' stupid, but I'm not as stupid as they think. It's that blonde, ain't it?"

"That's right," Tom yelled, and he grabbed Waldo by the collar and shook him. "Where is she?"

Waldo squirmed loose and stepped back, breathing hard. "Keep your fuckin' hands offa me, Tom. Dave told me you guys might be around lookin' for her. He says, 'The bond between them is strong,' that's what he says, and he told me I better never tell you guys nothin' 'bout that cunt, if I know what's good for me."

"What a second," I said. "Something's wrong. Where the hell is Karlovitch? You two are always together."

"Man," Waldo said, "you don't know nothin', do ya? Stan's in the army. He got busted again, and the judge he told him this time he has to choose between jail or joinin' up. So Stan, he choosed the army. He's at Fort Ord now, trainin', and Vietnam's probably his next stop.

"But 'bout that blonde," he continued, "She wouldn't give me the time of day. She's using junk, Dave gives it to her." My heart felt like stone when I heard this, but I gave no sign. "Dave gives it to her," he repeated, "and she stays stoned all the time so she won't feel nothin' of what she's doin'. That's what Dave says. She's his slave, he says, she's his property. When he first came back from Mexico he says, 'Look at this, she belongs to me, she'll do whatever I tell her to.' Dave's makin' her turn tricks, and he keeps the money. He says he's gonna get rich off her. But I never touched her. I ain't got money like that to spend on pussy. Now," he said, "that's all I'm gonna tell you two fuckers. The two of you can just go fuckin' to hell!"

"Okay, you motherless fuck," said Tom. "You don't want to talk to us? Then think this over: How would you like to explain to the cops where you were one night last September, when somebody we all know had his throat slit from one ear to the other?"

"That was suicide!" Waldo screamed. "Deacon killed hisself! Everybody knows it!"

"The hell he did!" I yelled. "You were there, Waldo, you know who did it! That makes you an accessory!"

All the resistance drained out of Waldo. He sagged against the rock. "Oh Christ," he breathed, turning pale. "Don't say no more about that," he begged. "Please don't say nothin' more about that. I ain't been able to sleep since it happened." He swallowed hard, then looked at me and then at Tom. "You guys swear you won't never tell Dave where you heard this, nor Larry either?"

"We swear," I said.

"Okay," said Waldo. "This is all I know, I swear. Over in Long Beach there's a new hotel just got built, near the old Pike."

"I know where it is," Tom said impatiently.

"Okay. Well, Dave, he heard about a convention that was gonna be there, a convention of doctors. He says he can take that Anjanette over there and make a fortune, charging all these rich doctors a couple hundred bucks a pop with her. That's all I know, man. I thought it might even be over by now."

"Is that it?" I asked coldly.

"Yeah," Waldo said, going sullen again. "That's all, I don't know nothin' more."

"You haven't seen us," Tom said.

"That's right," Waldo agreed. "I ain't seen you guys, you ain't seen me. An' I hope I never see either of you again, 'cause it'll be too fuckin' soon if I do!"

Chapter 29

The Pike

"What do you want?" the desk clerk asked sullenly.

"We're looking for some friends of ours," I said. "One in particular. They're staying here." I gave him a quick but vivid description of Anjanette. "Have you seen a woman like that?"

"No," the clerk snapped automatically. He had been studying a large, ledger-type book when we approached him, and he went back determinedly to that now, ignoring us.

"It's important that we find them." I gave him Dave's name, then Larry's, and asked if they were registered here. Once again came the automatic no, like a door closing, without looking up.

The clerk looked like a college student, as if he worked here in between classes at Long Beach State. His face was marked with pimples and he wore his hair unfashionably short and angry-looking, like he had to keep it buzzed off around the sides in order to retain his job.

"Listen you," Tom began, but I dragged him away from the desk and off to one side.

"Creep," said Tom. "Can't you see he's lying? The bastard just doesn't want to bother with it. But what are we gonna do? We can't search the whole fucking hotel."

I looked around the crowded lobby. People stood about smoking, talking, rushing to elevators. There there was a sense of money changing hands, deals being made, of everything being for sale, like honor, life, and integrity, if you were willing to pay the price.

The convention was still going on, we found out that much. But today was the end. Tomorrow the doctors would be going home.

Suddenly I had an inspiration. "You wait here," I said to Tom.

I went back to the desk, and elbowed my way through the people until I stood in front of the clerk once more. I put my hand into my pocket and took out a one hundred dollar bill, part of the wad I had taken from Robert. I held the bill, hidden in my hand, and looking straight at the pimply-faced clerk I said, "Hey?"

He looked up, the way he would if he heard a mangy dog bark. "Yeah?"

I put the bill in front of him, standing it up on its side. He stared at it, then at me, and I nodded for him to take it. He looked around quickly, then snatched the money with a quick grabbing motion.

"So?" I said.

"So," he replied, *sotto voce*. "The people you're looking for are here."

"Where?" I parried.

"9th floor. Now get lost."

"What room?" I insisted.

He stepped away for a moment, looking into an oversized card file. "929," he said softly. "Now will you beat it?"

"What about a key?"

"A key! You want a key?"

"So I can go in and surprise them," I explained. "It's a family reunion. Boy, will they ever be surprised when they see us!"

"There's no way," the clerk said.

"Sure there is," I said. "Just take a look at this. Fifty more. I'll bet that's two weeks' pay for you."

"It's more than that," the clerk said. He looked at the money hungrily.

"Make it sixty, kid, make it sixty and you can have the key."

I put another ten dollars on the desk. He snatched it away and then turning, got a key from a row of small, innumerable wooden boxes that were behind him. He looked around guiltily, then dropped it over the side of the desk so that it fell to the carpeted floor.

"Now get out of here," he said.

"Pleasure doing business with you," I said.

"What did you find out?" Tom asked. "Did you get the room number?"

"I did better than that," I said. "Look!"

"The key! Man, you scored this time, Pete. Let's move."

We hustled over to the elevator, and took it up to the 9th floor. We weren't long in finding the room, and when we did, Tom was all for rushing in.

"Wait," I said. "Let's hang loose for a second." We waited, and a while later a maid came along, a young Mexican woman, pushing a cart full of towels and other amenities. She used a pass key to open the door after knocking lightly and getting no response. We looked, eagerly, as she went in, and it appeared no one was there. When she emerged, a few minutes later we waited until she was gone before opening the door ourselves.

"She's around," Tom declared, for we could smell Anjanette's patchouli oil. "This is hers," he said, poking in a closet carefully. "Let's look in the bedroom."

"When Dave stays in a hotel he stays first class," I observed, for this was a suite even larger than Robert's in Cabo. There were two king-sized beds, and a sofa and chairs. We saw several packs of Dave's black Russian cigarettes and a brown leather jacket tossed carelessly over a chair. Then we heard the front door open and somebody came in. Quick as two cats we scrambled under one of the beds, and waited, our hearts pounding.

We heard Dave's voice, there was no mistaking it, that high, almost feminine voice that did not seem to fit him. Then a distinctly female voice spoke, and we looked at each other. I said to myself, if it's only Dave we can do it, we can get Anjanette away from him and run, if only Larry isn't there. I saw that Tom was thinking the same thing, for he was tensed and coiled up, like a cat ready to strike.

But it was not Anjanette. From where I was I could see through the bedroom door and into the other room. I saw Dave, strutting around in his black boots, and a slender black woman who looked like a model, whose hair hung straight to her shoulders. Wait a minute, I thought, I know her, it's Shawntel, Shawntel from Hell, I met her at the Pike that night. She was dressed all in black too.

They came into the bedroom now, and we couldn't see anything but feet moving. But we could hear every word.

"I need white powder," Dave said. "For you-know-who I need white powder."

"Where is that whore?" asked Shawntel.

"She's with one of the doctors, getting another mile or two of cock run through her."

"Get me a drink," said Shawntel. "That fucking blond bitch. I don't like her."

"She won't last long," said Dave.

"Not the way she uses white powder," Shawntel agreed. We could hear the clink of ice cubes. "She uses white powder like candy, that girl. And for white powder you have to wait, I can't get any until 9:00 tonight, at the Pike."

"White powder I can wait for," Dave said mockingly, and I could imagine those deadly-nightshade eyes arching. "What I want now is some black pussy!"

We heard, even though we couldn't see, Dave grab Shawntel and throw her onto the bed above us. The mattress squeaked and sagged, and we looked at each other, wondering what was coming next.

The battle on top of the bed went on, wrestling and kicking. "Let me go, get off me, you bastard," Shawntel kept saying, but Dave only laughed.

"I want some nigger pussy and I want it right now!" he said, and we could hear her hitting him.

Finally she got away, breathing hard. "I don't like your perversions," she said. "Save that stuff for that blond bitch."

Dave laughed. "9:00 tonight," he said. "Don't forget. In the usual place?"

"Yeah," she said, straightening her clothes and speaking in more normal tone. "Are you bringing that cunt along?"

"Of course," Dave said. "It's her reward. I'm giving her a break from all her hard work. All work and no white powder maketh Anjanette a not-so-good whore."

He and Shawntel both laughed, and they went into the other room where Dave fixed her another drink. She drank it off quickly, and he put his jacket on and they went out the door. We waited a few minutes and then got out from beneath the bed. When we went out into the long hallway we looked both ways cautiously, like children about to cross a busy street for the first time, but there were no signs of anyone. Nor were there any downstairs in the lobby, and the clerk at the desk pretended not to notice us as we went by.

·   ·   ·

At a quarter of nine we were at the Pike, coming in through the Walk Of A Thousand Lights, then waiting in the same place near the tattoo parlor where I'd gone with Dave last year. That seemed a good place to begin.

We made sure we blended in with the crowd so we couldn't be seen easily. We kept looking around, standing with a group of sailors who were waiting to get tattooed. We heard the screams of the people on the Cyclone Racer and saw the lights of the Ferris Wheel as it turned around and around.

I kept thinking of Anjanette and what was happening to her and then I did my best not to think about it anymore. It was too horrible a thing to think about, especially because it was my fault. Tom's face was set and I imagined her was feeling the same way.

I looked over at the tattoo parlor. There were hundreds of pictures on the walls, all of people who had been tattooed there. There was one enlarged picture of a guy with his shirt off, and every inch of his upper body was covered with tattoos, his stomach and his arms and his back and his chest, so the tattoos looked like a shirt he was wearing and not like his skin at all. And there was another, this time of a woman, a rather fat woman, with absolutely enormous breasts that you could see just about all of, and she was tattooed all over too, but hers were snakes, every single one, and it looked as if the snakes were crawling all over her. They both made me kind of sick to look at.

What I had done weighed on me like a heavy, heavy load that I'd never be able to set down. It was getting heavier, in fact, the more I learned of what Dave was doing to Anjanette. This added to my load and added to the lump of poison growing inside. I looked at the sailors and the whores, thinking there was an unnatural blackness to this place, there wasn't enough light even on the Walk Of A Thousand Lights to shut it out, a black mist of evil hung in the air here. It was almost subterranean, this feeling here, as if we had gone underground and were in a cavern.

Tom gripped my arm painfully and pointed. I saw Dave, and then Shawntel. They moved into a clearing amidst the crowd, then stopped.

"Where's Anjanette?" Tom whispered.

I shook my head, for I couldn't see her. People kept passing in front of us, blocking our view. We were standing alongside the merry-go-round now, hearing the music and the sound of a hundred voices speaking at once, some of them laughing, some of them angry. Once more, looking at Dave, I had the same feeling I'd had in Cabo, that he was Death, and his outward appearance was not real but only an illusion, a mask he wore so people wouldn't run away when they saw him. He looked, here in this place the resembled Hell, to be in his element, exactly where he belonged.

Now two men appeared, and began talking to Dave and Shawntel. It looked as if a deal was being made, negotiations were underway, for there was much finger-pointing and gesturing in the air. Then we saw Larry, and Tom hissed, because Anjanette was trailing him.

"Oh Christ!" Tom breathed.

I was too seized up to speak. I felt as if my heart was being squeezed, it was a balloon that would pop, if I didn't do something to put an end to this, stop it, bring it to a halt once and for all.

I hadn't seen Anjanette since that night in Cabo, and that seemed like centuries past. When I thought of her I thought of her as I knew her then, walking around with her hair glowing aureately, as if it had a halo around it, the girl who always had time to listen when nobody else did, who painted and sketched and loved nature and being outdoors. What I saw now gave me the chills, all the way to the farthest recesses of my soul, prying and picking its way like a cold rain, seeking out every corner, no place could be hidden from what I felt, no part of me was protected, for now I had to see what I had done, it was there, and no escape. There she was, all dressed in black, which made her blond hair jump out at you. Her face, normally so happy, was drawn and haggard, and she walked wearily, and hunched over. Looking at her face I sensed she wasn't really there, not actually in her body, she had taken herself out, as far from all this as she could go, because if she didn't and experienced it in full force she would go mad.

A kind of numbness came over me. Everything took on an air of reality times ten, all was tuned to the highest possible volume and intensity. Tom and I stepped through the crowd and attacked the small circle that had formed in the clearing. Tom's fist arced out of the black mist that hung in the air and smashed into Larry's face, and the short burly man's dark sullen eyes drooped tiredly. He fell backward, sprawling onto the blacktop. At the same time I sprang forward and pushed the unsuspecting Dave as hard as I could. He fell also, grabbing at the air and cursing, all of it happening too fast for either of them to react.

Anjanette cried out, inarticulately. "Come on!" I yelled. "Run!" Then Tom was on one side of her and I was on the other, and we were clear of the circle. We pulled her along, through the crowd, moving as fast as we could.

We ran straight through the open door of the tattoo parlor, knocking and kicking tables and wooden barstools out of the way. "Hey," yelled the proprietor, a bearded, greasy-looking man with a dagger tattooed on one arm and a mermaid on the other, "what the hell do you think you're doing?" But we went right on by, through another door where a guy was busily tattooing a heart between a woman's breasts *a la* Janis Joplin, she letting out a shriek when she saw us and trying unsuccessfully to cover herself. We knocked a table aside as we went through, the man yelling angrily but too astonished to try and stop us, dies and marking tools falling to the floor and scattering. We went through the back door, literally kicking it open, and then we were out, into the next row of stands and booths.

We heard the rat-tat-tat of the shooting gallery, and ran to our right. Then I saw Dave's form explode through the back door of the tattoo parlor and knew we were being pursued.

"Faster!" I said. "They're coming!" We kept running, bumping into people, shoving them aside, getting cursed and having fists shaken angrily at us. At last we came to a regular human wall where people were waiting to take the Ferris wheel.

"What'll we do?" Anjanette cried. She had come out of her stupor somewhat by now. "Please don't let them get me back! No matter what happens don't let them!"

We stopped, unsure of what to do next. Dave was getting closer, I saw his tall form pushing and shoving his way brutally through the crowd. Then I saw an open area, between two booths, and we plunged into that, single file, me leading the way, but then thinking, This is very stupid, Pete, because this goes nowhere and now we're really trapped. I could hear bells clanging and whistles blowing. "Here they come!" Tom called from the rear of our little column, and Anjanette let out a wail. Okay, I thought, they'll have to kill me first, before they take her back, for she sounded like a hurt puppy crying, holding onto my arm. Then I saw a door marked "Emergency Exit Only" and stepping over there, I managed to wrench it open.

I saw tracks on the ground, and then a car came slowly toward me. We were in the fun house. "Hurry up, in here," I yelled. Tom slammed the door and we all three jumped into the car, and it shot forward like a rocket, heading, it appeared, right for a wall. But at the last second the wall opened up, and I saw where it was divided in half, and then we rocketed to the left and a pair of blinking lights came at us out of the total darkness. The car stopped, and started again, bells clanged, and it looked as if we were going into a tunnel, straight at an oncoming train.

But we turned aside again, and went upward at a sharp angle, and then went down, as if on a slide or a roller coaster, down deeper and deeper into the blackness, then burst through some barn doors into the light outside. The operator sitting at the controls saw us and roared, "Hey! Where the hell are your tickets, you three?" and punched impotently at some buttons in front of him, then jumped to his feet.

"Sue us, dickhead," said Tom, and we got out of the car and ran for an open area that was like a runway, toward the stairs that led up and out of there. On the broad stone stairs sprawled some winos drinking from bottles covered in paper bags, and some whores stood under the big lion heads that sat on either side. Then I saw a flash of light, as if reflected off a mirror, and saw Dave standing there, as if standing guard, waiting, with Larry close by, straining at the leash.

"We can't go that way," I said.

"They're coming," said Tom.

Once again I heard the screams of the people on the Cyclone Racer. "This way," I said, and we headed toward the sound of the screams and into the hanger-like entrance to the roller coaster. "I always wanted to ride this," I said.

"You want to ride the roller coaster now?" Tom asked incredulously.

"Come on, I know just what to do," I said.

"I'm getting a bad feeling about this," said Tom, but pulling Anjanette along with us we went through the turnstiles and got onto the roller coaster.

"Be ready to move fast," I said.

Anjanette sat between us, holding on just like we were, as the car shot off and began making its loops and hooks, going slowly up a rise and then shooting downward like a rocket. We could feel the old wooden tracks creaking and groaning and I understood why some people said it wasn't safe and wasn't far from collapsing.

"Get ready!" I yelled over the rush of the wind. The car made one of its loops, came around slowly, and stopped, right where I thought it would, just over the place where the sand ended and the water began twenty feet below, pausing, as if to let the passengers recover for an instant before shooting off again. Two cars were ahead of us. I counted the seconds. "Now!" I shouted, and pushing the bar that held us in back to release us, I jumped up on the side of the car, pulling Anjanette behind me. I climbed up onto the rail and looked down. "Hurry! We're going to jump!"

The three of us stood on the rail, and just at that second the cars roared off. The structure of the roller coaster creaked and groaned, and we all three leaped at the same time, plunging down toward the sand and water below.

•   •   •

"Now I know that prayers get answered," Anjanette said, her voice shaky. She lit a cigarette with trembling hands. "I prayed and prayed that you would come, but there were times when I thought I'd never see you again. And when you weren't there I prayed to die. That seemed like the best way. It was all like a nightmare I couldn't wake up from. I wished, I just wished, that we were back in Baja again, because I think that was the happiest time of my life."

"We'll go back," promised Tom. "Just as soon as you feel up to it, we'll go. Won't we, Pete?"

"I swear we will."

We were at Casey's house. The three of us sat in a circle in the living room, the doors all carefully locked and the curtains drawn. The lights were out, and I had lit a few candles so we could see. They knew about Kekaha and could go there, but we didn't think they would look for us at Casey's.

Anjanette hadn't said much up to now. She had just cried, sitting in the back of the van, with Tom holding her. When we got to Casey's she held out her arms to me, and I went to her and I cried too, and then we sat on the floor, all three of us weeping by now.

"I'm not the same as I was," Anjanette said sadly. "I'm poisoned now." Unhappily she removed her black top, revealing a white one underneath, and rolling back her sleeve, showed us the needle tracks on her arm.

I started to cry again when I saw this. "It's my fault," I said through my tears. "God forgive me. I won't ever be able to forgive myself."

She held both my hands in hers. "I forgive you," she said.

"Oh God," I wept. "How can you? After what I did? I don't deserve it."

"I forgive you," she said again, and then she hugged me. "You came for me, didn't you?"

But I knew I would never get those needle tracks on her arm out of my mind.

Now she began to shiver again, and it took all I had to stand watching it. "I have some methadone," she said. "One of those doctors gave it to me. But I am so frightened of kicking again, I don't know if I can make it."

"You can make it," Tom said. "We'll stay here with you. All the time, you won't be alone for a minute. We'll take care of you, you're gonna make it."

"I brought something for you," I said. I got her sketchbook and handed it to her. "You left it behind, but I thought it might cheer you up."

She cried some more then, but these were happy tears, and she held the sketchbook to her like her favorite doll returned after being taken away.

We sat on the floor, huddling together like frightened children. Then Anjanette raised her head sharply. "What if *he* comes?" she gasped. "What if he finds me here?"

"You mean Dave?" I asked.

"Look," she said. She held up her wrist and showed a fresh cut, small, perhaps a half inch long, that had barely started to heal. "This is where he cut me," she said. "He cut himself in the same place, and pressed our wrists together. He said that joined us, made us one, bound me to him. He says I'll never be able to get away from him, ever, he says he can find me wherever I go."

"Bullshit," said Tom, but like me he felt a tremor, a sort of fear spasm, at what she said. He looked at me quickly, then looked away so Anjanette couldn't see his concern. "He won't find you here," he said.

She wasn't convinced. "Do you know who he really is?" she asked. "He's the Devil."

"He is not," said Tom. "He's just a--"

"He is the Devil," she insisted. "He says he's thousands of years old, he says he'll live forever, that he can't die. He says I served him before, for centuries, in other lives and in other guises, and I have to serve him again, now, in this life. He has powers," she said, "strange powers."

"He doesn't have any powers," said Tom.

"He does, he does, I tell you. His eyes are hypnotic. When I look into them I belong to him, and I do. Because I'm evil, just like he is!"

"No you're not, you're not!" Tom grabbed her by the shoulders and shook her. "He is, but you're not." He went and got Casey's .38 Police Special. "If he shows up here we'll find out if he's immortal or not," he said.

"Let's never be apart again," Anjanette said. "Never never never."

"We won't," I said. "I promise we won't."

"Do you really promise, Pete?"

"Oh God, yes."

"Because we have more to do in this life."

"We'll do it," I vowed. "And we'll meet in the next one too."

"But it's going to be terrible," Anjanette said, softly now. Her eyes were hollow, and there were dark rings beneath them. She shook and trembled all over.

"You won't ever let him near me again, will you?"

"He'll have to kill me first," Tom vowed.

"Same with me."

"Let's get some rest," Tom suggested.

We laid down like we did in Mexico, Tom on one side, me on the other, Anjanette in between. I hadn't realized until I laid down how tired I was from all this. I felt anchored to the floor. I was happy to have gotten Anjanette away from Dave, I was part way redeemed, but not all the way, I could never be all the way redeemed, I thought. Never, as long as I lived. Nothing I could do would make up for it. Even if I lived perfectly from now on all those bad things would be piled up like boxes reaching to the clouds. I'd better never do anything bad again, the rest of my life. I listened as Tom snored a little and Anjanette moaned as she drifted in and out of sleep. I thought I might stay awake just to watch over her but I kept nodding off, I was so tired.

I heard her cry out, "No! Get away!" in her sleep. I saw that we were lying beneath some hanging plants in wooden boxes. They were suspended by wires from the ceiling and they looked as if they weighed a lot, and I hoped they wouldn't fall and hurt one of us. Anjanette tossed about and I patted her on the arm and told her it was all right. She woke up for a second, held my hand, smiled, and we fell back to sleep that way, our hands tightly clasped together. And in the morning when I woke up the hand was empty, and there was an empty space between us where she'd been, and there was no trace of her, anywhere. All that was left was her sketchbook, lying on the floor where she had been.

Chapter 30

Waldo

She might have vanished off the face of the earth. We spent all day searching the town for her, but with no results. She was simply gone. Neither of us had heard a thing when she left Casey's, it was as if she had been lifted and carried out of there. We went to Dave and Larry's house over and over, but there was no one there. We stayed outside all night in my van, but saw no one. At last, the next morning, not knowing what else to do, we went back to Kekaha, disconsolate.

We had just gone upstairs to our room, Tom looking unhappily out the window at the green hills, when there was a knock on the door.

"I have to talk to you," Rena said. "I've been waiting so long."

I went downstairs with her and then out the back and onto Meditation Rock, where we sat in the coolness of the morning. We sat looking at each other. Rena brushed at her hair, pushing it back with her hands, then folded them into her lap.

"Pete, there's something I have to tell you," she said.

"What is it?"

"I'm pregnant."

I stared at her, not able to speak, unable to respond to this, coming in the wake of everything else.

"When did you find out?" I asked at last.

"Day before yesterday," she said, woodenly, for she appeared to be trying hard as she could to control her emotions, she was not going to cry no matter what happened. She held her hands tightly together, fingers laced around each other, squeezing.

"Ginny took me to the Free Clinic here in Laguna," she continued, still very wooden and controlled. "I thought I might be, but I didn't know for sure until I went there."

She was still wearing the Sowelu necklace I had given her. She held it with one hand. "I keep asking you if you want this back," she said with a sad smile. "Do you now?"

"No," I said. "I want you to keep it."

"I saw you yesterday," she declared. "In Angels Beach."

"What were you doing there?"

"Ginny took me. I went to see *him*."

"Who?"

"Him," she said. "At the Church. So I could tell him, make him see what he's done."

"What happened?" I asked, and it was my turn to be wooden now.

"He clucked his tongue," Rena said. "He raised his eyebrows. 'By whom?' he asked. 'By whom are you pregnant?' That's what he said, Pete, that's what he said to me."

"And then what?" I asked. "What came after?"

"That was like a knife in my heart," Rena said. "I told him, 'You! You're the father, there isn't anyone else.'"

Her hands were so tightly gripped together now it was as if she had them around the Reverend's throat and was choking him.

"So he said, 'Well, if you're sure it's me, what do you want me to do about it? There isn't anything I can do. I thought you were taking precautions. If you didn't take precautions, then you have only yourself to blame, don't you? You led me down the path into sin, and now you want to lay this sin on me too? That just isn't fair of you, Rena, it isn't a fair thing to do.'

"So, I started to cry. I had told myself I wouldn't, not in front of him, but I couldn't help it, I did. And he said, 'Oh, there, there. I will help you. I am a kind and compassionate man, filled with love divine. I'll pay for the abortion.'

"He started, then, to tell me about a doctor he knows that is safe and reliable, but I ran out, I couldn't stand it anymore, and Ginny brought me back here. I wish I had told him what I planned to say, that he makes me sick, and I hate him, and that I wanted to throw up after he touched me. But I didn't, I ran out, back to where Ginny was parked."

It was a beautiful morning when Rena told me all this. I looked at the sun which was steadily rising, beginning the arc it makes every day that ends out over the ocean.

"I'll marry you, Rena," I said.

She started, at this, tossing her head back as if pushed.

Then the tears gushed forth, her body shook, and she reached over to hold one of my hands in hers.

"Every time I think you've done the most beautiful thing anybody could do, you come up with something better," she said through her tears. "But you don't mean that, Pete."

"Yes, I do," I said.

"You don't care?" she asked. "About what's happened to me? About what I've done?"

"No," I said, truthfully.

"Oh Lord," she said, weeping. "I never heard of anything so wonderful in my life. And I won't forget it, ever, and I won't ever forget this moment, either. I'm so lucky to know you, and I know I'll never meet anybody like you again. But you don't want me. I'm not any good."

"Don't say that," I said.

"And I love you, you know that, don't you?"

"It's nice to hear you say it," I said.

"But I won't let you do this to yourself. You deserve more than me."

"That isn't so," I said. "You don't know the things I've done."

"It wouldn't matter. I hope you can find happiness someday, Pete, and that all the things you've dreamed about can come true. Maybe we'll see each other again, someday, and things will be different."

"What do you mean?" I asked.

"I'm going away," she said. "I'm leaving with Ginny. We're going to New Mexico, to the commune she used to live in. She says they helped her with her baby."

"No," I said. "No, you can't go, Rena."

"We're all packed," she said. "We're leaving after lunch today."

"Today?"

"I just wanted to tell you goodbye. I couldn't leave without seeing you one last time. I won't ever forget you, Pete. And if we never see each other again, please remember that I wish--I wish it could have been different."

I saw her off a few hours later, her few belongings packed into the back of Ginny's old Ford. The kid, Falcon, was propped up in a car seat. I held Rena one last time and then they were gone, down the dirt road, leaving only a trail of dust, and I stood there for a long time, watching as the dust settled.

•　　•　　•

I moped about for several days after that, saying little to anybody. Tom was feeling as low as I was. Everyday we drove up the coast to Angels Beach, hoping to pick up Anjanette's trail, but we didn't have any luck.

Then on the fourth or the fifth day, for they had all become one long blend of pain and guilt and self-pity, we had a surprise visitor.

He came driving up in his clanking old 1956 Buick convertible, with its top in tatters and the engine groaning like a worn-out washing machine. Waldo loved this car. He said it was a car with a lot of soul. He and Karlovitch used to cruise all over in it, yelling bad names at people they didn't like, asking girls if they wanted a ride. It was odd to see Waldo in that car alone. Karlovitch belonged beside him, and he wasn't there, the empty seat looked incomplete, unfinished.

Tom and I stared, wondering why he of all people had come here.

He walked toward us, grinning in his sly, stupid way, wearing his familiar black bowler hat with the peace sign on it.

"I got somethin' important to tell you guys," he said.

So we went up to Meditation Rock and we all sat, cross-legged, while he put his words in order. He took off his hat and twisted it about in his hands as he spoke.

"See, it's like this," he said. "That Dave is a real shit, and I'm sick of how he treats me. I never been friendly with you guys. Stan was the only friend I ever had, and we always hung out together. Then when Dave and Larry hit town we hung out with them, 'cause they was big shots and no big shots ever paid no attention to me, never.

"But that Dave, he was always mean as hell to me. Lately it's been worse, worse'n I can stand. He's always sayin' how stupid I am. Well, I *am* dumb, I ain't ever pretended to be nothin' else, did I? Ever'body always said I was, ever since I been a little kid, so I guess it must be true. I never been known for my *smarts*, but that don't give people the right to keep rubbin' it in my face."

As long as I could remember people had made fun of Waldo, imitating his slow speech and ponderous manner. That made him mean, and now I understood him a little, and didn't hate him as much as I used to.

"I never felt like nobody, 'cept when I was drunk or stoned. How does a guy get to feelin' like anythin' inside, anyway? I never knew. I hung out with Dave and Larry because sometimes I felt like somebody then, even though Dave puts me down all the time. He calls me names I don't even know what he's talkin' about. He says I'm a Nanderthal, a Cromagnet man, and a Grecian--I don't even know what any of them things are, do you? So I told him, the other night, I was sick an' tired of him doin' me like that all the time. I didn't care that Larry was right there, I told him. I done all kinds of dirty work for him, an' took lots of risks, and got practically nothin' for it, an' I said it ain't right, what you do to me.

"Well, he laughs. You know how he laughs. See, he's been doin' a lot of that MDA lately, more than any human bein' ever did. He never sleeps, an' he don't eat, neither. He's high all the time on that stuff. He's got—what do you call it—allusions of grandeur, from all that stuff he does. He says he's a god, sometimes, and other times he says he's the Devil. He says he's a thousand years old. He says he's immortal, gonna live forever. Mostly he says he's the Devil. He says he can do anything he wants to do, an' there ain't nobody can do anything about it. It's weird, I tell ya. Real weird, and spooky. I think he's nuts, or goin' nuts, but he's awful smart, the bastard. We use to go down to the jetty at night, and do these ceremonies. Dave, he'd draw all these weird pictures on the rocks, which he said were symbols for the Devil, and then he'd kill these cats and dogs we caught for him. Sacrifice 'em. He said he got power from doing that. He said it was black magic. He says he can control people's minds with his mind. He says he casts spells on people, and can make 'em do whatever he wants from that.

"But anyway, now, when I said that, he says he's sorry. He says he has treated me mean, an' he says he wants to make it up to me. So he gets out some pure crystal meth he's got, and we do a line together. Then he says he'll gimme the whole ounce for only a hundred bucks, as a favor, to make it up to me. Now I says to myself, I can clear two, maybe three thousand dollars from a deal like that, and have plenty left over for myself too. So I give him the hundred right there, and I go out and sell that speed all over town. But you know what? The son-of-a-bitch done to me what he's been doin' to a lot of people lately, he gimme fuckin' talcum powder! Now there's a whole shitpot of people out there who want to kick my ass, they think I burnt 'em! I give some their money back, but there's some still pissed as hell at me, and won't never trust me again."

"So what did you do, Waldo?" asked Tom.

"Do? Well, I went to his house again, last night," Waldo said. "Told him about it. He just laughed at me. Him and that gorilla brother of his, they just laugh at me. Dave says anybody as stupid as me deserves what happens to him. It's just tough shit, he says. I found out there's some low riders, over in Long Beach, that he done the same thing to, and they say they'll kill him if they can find him. I wisht I knew who those guys were, 'cause if I did I'd go tell 'em where they could find the bastard."

"Where is he?" Tom asked eagerly, when Waldo paused for breath.

"We've been looking all over."

"That's what I come to tell ya," said Waldo. "You know he's got that girlfriend of yours back again?"

"Where is she?"

"I'm gettin' to that," Waldo said ponderously. "I heard about what happened at the Pike. That orangutan Larry has a big bruise on his face where you belted him, Tom, an' I'm real glad you done that. But I gotta warn ya, Larry says for that you're gonna die."

"He'll have to catch me first," Tom said grimly. "So go on, Waldo, where is Anjanette?"

"That Dave is awful fuckin' smart," Waldo said. "He figured you might hole up at Casey's after that scene at the Pike. So he went there, and stayed outside, all by himself. He stayed outside all night—I told ya, he never sleeps. And he sends messages to Anjanette with his mind! This is what he says, I swear! He even says he knows how to conjure up the Devil now, but I don't know if that's true, 'cause the rest of the time he says he *is* the Devil. But he did this all night long, and at last, around daylight, when you two was asleep, out she comes. He give her a fix, and took her off."

"Did you see her last night?" Tom asked.

"No, she wasn't there. I don't know where she is now. If I did, I'd tell ya. But this is what I come to say: There's a big deal gonna go down at Top of the World tonight. This is the biggest deal Dave's ever done. He's doin' it with some Hessians from Santa Ana. This is the big leagues, man, and if he pulls any of his shit with them he'll be dead meat. But I guess that's too much to hope for."

"He's too smart for that," I said.

"You'd think so, wouldn't ya?" said Waldo. "But I wonder."

"When is this deal supposed to happen, Waldo?" asked Tom.

"Sundown."

"Well," said Tom. "Thanks, Waldo."

"It ain't nothin'," Waldo said. "Don't mention it."

He put his hat on and made as if to leave.

"What are you gonna do, Waldo?" I asked.

"Man, I don't know," he said sadly. "I fucked up so bad in school I can't graduate. Maybe I'll join up, like Stan done. But I think I'll go in the Navy, if they'll take me, not the Army. I don't much want to have my ass shot off in Vietnam. I'm done doin' drugs, too. One thing I've learned if I've learned anythin' at all, drugs are just a road leadin' to nowhere. I been too far down that road as it is."

"I've been thinking the same thing," I said. "And I won't graduate either."

"So I guess we got something in common, Pete," said Waldo. "Who woulda thought it?"

We both shook hands with Waldo and told him thanks. We said he could stay at Kekaha if he wanted to, but he said no, and got into his clanking old car and drove away. That was the last I ever saw of him. I had known him since kindergarten. We had gone all through school together. He was the class bad boy, the kid who always got in trouble and was sent to the principal's office. When he was called on to read out loud the result was a torture both to him and everyone who had to listen, as he struggled to pronounce the simplest words and mangled sentence after sentence and at last threw the book on the floor in frustration while around him the kids who knew how to read sat laughing. Kids made fun of him, called him stupid and said he was retarded, and he went home after school to a ramshackle trailer park and tried in his own way to make sense of it all. When he met Karlovitch he found a friend, and when Dave Myers came to town he at last discovered something he thought he could believe in. Now it was all gone.

"What do you think?" I asked Tom.

"It might be a trap," said Tom. "Dave coulda sent Waldo here. It sure seemed like he was telling the truth. I don't think he's that good a liar or an actor. But it could be like I said--Dave may be trying to trick us into coming to Top of the World and kill us. Now I wish I'd brought Casey's .38 along, I'd take it with me tonight."

"You couldn't shoot anybody," I declared.

"I could shoot Dave," Tom said grimly. "I'd be doing the world a favor, too."

"What if it's true, what he says, that he can't be killed?" I asked, recalling how I'd seen him those times, his face like the face of Death itself.

"Then I'll find a stake, and drive it through his heart!"

"I'll sharpen it for you," I said. I'll kill him myself, I thought. He's evil and I'll kill him. Or die trying. I don't care anymore if I live or die, so it won't matter if he kills me. But if I can I will rid the world of something evil, and I'll also help kill the evil that's inside of me.

Chapter 31

The Top of the World

Tom said, over and over, that it could be a trap, one of Dave's tricks, and so when we went to Top of the World we were very careful. We went from Kekaha up a back road through the hills, parking the van and walking a long ways, keeping our heads low and eyes open, thinking that if Dave and Larry were waiting for us they wouldn't be waiting for us here.

From Top of the World you have the most spectacular view of the city of Laguna and the coastline, as well as the hills of Laguna Canyon. The grass grows tall there and it's easy to hide out. We went along a pathway and at last came to a clearing, and we saw Dave and Larry there, just like Waldo said they would be, right before sundown.

Larry was sitting nonchalantly on some rocks, looking calm and brutish like always, his pig's eyes gazing out from his wide, brutal face. Dave smoked and paced about feverishly, then sat, then got up and paced some more, not saying anything. A few feet away there was a ledge, and the hill ran sharply down to a ravine perhaps one hundred feet below, strewn with rocks and brush. Black birds flew in and out of it. Dave kept going over and standing there, looking down as if he was thinking of taking a dive that way, then stopping and gazing contemplatively. We waited, keeping out of sight in the tall grass.

We waited for a while and then, just as I saw a hawk flying overhead, two giants walked into the clearing, looking as if they had just come right out of a Wagnerian mountain in the Black Forest, Fasolt and Fafner taking a break from their forges. The one I'll call the leader—since he did the talking—stood a good six feet four inches tall, and he walked with heavy, plodding steps, swinging his arms loosely, like an old, battle-scarred fighter does who expects anything and is ready for it. The other giant was even bigger, and carried himself the same way, slab-footed, like a dinosaur, prepared to trample anything in his path. They were identically dressed, each wearing a black leather motorcycle jacket, with the words "Vandals, Santa Ana," stenciled in big letters on the back, jeans, motorcycle boots, and each had a piratical black beard and long tangled greasy hair. There was nothing pleasant about them. They exuded only menace and danger.

The leader walked right over to Dave and began poking him in the chest.

"This deal better be on the level," he snarled. "Don't even think of pulling any of your shit with me," he went on, stamping his huge foot for added emphasis. The other giant stood back, glowering, his arms folded across his chest.

"I guess they haven't heard that Dave's immortal," Tom whispered.

Dave didn't bat an eye, although Larry looked a little nervous, like a star minor league player making his first appearance on the field where the real professionals play.

"Now, now, gentlemen," Dave said expansively. "There's no need to get suspicious." He carefully pushed the giant's angry finger out of his face, and spread his hands, as if to show that he was the most honest of men and being done a terrible disservice. The two Hessians did not look convinced, but glared at him menacingly.

So Dave made a signal to Larry, who, like a magician producing a rabbit from his hat, caused a sample to appear, a small sniffing spoon with some white powder in it. He handed it over to the first giant, who put it expertly to his nose. The silent giant took some too, and they snorted and hawked and worked their noses and swallowed, then looked at each other. The silent one made an expression, as if to say, "It seems all right."

"This don't prove nothing," said the leader. "Show me the real thing."

Now Larry now produced a package, a small brown paper package which he handed to the leader. The leader examined it carefully. Then he took some powder from it, and put it to his nose carefully. The other giant did the same, and once more they both nodded.

"Okay," said the leader. "But if this ain't right, there ain't no place you can go where we don't find you."

"You do us a dreadful injury," Dave protested. "I leave nothing but satisfied customers behind."

"That ain't what I hear," growled the leader.

A huge wad of money now changed hands. Larry gave the silent giant another package. If this isn't on the up and up, I thought, I wouldn't want to be in Dave and Larry's shoes. But when the deal was over Dave insisted they all shake hands, and said he hoped they could do business again soon. The two Hessians took off down a path nearby, after telling Dave and Larry to wait a while, just in case there was anybody watching.

As soon as they were out of sight Dave and Larry burst into laughter. They shook hands. Dave held up the wad of money, and they did a kind of dance of celebration. Dave moved gracefully, like a fencing master, with flowing, catlike motions. He pirouetted around and preened. "Am I the greatest, or what?" he said to Larry. "Are we rich now? Are we? Ha-ha! We've done it this time. Look at this!" He held the wad up again. "It's the mother-lode! We're rich! The mother-lode!"

"Let's go," I said softly to Tom. "This is the time to do it. I'll go first, you keep behind me."

"What is this?" Tom said. "You tired of living? You got a taste for martyrdom now? Let's go together, we've done everything else that way."

"I have to do this way," I said.

"No," he said, gripping my shoulder now, holding me back. "We went together into that black tunnel, remember? I never told you, but if you hadn't come along I never would have had the nerve to go on alone."

"I gotta do this by myself."

"Why?"

"It's what she always said--that you only have so much time to live, and when it's up, it's up. Maybe my time is up, there's no more for me to do, this is the end."

"You really feel that way, Pete?"

"I don't know what I feel, to tell you the truth, because I'm so mixed up about a lot of things. But you know, I did it, I'm at fault for all this, and somehow it's gotta be made square. Does that make sense?"

"One day you'll be a real deep thinker," he said, "if you aren't careful. If that's how you really feel, then you gotta go for it."

"Don't forget I have this," I said, taking the magic circle out of my pocket and holding it up for him to see. "It'll make everything right. It's been good to know you, Tom," I said. "If this is it, then I'll see you next time around."

I looked at him and grinned, and he grinned back, and then I leaped out into that clearing, expecting to die.

I thought, with that first step, that eighteen years isn't really very long to live. There is so much I still want to do, so many more sunrises to see, and waves I'd like to ride. And I wished, at that moment, I could see my mother and father again and tell them goodbye, and maybe say something--I couldn't think of what, maybe something like I wished it hadn't been the way it was. I was outside myself now, death would be release, perhaps I'd had this date with death from the time I was born. The whole thing had a feeling of *deja vu* to it, as if I had done all this before, and I realized I did know what death was like, a long journey into a tunnel of darkness, back to the place I had come from.

I stood there, looking at the two of them, and Dave saw me he ceased his ballet and threw back his leonine head in surprise. I waited for the fusillade of bullets from Larry's gun, the one he always kept in his pocket, looking, though, not at him but at Dave.

But Larry didn't shoot. The porcine eyes focused on me and one hand went to the ugly purple-black bruise on his face below his eye. He didn't see Tom, who was still in the grass behind me, but if he couldn't have Tom I would do, and he gave an inarticulate grunt and charged. I braced myself, waiting for the onslaught.

But before he could get to me Dave stopped him, telling him to wait.

"You'll have him," he promised. "Just wait and you'll have him."

Once Larry was safely under control Dave began to laugh. It was a menacing, mirthless laugh, mocking and frightening, and he put his hands onto his hips and let loose a long burst of it, laughter that had a ring of madness to it. I recalled what Waldo had said about Dave being insane, and at that moment it certainly seemed he was right.

"Well," Dave said when the fit of laughter had passed, "I must admit even I didn't expect this. Your persistence amazes me. Tell your friend to come out, he must be over there behind you, you wouldn't come here without him."

"No sense in my asking how you found out about this, or about that deal at the Pike either, is there? You two," he went on, "are extremely resourceful, I have to say it."

"Where is she?" I asked.

"If you came to find that blond slut, you came to the wrong place, she isn't here."

"Where is she then?" I repeated.

"All in good time, boys, all in good time."

"You don't have that much time, Dave," Tom said.

"Oh?" said Dave mockingly. "Pray tell me why, Mr. Surfer-of-the-Century."

"Because," Tom replied, "if you did what I think you just did, and burned those two Hessians, by tomorrow you're going to be in Hell. And I sure won't send you any ice water."

"You think Hessians scare me?" Dave snarled. "Those two iron riders can't do anything to me, *not to me*, do you dig?" I saw, again, the madness, shining through now like a light. "You two little punks! Following me around like harpies! It was amusing for a while but no more. Waste them both, Larry," he said to his brother, "and let's move on."

Larry's hand went eagerly to his pocket and I thought, this is it, I'm going to be in that tunnel again real soon, but Tom, cool as a spring lake, said, "People know where we are, Dave, and who else is here. If we don't come back, they'll tell everything to the cops, and even you don't want that, do you?"

"It's a lie," said Larry, but he stopped, hand still outside his pocket, the gun staying where it was. He looked to Dave for instruction.

Dave looked us over thoughtfully. "It's possible," he said. "Don't kill them yet, Larry. Let's hear what they have to say."

"Where's Anjanette?" I repeated. "That's all we want. Where is she?"

Dave looked at Larry, and they both laughed, unpleasantly. Then Larry walked close to me, looking me in the eye.

"What's it worth to you, to have that bitch back?"

I took one of Robert's hundred dollar bills out, and gave it to him.

Larry looked at it, turning it over in hands as if to make certain it was real. He seemed impressed, and glanced over at Dave. "Who knows you're here?" he asked.

"We told some people we were coming to Top of the World," I lied, making it up as I went along, "and I wrote down the names of who we were going to see here, and put them and your address in an envelope, sealed it, and gave it to them, to be opened if we didn't come back. Tell us where she is, and you've got nothing to worry about."

Larry seemed satisfied. He put the bill into his pocket. Then Dave came over and stood beside him, and they both began to laugh again, doubling over and thumping each other on the back.

"I don't know," Dave giggled, "why you would want her back, now, because she isn't like she was, not like she used to be, not as pretty, I would say, and she's had a good ten miles of *cock* run through her since you saw her last. She's been busy! All that junk she does is making her waste away, fast, I want you to know. I could see she wasn't going to last long in this game, I couldn't get much more out of her before she was used up, and so," he paused here, giggling uncontrollably, "and so--hee-- hee-haw--haw-ha-ha-ha," he stopped now, and rested one arm on Larry's thick shoulder, "we sold her, ha-ha-ha."

Tom and I stared, speechless.

"She isn't far from here," Dave continued, still laughing. "We sold her to some weird hermit named Whalebelly. So that's where your sweetheart is, fellas, that's where we left her, anyway, no telling what *he's* done with her by now, ha-ha-ha."

We were standing near the ledge; beyond was the hill. Dave had his back to where the drop-off began, standing there arrogantly, confidently.

Tom shook all over.

"You sold her?" he gasped. "You sold her? The way you'd sell a dog?"

"That's right," Dave said, sensing that maybe the time for laughter had passed. "I did. Not that I got much for her."

"You can't," Tom sputtered. "You couldn't, you couldn't do that."

"Who says I couldn't?" Dave snapped. "I do anything I want to do, I please myself, Surfer Joe, and I do a good job of it, too!" He turned and looked at Larry, then with a toss of his head, indicated it was time to turn the knuckle-dragger loose.

Larry's hand shot into his pocket, and with incredible speed withdrew a big stiletto with a black handle and a button on the side. I heard the click as the blade shot open and he charged for Tom, the knife in front like a lance. He had forgotten me completely, he was so focused on Tom. I lunged, and did a kind of sit-out, throwing both my legs horizontally for Larry to trip over. He never saw them and went head-over-heels, flying right over the ledge and down the hill with a howl of surprise, dropping his knife so that it fell into the dirt. He rolled over and over, unable to stop himself, picking up speed as he went, clawing at the rocks and bushes in a vain attempt to slow down. At the bottom of the ravine he came to a halt and lay there, not moving.

Tom went straight for Dave. They crashed together like a pair of sumo wrestlers, hitting with a bang that sent Dave's mirrored glasses to the ground like a wounded bird falling out of the sky, the big wad of cash landing nearby. Dave shook Tom off, raising his arms to break the hold Tom had on him, then with a quick spin about and a slashing move with his elbow, drove him back. Tom cried out in pain and surprise, retreated a couple of steps, and then looked over at me, as I clambered to my feet as fast as I could, picking up Larry's knife so that it's blade glinted in the late afternoon sun.

"Get back," he said. "Stay out of this."

A second later he was so focused on Dave, and Dave on him, that it was as if no one else in the world existed but them. I also saw right away the same thing I had felt when I was at Dave's house that night—that in spite of his sissyishness and effeminate manners, Dave was not someone anybody in his right mind would want to pick a fight with. He had lost weight, just as Waldo said, and had this been a contest of strength alone Tom would have won easily. But this wasn't going to be that kind of a fight. Dave moved with a practiced, lethal ease, cat-like, every move controlled and every move dangerous.

Tom charged again, aiming punches and kicks that would have destroyed most people, but were blocked easily by Dave with round, fluid motions. He smiled, mockingly.

"You got a lot to learn, boy," he said.

He moved to the offensive now, and I began to get a sinking feeling that Tom had started something he couldn't finish. Dave faked to the right, then faked to the left, landing a blow in between, the smile never leaving his face.

"You should stick with surfing," he taunted.

But Tom was unfazed. He redoubled his efforts, moving in, then out, just beyond Dave's range, making him miss, and landed several blows of his own. The sneer on Dave's face faded and for the first time he started to look worried. Tom drove him back, and it began to look like, with a few more moves, he would be able to get through Dave's defenses.

"All right!" Dave shouted suddenly. "Hold it, man! You're better than I thought." He threw his arms up in a gesture of submission.

I could see it coming. Just like when someone is drowning and their life flashes in front of their eyes, I saw what was about to happen. But before I could shout out a warning to Tom he fell for it. His native goodness and natural kind heartedness made him pause and drop his guard just long enough for Dave to spin about with amazing speed and drive an elbow into Tom's unprotected mid-section. Tom cried out, in real agony, and doubled over, arms across himself, moving backward, away from Dave.

Dave laughed, mockingly once more, heaved his chest and moved forward for the kill. He drew both his arms up and out, but before he could strike Tom exploded, knocking Dave's arms to either side and driving forward so that his head landed solidly on Dave's chin. It was the same move Dave had shown me. I didn't think Tom had actually taken it in when I showed it to him. Dave went backwards and down, stunned, falling onto the dirt. The smug, mocking look was gone.

I saw his glasses lying nearby and I went for them, stomping them into a thousand pieces, smashing the frames into the ground. I also swept up the mother-lode and put it in my pocket so quickly no one could notice.

The point of Larry's knife was sharp as a hypodermic needle. I could visualize, in my mind, exactly what was going to happen, I could see, I could feel, the blade going into Dave's heart. An instant later and I was sitting astride him, and I looked into the deadly nightshade eyes of pure evil and I saw that I had to do this, he had to die and I had to be the one to take his life. The heart was pumping, life was near the surface. I drew the knife back to plunge it in, and as it started its descent Tom seized my arm with both hands.

"Let go!' I cried. "I'm gonna stick it right into his heart, that's the only thing that'll kill him!"

"Don't do it!" said Tom.

"Why the hell not? Don't stop me, let me kill him, he's evil!"

"Let somebody else do it," Tom said. "Or else you'll be no better than him."

I ceased my struggles then, and let the knife fall from my hand.

"Then we better get to where we gotta go," I said, getting up.

Dave, with my weight off his chest, struggled up onto one elbow, spitting blood. He saw that we weren't going to kill him, and a touch of his old arrogance returned. But there was more madness than arrogance.

"You better go," he said ominously, a slight wheeze in his voice, for his exertions had left him winded. "Yeah, you better. You better run just as far as you can. You two punks. You don't know what you've done. You can't run too far. Not to where I can't find you. You're messing with the Lord Satan himself, and you'll pay."

"Say hi to him from me, next time you see him," Tom riposted, his chest heaving. "I bet it won't be long. And when you do ask him to start thinking about how he's gonna help you get out of this: We were in the old power plant that night you slit Deacon's throat, and we're going to the cops and tell them about it right now! So you better start some more conjuring pretty damn soon, and skinning more cats and making your signs on the rocks, 'cause you're gonna need them!"

Dave sat all the way up now, his bloody face twisted, pointing with his hand. "So it was you! I should've known! You two bastards! You can't get in my way and not suffer for it! You're dead already! You're dead, do you hear me? Dead! Dead! Dead!"

Dave screamed, then, the madness taking him over completely. We left him there screaming, and ran back down the hill and down the long trail to where the van was parked on the road.

"Now I really did it," said Tom. "Just what I said I would never do. So now we *gotta* tell. But first let's pay a call on Whalebelly."

I drove into the Canyon, past the road that leads to Kekaha, then up another dirt road toward the string of old cabins and wooden shacks. When we got to the end where the very last one sat by itself I killed the engine and parked. By now it was dark and I shut the lights off and we went up a long pathway, well-worn from footsteps, to where a red light shone on the small wooden porch.

We knocked at the door, but there wasn't any answer. We kept knocking, and still there was no response. "He's here," said Tom, indicating the old Ford pickup parked nearby, "or else close around somewhere." Finally he tried the door, which opened, and we stepped inside.

The place was dark inside, and there was that same awful smell of stale beer, cigarettes, trash that needed to be taken out that I remembered. The air was heavy, like the windows were never opened, no fresh air was every allowed inside this place. We went haltingly inside, walking with short, careful steps. There was no sign of anyone, no indication of Anjanette being there. As my eyes adjusted to the dimness I saw the Playboy centerfolds and the poster of Raquel Welch on the walls, a regular collage of Miss Octobers and Miss Augusts, naked breasts and legs striking one sexy pose after another. Then I saw, in a corner, what appeared to be the high-heeled boots Anjanette had been wearing the last time we saw her. Going over, I held one up, wordlessly, and Tom nodded his head.

There was a hallway nearby, very dark, but out of it there came a glow, a dim light, and then we heard noises, as if coming from far away. We walked, slowly and silently, into the darkness, still stepping lightly. The light grew a bit brighter and so did the sound, someone crying out softly, as if in pain. I went first, and we followed the light, until I was looking through the open door of a bedroom.

A candle was burning, enclosed in a red glass, giving the room a reddish dark look. There was a bed in the corner and Anjanette was on it. She was naked and on all fours, rocking back and forth, and crying. Whalebelly was kneeling beside her, his shirt off, exposing his monstrous white bulk that made me think of the elephant seals I had seen down in Baja, so horribly fat and blubbery they could move only by undulation. "No, please, no more, please no more," she was saying. "Come on baby, take it all, take it all, I don't want to have to whip you again."

We yelled, both of us at the same time, a yell that brought everything to a halt. The torture stopped, and Anjanette collapsed onto the bed. Whalebelly leaped to his feet, staring at us, frightened and startled, his big blubbery white mass heaving up and down and shaking like jelly.

"That's our sister you've got there," Tom yelled, "and we come to get her back."

"But I bought her!" Whalebelly protested. "She's mine!"

"We'll buy her back," I said.

"But I don't want to sell her," Whalebelly cried. He hung his head. "Still, I don't want to keep nobody's sister. How much will you gimme for her?"

I have him a hundred dollar bill. He took it, and said, "But this is exactly what I give for her," and so I gave him another hundred. He looked satisfied. "Go on, take her," he said, and stood aside.

I got a blanket from the van and we wrapped Anjanette in it. We saw that her face and arms were badly bruised, and when he realized we had seen this Whalebelly went and got a big heavy .45 automatic from a drawer. He didn't point it at us but stuck it in his belt.

"They said I could do anything I wanted with her," he said.

We drove over to Kekaha. Anjanette didn't say a word, but sat and trembled the whole time. When we got there we carried her inside and put her in her old room upstairs. The Professor said he had some herbs that would help her and she took them passively, still not speaking, looking at us with these hollow eyes, and after a long time she went to sleep. Tom and I sat up all night with her, taking turns sleeping a little, and in the morning we drank some strong coffee. Duke said he would sit with her now, and we set off for Angels Beach, to put the last piece of the puzzle in place.

Chapter 32

The Red Tide

A strange peace came over me now. It was as if something had come to an end, and I knew it. I couldn't say what this was, but I felt it deeply and for once didn't question anything, just let it be. I no longer had any fear, but had more a sense that I was acting something out, going through motions that had to be gone through, like an actor doing a play he knows so well he can do his part without effort.

I could see Tom felt the same way. Something had happened, to both of us, during the night while we sat up with Anjanette, something had been lifted and we were no longer the same. Neither of us spoke as we drove up the coast. As we passed 11th Street and were about to turn to go toward the police station on 8th Street we saw a clump of police cars and fire trucks, and heard sirens wailing in the distance. Still without speaking, but with mutual consent and understanding, I turned down the street and got as close as I could, then parked, and we got out to get a better look.

The knot of people was growing, and all the attention was focused on a house with a white picket fence that had a black eagle on the mailbox.

One of the wings of the eagle had been broken off and was lying on the ground. The crowd was surging closer, and there was talking, muttering, running through it as everyone tried to figure out what had gone down. Evidently whatever it was had just been discovered, people were going to and fro freely, the cops were only now setting up a line to keep them back. Police cars were still arriving, and in the distance was the cry of an ambulance, followed by the squawking of a blackbird on the roof.

We pushed through, went across the yard, and onto the front porch. We stopped there, because we didn't need to go any further.

We saw through the big front window everything we needed to see, before a cop built like a professional wrestler yelled at us to get the hell out of there.

The cops were nervous. This didn't happen in Angels Beach. Their faces were red and distorted, and they were yelling at people to get back and make room, and the siren got closer and the ambulance arrived, useless now, for there were no lives to be saved, not here, for there were no living people, only dead ones.

This was worse, in some ways, than Brian, worse even, than Deacon. The difference is, I said to myself, these guys deserved it, but whether they deserved it this way only God could say. They were shot full of holes, both of them, dotted with holes, in fact, and there were pools of blood on the floor. Dave was in a chair, sprawled backwards in an especially lifeless posture, his eyes wide and staring at nothing. The holes were in his chest, small, neat round holes, with a corona of blood around them. His face was like the face of a wax dummy, the life drained out of it. It was funny, I thought, how different the face looked without the life behind it. It resembled a burned out bulb. All the meanness and cruelty was gone.

Larry was the floor beside him, face down. There were dark stains on his back. Nothing else in the room was disturbed, no furniture overturned or dishes broken.

"They never knew what hit 'em," the big cop said, coming closer to us and studying us carefully, the way a cop will. "Professional job, looks like. They friends of yours?"

"We're just looking," I said.

"You better go look somewhere else," he ordered.

We obeyed, walking back up the street. "What goes around comes around," said Tom, his voice shaky. "But my God, that was awful to see."

We got into the van and drove back to Kekaha. There wasn't any point, now, in going to the cops about Deacon. The dead could bury the dead.

·   ·   ·

Tom put his watch back onto Hawaii time. He got out his ukulele and plucked at the strings, but he didn't sound any better than he did back in Angels Beach.

"Tom," I said, "give my ears a break."

"How much is a plane ticket to Honolulu?" he asked. "That's what we need, enough money for three tickets to Honolulu."

"Are you kidding?" I said. "After what happened on our last trip, which was also your big idea, remember? No thanks."

"What about you, Anja?"

She reached behind her and took out an envelope. Her name was written on it, in a child's handwriting. "This is from my daughter, in Arizona," she explained. "She wants to know if I'll ever come see her. I just wrote and told her I would, as soon as I was well. I'm going to get her back."

"So you're going to Arizona," Tom said.

"Yes. I can be with my daughter again. There's a junior college nearby, so I'm going to take some art classes."

"So you need money for a bus ticket to Mesa, and I need money for a plane ticket to Honolulu. How are we going to make that happen?"

"Maybe it will appear," I said. "Like magic."

"What do you mean?" Tom demanded.

"Wait and see."

Anjanette healed fast. The Professor's herbs helped her get through the worst of it. We stayed with her day and night until the withdrawals were over. She began to eat, she gained weight, and began to look like herself again. When she learned Dave was dead she improved even faster.

A couple of weeks later we were all sitting in the room Tom and I shared.

"Do you remember a drawing I made a long time back, of us three, and there was a thundercloud in the background?" she asked.

"Yes," I said. "That sure turned out to be true."

"Well, I just made another one."

She showed us this new drawing. The three of us were on a long white beach, the waves gracefully rolling in beneath a cloudless sky.

"But we're all walking in separate ways," I protested.

"I told you that's how it came out," she said.

"So you're leaving. But you'll come back, won't you?"

"Of course I will," she promised. "But even if I don't, it won't matter. Wherever I go, you'll both always be with me. And wherever you are, I'll be there, watching you and laughing."

"We could go to Baja again."

"That's right," said Tom. "Why, we could get a boat this time, and explore some of those islands in the Cortez we heard about. We could all become *vagabundos*, couldn't we, Pete?"

"Gypsies of the sea," I said.

"So as soon as I can get the money, I have to go," said Anjanette.

"Now is the time for the magic," I said. I reached under the mattress and took out what remained of the money I had taken from Robert. "There's enough here for a ticket to Honolulu, and to Mesa, and some left over."

I divided the money up three ways. "What about you, Pete?" asked Anjanette.

"I'm thinking about taking a trip myself."

"Where?"

"I might go to New Mexico. Taos, New Mexico."

"There's someone there you want to see again, isn't there?"

•   •   •

We saw Anjanette off at the Greyhound Station in Laguna. "Don't you start crying again," she said to me, holding back her own tears. "I couldn't stand it if you do."

"I'm not crying," I said, sniffing. "It's just that I don't know what I'm going to do without you."

"We'll see each other again," she promised.

"In this life?"

"I hope so."

"Because I don't want to start worrying about the next one already."

"I've got something I want you to have," she said.

She put her sketch book in my hands.

"Think of me," she said, "when you look at my drawings. And for you," she said to Tom, taking the crystal from her neck, giving it to him, "I want you to have this. You'll see me," she said, "In there, if you look hard enough. Now don't you start blubbering," she said to Tom.

"I can't help it," he said.

"I have something for you too," I said, harding her an envelope, tightly taped closed. "Take good care of this. And promise me you won't open it until you get to Mesa."

She looked at it curiously. "What is it?"

"It's more magic."

"The bus is leaving," she said, and after hugging and kissing us both, she got on board. We waved to her as she left, and through the windows above us she waved back. The bus roared off, out the canyon road and out of sight, and we stood below a palm tree, watching.

"What was in that envelope you gave her?" Tom asked.

"I told you, magic."

     •   •   •

I drove Tom to Los Angeles Airport. "Sure you won't go with me?" he asked.

"I'm sure."

"How come?"

"I don't know, exactly—it's just that I know it isn't what I should do right now."

"Still thinking of going to New Mexico, eh?"

"I'm thinking about it."

"It's hot there."

"It's hot in Hawaii."

"Yeah, but it's not the same."

We went through the terminals and through check in, and then sat in the waiting area for his flight to begin boarding. Nearby a girl turned on a portable radio and a song by the Beach Boys came on.

"It's automatic when I talk with old friends/The conversation turns to girls we knew

When their hair was soft and long/And the beach was the place to go...
"Let's get together and do it again..."

"You really think we'll all see each other again?" he asked suddenly.

"Sure," I said, although secretly I wondered. "Don't you?"

He looked through the huge glass window at the 707 outside.

"You know what? I never flew on a plane before."

"Me either."

"Remember when we went into that tunnel at the old power plant?"

"There isn't much chance I'll ever forget *that*."

"I was scared."

"So was I."

"But I always figured, after we went through that together, that we'd done something, you know, something that bound us together. You feel that?"

"Yeah, 'course I do."

"So that's how I know we'll be together again, someday. I feel like wherever I go, you're with me. Doesn't matter if you're really there or not, you'll be there still. And hey, don't forget, we said we'd all meet again in 1988." He took out a piece of paper, the one we'd signed along with Denny at the dock that time. "You still have yours?"

"Someplace I do."

"Well, we gotta get together for that. It's only nineteen years from now. Every end is a new beginning. And if we don't make it then, we'll meet some other time, but maybe not in this form. Do you ever get the feeling that we did all this before, and that we'll do it all again someday?"

"Are you gonna start that next life stuff now?"

"No. Yeah. I mean, maybe it won't be for another hundred years, but we'll have more to do together, more adventures, sometime, and we'll be together then, and we'll do it. Do you think it could be?"

"You're gonna become a real deep thinker," I said, "if you keep this up. And besides, I'm having trouble enough with this life, I don't want to start planning for the next one yet. Still, it's all--"

"Goodbye old way—"

"Hello new day!"

His plane began to board. He stood up. "Now I don't want to go," he said. "It's not gonna be the same, without you."

We shook hands, then embraced. "Say," I said, hugging him, "you're not going to forget any of this, are you?"

"No. How could I? It'll all be with me, every minute of my life. Do you suppose it's all a dream, like Anjanette always said?"

"If it is," I said, "I'll see you in the next dream. But wait. Take this. Don't open it until you get off the ground."

"What is it?" He looked at it keenly, for it was identical to what I had given to Anjanette, an oversized envelope tightly taped all around.

"Just promise me, all right?"

He boarded his plane. I saw him give his ticket to the stewardess at the gate and then I watched him disappear through the door. I sat on the chair after he was gone and let the tears run, and when I was done with that I made my way through the airport and out into the parking lot to where my van was parked, then got onto the freeway heading south.

•　　•　　•

I got off at the Angels Beach exit, and drove down to 1st Street. I parked, and went across the street to look at the old power plant, stopping with a start when I looked up and saw cranes and bulldozers at work there.

There was a roar of powerful machinery. A worker shouted instructions, and somebody shouted back. A wrecking ball flew through the air and crashed ringingly into the bricks, smashing them, jarring them loose, they fell in long pieces and clattered to the ground, where there were piles of broken brick already. A haze of red dust from the bricks hung in the air. Then the bulldozer came along and scooped them up, pushing them rudely to one side. The man working the crane shifted the controls, the boom swung back, then came forward again, slamming the wrecking ball once more into the bricks, bringing forth another small avalanche. Nearby a big dump truck waited to haul the rubble away. I saw now the entire wall was cracking, a few more blows would bring it all the way down.

I watched this for a while, then went down the path to the jetty. I stood on the rocks, noticing now a smell in the air. No one was in the water, I saw, even though it was early summer now, and warm. It's red tide, I thought, but it's fading, in a few days it, like the old plant, won't be here anymore.

I thought about going up to my secret place behind The Hill but decided not to. I sat on the rocks by the water of the bay. Behind me I heard the wrecking crew at work as they demolished the old plant. I sat there for a good long while, taking rocks and flipping them into the water. A jet plane passed overhead, heading out toward the ocean. I knew it was the plane Tom was on, and I stood up and waved to it. I could imagine him up there, waving back at me, and I thought of him opening the envelope I'd given him and seeing all that money. For I had divided up the money I had taken from Dave at the Top of the World, and given one-third to Anjanette and one-third to Tom. It was a lot of money, more than enough to pay for her tuition to the art classes she wanted to take and plenty to keep Tom going for a good long time while he lived in a grass hut on the North Shore.

Now the words of his favorite song came to mind:
"We come on the Sloop John B./My grandfather and me
Around Nassau town/We do roam…"
I went walking by the bay, throwing rocks into the water, watching

them skim across the surface. The sun was going down by the time I got to the bridge. I took a last look at it, then took a flat rock and heaved it, watching as it sank out of sight in the water. It was still red tide.

Or, maybe, I thought, it was all just a dream I had.

I threw one last rock into the water, a bigger one, and watched it go ker-plop and be gone. That was for Pete, I said to myself, for it is his voice I always hear, and he's always trying to talk to me.

"But what is it you're trying to say?" I asked out loud, looking at the ripples in the water where the rock had sunk.

I felt the answer, I didn't really hear it. But I knew he had spoken it at last, finally I knew what it was. Life is like that rock, it can be gone any time, so get hold of it while you can, and don't let go.

"Thank you, Pete," I said. "I'll do it," for I could see in my mind Tom getting off the plane at Honolulu Airport, getting his first look at Waimea Bay and Sunset Beach on the North Shore, then taking his surfboard and getting his first ride in the waters of Hawaii. I could see Anjanette in a drawing class at the community college in Mesa, Arizona, and I wondered how surprised she would be when I showed up there to say hello, and I imagined meeting her daughter and telling her who I was. And then I saw Rena, in Taos, New Mexico, and saw myself driving that way out Route 66. What would I find when I got there?

I went up the pathway to the road, and then got onto the bridge. I looked down at the water flowing beneath me, flowing out toward the ocean. I saw Tom's face in the ripples of the water, smiling up at me, and Anjanette's face too. They were going out to the sea, to mingle with the vastness of the Pacific. I saw my own face go by, going the same way. I waved to it, I waved to all three of them, then turned and began walking. For there is a new beginning in every end, and every cup that was full has to be empty one more time. I did a hop and a skip as I walked, dancing a little jig of joy. I took another look at what was left of the old power plant, and kept on walking toward the sun.

Songs

Blackbird. John Lennon, Paul McCartney. 1968.

Come Along Home—Tom's Song. Tom Paxton. No date.

Devil with a Blue Dress On. Shorty Long and William "Mickey" Stevenson. 1964.

Do It Again. Brian Wilson, Mike Love. 1968.

Groovin'. Felix Cavaliere, Eddie Brigati. 1967.

In the Midnight Hour. Wilson Pickett, Steve Cropper. 1965.

Jumpin' Jack Flash. Mick Jagger, Keith Richards. 1968.

Lemon Tree. Will Holt. No date.

Sloop John B. Traditional.

Sympathy For The Devil. Mick Jagger, Keith Richards. 1968.

The 9th Symphony. Ludwig van Beethoven. Lyrics by Friedrich Schiller Traditional.

The 59th Street Bridge Song. Paul Simon. 1966.

The Great Pretender. Buck Ram. 1955.

What The World Needs Now Is Love. Hal David, Burt Bacharach. 1965.

Wouldn't It Be Nice. Brian Wilson, Tony Asher, Mike Love. 1966.